WORKS BY S.M. PERLOW

Vampires and the Life of Erin Rose

Novels
Choosing a Master
Alone
Lion
Hope
War

Short Stories
Alice Stood Up

—

The Grand Crucible

Novels
Golden Dragons, Gilded Age

—

Other Works

Short Stories
The Girl Who Was Always Single

CHOOSING A MASTER

VAMPIRES AND THE LIFE OF ERIN ROSE

S.M. Perlow

Bealion Publishing

A Bealion Publishing Book

Editor: Stefanie Spangler Buswell, Red Adept Editing Services
Cover design: Streetlight Graphics
Formatting: Polgarus Studio

smperlow.com—updates, social media links, and more information about the story

ISBN: 978-0-9992858-0-0

1.0.1-p2

1

ETHAN

Saxophone notes meandered high and low. The old instrument's older owner played from a wooden stool on the small club's low stage, while a young New Orleans local rolled his fingers along the piano's ivory keys. On a booth seat at the back of the dim, packed room, just east of the French Quarter, I held Karen's tanned wrist. She wore a white cotton dress with red roses on it, and leaned against me with her eyes shut, but it wasn't the music that had captured her attention.

I pulled my fangs from her wrist. She formed a warm smile, while I scowled. Her blood did not contain what I sought. It satisfied lingering wants of my inhuman thirst that had been fed earlier that evening, but Karen's blood, like all the rest, was not my answer. I scooted away from her.

Her eyes opened, and she sat upright. Her lips parted, but no words came, until she held out her bitten wrist. "More?"

"No." I stood. "But thank you." It wasn't her fault about her blood.

Her shoulders slumped. "Okay."

Weaving between crowded tables, I headed out to the sidewalk on Frenchman Street.

Gaps in clouds revealed bright stars. Up the street, a clean sign with a new name hung where a dive bar's worn wooden plank had always been. Half a mile south, the Mississippi River ran steady where it curved—unless that, too, had changed since I had seen it the night before.

Nothing to do but keep walking. So I did and would continue to until I found the blood I needed, or any hint of it.

Those who knew Frenchman Street to be a saner area than Bourbon Street smiled and laughed over dinner or drinks inside the restaurants, bars, and clubs I strolled past. Mostly fresh faces, tourists surely, walked inside. I recognized the occasional local, two of whom I had met on nights past and enjoyed conversing with before sipping their blood.

Jazz, rock music, and solo voices over strumming acoustic guitars came out louder when the doors opened. My time hunting in the neighborhood told me some of those people leaving the bars here were headed for Bourbon Street. "Start with a civilized meal around here, have a few drinks, then let sanity be damned," many thought.

Not that I wouldn't hunt on Bourbon. The more I could drink from, the more thoughts I could read with my prey's blood, and that was better for my purpose. Usually, Bourbon Street was just the spot for quantity, though quality tended to suffer.

My old watch read 12:30. I had more than half the night before sunrise. I noticed couples holding hands, as I used to with my love, Ellie. I couldn't bear to watch them, though, because Ellie couldn't hold my hand any longer, the way she used to back in high school, when we met. I slid my hands into the pockets of my navy slacks. A light-gray shirt and nice brown shoes completed my outfit. To the men and women I passed, I appeared to be about eighteen years old. But I had appeared that way for eleven years, since 1995.

Broad-shouldered and not quite six feet tall, I had dark-brown hair and skin on the paler side. And when I smiled wide with my teeth showing, my two sharp fangs gave me away as a vampire. I wasn't a Spectavi vampire. I hadn't sworn loyalty to them, and I didn't work in cooperation with the police and human governments. I had no role in Eure, their global conglomerate corporation. I was a Sanguan, free and on my own, with no allegiance to anyone, except to Ellie.

Older Sanguan vampires, some far older, walked the streets of New Orleans. Spectavi did, too, right along with me, maybe dressed to blend in, just like me. But the Spectavi drank only synthetic blood, so they weren't out hunting. Whatever else they did with their immortal lives, the Spectavi kept the peace, and they were part of the reason I didn't sink my teeth into every man and woman nearby, in hopes that one of these people's blood was what I searched for—blood unlike any I had ever tasted. Rich, pure... sublime, it was supposed to be.

In my pocket, my phone buzzed. I pulled it out and saw

the icon for a new text. I flipped it open to the word, "Arrest."

Faster than human eyes could see, I ran west on Claiborne Avenue, then northwest on Esplanade. I couldn't sprint at that speed forever, but zigzagging through short city blocks, dodging mortals and cars, both advancing and parked, I kept up my pace the entire two miles to the nursing home.

I pulled open the glass door to find the receptionist standing at her long desk in the carpeted lobby. I darted past her, yanked open the stairwell door, then bounded up four concrete flights to the third floor.

Beeeee—the flat tone from Ellie's heart rate monitor filled my ears as I raced down the beige-walled hall to the end. I burst into her room on the left.

"Clear!" Diane called, electrified paddles in hand, poised over Ellie—my Ellie—my painfully mortal, fair-skinned, blond, twenty-eight-year-old Ellie.

The two younger nurses, both wearing blue scrubs, leaned back, and when the paddles touched Ellie's chest, I recoiled as she jolted up in her bed. *Beeeep—beep—beep.* The monitor relayed her resumed heartbeats.

I breathed, finally, as the beats continued. Ellie rested in the coma she had been in almost continuously since before I became a vampire.

I went to Ellie and took her hand as Diane put away the paddles. "Thank you," I said to the nurse.

"Ethan," Diane said, "this is the second time."

"I know." I fixed my gaze on Ellie. At sundown, three weeks prior, I had woken in my coffin to the same alert on my phone, sent from the automated system attached to her heart monitor. Thankfully, a second text reported that her heart had been restarted. I had rushed to her side, regardless.

Diane came over. "Maybe her body is telling us that it's time. Maybe she wants to go."

I snarled at the middle-aged woman. *"Time?"*

She stepped back.

I moved toward her. "It's *time* when you can do no more. Do I pay my bills?"

"Yes." Diane nodded hurriedly.

"Do I pay *extra* to ensure Ellie has the best care she possibly can—night *or* day?"

"Yes, of course. It's not money." She shook her head. "I'm only asking—"

"What?" I leaned closer. "What are you asking?"

"Her body's dying. Is it cruel to keep this up?"

I opened my mouth wide and sized up Diane's plump neck. Would she have asked if I didn't look so young? Would she have asked if Ellie and I had been married, like we surely would have been by then if Ellie hadn't gotten sick?

I shut my mouth, leaned back, and turned to Ellie. "It would be *cruel* to do any less than all I could." I looked to all three nurses. "You will not give up. I will not give up."

2

VERA

Lukewarm shower water hit the top of my head and ran down my long chestnut hair, my face, and my chest. I sat in the porcelain tub upstairs in Edmond's palatial home, holding my knees to me, staring at the white wall but not seeing anything in front of me.

Fire that wasn't really there—lots of fire—burned in my mind. Red flames dominated the oranges and yellows. Almost pure red, as usual, they flashed, searing the back of my neck and out to my temple.

Bam! Red beat on my forehead.

Bam—Bam! Red fists pounded my skull.

I held the sides of my head as tightly as I could, and the pounding calmed.

My mother, her throat torn open, shot to mind. I let go of my head and held my long legs, but the vision persisted while I rocked to and fro. Tears mixed in with the water cascading down my face.

I saw my mother again, her soft, unblemished skin torn

open, blood pouring out of the jagged wound. Fire spread across her body. Red flames enveloped her.

She burned, and I sat there, imagining Edmond drinking from me. I imagined the fire that came from his bite—all the shades and the nuances, most of all the blue driving away the red assault, as it always did.

Three things could end my patients' attack on my mind. One was time. The effect of their attacks did not last indefinitely. But it might take days to run its course. The second was distance. My patients, two vampires, were with me at Eure headquarters in northern Virginia. If I were farther from them, my pain would be lessened. The third was a vampire's bite. Edmond, lord of the Spectavi vampires, was who I preferred to drink my blood and give me peace. Victoria, another ancient Spectavi, ranked a close second. While nearly every Spectavi drank synthetic blood, as their laws and official policy stated they *all* did, many of the oldest of their leaders did not, opting instead for real human blood to satisfy their thirst.

Blood poured from my poor mother's throat again in my mind. Fire roared over her. She could not move. She could not resist the flame. I thought of Edmond's soothing bite.

Edmond led the Spectavi and also served as CEO of their worldwide business, Eure, a conglomerate involved in everything from semiconductors and defense to manufacturing and pharmaceuticals. He had been running the company for hundreds of years, as long as it had existed. At nineteen, I was a mortal woman, working as a chemist at Eure. For my two patients, I applied those scientific skills like a doctor trying to bring them lasting peace, but to them, based on how they lashed out at my mind, I must have seemed like a torturer.

A thunderclap of red shut my green eyes. I opened them to fading red. Crackling red hit hard, faded, and smashed me again.

I could wait no longer.

With hands on opposite sides of the tub, I got to my feet. I stepped out of the tub, grabbed a white towel, and dried myself off a little before dropping the towel to the floor.

Red flashed, and I fell forward, getting my hands up just in time to stop my head from smacking the bathroom door. I pulled my long green silk robe from its hook and wrapped it around me. I tied the belt at my waist and, with wet feet, headed across the bedroom's hardwood floor.

Red boomed in my brain. At the closed door to the hall, I held myself up, letting the red fade before I opened it.

"Yields are as expected?" Edmond asked, downstairs.

I kept a hand on the wall in the hallway then hugged the wood railing, making my way down the L-shaped staircase.

"Right on target," Guoliang responded in the drawing room. I recognized the voice of the Chinese vampire in charge of our semiconductor operations.

"Good," Edmond said. "Our average selling price dipped a little, I noticed."

"Should be higher this quarter with our new chips," Guoliang said. "Will more than make up for it."

"Mm-hmm," Edmond responded.

I continued down and spotted the top of Edmond's full head of black hair. Seated a quarter of the way around a small coffee table from Guoliang, his big frame filled out his old leather chair. Edmond's dark-gray suit jacket hung on the chair's back, and his pale white hands flipped pages of what I presumed was the report they were discussing.

I stepped off the last stair and onto the marble floor.

Guoliang, who was not as pale or nearly as old as Edmond, stood up, staring at me.

Edmond turned. "Vera." He rose, and his kind brown eyes met my gaze.

"I'm sorry." I held myself up against the banister.

"I'll leave you." Guoliang collected papers from the table and placed them into his briefcase, which he carried to the door.

"Thank you." Edmond hadn't looked away from me to say it. The ancient French vampire came over and reached for me.

I let go of the railing and fell into his arms. "I'm sorry."

"Shhh…" He moved my wet hair aside, exposing two fang marks on the right side of my neck.

I heard Guoliang leave and the door close behind him.

Edmond held me more tightly. "It's all right." He opened his mouth, I shut my eyes, and his fangs broke my skin.

Fire! Red. I felt Edmond suck. The fire within me burned orange.

Blood ran out of me, and the fire turned yellow. My head still pounded red. Edmond sucked. Orange hit like a drum, yellow like a rattle, then blue-hot fire cooled my mind.

I couldn't feel Edmond's arms around me. I couldn't feel

his fangs at my neck. I no longer felt anything except blue pulsing down my spine.

Soothing blue flame built in my core. Then it burst out to my arms and legs. Out to my fingers and toes, blue fire touched me.

Blue at my center rolled into a ball. Streaks of yellow and orange mixed in. The sphere stretched and cracked… then ruptured.

Orange, red, and blue raced through me. Then glorious blue was everywhere.

His fangs left me, and I opened my eyes. Edmond lay with me on the big bed upstairs. The thick white comforter had been pulled down and only covered our feet.

I breathed easy. "Thank you." No red flashed to mind.

"Of course." Edmond kissed the top of my head. "But you are made to endure too much, Vera."

"I will heal them."

He shook his head. "It kills me to see you like this."

The notion of never again being struck by that red called out to me, but I wouldn't listen. "I made you a promise." I leaned up to Edmond and ran my fingers across his cheek. My lips met his. My tongue found his.

I turned my head and pulled my hair off my neck. "I won't give up."

3

JOHN

So this is what giving up feels like, I thought. In Reims, in northeast France, I sat on the short side of the bar and gulped bland beer from a heavy glass mug. Electronic dance music pulsed through the dark Sanguan vampire club.

Around the bar's corner, from just past the stools to the wall of the narrow room, bodies packed in tightly with other bodies moved fast to the music. Most were human bodies, it seemed, but from the bites illuminated by occasional bursts of light timed to notes in songs, some were clearly vampires. The scent of fresh sweat permeated a stale one. It was my first visit to a Sanguan club. I had searched online from my hotel earlier, and the scene before me matched most of the reviews I had read.

I drank and glanced at the two females halfway around the bar, their backs to the edge of the dancing crowd. The pair chatted with each other, probably in French, occasionally smiling widely enough to reveal their pointed fangs. Giving up could have been worse, I thought. Those vampires were hot.

I hadn't found what I'd hoped to in Europe, just like I hadn't found it back home in the States. I had been married once, but even though I was only thirty-one, that had been years before. The marriage shouldn't have lasted as long as it had. Looking back, I understood it never should have begun, and since it had ended, I was better off for it. I had no doubt about that. Nevertheless, the whole ordeal had left me alone, and as the months and years wore on, I hated being alone more and more.

Finding dates was never my issue. Six-one, thin, with a stable income was apparently appealing enough to most of the women I found interesting. But appealing and interesting on the surface never cut it for long with me. Getting to know people, *really* getting to know them, took time and effort, and that came at a huge emotional cost. After years of all that effort going nowhere—or worse, leading to promising relationships that died a couple months in—I had been spent. I'd needed a change.

England for a month had been first, and excitement greeted me each morning, but only for a while. I didn't meet many people. In between seeing the major sights, I talked to hotel receptionists, coffee shop baristas, waiters, and bartenders, but I didn't really *meet* anyone, and the excitement faded.

The idea of visiting a Sanguan club had come to mind while I was in London. I'd googled to find a few and walked past one, planning to go in, but I'd chickened out and had a pint of beer at the bar up the block before returning to my hotel. Then I had taken the train across the Channel to France, and after an uneventful night in Paris, I took another high-speed train the forty-five minutes east to the old city of Reims.

Staring at the ceiling in my hotel earlier that evening, with nothing in particular to do, no one to meet, and hardly knowing the language of the country I had dragged myself to, I decided to finally give it a shot. I would meet *someone,* I figured. Sanguan vampires *lived* off human blood, so whether they could tell me in English or not, one would find my blood to their liking.

I assumed one would, at least, even as the notion unsettled me. I had never been bitten by a vampire.

"Another?" the vampire behind the bar called to me over the beating music.

I glanced at my nearly empty mug. "Please." I finished the watery brew.

The bartender wore a black tank top, and I had seen her fangs earlier when she guessed correctly by beginning our conversation in English. She came over with my new beer and grabbed the old mug.

"Breen." I gave her my last name.

She nodded and went to her computer to record the order. She was fit and very pretty, not that I could ever recall seeing an unattractive vampire in person. But the bartender did not strike me the same way as the two vampires chatting around the bar. One, also in a black tank top, wore a thin choker around her neck and had her brown hair pulled up in a tight bun. The other wore a cropped leather jacket over a gray top and had short blond hair. More makeup, I decided, differentiated them from the bartender, as well as jewelry, and… Whatever it was, the two of them were gorgeous.

I took a long drink of flat beer. How did it work? I wanted one of them to bite me. That's what Sanguan clubs were for. Willing prey walked into places where they wouldn't be killed by the predators or where they were at least hardly ever killed. Dying customers kept people away.

Regardless, I had made my decision when I finally came in, so how did I get one of those two to drink my blood?

Vampire bites felt incredible, according to almost anyone I'd asked. They were supposed to be like a drug shot into a human's system, full of warmth and an eventually overwhelming rush of feelings and sensations. The rush ebbed and flowed, depending on how exactly the vampire drank.

The pair of Sanguans glanced my way. My God, they were pretty. They giggled and resumed chatting.

I swigged my beer. I wanted to hold them while they drank from me—the short brunette in the little black skirt, if I could pick. I liked her feline eyes. But the blonde would have been fine. It didn't matter which. And *she* would hold *me* when she bit, when she commanded that rush inside me.

She would know all my thoughts, all my memories and emotions, when she drank. Those things came with the blood of humans, and much to my initial surprise, I looked forward to being so naked to another. There would be no first-date chitchat, no avoiding topics or worrying if they cared I had been married. She would just have a drink, know me, and let me lie beside her and hold her. For a while, I wouldn't be alone.

The brunette got up. I held my mug halfway between my mouth and the bar as she walked over. Her knee-high boots with tall block heels accentuated her toned thighs.

"Hello," she said with a thick French accent. She held out her pale hand. "Collette."

I shook her hand. "John." Her fingers and palm felt firmer than her delicate, youthful appearance suggested. "Can I get you a drink?"

"You can." She glanced at the liquor bottles behind the bar. "But not those."

Stupid. Any of them would have tasted like nothing to her, like flavorless water. Vampires didn't eat or drink, aside from blood.

"Downstairs?" She gestured to the back of the club, past the bar, away from the dance floor.

Where the blonde had sat was an empty stool. I didn't know why I'd checked. A song faded into another, and the dancing continued uninterrupted.

"Will you come?" Collette asked.

I would, and I would kiss her deeply, after kissing her neck near her choker. I would hold her bare shoulders while I did it.

Or I wouldn't, and I would set my beer on the bar, run from her and that club, and never return.

I needed time to think. Collette had forever to live; she would be patient.

"Will you, or no?" she asked.

The Sanguan vampire didn't need to be patient, not looking like that, in a club full of willing prey.

"Sure." I chugged the rest of my beer and felt dumb for having done it. But Collette smiled while I slid off my barstool.

"Come." She held out her hand, and when I took it, she led the way to the back of the club, between the barstools and encroaching dancing bodies. Downstairs, she had said. The clubs had private rooms, I knew that, but none of the online reviews described the basement.

Collette looked back at me.

I stopped staring at her legs running up to her skirt.

"You are new to France?" she asked.

"Yes."

She turned around and kept pulling me onward.

Did it matter? Did she care how I gawked at her? Surely she had dressed like that for a reason.

At the corner of the room, she stepped down into a spiral stone staircase. Keeping hold of my hand, she descended. The music grew quieter, and stone walls surrounded us.

A hallway opened up to the right, with rows of closed wooden and iron doors on both sides. Two yellow-orange lightbulbs at the end of thin wires hung from the ceiling, but we kept spiraling downward. The music above faded further. I wondered how long the little creature had been a vampire.

At the bottom of the stairs, Collette pulled me into a hallway like the one above, where a lonely bulb glowed. Rows of doors lined both sides, but unlike above, a few doors were cracked open. Collette brought me into the first room on the right and finally let go of my hand.

I had expected to find a plain stone slab or a crude iron

torture rack. But the king-sized bed with pillows and a maroon comforter didn't look so bad.

Ah—manacles dangled from high on the wall. Good to know I wasn't that far off.

"You like those?" Collette closed the door and pointed to the wrist shackles.

"Uh… I dunno." Not that I could have stopped her from using them. Not that she needed to use them. Despite being petite, like all vampires, she possessed strength far greater than any mortal's.

She walked to me.

Surely the rules about safety in vampire clubs extended to their basements, right?

Collette's blue eyes flared. *Or did they?* She kept coming. I didn't know what to say—I couldn't do this.

She stopped inches away and looked up at me. I wanted to kiss her. She put her hand on my chest and brought her soft lips to mine. She pushed me back a step, and I glanced at the stone wall behind me.

She kissed me again and pushed me backward. Holding her sides, I went to kiss her, but she shoved me, sending me stumbling backward into stone.

She pounced. In the blink of an eye, she covered the distance between us and pinned me against the wall. She chomped into my neck.

Warmth shot into me. Collette sucked blood out of me, and heat—glorious heat—surged into my body.

She withdrew her fangs. Her chest heaved. "*Mon Dieu…* John, do not move!"

Then the door was open, and she was gone. She had moved too quickly for me to see. I stood alone in the cell, wondering what in the world I had done wrong. Why had she left and taken that warmth with her? I wanted it back. I *needed* it.

Blood trickled down my neck. Or should I have been thankful to have had only a taste and taken that chance to leave… but leave and do what? No one out there made me happy.

Collette reappeared at the doorway. The blonde who had been with her at the bar followed her in and sat on the bed, her hungry eyes fixed on me.

"Come." Collette held out her hand once more. Once more, I took it.

Collette sat me down between her and her friend. Together, they pulled my shirt over my head and dropped it on the floor. The blonde took my wrist in her hand. Collette slid her fingers across my bare chest, held my neck, and bit back in. Heat poured into me. I closed my eyes. Two pricks at my wrist sent flame up my arm, swirling to my center.

Both vampires sucked. Blood ran out of me. Heat poured into me, pulsing through my arms and legs, crashing against my fingers and toes.

Let it crash again…

They sucked harder. A wave of flame radiated from my neck. Another from my wrist. From my neck. From my wrist.

The waves slowed. They drank more slowly. I grew warmer, ever warmer.

Fire burst at my side, and I cracked open my eyelids.

Leaning on the bed, a shirtless male vampire in tight leather pants had sunk his teeth in. A female in a bright-red dress entered the room, and the blonde held my unbitten wrist out to her.

I burned in waves from every corner of my body and couldn't keep my eyes open any longer.

4

ETHAN

Rich, yet pure blood. With my hands in my pockets, I walked Magazine Street's uneven sidewalk, in the Garden District west of the French Quarter. I hadn't fed that evening and imagined yet again the nuance of the blood I searched for. What would the contradiction taste like? How would it feel running over my fangs and into me? Ellie had been resting comfortably when I left her at the nursing home an hour earlier. If her heart failed, I'd be alerted like last time and back there immediately.

Trendy restaurants, bars, boutique shops, and sure enough, nationwide-brand stores were mixed in among private homes on up-and-coming Magazine Street. The majority of the buildings shared the same narrow, shotgun-style layout that permeated that part of the city. The eclectic mix of consumer locations attracted an equally varied mix of patrons. Young professionals fresh out of college frequented the inventive, artisanal eateries and craft-beer bars, along with older residents who had lived in the area since before the new wave of businesses.

Purple, green, and yellow ball gowns filled the windows of a shop across the street from me, next to a more traditional women's clothing boutique full of attire in always-fashionable black. The veterinarian's office just past it was always closed by the time I woke, except during the shortest days of winter. On my side of the street, just ahead, a young woman in a business suit led two others out of a windowless bar. In the midst of a conversation that hadn't ended inside, they smiled and laughed. One woman had to warn their leader not to run into me, and I halted to make it easier for her to pass.

The women were lawyers or legal assistants, I guessed, based on their clothes. Watching them cheerfully walk away, I opted against following and finding out their professions for sure. It wasn't for lack of thirst, but I aimed to reach a particular antique shop before its owner closed for the night. The group turned off the street at the corner.

My thirst called out to me. The inhuman need, like a violent hunger at my core, screamed in my mind: "Catch up with them! Hold them! Sink your fangs into their soft flesh. Pick one, at least, and do not wonder—*know* if she is a lawyer! Know the taste of her blood, know her completely, and calm the storm raging within you."

I had woken with that hunger at sunset. I'd climbed out of my coffin with it, as always, and would carry it with me through the streets of New Orleans until I satisfied it. Often a particular craving came with the thirst—the blood of the innocent or, on another night, the blood of the very guilty. My body would urge me toward someone of this race or that.

Usually, it was a woman, but sometimes, the blood of man called to me louder than the rest. "Find someone who has never been bitten by a vampire," that lust sometimes said. "Or someone who would drop their guard the moment they noticed you, because as much as you desire their blood, they crave the rush and the high that comes with your bite." Or it might insist, "Find someone fascinated by your apparent youth."

In addition to that unchanging appearance, I was also inhumanly fast and strong. But the gifts had not come without a price. College had become impossible, and I'd dropped out. I never got to work on Wall Street like I had planned. I missed the sun's bright rays warming my skin, but I'd become accustomed to hiding from them. Hiding from my thirst, however, had proven impossible.

When I was a new vampire, back in New Jersey, I'd tried to hide from it. Ellie had awoken from her coma then, long enough to tell me that she had loved the three years we were together. She had never been happier her whole life, but despite that, she would not drink my blood and join me as a vampire. She would not be healed by unholy demon blood, even *my* demon blood.

The night after that, instead of hunting for blood, I sat at Ellie's bedside, but she didn't wake to reconsider. That still scene played out the following nights, while my vampiric thirst grew. Nurses came to her room, one after another, night after night. They checked Ellie's monitors, and my gaze wandered to the nurses' veins and delectable arteries while I listened to their beating hearts pumping blood through them. But why go on? Why feed my body and nourish the home of my immortal blood if Ellie would not take my blood and be healed by it? Why live, if she would not truly live with me?

My thirst did not share my melancholy, though. While potential prey came and went from Ellie's room, the thirst beat against my insides like a drum, growing, clamoring louder, berating me from ever deeper within, becoming deafening.

So, on the fifth night—or the sixth, I couldn't remember—I leapt from my chair and grabbed a male nurse. He resembled a jerk from high school I had gotten into a shoving match with freshman year. I chomped into the nurse's throat with such force that it looked like a bite from a dog, not a vampire. Mere feet away from Ellie resting calmly in her bed, I sucked that young man's blood with all my strength. I slurped and gulped it down. I took so much blood I almost killed him. He quit his job after that.

Eleven years later, I could surely have made it longer than five or six days without mortal blood. Eleven years, while hardly a long time by vampire standards, was not nothing, either. I was no longer a newborn creature of the night. I could control myself. I was also no masochist, and starving myself would have been pointless, unless I truly sought to die. And I did not. A year into my nocturnal existence, I had found hope in an antique shop.

Past a private home, the yellow light in that shop shut off. Mr. Rutherford must have been closing up. I checked my watch—he was closing a little earlier than normal. But no matter, I would visit him another evening my walk brought me across his path. Hands back in my pockets, I kept walking.

My hope did not stem from fact I had yet verified, and it grew increasingly fleeting as mortal Ellie neared thirty years old and would not stop getting older.

"Rich, yet pure." Mr. Rutherford had translated the Latin from beneath a drawn image in a deteriorating mid-Renaissance book that had allegedly been written by a Sanguan vampire. In the middle of the two hundred and thirty pages, a map of Hungary took up an entire left-side page, with a dot in its east and the year 1282. On the right-side page, at the top, a black-and-white drawing showed a young man at the bedside of an old, sickly woman who had a grim face. The sun shone brightly outside—its rays could not be mistaken. Blood dripped from a cut in the man's hand, held above the woman's mouth.

In the drawing below it, with the sun clearly overhead, a sun no vampire could have tolerated, the old woman had risen from her bed and gazed to the heavens, smiling.

"The taste is most sublime," the Latin below read. "Rich, yet pure. Blood of a mortal, like the blood of God, if only God still walked this earth for us to drink from."

Human blood, not vampire blood, had healed that woman. Not *demon* vampire blood, like mine. I copied the text to paper Mr. Rutherford supplied, word for word. I searched the book for any other trace of related information but found none. Seeing my excitement, Mr. Rutherford apologized profusely that he could not sell me the book, as it had already been purchased by a regular customer, an anonymous Spectavi vampire, via an agent.

I had considered stealing the book. Mr. Rutherford couldn't have stopped me. But the Spectavi would have retrieved it eventually. Making enemies of that worldwide organization seemed unappealing. My purpose was far better served remaining ignored in their war against the Sanguans. Since I didn't drink synthetic blood, I absolutely was a Sanguan, and the Spectavi despised me for it. But following the law and not fighting actively against the Spectavi meant they had no cause to bother me. They left me alone and focused on the Sanguans who openly opposed them or the ones they could prove had committed crimes against humanity.

So why upset my personal peace with them? I had the information I needed. I had written out the words in Latin and English. I remembered the drawings completely. I asked Mr. Rutherford to contact me if he came across anything else that might be connected. Even if he had to sell those items to the anonymous Spectavi, he gave the impression that he really would give me a chance to see them first.

Best I could find, the book had been written by an ancient Sanguan, but under a pseudonym. Either no one I spoke to knew the true author, or no one would tell me if they did.

I discovered nothing about those particular drawings' subject, the man with the sublime blood. I asked around and met one Sanguan who recalled seeing the book, but he hadn't paid the drawings special attention before turning the page. He found my interpretation of what they represented intriguing, but not conclusive. He seemed sincere, and I had to take him at his word. Drinking his blood wouldn't have revealed more than he'd told me, since memories and emotions came only with mortal blood, not the blood of other vampires.

Out on the busy street after that meeting, I'd smelled the stench of Spectavi synthetic blood and assaulted the vampire whose veins it ran through. Despite having no idea who he was, I screamed questions at him about the book and drawings as I shoved him down to the sidewalk.

He proved considerably stronger than me, when he got up and pinned me against the brick building side. He explained with clear precision that he hadn't the faintest notion of what I was blabbering about. Over the years that followed, I questioned a handful of other Spectavi more politely, and all echoed that response.

Past Mr. Rutherford's antique shop, I continued down Magazine Street with nothing but my faint hope. The year 1282 was a long time before 2006, and Hungary was an ocean and half a continent from New Orleans, but there *had* been a mortal whose blood healed another mortal. If only such a person would exist in my time, and I found that person before Ellie died her mortal death...

5

VERA

In the steel box of a laboratory beneath Edmond's home, filtered cool air gently circulated. Machines hummed, pumping and analyzing blood. I slid a slide under my microscope lens and inspected the sample of the most-recent blood mixture I had sent through my patients' bodies. The red synthetic cells appeared as expected. They hadn't been damaged. My patient hadn't modified them when responding so poorly to them. The molecules I had added remained present; they just hadn't produced the desired result.

"Good evening, Vera."

I looked up from the microscope to the propped-open glass door. "William."

The Spectavi scientist had led the Eure team that created synthetic blood. The thin vampire nodded his bald head at the wide window separating our work area from the rest of the room. "Any luck?"

"No." I shoved my hands into the pockets of my lab coat

I wore over a white blouse then looked through the glass at my patients. The two shiny steel coffins stared straight back at me as always, horizontal on stands, an unmoving body beneath each lid. "And it won't be luck when it works. I just haven't found the right mixture yet."

"Of course." William sat down at his laptop behind me, facing away from me and the coffins.

I took another look into my microscope.

World War II, for all its horrors, had led to very significant advances in almost every scientific field. I had read, and Edmond had recounted the tale of how in 1951, based on projects begun during the fighting, he and William's team of scientists at Eure had finally succeeded in creating what they had for so long sought—laboratory-made blood that could satisfy a vampire's thirst.

Vampires were drastically stronger than mortals, and they moved at superhuman speed. Decapitated or burned to ash by sunlight or persistent fire, they would perish, but vampires healed from almost any other injury and healed quickly if supplied fresh blood. A vampire's powers grew over potentially endless years, rising with each setting sun. Pitted against such creatures, mortal humans had little hope. They couldn't fight vampires, and they would have been dominated by those immortals bent on subduing the human race if it weren't for the Spectavi. Edmond's Spectavi vampires protected humanity from Sanguan vampires who acted as they pleased. No law would restrain them, Sanguans declared, so the Spectavi took on the task of policing them.

Having played that role in the interest of humanity for more than a thousand years, the Spectavi had long held positive relationships with governments all over the world. The advent of synthetic blood cemented those ties, which made perfect sense to me. Imagine a meeting or mission with human police or military personnel together with Spectavi vampires. Of course the humans would feel more comfortable alongside vampires who didn't crave their mortal blood.

"Good evening, Vera."

I looked up again and smiled.

Edmond, wearing a dark business suit, stood in the doorway, holding a thermos in his almost perfectly white hand—vampires' skin lightened as they aged, and Edmond was very old.

"William." Edmond nodded to him then set the thermos on the counter in front of me. "Coffee. That blend from Guatemala you liked when we visited."

We had been there the year before, and he remembered correctly. I had loved it. "Thanks." I usually kept the vampires' nocturnal schedule, though I did sometimes wake a couple hours before sunset and begin my day while they still rested in their wooden coffins.

"How are things going?" Edmond asked.

"With them." I motioned at the steel coffins. "Not well."

"And Protice?" He was referring to the project I was leading to enhance the synthetic blood.

"Protice…"

William turned to me.

"Also not well," I said. "But differently badly, if that helps."

Edmond smiled.

"With Protice, my test subjects don't lash out at me day and night, like those two do." The comparison didn't have the amusing ring I had envisioned. "So that's something."

Edmond glanced to the steel coffins. "It's been quite a while with those two."

"I'll figure it out," I said.

"What if you don't?"

"What?"

"What if you can't?" Edmond asked.

I crossed my arms. "Have I let you down yet?"

"No."

"Do you trust me?"

"Yes."

"This is science," I said. "It's hard."

"That, I can attest to," William said.

"That it is difficult, I certainly appreciate," Edmond said. "The work you two do is extremely complicated and, at this point, so complicated that it is beyond me. But with your patients, I wonder if it simply goes beyond science."

I threw up my arms. "Really? This *again*?"

William said, "The way they send visions to your mind is so rare. Almost unheard of."

"Blood runs through them!" I pointed at the coffins. "Blood can heal their madness. We've seen changes in their brain patterns when we've altered the synthetic blood running into them. We've documented the changes. We've modified what we sent to them and documented those results. That is *science*."

"Temporary changes." Edmond wagged his finger. "Only temporary. And the pain they inflict on you…"

I pulled off my lab coat and hung it on the back of my chair. "I can't deal with this from both of you." As I grabbed the thermos and marched toward the doorway, Edmond stood aside. I turned around before leaving. "Well, I could deal with it, but I won't." With a nod, I left and headed up the steel staircase.

Beyond the basement door, Edmond's fine wood floors were covered with intricate rugs brought back from the Orient, and all the ancient sculptures and artifacts made his home undeniably impressive. But I had walked those floors and seen all the art before, as I had before endured listening to Edmond's doubts and concerns for my well-being. I didn't *like* that my patients attacked my mind, but it came with the job. I had promised Edmond those patients would find peace, and I meant it, however long it took.

In the foyer, I pulled open the heavy wooden door and slammed it shut more forcefully than intended. Warm, humid air filled the early summer evening, but I sipped my hot coffee anyway.

Toward the main entrance, downhill from the private homes, white office buildings—some high, some low—lined the campus streets. On a desolate uphill street, heading for a particular private home, I traversed Eure's global headquarters, where nearly a thousand Spectavi vampires worked each night, along with a few dozen humans who all longed to be vampires. While I had access to everywhere, security was tight around the clock. After sundown, Spectavi guards took over for the stout human force that worked the daylight hours.

I *would* help my patients, I assured myself. Edmond hadn't told me their identities, only that they were vampires. Since he cared so deeply for them, I assumed they were his family or dear friends afflicted with vampiric rage they could not control. Maybe brothers-in-arms from his centuries of fighting Sanguans or perhaps old brides. I no longer dwelled on it, though. Edmond said he kept their identities from me for my safety, so I didn't press him on it. He had given me so much, and I trusted him. What I really cared about was the challenge he had set before me.

But why didn't *he* trust *me* when I said that I would finish the job?

Clearly, mixing my own blood in with the synthetic when I was sixteen had been a mistake. That had started my patients' assaults on my mind. Or it had allowed them to start. If I was going to scream about science, I needed to be precise in my descriptions. Mixing my blood with the synthetic blood that ran to their bodies had apparently allowed them to identify *me* as the person in charge of the tests on them.

For hundreds of years, my two patients had been locked in steel coffins. Before the invention of synthetic blood, they'd lashed out against their confines, battering the walls that held them. Deprived of blood, their bodies withered and weakened, but would not die. Yet their minds did not weaken or slow. Their minds raced with the overwhelming rage that Edmond sought to cure them of. He had told me as much years ago.

Then, in 1965, Victoria moved the two patients into their current shiny steel coffins. From vats in our lab control room, out through plastic tubes, a special synthetic mixture that William had devised was pumped into their wrists. It nourished them like normal synthetic blood would have, but it also kept them paralyzed, unable to beat against the walls of their coffins or move at all. But that special synthetic blood did not calm them mentally. The monitors on their brains reported frantic activity, and we knew in a different level of detail because of how they lashed out at my mind.

Edmond had failed to cure them of that rage, but I would not. I saw my destination ahead, up the hill: a home built of black stone, with plain columns at the entrance and metal bars covering all the windows. Grim and uninviting in appearance, it was always open to me. I bit my lip and wondered if she would be home.

I stepped onto the porch and, with some effort, pulled open a heavier, darker wooden door than the one at Edmond's. Inside, the only light came from outside, mostly from out back, broken by the bars on the windows. The door slammed shut behind me. Dust lifted off the hardwood floor, old furniture, and ornately framed artwork from centuries past.

I covered my mouth. "Hachoo!" The echoes of my sneeze faded to silence.

To my left, a ray of artificial light hit a statue of the archangel Michael. Sword in hand, he stood on a pedestal, foot at the throat of the serpent, poised to strike down Satan. Michelangelo had carved it for the home's owner in 1542.

On the creaky hardwood, I headed through the foyer, past a rarely used kitchen, and out the back door. A winding dirt path led to a circular wall of tall wooden planks with banks of lights at the top, aimed inward.

I went into the arena, where two vampires—they had to be vampires because they moved with such speed that I couldn't make it all out—fought with short swords. Spectavi vampires. When they slowed enough for my mortal eyes, I recognized them both, and that meant it was practice. In the box seats, separated from rows of empty bleachers, Victoria sat watching, with her long, toned, pearly white arms draped over the chair backs beside her, and her long black hair in a single tight braid. As she often did, she wore leather. The loose skirt reached halfway down her muscular thighs, and her tight top concealed the red cross that always hung from the end of her black chain necklace.

I made my way up the steps and down the row to the eight-hundred-year-old warrior. She moved her arm, and I plopped into the chair next to hers.

"Who's winning?" I asked.

"Stosh," she said, without taking her eyes off the fight.

"Wow." I sipped coffee from my thermos.

"Niall isn't showing me much at all tonight."

"How was Australia?" I asked.

"Fine."

"What was going on there?"

"A horrible Sanguan."

"Horrible how?"

She looked at me then back at the arena.

"C'mon... I'll get Edmond or William to tell me, if you won't."

"A female in Perth murdered a human couple every night at a restaurant," Victoria said. "A man and woman out to dinner, a man and a man on a date, or two women—this Sanguan didn't discriminate. Somewhere in the city for nine consecutive nights, she hacked apart her victims with a short sword. The local Spectavi tracked her after she struck, but whenever they confronted her, she slaughtered them. So I flew over. The Sanguan had some skill, but it didn't take me long to slash off each of her arms before separating her deranged head from her body."

I pictured Victoria swinging her mighty longsword through the Sanguan's neck. "Why'd she do it?"

"It was hard to tell amidst her ranting and raving. Something about unreciprocated love, maybe."

Damn the Sanguans. I heard stories like that all the time, often worse and in more gruesome detail from Victoria, Edmond, and more Spectavi than I could remember, so it didn't strike me as a new horror. But still, damn those Sanguan vampires to hell.

Stosh sliced across Niall's thigh, sending Niall to a knee.

Victoria shook her head. "Want to fight?"

"God yes." I stood.

"Go get changed. I'll call someone."

"Who?"

"It shouldn't matter."

"It doesn't!" I spun and hurried out of the arena.

Inside Victoria's home, I bounded up the old staircase

two steps at a time then rushed down the hall to my room—my other room, as mine in Edmond's home was my first. I flicked the switch, and dim lamps on each side of the old bed lit.

My sword, a Japanese katana I had named *Tomori*, rested in its black scabbard on its stand atop the oak dresser. I wouldn't need my sword, because surely we would spar with wooden weapons, but seeing it always made me happy.

I set my thermos on the dresser and pulled out what I needed. I switched my black dress pants for leggings of the same color and changed into a green-and-black sleeveless top that clung to my lean body and had a high collar that covered the two fang marks on my neck. I slipped on flat shoes and pulled my hair into a ponytail.

My sword *really* looked like it wanted to come with me. I grabbed it off its stand and headed outside as quickly as I had come.

In the arena, Victoria had gone down to the fighting ground. Niall stood only a couple inches shorter than her, but the difference appeared more pronounced while Victoria scolded him. I slowed my approach, already sweating from my haste in the sticky air. Bleeding from wounds to his leg and shoulder, Niall nodded to her repeatedly, before limping away with his head low.

Victoria looked to me. "You brought your sword?"

"Ya." I tried to slow my breathing. "Yes."

"That would be a dangerous game," Victoria said. "Against Primo."

"What's a Primo?"

"Your opponent. He's visiting from our office in Barcelona."

"He has a silly name."

Victoria smiled.

I savored the rare accomplishment. "Human?"

Victoria raised an eyebrow. "As long as *you* are human, fast as you are, you won't be a match for my kind." So yes, human. She nodded past me.

I turned to a Spectavi guard in gray fatigues, carrying an assault rifle, leading a tall, broad-chested man up the path. Primo wore loose black pants and a tight sleeveless top. He did not have a silly demeanor.

"Why does he look so angry?" I asked Victoria.

"Focus, Vera. That's focus on his face and in his body. You might try yourself to find such a state."

"I focus," I said. "I just don't look miserable when I do."

"Primo," Victoria said. "Welcome."

He extended his hand. She put out hers, and he bowed and kissed it.

"This is Vera," Victoria said.

His determined countenance remained. "Vera."

Six foot four, I guessed him to be, a full seven inches taller than me. He had long, muscular arms and was almost certainly a few years older than me. Purely as a soon-to-be adversary, he did demand more respect than I naturally offered anyone, so I attempted to appear serious. "Primo." I asked a question I knew the answer to: "What do you do at Eure?"

"I am a warrior." He looked me up and down. "Like you, yes?"

"No. I'm a scientist. This is for fun."

"Bu—"

"Primo." Victoria pointed at him. "I assure you, I did not call you out here to waste your time."

He shook his head. "To teach her a lesson, maybe?"

"Please do." Victoria walked to the variety of swords, axes, and other weapons leaning against the arena's tall wall.

She threw a slightly curved wooden bokken—a practice sword shaped like my real one—in my direction. I snatched it out of the air and tossed her my sheathed katana. She threw a bokken to Primo.

"First to three," Victoria said.

Primo and I looked to her.

"Well?" She shrugged. "Go."

One handed, Primo sliced his bokken at my head. I ducked. He swung low, and I jumped over it.

He got his second hand on the bokken handle and chopped down at me, but I stepped aside.

He lunged forward and sliced. I dodged.

Bam! My cheek collided with his rising elbow. I dropped to a knee.

"One," Victoria said.

He towered over me. "Scientist?"

I stood and backed away.

Primo tapped the end of his bokken to his palm. "Do you know how to use this?"

I finally got my second hand on mine. "Uh-huh."

I stepped to him and chopped high. With a loud *crack* of his bokken against mine, he blocked. I swung low, but he blocked. I moved forward and swung high. Block.

Low. Block. High. His blocks kept coming, so I pressed forward, swinging faster, switching sides while he retreated. I switched back and swung high. Faster, I swung. High! High! High! *Smack!* My bokken finally connected with his skull.

"One to one," Victoria called from the far wall.

Primo looked left and right.

"You backed up a *long* way," I said. "Lose track of where you were?"

He glowered at me.

"Do you fight often?" I shrugged demonstratively. "Am I wasting my time?"

Two hands on his weapon, Primo stepped to me and swung hard.

I ducked, shifted backward, and returned to a fighting stance. When he swung low, I blocked.

His next strike hit high, driving my bokken to my cheek. He struck harder, and it took all my strength to block effectively.

I swung my foot under his ankle, and feet flying into the air, he fell to his back. He blocked two swings at his face before I smashed my bokken into his ribs. For the best, I decided. I didn't *actually* need to break the Spaniard's pretty nose. He pushed himself backward in the dirt.

I glanced at Victoria.

"Two to one," she said.

Chest heaving, Primo got himself up and walked away from me. He turned, and his nostrils flared. Then he slowed his breathing.

Good to see he wasn't a total waste. Eventually, he would be a Spectavi vampire, and we would need him to fight well in the war against the Sanguans.

But that was eventually. In one hand, I spun my bokken end over end—three to one sounded a lot better than three to two. I got my other hand on my weapon and ran at him.

He waited, and when I got there—*crack!*—he blocked. I dodged his fist flying at my face. With his other hand, he swung his bokken, and I ducked. He finally used his reach to his advantage, but I moved faster.

I dodged then blocked. I dodged again then swung. He blocked, but the look on his face told me he hadn't expected my attack.

I was faster than he was—I was faster than *everyone*. But he got his bokken up just in time for my next attack. He swung. I smashed it away.

He would make a mistake eventually, but I wouldn't.

Red! Everywhere.

Smack! Wood hit my hip, driving me to the ground.

Red filled my world. My hip didn't matter. Thundering red fire beat against my forehead.

Victoria stepped toward me. I put up my hand, and she stopped.

"What's this?" Primo shouted. "Learn to take a hit, girl!"

"Vera, are you all right?" Victoria called.

I saw half red. Ringing filled my ears between crushing, violent screeches. Surely Victoria understood that my patients, from their coffins beneath Edmond's home, had launched a fresh assault on my mind.

"Yeah." I pushed myself off the dirt and got myself to my feet. "I'm fine."

"Hm." Primo gestured to Victoria. "Well?"

Victoria crossed her arms. "Score's two to two."

Primo charged.

Red flashed, and I saw only a wall of the color.

I screamed and cut down with my bokken.

Crack! Primo blocked, and the red faded.

I cut high, and our bokken met. Low, he blocked.

Bloody bubbles popped in my mind. I screamed and kicked at Primo's ankle, but his other leg hit mine to block. I could barely see, so I raised my bokken and—*crack*—caught his. I swung high.

Seeing only red, I fought using sounds and moving air.

Low, high, low. I fought from memories of earlier rounds.

High, low, high. *Smack-smack!* His bokken hit my face as mine hit his. I fell backward and hit the dirt hard. The black sky gave way to red, except the stars still shone above.

A star snuffed out by red became a drop and hit my sweaty forehead. Then another fell.

I watched as each star in the sky ceased twinkling. White light changed to bloodred then liquefied and fell. A steady stream rained down, pelting my exposed skin hardest.

My skin ignited in flame. I opened my mouth to scream, but no sound came. I could not move. I lay there, mute, motionless, as drops of red set my face and arms afire.

Then sweet blue shot through me. I breathed a full breath.

Blue flame ran cool over my skin, healing the fresh burns. It traveled up from my neck and met each beat of throbbing red. And blue won! The red beats became weaker as blue hit harder.

The red fire diminished until blue remained unchallenged. Then it, too, died out.

I opened my eyes. In the center of the arena, with white stars twinkling in the black sky above her, and my skin unblemished, Victoria held me, kneeling. A stream of my blood trickled from the side of her mouth.

I looked around for Primo.

"I sent him away," Victoria said.

"Thank you."

"End this," Victoria said. "End your torture! I'll do it right now."

"No," I said.

"I'll get Edmond, if you'd rather."

She offered a fourth cure, a way my patients would never be able to attack my mind again.

"Let him make you a vampire," Victoria said.

"No." A tear slid down my cheek. I held her more tightly. "Never."

6

JOHN

I opened my eyes to find a blue glow along the floor coming from the stone wall. I lay on the bed atop the comforter, alone in the room. The wooden door was shut.

Dots covered my abdomen in pairs. My shirt was on the floor, but my pants, socks, and shoes were still on. I shuddered. I had woken up on my back—like a corpse.

Sitting up, I pressed my fingers to my neck. Two small indentations marked where I had been bitten. On the other side was the same thing.

A thin wire under the door ran to the source of the blue glow, a night-light propped against the wall. *How thoughtful of the Sanguans.*

I pulled my phone from my pocket. *8:17 a.m. Daytime.* That meant no vampires could be around. Was anyone else?

What had I done? I remembered the vampires on the bed with me, all of them with their strong hands and firm bodies all over me. *That* had not been my aim when I'd sat down at the bar.

I laid my head back on the thick pillow, stared at the rough stone ceiling, and took a deep breath. I was alive. I was okay.

My eyes closed. Heat, fire… Collette sucking blood from my neck. God, that had been good.

"Never again," I felt as though I should have thought. I should have pronounced it or sworn it.

Instead, I wondered if Collette's coffin was nearby, how soon after nightfall she would wake, and if she would pounce on me the same way the next time I saw her. Would she be at the same club that night?

My wallet and hotel room key were also still in my pocket, along with two unexpected pieces of off-white folded paper. I unfolded a piece. Written in pen, the note said:

Come back tonight. We'll take our time.

Argo, Janet, Felipe

How many had drunk from me? Those three and Collette. But there had been others… Vampires had streamed into the room before I passed out.

I unfolded the other note.

Let's meet up again. Text me.

- Collette

P.S. You shouldn't stare. You are correct. I dress like that to be noticed. But how about a glance when you notice, a smile, and you come talk to me?

I read her phone number at the bottom then let the notes rest on my chest. She knew the questions I had asked myself about how she was dressed because she'd learned all my thoughts and memories when she drank my blood.

Should I wait to text her until nightfall?

I could decide later. I had all day.

I folded the notes, slid them into my pocket, and got off the bed. I grabbed my shirt from the floor, and as I stood, my head spun. I steadied myself on the bed. I had lost a lot of blood. More accurately, it had been taken from me.

But I was fine. And Collette had been beyond fine. So had her blond friend. Wondering if it was normal for so many to rush in to drink my blood, I put on my shirt and felt my neck again. A turtleneck would be good to cover those marks.

I rechecked my pockets, making sure I had everything. I collected myself at the door to recover from the long four-step walk and to take a moment before testing my freedom. I wrapped my hands around the iron handle... and pulled open the door. Thank goodness.

The overhead bulb was off in the hall, but a blue night-light opposite the staircase was glowing. Most doors were open, though a few remained shut. I didn't hear anything.

My fingers running along the stone wall helped steady me up the spiral staircase. My stomach growled loudly. Breakfast had to be my immediate destination.

At the first basement level, all the doors were open except one. I kept ascending until I saw into the quiet club. A shirtless man lay against the nearby wall, breathing. A woman in the far corner rested in the arms of a man with a loosened necktie. Others slept scattered throughout the place, which still reeked of sweat and stale air.

Thunk-creeaak. A door opened below. I couldn't see into

the basement hall, and I was blocking the staircase, so I finished going up, got off it, and continued toward the bar. The hallway beyond led to the exit.

Footsteps echoed up the stairwell. Near the stool I had sat on the night before, I held myself up against the bar and turned back to a tall woman emerging from the basement. Beneath long, straight black hair, she had such a pretty face and very fair skin—what I could see of it anyway. She wore black pants and a matching long-sleeved shirt.

I wanted to introduce myself as she approached, to say hello or to say anything. But I failed to get a single word out of my mouth.

She gave a small smile then shifted her eyes down. I couldn't think. Could I blame my inaction on having lost all that blood? I pictured Collette at the bar with me but shook the image away while I watched the girl walk down the hall and turn out of sight.

I followed. By the time I made the same turn and got to the first of the doors, the girl had disappeared. Around the second corner, beyond the second door, outside, I squinted in the sunlight and spotted her up the block.

"Hi, I'm John. Are you from Reims?" would have worked. But even if I had been able to muster the energy, I would have had to yell it at that point.

The other way, down the street, I spied McDonald's golden arches in the distance. I had missed my chance with the girl, and experiencing local cuisine be damned, I needed food.

I ate two breakfasts then slept in my hotel until almost three before going out for lunch at a nearby cafe. It all helped significantly, but I still felt tired. I had never donated blood or had it drawn by a doctor, but what all those vampires drank from me surely amounted to more blood lost than either of those would have. Everything I did that day was unusually exhausting.

At nearly five o'clock, the sun shone between occasional clouds, and I slowly walked the sidewalks of light-gray flat stone toward the huge thirteenth-century cathedral in the center of town. The destination did seem ironic considering the events of the prior night, but it had been on my list for that day, and it would have taken more energy to come up with something other than the sightseeing I'd already planned.

I'd decided to text Collette shortly before nightfall.

My heart beat quicker. I would hold her. She would bite me.

Vampires couldn't have sex. They lost that when they ceased to be human. Drinking blood was said to replace that sensation for them, but only to a point. After experiencing the bites myself, I agreed with that assessment. The bites had been a different pleasure that offered a different kind of connection. In my tired mind, I searched for details of the Sanguans' bites, and amid the fire, the sun didn't seem as warm or bright as usual.

The cathedral and its two square-topped towers dwarfed the city buildings around it. Though my mother was

Catholic and had tried to lead me down the same path, it had never stuck. By high school, I had quit going to church altogether. I will admit that during especially lonely hours in the wake of my divorce, I had conversed with God in my mind more than ever before. But that had been years ago, and it hadn't lasted.

Yet I remained alone. Collette might change that. The notion that she knew my whole life and all my emotions pleased me. What would she say when I texted? What would I write to her? How many texts from others like me would Collette have waiting when she woke that night? Maybe it wasn't an appropriate time to be thinking about a Sanguan vampire.

The cathedral grew before me as I neared—those tall towers, its three arched portal entrances, and the big rose window at its center. The building cast an imposing visage.

At the door of the portal on the right, along with the other tourists—mostly tourists, presumably—I entered. Massive Corinthian columns ran up to a ceiling vaulted more than a hundred feet in the air. Ornate stained-glass windows glowed deep blue and vibrant red, yellow, and green in the sunlight.

And it was cavernous. Fine craftsmanship and intricate details abounded, sure, but the space just opened up so big. Construction had been completed in 1275, I remembered from the guidebook I'd left in my hotel room. French kings had been crowned in the cathedral, back when there had been French kings, and the church had served as a hospital in World War I. Though it had been damaged by German shellfire, the structure had since been repaired.

A path ran the length of the nave, flanked by rows of simple wooden chairs, nine on each side. Nearly all were vacant. At the opposite end of the cathedral, below narrow stained-glass windows, was an illuminated altar, but I could hardly see it from that far away. I headed up between the chairs for a better look.

Golden chandeliers hung at the end of long cords. I imagined their candles lit at nighttime, which seemed worth coming back to see. A simple, small wooden crucifix adorned one column. The people scattered among the chairs checked guidebooks, chatted quietly, or gazed to the ceiling or at the walls, taking it all in, the same as I did. No one prayed, though I figured more secluded places away from the tourists had been set up for that.

I neared the space separating the first set of chairs from the set in the choir, nearer the altar. In the front row of seats, in the middle chair on the right, sat a woman with long black hair.

A few rows behind her, I stopped. Could it be the same girl I had seen leaving the vampire club? What were the odds?

I veered down a row of chairs to put more distance between us. Maybe I would grow bolder eventually, but not without being certain. Out in the aisle on the opposite side of the church, I looked over at her as I walked until I could see her face. Her thick black turtleneck puffed up under her chin. Same girl. Holding a notebook, she glanced up at the far end of the cathedral and appeared to be drawing, her long legs in black pants, stretched out in front of her. She wore simple flat shoes.

A column blocked my view, so I backed up a step. Late twenties, I guessed, a few years younger than me. Her skin seemed so fair compared with the harsh cathedral.

All I had to do was walk over and introduce myself, but... I didn't even know if she spoke English. I wished Collette were with me. Collette knew everything about me. She knew my secrets and had already said she wanted to see me again. The girl in the chair didn't know me, not one bit. What if she didn't want to talk to me? Even if she did happen to speak English, she was busy with her notebook.

It dawned on me that I didn't know Collette at all. She had drunk my blood, but information hadn't flowed both ways. And Collette had encouraged action. With regard to herself, perhaps, but surely, she also meant it as a life lesson. I headed for the girl, thinking that when it went horribly, it wouldn't matter, because I was in France, and I would never see her again.

Still holding the pencil between her fingers, she suddenly looked up at me with a puzzled expression.

I had to say something. "Hi, I'm John." Could have done worse.

"Madison," she said.

"I saw you at the club earlier."

"I remember." She sounded American, but no regional accent jumped out.

"How... uh... how was your night?"

She tapped her pencil's blunt end against her notebook. "Fine. Yours?"

Mine had not gone as expected. It had been very confusing. "Fine," I said.

"Want to sit?"

"Sure." I sat in the wooden chair beside her.

The soft red of her lips, the bold raven color of her hair, even the silver of her eyes all stood out from her very light skin.

"So… What brings you to Reims?"

"Traveling," she said. "Really… just traveling. How about you?"

"The same, actually. I was in England for a while. About a month. Then headed here. Did a night in Paris, but then here."

She looked up and around at the cathedral. "What do you think?"

"It's magnificent."

She nodded.

"What do *you* think?" I asked.

"It's big."

"Ha. It *is* big." All signs pointed to her traveling alone, but asking didn't seem appropriate. I glanced at her notebook then at the altar at the far end of the cathedral— in her drawing, a man lay sprawled atop it. "Interesting."

"Is it?" she asked.

Her drawing detailed the wide marble altar, the gold carving on its front, angels at its side, six candles atop it, the narrow stained-glass windows behind, and the crucifix that hung before the glass. However, she'd added Jesus sprawled atop the altar, with a serpent slithering across his bare chest and wrapped around his legs. Blood dripped from the serpent's fangs, and a prominent bite mark marred his side.

"Doesn't the snake usually lose?" I asked.

"I'd argue differently."

I nodded. "It's good, though. The drawing."

"Thanks." She smiled, which seemed a little forced, then closed her notebook. "Any interest in getting dinner?"

"Uh, yeah, okay."

"You don't have to." She cocked her head. "But the club doesn't open for a while."

"No, no. I want to. Yes."

"Do you know Le Café du Boulevard?"

"No," I said. "But I can look it up."

"It has a maroon awning." She pulled out her phone. "A little after five… See you there at eight?"

"Sure."

She nodded, got up, put her pencil behind her ear, and walked down the center of the nave and out of the cathedral. I watched every step.

———————————

After Madison left, I ambled around the cathedral. I had never enjoyed another as much as that one. I had also never been as distracted from the Gothic architecture and art.

Later on, my hotel's concierge gave me directions to Le Café du Boulevard. Wearing a white dress shirt with a blue sweater and khakis, I headed out so early that I couldn't possibly be late. In fact, I ended up at the half-full restaurant fifteen minutes ahead of schedule. I got a table and waited, saving the booth side for Madison.

Paying me no mind, the couple at the table beside me chatted happily over their plates of sliced meats and cheeses. They spoke French, like everyone else in the restaurant. I couldn't understand them one bit, and in between glances at the front door, I tried to decipher the menu.

"A drink to start?" the waiter asked in heavily accented English.

"No," I said. "Not yet. We will, just not yet."

The waiter walked away. Then the door opened, and Madison walked in. She hadn't changed her outfit. She was so pretty.

"Sorry if I'm late," she said as I stood.

"You're not. I was early."

We both sat down.

"How's your evening been so far?" I asked.

"Fine." She set her purse beside her.

"Well, I got some more rest," I said. "Much-needed rest."

She smiled. "That *will* be needed."

I smiled. Apparently, the previous night had not been her first visit to a vampire club.

The waiter returned. "Something to drink?"

Madison looked to me.

"Uh, yeah. Red wine okay with you?"

"Sounds great," Madison said.

"A bottle of this Bordeaux then." I pointed to my selection, having picked it out earlier along with a bottle of Chardonnay, in case Madison preferred white.

"*Bon.*" The waiter nodded and departed.

I glanced around the restaurant. "This is a nice place. Have you been here before?"

"Yeah. I really like it."

"How long have you been in Reims?"

"Uh…" She squinted. "Three weeks, maybe? Or four. I'm leaving tomorrow, actually."

"Oh." The gulf my heart fell into was cavernous. "Where for?"

"Paris."

Hope. From a trampoline in the gulf, my heart bounced back up toward its surface. "Nice," I said.

Madison examined her menu, so I did the same. She said she didn't know much French, either, but had been to the restaurant often and could explain most of the menu items to me. She went with smoked salmon, and I ordered pasta with chicken and a thick Alfredo sauce. Our entrees were not perfect matches with the wine, but she didn't seem to mind.

"So why Reims?" I asked while we waited for our food. "For almost a month."

"I didn't really plan it. I've been traveling for a while." Her eyes shifted away. "I got comfortable here."

"Then why leave?"

She shook her head. "That Sanguan club—I joked before about what time it opened tonight, but I'm not going back." Madison reached for her wine glass. "I had been *seeing*, I suppose, a vampire there." She took a long sip. "But he's leaving Reims and won't tell me where for, except that it's some mission in their war. He said I couldn't go with him."

I drank, noticing the fading light outside the window. I hadn't texted Collette yet.

Madison sighed. "Probably for the best."

"Right."

"Why'd you come to… England, you started in? Why England in the first place, and where from?"

"From exotic Maryland." The phrase usually garnered a positive reaction on dates, and Madison's smile told me it had once again. "To get away. I needed a change."

"I can certainly relate to that."

"Where are you from?" I asked.

"Seattle."

"Oh, cool." I put down my wine. "I can work from wherever—I'm a web developer, freelance at the moment—so I figured why not pick somewhere that was *actually* more exotic than Maryland."

"How did you *ever* find such a place?"

"Exactly." Our glasses were close to empty, so I took the bottle and tilted it near her glass.

"Mm-hmm."

I poured hers then refilled mine. "How about you? How long have you been in Europe?"

"It's June, so… getting close to a year."

"Wow."

"Yeah. Portugal, Spain, France, England, Italy, now France again."

"Do you speak any of those languages?"

"English," she said.

"Ha, right."

"And some Spanish. People haven't given me a hard time about the languages, though. Most people, anyway."

"That helps," I said. "What do you do for a living?"

"I was a high school art teacher."

"Was?"

"Was. And a painter."

I pictured her drawing of the victorious serpent. "Always such grim art?"

She looked to the table. "Not always."

"The salmon." Our waiter set her plate down then mine. "And the pasta."

Madison got up and grabbed her purse. "I'll be right back."

I watched her and was relieved when she headed for the restroom behind me, and not the front door. Enough personal questions, I decided. That aside, things seemed to be going well. As usual, I was more comfortable once we were *in* the restaurant than I was while getting the girl there.

When Madison returned, we ate and chatted about our time in Europe traveling solo, something new to both of us. She, of course, had more stories from more countries, but my time in England had given me a couple interesting moments to recount.

She had visited the major museums in every city she'd stopped in, and because her trip didn't have a planned ending, she'd also taken the time to visit lots of smaller ones. Some days, she did nothing but draw. When she had said that, her face grew grave.

As she described how beautiful Italy had been, she brightened. The art in Florence reminded her of art that had inspired her growing up, and she had found the quieter canals of Venice especially peaceful. Barcelona, Spain, and Porto, Portugal, were other favorites. The Christmas lights in Nice had brought her to tears, but she didn't elaborate as to why.

And my guess had been close—she was twenty-nine, two years younger than me.

After our waiter cleared our plates, he returned. "Some dessert?" He picked up the empty wine bottle. "*Un autre verre*—another drink?"

"Not for me." Madison gestured across the table. "But you go ahead."

"No," I said. "Thank you."

"*Bon*." The waiter set down our check in a small tray.

I grabbed it and reached for my wallet.

"Thank you." Madison glanced outside, where night had fallen. "Headed to the club later?"

The waiter took the check and my credit card away.

"Oh, uh… I don't know if I'll go, either."

"No?" She tilted back her wineglass and finished the last of it.

"We'll see."

"In that case, I wish we *could* stay for another drink, but my train is very early, and I haven't packed."

"That's all right."

Madison bit her lip but didn't say anything.

The waiter returned, I signed the check, and we got up. I held the door for Madison, then stepping into the night, I wondered if Collette was out there, nearby, waiting to pounce or watching from across the busy street. Were other Sanguan vampires strolling past or lurking in the shadows? How old might some be in a city as old as Reims?

We walked toward Madison's hotel, and I stayed close to

her, despite how futile my effort to resist would have been if a Sanguan attacked, and a Spectavi vampire didn't happen to be around at that very moment.

After a few blocks, Madison pointed, and we turned onto a smaller street. I wondered if she worried about vampires the way I did. We made a left onto an even quieter street. Would I ever see her again? I had to try.

"This is it." Madison pointed to the blue-and-white sign protruding from a four-story building.

"Well, thank you for asking me to dinner tonight."

"Thank *you*," she said. "I'm glad we ran into each other this afternoon."

"I am, too. How long are you going to be in Paris?"

She shrugged. "Who knows?"

"Can I call you?" I took out my phone.

She shook her head.

"Oh."

"Come with me."

I couldn't help smiling. "Really?"

"Really. I don't know if it showed, and I guess you couldn't know, but I smiled more today than I have in a long time. I enjoyed being with you."

"Me, too. I mean, the enjoyed part. I enjoyed being with you."

"Train's at six twenty-five. See you at the station?"

"Definitely." I got that one out correctly.

Madison leaned to me, and I kissed her. When she leaned away, her expression told me I had also done that correctly. She turned and went into her hotel.

7

ETHAN

After waking in my coffin in the larger of my house's two bedrooms, I walked the two blocks to visit Ellie in her nursing home. I sat with her for an hour, holding her hand, remembering the time we'd spent together before that time was confined to nights in that small room.

From there, I headed southwest, into the Warehouse District.

Crack! Billiard balls broke across the street at Billy's. Its front door and the garage door into the bar were both wide open. Two guys were shooting pool under a dirty light hanging above the table. Two men were eating at the bar, and a woman farther down sat alone with a glass of wine. She was forty years old, maybe forty-five, and I needed her blood.

I crossed the street and headed in. The gruff, gray-bearded bartender named Billy glanced at me before getting back to cleaning a mug. He might have guessed such a youthful face belonged to a vampire, but just the same, he might not have. It wasn't the kind of place where anyone received a merry greeting upon entering.

The two men at the bar chomped on chicken wings and occasionally glanced at *Cops*, or whatever police show was playing on the little old TV up in the corner. I headed for the woman at the bar's end, who was focused on a newspaper folded in front of her, while holding a pencil in one hand and her red wine in the other.

Up close, she did indeed look on the older end of my estimated range. Her blond hair was half up, and she wore a pink top, rich indigo-colored jeans, and short gray boots with small heels. She reminded me of my senior-year English teacher.

I motioned to the stool next to her. She shrugged, so I sat. She put down her glass and wrote "BURMA" in her half-empty crossword puzzle.

Billy came over. "What'll ya have?"

I pointed to the woman's wine. "How's that?"

"S'all right," she said.

"Then I shall have a glass."

Billy went to get the bottle.

"S'nothing special, actually," the woman added.

"Won't matter to me."

She raised an eyebrow. "Oh? Not really thirsty?"

The hunger within me screamed against my stomach and up to my chest. "I'm very thirsty."

"I see." She pressed her pencil to a blank puzzle space and stared there.

The bartender set my poured glass down in front of me. "You're twenty-one?"

"More and less," I said.

He grunted and walked away, having probably heard the line before—possibly from me.

Holding the glass by the stem, I swished the thin red liquid around its base. I could smell the fruity notes of plum, but once the liquid hit my mouth, it would taste like nothing, somehow more flavorless than even plain water. I stopped swishing my wine and watched as no legs formed on the side of the glass. Seemed I wasn't missing much with that particular vintage.

The woman put down her pencil. "I'm Sadie."

"Ethan."

"How's your night going then?"

I leaned my elbow on the bar and my head on my hand. "The same as all the rest. How's yours?"

"The same as all the rest." She set her elbow on the bar and matched my position. "Why me?"

Have this woman, my body told me. *Remember your teacher you found so pretty. Know what holding her and biting her would have been. Know it now!* "Because you're the prettiest woman in Billy's bar."

"I'm the *only* woman here."

I smiled. "Because from across the street, I could tell there was something to you. More than to the men shooting pool." I pointed my thumb behind me. "More than those two and their chicken wings. And more than everyone else out tonight I've crossed paths with."

Sadie smiled. The expression made her look less like my old teacher and more like her own person, whom I knew nothing about, yet *had* to know everything about.

"I want to know what it is," I said. "Why I want you so badly. You *are* very pretty, and I want to move your hair aside and kiss your neck, and then sink my fangs in there. While I drink your blood and hold you in my arms, you'll know the depth of my bite, while I'll know what drew me to you from across the street."

"Billy." She leaned forward and called to the bartender. "We're gonna need our checks."

I took out my wallet.

"My place isn't far." Sadie put her newspaper and pencil in her bag. "If there's okay."

"It is."

Billy set down the checks. I took them both and placed a twenty-dollar bill on top. Sadie slid off her barstool, and I followed her out to the street.

"What do you do?" I asked as she turned right.

"I'm a teacher. Fourth grade. But you'll know all that soon, right?"

"I will."

Her foot hit a raised edge of a concrete slab, and she stumbled.

I caught her. "Are you all right?"

Her heart raced. "Yes."

I needed her blood *immediately*. "Why wait?"

She glanced from side to side. "Here?" Her heart sped faster.

I leaned to her and brushed her hair aside. I heard the blood coursing around her body, pounding at her jugular. I kissed her there as I had said I would. I pulled her closer, tighter to me, opened my mouth, and sank my fangs through her flesh.

A spurt of blood teased my lips. I sucked, and blood streamed over them and my teeth. Hot and juicy, it was no flavorless wine, no plain water.

Harder, I pulled her blood into me. *Oh, mortal blood! Oh, Sadie...*

I clutched her beautiful body. The stream of fire ran down into me, fueling me and calming me all at once. She was indeed an English teacher. Her memories came with the flames. She taught in New Orleans and had been since moving back from Baton Rouge after college at Louisiana State.

I slowed my drinking but kept the stream coming. The fire burned lower. She had been born in New Orleans and had a brother and a sister named Jenna, who also lived in the city.

Sadie had just seen Jenna. They'd attended an orchestra concert at the museum of art in City Park the evening before. The quartet had been lovely. The brightly lit Great Hall had been a splendid setting for their beautiful notes. Sadie had enjoyed sharing the evening with her sister, but a real date—a husband or at least a boyfriend—would have been a lot better. In fact, Sadie almost hadn't attended the show, on account of not having a real date to bring.

Bitterness speckled Sadie's blood. Faces and voices of exes flashed to mind, along with memories of final parting meetings and disappointing phone calls from them. It had been a while since she had been with anyone long term.

Sublime. The word called me back to the museum, to a moment after the concert that night with her sister, to a room of dramatic baroque-style paintings.

Rich. I sucked Sadie's blood harder. *Rich, yet pure.*

But those words didn't describe Sadie's blood. She rarely let it show, but within, anger and sadness dominated faint moments of joy. Sadie had heard those words while standing in front of a painting of Saint Cosmas. While reading details of how he died in the late third century, Sadie had noticed a feminine voice from off to her right: *"Sublime. Rich, yet pure. If it hadn't been a mortal's blood I drank, I might have guessed it the blood of a god."*

What a strange thing to say, Sadie had thought. She turned to see who had uttered it. No one behind her. She started for the entranceway to the next room to check there, and her phone buzzed.

A text from her mother asked how the show had been. Sadie assumed her sister had told their mother about the concert, because she certainly hadn't shared her plans for the night.

Sadie responded that it had been good then went out into the Great Hall in search of her sister. Eventually, upstairs on the second floor, she found Jenna in a room full of paintings depicting the Gulf Coast region of the United States.

I pulled blood into me. Sadie slumped in my arms, but I had to keep looking.

Sublime. Rich, yet pure. I found that memory again. The words that matched what Mr. Rutherford had translated for me in his antique shop. Other trips to the museum stood out to me in Sadie's blood, but she had never heard those words in that combination before. She had been bitten by vampires over the years, not infrequently. I recognized four as ones I had seen around New Orleans, but their voices didn't match the one from the museum.

I pulled my fangs from her. Sadie's eyes remained shut. If I had taken enough blood to kill her, so be it. I had to know if she knew anything else of that sublime blood.

She breathed in my arms.

"Hey!" a voice boomed behind me.

I turned, and a rock-hard fist smashed into my cheek.

The stench of synthetic blood hit my nose just before the Spectavi vampire in a gray business suit smashed an uppercut into my chin.

I flew into the air, and he pulled a long knife from a holster inside his jacket. It was at my throat by the time I crashed down onto the sidewalk. My hand gripped the switchblade in my pocket.

"Wait," Sadie said, on her knees.

The Spectavi and I both looked to her.

Her eyes half opened, and she held her neck. "He's with me."

The Spectavi squinted. "Are you sure?"

Sadie widened her eyes. "Yes."

The Spectavi holstered his knife.

I started to get up, but he kicked his wingtipped shoe hard into my side.

"Have a good night." He straightened his jacket and walked away.

Sadie offered me her hand, but I stood without it. The kick didn't matter. The Spectavi walking by had been bad luck, but I was glad to pay that price to have found Sadie.

"Are you okay?" she asked.

"I am." I glanced skyward. "I'm so glad you decided to see that quartet with your sister."

Sadie gave a puzzled look.

"You overheard something," I said. "Words and phrases like ones I read in a book, years ago. I've been looking for any sign of them. And that you heard them not long ago could mean something important." I suppressed the instinct to ask follow-up questions about the event. "It could be *really* important." I had searched carefully for anything else relevant. Sadie had overheard those words, yet knew no more.

But I *had* to know more. I had to find out who had spoken of the sublime blood and if they had drunk it recently, in the thirteenth century, or during one of the seven centuries in between.

8

VERA

In Edmond's lab, ten minutes before midnight, I sat alone with my chair rolled back and my feet up on the countertop. My lab coat hung off my chair's back. To the hum of the blood-pumping machine, I read a printout of the results of my latest test with my patients—no significant brain function change from their usual wild fluctuations.

I looked at their identical steel coffins beyond the lab's long dividing window. Red synthetic blood filled the tubes, locking the patients in their physically paralyzed, but mentally agitated state.

The door at the top of the staircase opened. I only half hoped it was Edmond, as I didn't have anything positive to report about my work.

Footsteps descended the stairs. I glanced at my cell phone on the counter. I wouldn't flee to Victoria's immediately, but the prospect of sparring the following night had appeal. I would text her later, to see if she would be around.

Beyond the glass, Edmond, in a lighter gray suit than the

night before, but a darker one than the night before that, strode by. He rounded the corner into the lab. "How are you?"

"Fine."

He spun William's vacant chair around and sat in it. "And how are things with our little project?"

I figured I could stall him for exactly one second. "Which project?"

"Protice."

And my second was up. I added the printout about the patients to a stack of others just like it, got my feet off the counter, and spun my chair to Edmond. "No significant progress."

"Any progress at all?"

"Maybe, but nothing conclusive. I'm seeing different results, but I don't know if any of them are going to lead where we want."

He nodded.

"I just don't know," I said.

"What have you been trying?"

I recalled some of our advances with synthetic blood over the recent years. I'd added new molecules to cells, removed DNA, added DNA, reprogrammed DNA, and edited RNA to change gene expression.

Spectavi vampires all over the world lived on that synthetic blood. True, Spectavi also drank from other Spectavi. They still craved physical connection with others, though less, studies showed, than Sanguans craved it. And after Spectavi drank from one another, they required extra synthetic to feed their inhuman thirst. There was no getting the synthetic blood out of the equation.

So we had altered the blood to make it faster and cheaper to produce. We improved it so it would last longer in storage. We increased the blood's potency, meaning a vampire would be satisfied by less. We made the blood taste closer to the real thing and smell less fake—though work remained to be done in both areas. Then our more-classified work had begun—but I was stuck on Protice.

"New molecules in the blood cells was my latest attempt," I said.

"Hm." Edmond rubbed his chin. "You're confident you can produce the results we need?"

"I am."

"Why?" Edmond asked.

I shrugged. "I always do."

"I fear I may have stumped you this time. Except with your patients, who we've all been dealing with for quite some time, you've never been stuck this long in one spot. I've never sensed such uncertainty in you."

I loved how he knew me completely by drinking my blood. I never had to wonder if he understood where I was coming from in conversations. I couldn't hold on to secrets, so I confronted him about everything rather than harboring grudges.

He had loved me before ever drinking from me, I was sure of it. But once he had drunk from me, his feelings had grown into a different, deeper love. I couldn't drink his blood to know for certain, but I saw it and felt it. Knowing me completely let him love me completely.

Yet even with that sum of all my memories and emotions, he underestimated me. Knowing what I *had* done and *had* felt didn't tell him what I might do next.

"Don't worry about me so much," I said. "This work takes time."

"Mm-hmm. And those patients." Edmond motioned to the glass. "Any change with those two?"

"No."

He nodded. "I'll be traveling more, starting tomorrow. Our office in Singapore first. Would you like to come? We could make a vacation of it and put some distance between you and them."

The distance that would lessen the force of their attacks had appeal, but I would rather end the attacks for good. "No. I need to keep working."

"I understand." Edmond stood. "And in that case, you have eight weeks." He pointed his finger at me. "In eight weeks, I need to see demonstrable progress with Protice."

"Or what?"

"I take you off the project. It might be that a new approach is needed."

I shook my head.

"Or maybe you solve it tomorrow, Vera. I pray you solve it; you know I do. But I have a schedule in mind, which you also know, and we are behind in that schedule already."

I pointed to the glass. "What about them?"

Edmond turned that way. "Eight weeks, eight years… however long it takes with them." Edmond stepped to me.

"I dearly appreciate your work on their behalf."

I looked up at him from my chair. "I know."

He leaned down, grasped my shoulders, and gave me a long kiss on the lips. "Thank you." He headed for the lab exit then turned back. "I'll make sure that Victoria, William, or myself in between trips is on this campus at all times." He left and headed upstairs.

He meant they would be on campus in case the patients attacked me, I couldn't handle the pain, and needed someone to drink from me to make it stop. Eight years, he had said. I stared at the coffins and couldn't imagine eight more years of their assaults. I had to cure them *soon*, for my own good.

But first, Protice. I opened my laptop then glanced at my phone. I wouldn't text Victoria after all. Protice had to move forward, and I only had eight weeks.

9

JOHN

In Reims, the sun was rising when we boarded the commuter train, which wasn't as nice as the high-speed train I had arrived on. Well under half the thinly padded plastic seats were occupied in the first car I followed Madison through, carrying my big pack on my shoulder. She pulled a wheeled suitcase and held a large handbag.

More empty rows greeted us in the second car. In the middle, two seats faced two others. A small table between them created a booth. Madison threw her bag on the far seat, and I lifted her case onto the overhead rack, where I put my backpack. I sat against the window, which would face forward when the train moved, and was glad when Madison took the seat beside me, instead of one across the table.

"Why such an early train?" I asked.

"It was half the price," she said.

"Ah."

"And... I've been on a weird sleep schedule lately."

I wondered how often she had seen the vampire from the

Sanguan club. Had it been *every* night? A man in a dark business suit walked into our car and glanced at us before continuing to the vestibule that led to the next car.

The train began pulling out of the station.

Madison added, "I didn't fall asleep until after two last night."

"Me, neither." I had lain awake debating texting Collette. I never did, though. But as we left Reims, I missed the little vampire. A lot. I missed her fangs in my neck, my blood running over them, and the warmth running from her into me.

I spotted the man in the suit on the station platform, talking on his phone.

Madison grabbed her bag from the seat across from us. She took out her notebook and handed it to me. "Hold this, please," she said, rummaging around in her bag. I did, and she stuck her head nearly inside her bag.

I recalled what she had drawn in Reims and couldn't resist flipping open the notebook. In familiar black and lighter graphite shades, the Eiffel Tower in Paris stood tall above the grass of the Champ de Mars, with the Seine River beyond it. Corpses littered the park field, in every state of decay, from freshly wounded and bleeding to rotting and bare skeletons. Vultures picked at bones and eye sockets. Bodies hung on nooses dangling from the iron tower's base.

Madison emerged from her bag with ChapStick, which she applied while watching me examine her drawing. I turned the page and rotated the notebook ninety degrees.

Men and women of a noble court filled a wide scene from

left to the right, where the most fancily attired surrounded a throne. All the way on the right, the Pope—I guessed by his garments—watched as the figure at the throne crowned himself. It was almost a normal scene, void of anything macabre, except the figure at the throne wore a hood that hid his face completely. With one hand, he held his crown with fingers of bone. In the other, he grasped a tall scythe. It was the figure of Death.

"It's supposed to be Napoleon," Madison said. "It's in the Louvre. In the painter's original sketch, Napoleon crowns himself."

"Grim," I said.

"Indeed."

"Are they all?" There might have been a hundred pages in the notebook.

"Yes." Madison reached for it.

I handed it over. "Why? You said you didn't always draw things like this."

She put the notebook in her bag, along with her ChapStick. "It's too early." She threw her bag to the seat across the booth, hooked her arm around mine, and rested her head on my shoulder as Reims changed into countryside out the window.

———————

Our train pulled into Paris Est station a little after eight o'clock. Our car had been very quiet. I had watched out the windows the whole trip as the French countryside built up into the big city of Paris. I didn't think Madison had slept, either. It felt so strange traveling to Paris with a girl I had just met. But Madison was *so* new to me that every minute with her, even those in silence, I knew her better than the minute before.

And she was beautiful. A sadness blanketed her, clearly, but a light flickered within her. I couldn't wait for my day with her in Paris to begin.

Madison got up and grabbed her bag as the train eased to a stop. I retrieved her suitcase and my big backpack.

"Where to?" I asked. "Did you already book a hotel?"

"I did." She led the way out of the train car. "In Montmartre."

The area was a hilltop home to artists and the Moulin Rouge cabaret, but I knew nothing else about it.

"Same place I stayed before when I was here," she said. "We can drop off our bags now and check in later."

The downtown station was bustling with travelers, but outside, cabs were plentiful, and we got one quickly. It might have been early for our driver, since he kept quiet after asking for our destination. The winding route in traffic took twenty minutes to cover what couldn't have been farther than a couple miles. Madison stared out her window while we started and stopped, so I stared out mine at the shops on street level, the residences above them, and the people walking and sipping coffee. I wondered what Madison was thinking. Did she regret asking me to join her?

When I noticed the taxi driving uphill, it turned onto a side street and went half the block.

The driver pointed. "*L'hôtel.*"

The taxi stopped in front of the narrow white building, which stood five stories tall, and we all got out. The driver went to the trunk for our luggage.

"*Merci.*" Madison paid him while I held my open wallet. "You got dinner," she said to me. The taxi drove off, and Madison led the way to the hotel's door. "It's redone inside. Bohemian décor that gives it a… a quaint charm."

See, I thought, *she's not melancholy* all *the time.* "Sounds great."

The receptionist, a hefty black man wearing a little red hat, smiled and stood from his small wooden desk as Madison rolled her bag in. "Miss May."

"Oluwaseun!" Madison reached across the desk to hug him and kissed his cheeks. She pointed to me. "This is my friend, John."

"Mister…?" Oluwaseun asked.

"Breen," I said.

"Welcome." He took the handle of Madison's bag. "Your room will be ready at two p.m. Mr. Breen, can I take your bag, as well?"

"Yes, thanks." I handed it to him. "And is there another room available?"

Madison gave me a look.

"I just—"

"Nonsense," she said. "Stay with me?"

"Sure." I wanted to, *of course.* But we hadn't discussed it. "Thanks."

"Good." Oluwaseun threw my bag over his shoulder. "See you this afternoon." At the side of the room, he opened a door to a closet with other bags, cases, and sacks in it, and added ours.

Madison turned to me. "Coffee?"

"Absolutely."

"Have you ever been to Montmartre?" she asked.

"Nope. Aside from a bar and a coffee shop near my hotel, and a couple train stations, I haven't seen Paris at all."

"Well, let's go then. Might as well start with the best view there is, and I know a good place for coffee on the way up the hill."

———————

I wholeheartedly believed Madison had taken me to the best view of the city. On the steps of Sacré-Cœur Basilica, while the unobstructed morning sun gently warmed us, we sipped our coffee, and she pointed out her favorite spots. I suggested it would be fun later or the next day to find a good view back at the Basilica. We concluded that the Eiffel Tower would be perfect.

Paris seemed to move Madison, to brighten her. I wondered what had driven a girl eager to point out city highlights to draw corpses spread beneath its iconic tower. But I didn't want to interrupt her more positive mood, and it was still early, so I didn't ask.

We had crepes for breakfast, mine with ham and cheese, hers with fresh oranges and melting dark chocolate. Then we walked the hilly streets of Montmartre and talked.

Art in the high school where Madison had taught consisted of broad survey classes, as well as specialized electives. So she had experience in everything from drawing and painting to photography and sculpture. And she knew lots of art history, both from teaching it and her undergraduate degree in the subject from Stanford. We visited a home turned into a museum of the surrounding area, and I enjoyed her pointing out intricacies in different pieces that I never would have caught on my own.

For lunch, we had a second round of crepes. Breakfast hadn't disappointed, so we figured, why mess with a good thing? We sat outside at a small round table, and I kept it to myself when deciding that *surreal* had replaced *strange* in my mind, to describe enjoying Paris with a girl I had met only the day before.

Madison had been the black sheep in her family of doctors and lawyers, which felt like the beginning of an explanation for her dark artistic streak, but she didn't provide additional details. I told her I had a younger brother and that my father taught middle school history. When I asked how big her family was, she put down the last bit of her crepe, wiped her hands, and said, "Not as big as I'd like." She never resumed her meal.

Growing up, she had played violin. I told her I had played trumpet in the high school band, which made her laugh. She just couldn't picture it. But it was true, I assured her, though I admitted to never becoming especially good. Neither of us were very into sports, either playing or watching.

She asked about my work, and I explained that I would have to do some website updates and maintenance for clients in a few days, but that aside from checking my email for emergencies, I could put work off until then. I assumed she didn't need to rush back to work, and she did no more than agree with that assessment.

I asked her what she had in mind after Paris—and immediately regretted it. Why suggest a possible end to whatever we had just begun? But she took it in stride. She didn't know, but said she had a lot of Europe left to see, to say nothing of the rest of the world.

On Boulevard de Clichy, in front of the Moulin Rouge, Madison yawned and checked her watch. "One thirty. Should we see if our room's ready? I wouldn't mind a nap."

"Sounds good to me."

We walked back to the hotel, where Oluwaseun greeted us. "Miss May, Mr. Breen." He took a key from a cubby behind him and handed it to Madison. "Room 306. Your bags are inside."

We both thanked him, and Madison led the way to the cozy lift. *Surreal* didn't fade away completely, but it had begun to feel right to be going to *our* hotel room.

This is why I left Maryland, I thought. I glanced at Madison. I'd hoped—dreamed, more accurately, because it seemed such a remote possibility—for something *exactly like this.*

The lift opened to a short hallway with six doors. Ours was the last one on the left.

Madison used the key and pushed open the door—which brushed against the white cloth curtain of the tiny shower, next to a sink, a mirror, and a narrow open door to a toilet. A queen-sized bed immediately to our left nearly reached the wall and window at its foot. There were nightstands, a tall wardrobe, our bags on stands on the far side of the bed, and nothing else.

"Quaint," Madison said. "As promised."

"Very," I said. "But it's great."

Madison yawned again. "Could we nap? I'm going to nap. You don't have to, of course."

"No." I yawned, glad my body had done it. "A nap sounds wonderful."

"I'll wash my face later." She kicked off her shoes, sat on the bed, got under the covers, and slid to the far side.

I took the near side, lay on my back, and considered setting an alarm. She moved closer and put her arm over my chest.

No alarm, John, I told myself. *Because who cares when you wake up?* I was at a beginning, with no end set. *Nap as long as you want. Nap as long as* she *wants.*

I moved my arm so she could lay her head on my shoulder. She did, and I held her. I kissed the hair atop her head. She smiled, and we both closed our eyes.

———————

The bedside clock read six thirty by the time we woke from the longest nap I had taken in years. We were both famished, so dinner became our priority. She showered first and stepped out from behind the curtain with a fluffy red towel wrapped around her.

What color wouldn't look good on her? Against her light skin and with her jet-black hair, I could not think of one.

While she went to her suitcase, I got undressed beside the shower. In the mirror above the sink, I noticed that the fang marks on my neck had mostly healed and faded away. I got in the shower and turned on the water. The dots on my wrists and sides had faded, too. As long as repeated bites in the same spot hadn't made them, marks from vampire bites were supposed to heal quickly, which, thankfully, was proving true for me.

Blow-dryer in hand, Madison glanced at me when I emerged with a towel around my waist. My jaw might have dropped.

She was wearing a black dress that reached halfway to her knees, with white trim. I must have been expecting another turtleneck and pants, but her slender arms and most of her long legs weren't covered at all. She smiled then turned her attention back to her hair.

I put on dark-brown pants, a light-blue shirt, and a navy blazer—the best outfit I could pull out of my backpack. It would be good enough, I told myself. On the lift ride down, I told Madison I really liked how she had done her hair in a low side bun. Outside the hotel, I took her hand and led us down the quiet street.

Around the corner, on a street with more crowded sidewalks and more cars driving past, we found a menu in a restaurant's window. It looked okay, but we pressed on. We passed a few other restaurants before finally picking one with a chalkboard out front boasting of dishes themed for the season. We simply *had* to know what meals represented summer in Paris.

We were seated at a narrow table without much space between it and the adjacent tables. On my left, middle-aged men with glasses of wine and a plate of cheese between them chatted in French. To my right, a younger man and woman leaned close to each other, holding hands, smiling, and speaking softly.

Once we had picked a bottle of red wine from Burgundy, I noted that night would soon fall.

"It's like a whole different world once it does," Madison said.

"It really is." I looked around the lively restaurant, wondering if any Sanguans might stroll in with mortal companions or on their own, eyeing potential prey, while we ate. "There must be some very old vampires in Paris."

Madison shifted in her seat. She touched the two prominent marks on the left side of her neck. She had likely been bitten there often, because the marks had hardly faded.

"I'm sure lots of Spectavi," I added.

"I'm sure." She tapped the table with her finger and glanced at our neighbors engrossed in their own conversations. "I want to get it over with. Can I tell you why I came to Europe?"

"Of course."

"It's not a *fun* story. Not even a little."

Our waiter returned with our wine, and after I tasted, he poured our glasses. Madison bit her lip more than once while she waited.

When he finished and left, Madison took a sip. "You asked how big my family was. My family used to be bigger. It's... horrible. But I just want to tell you and be done with it."

"All right."

"My mother and my father…" She glanced away. "Three years ago, they were on vacation in Morocco, celebrating their thirtieth wedding anniversary, having lunch, when a bomb went off in the restaurant. Seven people, including the Islamic terrorist, died, my parents among them."

"I'm so sorry," I said.

"Two Christmases ago…" Madison's eyes glossed. "My brother and sister, along with her husband, were killed on the way home from church. Christmas Eve. A drunk driver, a high school kid who hadn't had his license a month. I wasn't in the car because I didn't go to church with them. I was home sick. Some virus. I was sick for… a day, really. The next day, I wasn't sick anymore, but my brother and sister were still gone, along with my parents. All dead, all for no reason."

"I… I'm sorry." That definitely explained the drawings.

"That's it, I guess. There isn't more to it. They're gone. After my parents, I managed to go back to work. Terrible things happen sometimes—I understood that. And I had my brother and sister. But after them…" She shook her head. "I tried to go back to teaching right away, to get on with my life, but I couldn't. I just couldn't. A few months later, I still couldn't. My parents left me money, so I could afford to not work, at least for a while. I came to Europe to get away from… everything."

"That's awful." My eyes watered. "I'm so sorry that happened to them. To you. I can't even imagine."

Madison wiped a tear. "I don't understand it. How can I

go back to living like I had? After both my parents and my brother and sister, gone, just like that. Am I going to be smashed by a drunk driver next time I get in a car? Is a terrorist bomber on his way to blow up this restaurant right now?"

"No," I said.

"My sister had a daughter. She's with her grandparents now. It's worse for her than me." Madison shook her head again. "I know that."

I had to say something. "I don't understand it, either." That was most certainly true.

Madison picked up her glass and appeared so delicate, under a freshly weighted blanket of despair.

I thought perhaps sharing my own pain might lighten hers. Maybe she would let me under her blanket, and we could carry the weight together. "I could tell you why I'm here. What I needed a change from, I mean."

"Please." She took a sip of wine.

"I'm divorced—it's been four years." I always followed those first facts up immediately with another. "My ex-wife had an affair."

"I'm sorry." Madison frowned. "That's terrible."

"Eh." I waved my hand. "It seems a small thing compared to what you've been through."

"No," she said. "It's awful. Just… differently awful."

"I guess. But in retrospect, it was for the best. I never should have married her. Something was missing in our relationship. Passion, maybe. We were best friends before getting married and had been dating for a while, so getting married 'made sense' as a next step. But I realize now that path wasn't leading where I wanted to go. I want *romance* and *passion* and... a life with a lot more excitement than routine. You read about couples like that and see them in movies, but I *know* that kind of life could be real."

Madison nodded.

"Anyway, her affair was a hell of a way to figure things out, and I don't wish that on anyone. But in the end, it was for the best. I know what I really want now. Or at least I know a lot better. Maybe that sounds cliché, and while I definitely didn't jump right to that conclusion after it happened, I really do mean it. And that's all well and good, but I couldn't stand dating anymore." I paused. "That sounds terrible. What you lost, and me, they don't compare. But the whole thing for years really wore me down. There were *so many* first dates over coffee or drinks, to get to know someone with potential to be a good match, only to find out later, three other things about her meant it wouldn't *really* be a good match. Or I'd find out she was also seeing someone else, and I was the backup. Or *I* would meet someone else and have to choose between two people, and I'd choose wrong. But who knows if the other one would have worked out any better?

"And meeting people in the first place... Often my friends knew a friend or co-worker who liked something I did—a TV show, jogging, a certain restaurant... We'd go out, and the common interest gave us something to talk about, but it never amounted to anything to base a relationship on." I took a deep breath. "I could go on forever, but suffice it to say: I hate being single, but the years trying not to be single have been exhausting. I needed a break from it. Badly."

"I understand," Madison said. "Or... I haven't been exactly there, but I've been single plenty. And I can imagine it being especially hard after thinking you had already found 'the one.'"

"Exactly." I stopped myself from describing how the stress of picking the wrong girl a second time weighed on me significantly—as did time in general. I didn't mention that, either. At thirty-one, I didn't feel old, but I had already lost the years when I was with my ex-wife. I hadn't wasted the years, because I had learned priceless things about myself during the experience, but that time was not coming back. Since then, as the months and years marched on, I saw "old" creeping up on the horizon.

The waiter returned, and I assured him that the *next* time he did, we'd have decided on food, so we studied our menus. As before, Madison helped me decipher the French. She chose salad with seared tuna from the summer-themed list, while I opted for steak au poivre from among the regular options.

We moved on to lighter subjects, like why neither of us had chosen to learn French in school and why, of all instruments, I had picked the trumpet. Our plates came, which we both enjoyed and shared with each other. After, we had dessert—chocolate mousse for me and crème brûlée for her.

I paid the bill after promising, at her insistence, that she could pay for the next evening's dinner.

"Where to now?" she asked.

I put away my wallet. "You know the city better than me. Or is there anywhere you wanted to go but didn't make it to last time you were here?"

Madison's eyes lit up. She leaned forward. "The Catacombs!"

"The Catacombs?"

"Tunnels with skulls and bones. Tons of them. Millions."

"Human bones?"

"Yeah," she said. "From the eighteenth century, when the cemeteries in Paris overfilled and they had to put the bones somewhere else. That's the gist of it anyway."

"Looking for fresh inspiration for your drawings?"

She smiled. "I might be. But c'mon, it'll be fun."

"Sure," I said.

"Wait." She leaned forward again. "Come here."

I leaned close.

"Thank you," she said. "For coming with me to Paris."

"Thank you for asking me."

"I haven't felt so good in a long time." She kissed me, and the kiss I had been waiting all day for met my high expectations.

We both leaned back, and I said, "Let's go see some skulls."

———————————

The remains of more than six million of the city's dead lay within the Catacombs of Paris. Madison recalled the number during our cab ride. Just off a busy intersection, we were dropped at the green hut entrance. To my relief, a woman was reading a magazine behind a cash register, meaning Madison had led us to a legitimate tourist destination, not some hidden passageway she had been tipped off to by a bartender or, more likely, by a vampire.

There was no map, just a narrow spiral stone staircase down, the promise of a few rooms of information, then one and a half kilometers of tunnel—a small fraction of the complete underground complex—before we would climb a staircase up to the street at the other end.

"Brave souls," the cashier said in heavily accented English after Madison paid for us both. "Visiting at night."

Madison smiled playfully at me.

I led us down, recalling the staircase in the Sanguan club, wondering if Madison was thinking of the same winding stone. But the Catacombs went much deeper than the club. Finally, we reached the bottom and stepped into a room with painted white walls, and on them, placards with text, diagrams, and maps providing context for what we were about to see. No one else was around.

Madison and I separated to read the placards. Parisians had begun to fill the tunnels with skeletal remains in 1785, when the city's cemeteries had no more room for proper burials. In fact, the cemeteries had been overflowing for years before then, and Parisians complained about the spreading stench and disease. When a basement wall around *Les Innocents* cemetery collapsed, decomposing bodies slid into an adjacent property. After that, the cemetery was closed, and from there and other cemeteries across the city, it took years of nightly work to relocate the skeletal remains of millions to the Catacombs.

I finished reading first and waited at the tunnel entrance. The long path before me made by walls lined with human bones and skulls turned far ahead. In the wan yellow artificial light, I saw more bones than I had ever seen in my life, counting all those from museums, textbooks, television shows, and movies. Rows of skulls served as decoration, support, or both, between floor to ceiling stacks of leg and arm bones, with their ends pointed out. The ceiling was low, but we wouldn't have to duck to fit. According to the introductory text, the oldest skeletons dated back over twelve hundred years.

Madison stepped beside me. "Crazy, isn't it?"

"It is."

At my side, she took my hand, and we entered the tunnel.

Bones upon bones, upon skulls and more bones, surrounded us, organized with carved stone signs indicating when those particular bones had come from:

September 1859

November 1804

1786, 1782, 1777

"It's almost unbelievable," I said. "That these were buried for centuries, then dug up and arranged here like this."

"I think you were right," Madison said. "I'll have plenty to draw based on what's down here."

"You could devote a whole notebook to it."

"Maybe." She raised her eyebrows. "Or maybe not." She leaned over and gave me a quick kiss.

I would have kissed her again, but a chill hit my neck. She rubbed her bare arms.

"Here." I took off my jacket and helped her slide her hands into its sleeves.

"Thanks."

Then I held her side and did give her that longer kiss.

We traded soft kisses, and when we might have stopped and been done, one of us would give a quick kiss or a long one that deepened. I supposed we could have stayed in that spot for hours at the same game, but we had a lot of tunnel still to walk, and I had begun to think about what we might do back in our quaint hotel room. I held Madison's hand, and we moved on.

Christian crosses, obelisks, and sculptures of cities broke up the otherwise continuous walls of bones. Tall gates blocked off access to passageways and other tunnels with stacked bones that were not part of the tour.

"Hear that?" Madison asked.

"The gate?" I thought one on our left might have rattled. "Yeah."

Still no one else was behind us or ahead. I checked my phone. No service. As we continued on, Madison kept close to me. The endless walls of bones and skulls might have become boring were there not *so many* bones.

"I can't believe we're under Paris right now," I said as we entered a very narrow section of the path.

"Me, neither," Madison said. "It's 2006, and this exists beneath the City of Light."

Ahead in the tunnel, a shadow of a figure came into view.

"They had little choice," his male voice called as he approached.

Madison clutched my arm. Behind us, nearer, stood a tall female with brown hair, light skin, black pants, and a leather jacket over a white top. She crossed her arms. She was beautiful.

I turned back to the male.

"Had you seen it and smelled it," he said, advancing, "the cemeteries overflowing, the rotting corpses in the streets, the foul smell of it all... you'd agree they had no choice."

The female hadn't budged. The male had gotten close enough that I could make out long dirty-blond hair and very light skin. He wore gray slacks and a black shirt.

"If you had been there, as I was," he said, "you would most certainly agree."

He had confirmed my fear—a vampire blocked our way—and I assumed another stood behind us. I didn't recognize either of them.

"Who are you? What do you want?" I asked.

His steady approach continued. "I am Bayard. Word from Reims is that your blood, John Breen, cannot be adequately described. It has to be tasted to be truly understood." In the blink of an eye, he darted to me. His arm wrapped around me, and his hand covered my chin and mouth.

The female held Madison the same way. Wide-eyed, Madison tightened her grip on my fingers. I struggled to free myself from Bayard, but he held me like a vise. His palm muffled my attempt to yell. I strained and tried to twist, but my efforts were utterly useless.

His fangs pierced my neck. Scalding, sumptuous fire ripped through me. Skull walls filled my view. Bayard sucked, and heat rushed into me. Flame in every shade roared in my mind.

It stopped. Bayard leaned up from me, tilted his head back, closed his eyes, and swallowed. "Sublime."

I wanted the fire back. And I wanted to be far away with Madison! Away from the Sanguans. Away from that place of death.

"Most sublime," Bayard said, still holding my mouth and jaw, preventing me from yelling.

The female leaned up from Madison's freshly bitten neck, swallowed, and shook her head to Bayard.

I felt him shrug. Madison cracked her eyes open.

Into Bayard's hand, I screamed!

"We must be off, John." Bayard lifted me and moved away from Madison until I had to let go of her fingers. Down the tunnel he ran, so fast I could only see a blur in all directions.

I screamed again! I screamed for Madison.

10

ETHAN

I walked to Sadie's sister's house in the Bywater District of New Orleans, east of the French Quarter around the bend of the mighty Mississippi River. I would have run, but Jenna wasn't expecting me until nine o'clock, so I had a little time to kill.

After leaving Sadie the night before, I'd visited Ellie to tell her there might be good news. If the words Sadie had overheard had indeed been the description of a vampire's recent drink, then mortal blood that could heal Ellie, that she would *allow* to heal her, flowed within a living, breathing person—assuming the vampire who had taken that drink left that person alive.

That last possibility made my stomach churn—that I might have missed Ellie's savior by days. I wouldn't let myself dwell on it or that someone could have found the same story and was simply repeating what they'd read. I didn't mention any of that to Ellie. She didn't respond, of course. I had been told that people who had woken from comas sometimes reported having perceived things while unable to respond, but only very rarely. And Ellie hadn't reported as much when she'd last woken from her coma, eleven years before.

If she had heard me, she wouldn't have understood the taste described by the text—rich, yet pure. The contradiction… I couldn't understand it exactly either, having not drunk it, but I had a sense of what such blood might be like. Or a guess.

But for Ellie, the taste would not matter. She would be healed. And not by "demon" vampire blood. With crystal clarity, I remembered the stinging word passing her lips. Ellie and I had not spelled out her precise definition of the word "demon," but knowing her strong Christian faith left me with no doubt what she'd meant. I had become a thing driven by a power from hell. To her, I had become an agent of Satan.

But was I a *demon*? Did I wake at sunset to do that fallen angel's bidding? I did not think so.

Yet *some* power allowed me to come alive each night, unaged by the passage of time, and with a thirst unquenchable except by blood. What gave me my gifts and whether Ellie had labeled me accurately, I did not know. But I most certainly did not consider myself to be holy.

As clearly as I remembered her dark label for me, her damning judgment, I remembered what came later, the last words Ellie spoke to me or anyone. Before closing her eyes and forming the smallest, barely perceptible smile, she'd said, "I still love you."

With those words buoying my soul, I reached Jenna's

house, which had the white siding and blue shutters I had glimpsed in Sadie's memories.

I had to find out who had described the "rich, yet pure" blood at the art museum. If I had a clear image of who had that feminine voice with no discernible accent, I thought I might be able to track them down. With a name, I felt sure I could. Jenna had been at the museum that night, and I needed to know what she had seen and heard.

I climbed two steps and knocked on the front door.

Her husband, a heavyset man in khaki shorts and a T-shirt, opened it.

"Evening," I said. "I'm Ethan, a friend of Sadie's. She let Jenna know I would be stopping by."

"Yes." He opened the door farther. "Come in. I'm Grady. Jenna's upstairs putting the kids to bed."

I stepped inside.

"Please." He motioned to a living room, where military action figures and small toy robots littered the floor. "Have a seat. I'll tell her you're here."

"Thank you." I made my way to the couch.

Grady went halfway up the staircase in the foyer. "Jenna," he called. "Ethan's here."

"I'll be right there!"

Grady returned to the living room. "Can I..." He scratched his head. "Can I get you anything? Water? Do you drink water?"

"No," I said. "I don't. I'm fine, thank you."

He nodded. "Jenna shouldn't be long." He sat in the recliner past the far side of the couch. "How old... How long have you been a vampire?"

"Eleven years."

He rubbed his chin with his thumb, and I wondered if he was disappointed I hadn't said a hundred years or a thousand or if he was relieved to not have a creature those years had made more powerful than me sitting in his living room.

"How old were you?" he asked.

"Eighteen."

"From around here?"

"New Jersey," I said. "Then New York City before here, but I've been in New Orleans awhile."

Footsteps thundered down the staircase. In faded jeans and a blue T-shirt, Jenna stepped off the last stair. "Sorry!" She was younger, but had the same blond hair as her sister and clearly resembled Sadie.

I stood. "No problem at all. Thank you for seeing me."

"Of course." Jenna walked over. "Sadie explained your situation. I'd like to help, if I can."

"Thank you."

She gestured to the couch, and I sat back down.

Jenna took the cushion beside me. "I hate to say it, but I don't remember anything like those words you're looking for."

"That's okay. You might remember something helpful, without even knowing it."

She nodded.

I reached for her wrist, which she placed in my hand.

"Have you ever been bitten by a vampire?" I asked.

"A couple times. Years ago. In college."

Grady crossed his leg in his chair. "All right if I watch?"

I considered asking if I should grab him a bowl of popcorn for the show. "Jenna?"

She shrugged. "Sure."

I brought her wrist toward my mouth. "If this hurts, it only will for a moment." I rotated her arm slightly for the appropriate angle to bite her artery. She repositioned herself nearer to me on the couch. And then, gently but swiftly, I sank my fangs through her skin.

Fire rose quickly, sweet fire… but I hadn't come for that.

I saw Jenna bitten by vampires in college. It had been more than the "couple times" she had admitted to, and she had sought out Sanguans for their bites after college, but it had been years since the last time.

Her molten blood flowed into me. Sure, my visit excited her. My broad shoulders and narrow waist reminded her of a high school boyfriend who had played on the baseball team. And I was certainly a change from her daily routine with the kids and Grady, but she found comfort in that routine, and she loved her family very much.

I searched for "rich" and "pure" qualities in her blood but did not taste them. I sipped and found the night at the museum.

In the bright column-lined Great Hall, she had sat with Sadie and enjoyed the quartet's music. No bitterness in Jenna's blood—she had been excited when Sadie invited her to the show.

As with Sadie, Jenna had let her eyes wander to others at the event: women in dresses and business suits with carefully made-up faces, adorned with gold, silver, and sparkling jewelry, along with neatly groomed men in suits and ties, wearing polished shoes and nice watches.

If it had been a dingy bar, picking out a vampire from the crowd of sloppy mortals would have been an easier task. But no such luck.

Jenna fell into me. I held her and drank on.

When the music ended and Jenna gave polite but heartfelt applause, she and Sadie decided to stick around, along with lots of others. The pair took flutes of champagne from a circulating server on their way to rooms dedicated to Dutch and Flemish paintings.

Sadie liked it, but the art didn't resonate with Jenna, so she left her sister and went to see the contemporary art on the second floor. On the way across the Great Hall to the staircase, people more social than Jenna smiled and introduced themselves to each other. Couples and solo guests shook hands, sipped on drinks, and laughed. No one stood out to me as an obvious vampire. I didn't recognize any of the names I heard.

Jenna climbed the stairs, and from her second-floor vantage point, she saw Sadie walking across the Great Hall and into the room with the baroque art—the room where Sadie had overheard the description of the blood.

I sipped Jenna's blood and focused.

Jenna noticed four people walk into the baroque room after Sadie—two women. Then six other people—four women and two men—walked in the far entrance to the same set of rooms.

Red dress, blue dress, black suits and dresses… it could have been any of them. Then Jenna turned away, and any number of other women could have walked in or out of the area near her sister.

Jenna proceeded to the rooms of contemporary art, which she liked significantly better than the Dutch and Flemish. Sadie found her up there later.

I withdrew my fangs.

Jenna smiled. "Ehmm…"

Grady sat on the edge of his seat.

Jenna slowly opened her eyes. "Did you find what you were looking for?"

"Some helpful clues, I think." I smiled. "Thank you. Are you all right?"

"Mm-hmm."

Gently, I leaned her against the couch's back, then stood. "Thank you both."

Grady got up and kissed Jenna's forehead, then followed me to the door. He opened it, and I left.

———————

Jenna's blood really had helped. Though I hadn't found the name of the vampire who had described the rich and pure blood, I had a fuller context for future images I intended to find.

After leaving Jenna's house, I drove an hour and a half west, through a line of thunderstorms, to a small theater in Baton Rouge. The quartet that had played at the museum had a simple website that hadn't been updated in two years, but googling the group's name had produced its upcoming schedule. I parked my old Ford Escort a few blocks away, and despite the ticket woman warning me that they had nearly finished, I paid her then sat in a plastic folding chair in the last of eight rows to listen to the end of their set.

The two violinists—a man and a woman of perhaps forty—sat to the left on a low stage in front of a maroon curtain. To their right, a younger woman ran her bow across the viola, and on the far end, an older, larger man played the cello. As they had at the museum, they all wore black, dresses for the women and suits for the men. Unlike at the museum, they were the best-dressed people at the event.

They sounded glorious. From their wood and string instruments, they laid long, low groundwork for shorter dynamic highs that made me smile. I understood Sadie's and Jenna's reactions to the music, and I could also reach farther, for details they had perceived but couldn't recall and relive. They had enjoyed the music, but aside from a few moments here and there, they couldn't replay the notes as they had happened. But I had been able to piece together their memories and replay the sounds while I drank.

But listening to them, I realized the gap between what I had discerned in blood and what I heard and felt in person was more truly a gulf. The rich, full notes warmed me deeply, and I enjoyed watching the four onstage for the care they took with each stroke, to ensure it would join in harmony with the three beside them.

I had to help Ellie and had taken the rare trip away from her to find information to that end, but my mind could be patient for the length of a song or two. My needy body did not know patience, but because Jenna's blood had met its demands, I could sit and enjoy the performance in contented peace.

Soon, Ellie might sit beside me at a show like that, I thought. In a nicer place, I decided, but music exactly like that. Just as I had when we rode the train into the city to see *The Phantom of the Opera* on Broadway, and I held her hand during the whole second act, I would hold her hand while we enjoyed a quartet together. Then I wouldn't let it go when the performance ended or when we walked out of the theater. I would never let go of Ellie's hand the next time she had the strength to hold mine back.

With final notes, the musicians stopped their bows and smiled at one another. The quartet stood and bowed to the applauding crowd. When everyone rose and continued applauding, I joined them, even as I steeled myself to my purpose, whatever direction it went.

The performers carried their instruments backstage, behind the curtain. Against the current of spectators filing out, I headed for the front. Onstage, I pushed aside the curtain and found the four musicians placing their instruments into cases.

They stopped and looked to me.

Wanting to do it the easy way, I gave a low wave. "Hi."

"Can we help you?" the cellist asked.

"You guys are great. I saw you in New Orleans, at the museum of art," I said. "You played even better tonight."

"Thanks," the female violinist said.

"But I wanted to ask you about New Orleans," I said. "Do you remember any vampires being there?"

The four shared concerned looks, then turned them to me.

"No," the cellist said. "But it's hard to tell, you know?"

"Yes." I clasped my hands. "It most certainly is. Thinking back, did anyone or anything stand out to you as, well, odd in any way?"

They shook their heads.

"What is this about?" the cellist asked.

"I believe there was a vampire there, in the museum that night. I don't know who she was or what she looked like. But I need to. I really need to know."

"I'm sorry," the cellist said. "I don't recall a vampire. I don't think they do." More shaking heads from the group. "I don't think we can help you."

"Ah." I stepped toward them, until I could have reached out and grabbed the viola player. The two violinists were right past her and the cellist farthest, but not far as fast as I could move. "You *could* help me, actually, if I could know what you knew. If I drank your blood."

Eight eyes widened.

"Just sips," I added. "The vampire has important information. Information that could save my—"

"Sa—" the cellist called, but I darted over and had my fangs in his neck before he got out "—nguan!"

I sucked hard, swallowing his blood, and the fire ignited.

His was a lonely fire. No wife. No family. The quartet was his family, and he was terrified of what I would do to it.

In the blaze, I found the four of them arriving at the museum, setting up, chatting before the show, meeting a few guests, then playing. If I had no other agenda, I would have remained there—feeling how he played, knowing what it was like to make such fine music. He believed what the group played was indeed beautiful.

But I moved on and found Sadie and Jenna in the audience, their attention focused on the musicians.

After the quartet had finished playing, the cellist joined the reception. He shook hands with person after person. Face after face, name after name.

Mitchell, Jaimie, Deidre, Shanta, a museum curator, Nancy... Among the faces, he hadn't seen any fangs. He hadn't suspected a vampire sat in the audience. He hadn't noticed Sadie go into the room of baroque art.

I pulled my fangs from him.

The other three musicians watched in terror. The women covered their mouths with their hands. I pushed the cellist, sending him stumbling into the violinists, and together, the pair managed to catch him.

I raced to the viola player. I wrapped my arm around her, moved her brown hair off her neck, and sank my fangs in.

She had never been bitten by a vampire. Watching me at the cellist's throat, she had tried to scream, but couldn't manage to make the sound. She feared my bite, especially how she would feel during and after, and that I would know her whole life if I drank from her. At that thought, I went straight to the museum.

Her arrival, preshow, and playing generally aligned with

the cellist's experience. After the show, she shook hands with a few people. She received their thanks and congratulations for the performance and found a reluctant but eventually gratifying joy knowing that while she recalled small mistakes, small things she vowed to correct next time, people had thoroughly enjoyed her playing.

Henry, Vivian, Darren—more names, more faces. Again, I saw Nancy Evans, the museum curator, who was an older woman with shiny shoulder-length gray hair, wearing a black suit and no wedding ring.

I sucked blood and reached backward in time, to moments earlier. Ms. Evans had been shaking hands and introducing herself to others on the way to the viola player. Before the show, it had gone the same. The viola player had noticed Ms. Evans moving around the room, making lots of short introductions.

I withdrew my fangs from her neck.

Hands gripped my shoulders and pulled me away from the viola player. I let the cellist shove me to the ground.

"Sanguan!" he cried.

The two violists hadn't moved, except to clutch each other tightly. The cellist asked the viola player if she was okay. She nodded.

On the ground, I pictured what Jenna had seen in the museum, looking down from the second floor.

Two women had gone into the baroque room after Sadie, using the same entrance Sadie had. Four had gone into the far entrance of the adjoining room, and among the four, one was an older woman in a black suit, with shiny shoulder-length gray hair. I knew that woman's name: Nancy Evans, the museum curator.

I spotted an emergency exit door, got up, and ran outside into a steady rain.

At Ellie's bedside the following evening, I sat holding her hand.

I had the museum curator's name but didn't know where to find her, beyond looking at the museum. And it wouldn't be open in the evening until Tuesday, three long nights away. I decided against asking a human friend to go during the day to investigate, for fear of them raising suspicion when it would be hours before nightfall and I could act on their information.

I rubbed my thumb over Ellie's. We were together for three years before she got sick. Sometime before the end of the first year, I knew I loved her. And I had loved telling her that I loved her.

It wasn't fair that she could no longer hear me tell her how much I loved her. Others from my high school class had gotten married. All my friends had gone to college. Ellie and I got a decade in a nursing home room.

It wasn't fair.

Under a canopy of old oak trees, I walked along Esplanade Avenue, toward City Park, where the museum of art was located. If I was lucky, Ms. Evans was working or someone could tell me where to find her.

Only a scattering of parked cars lined the street near the museum. No special event was scheduled during the evening hours. I climbed the wide stone staircase, feeling for the switchblade in my pocket, hoping not to need it. I entered through the door beyond the Ionic columns.

Inside, across the Great Hall, a security guard watched the big, brightly lit open space that rows of chairs had filled when the quartet played. Above him, where a surveillance camera should have been, was the vacant mount I had noticed in Sadie's and Jenna's blood. To my left, a young woman stood behind a cash register and computer monitor at a small desk. I smiled at her and walked over.

She smiled. "Good evening."

"Evening."

"One student?" she asked.

I reached for my wallet and glanced at the security guard, who had turned his attention to us.

"Yes." I handed the cashier a twenty. "Do you know Ms. Evans?" I asked as she gave me my change.

"The Curator for European Art. Of course."

"Is she working tonight?"

"No," the woman said. "She doesn't usually work nights."

"Do you know where I might find her?"

"She'll be here tomorrow morning."

The guard still watched us.

"I need to see her tonight," I said. "It's important."

She gave a puzzled look. "I… I guess I could call her. Maybe. What is it about?"

"It's a private matter. Do you know where she might be? Or where she lives?"

"Um… I don't." The woman glanced at the guard, who began walking our way.

Human, the smell of his blood told me.

"It's really important I see her," I said. "Are you sure you don't know? You don't have an address or anything?"

The guard's footsteps became more urgent.

"I don't," the woman said. "And if I did, I don't think that's the kind of information I'm allowed to give out."

I ran at the guard and whipped my forearm against his forehead. He hit the floor rear end first, and I caught his head before it smacked the marble. I laid him the rest of the way down. He might have a concussion, but otherwise, he would be fine before long.

I turned to the cashier, pulled my knife from my pocket, and flipped open the blade. "Is there a paystub you can check for her address? Anything like that?"

"I… um… no." She slowly backed away. "No paystub."

I darted behind her and held the knife to her throat. "I *need* an address."

Her heart raced; her breaths came fast.

I moved the knife away. "Just an address."

She reached her arms out and let them guide her to the computer keyboard and mouse. "There's an emergency contact list. Let me… just let me—"

"All right," I said. "Calm down."

"I'll find it." She opened Microsoft Outlook and scrolled down a list of email subjects.

I closed my knife and put it in my pocket. "Once you do, I'll be on my way."

"Here." She pointed to an open spreadsheet. Row eight contained Nancy's name and the address of an apartment in the city.

I sprinted to the street then for that address.

In the Garden District, I found Nancy Evans's apartment building. Beyond the pair of glass doors, a black-and-white checkered pattern covered the narrow lobby floor. Ornately framed paintings hung on the straw-colored walls, and a concierge in a light-gray suit sat behind an old wooden desk. He had his attention on a bulky computer monitor as I pulled open the door and stepped inside.

The concierge stood and pointed an assault rifle at me. "A credible threat was called in."

I smelled his synthetic blood. "I just need to speak with her."

"Not a chance." The Spectavi vampire flipped open a cell phone.

I ran at him. He fired. I dodged the bullet and grabbed my knife from my pocket.

The Spectavi dropped his phone, got both hands on the rifle, and fired again. The bullet ripped into my gut as my blade flipped open. I fell forward over the desk onto the vampire, tackling him to the floor.

He smashed the butt of his gun across my face. I stabbed my knife into his chest.

Silver! I clutched my burning side. The melting silver bullet oozed into me.

The Spectavi smashed my chin with his gun. He pushed me off him and got up, staggering backward.

He aimed his rifle as I launched myself at him. The sharp edge of my blade sliced through half his neck, and he fired after I had passed.

Blood poured from his cut veins and arteries. He dropped his gun to clutch his neck with both hands. It wouldn't matter, though. He needed to drink blood to heal such a bad wound.

The Spectavi fell to a knee in a growing red puddle then crumpled the rest of the way to the floor. I kicked his rifle away from him, and his hands slipped off his neck. His head tilted sideways, and I heard his heartbeat slow, then stop.

Knife in one hand, holding my side with my other, I made my way to the elevator. But when I pushed the button, nothing happened. I noticed an electronic pad beside the buttons, and I didn't have whatever device would activate it. The stairwell door behind me had a similar reader. I put away my knife, gritted my teeth, pulled hard, and ripped the door off its hinges.

I dropped the door and ascended the five floors as quickly as I could. The silver flowing through my entire body slowed me, but it wouldn't kill me. I would drink someone's blood later and feel better. A day in my coffin would likely complete the job. But another job needed completing first.

Down the hall carpeted in brown and orange, I found room 507. Covered in blood—real and disgusting synthetic—I knocked on the door.

A heartbeat approached, and with rosary beads in hand and wrapped around her wrist, Ms. Evans opened the door halfway. "Terrence is dead?"

"The Spectavi downstairs?"

She nodded. A shaded lamp glowed in the dim living room behind her.

"He is dead."

"Am I next?"

I put up both hands. "No."

"They told me to leave," Ms. Evans said. "I refused. I said, 'Whatever God has in store for me, I will stay and face it.'"

"I just need information."

She crossed herself—up, down, left, right—opened the door wider, and stood aside.

I entered, sat down hard on her suede sofa, and winced.

She sat straight in a recliner adjacent to the sofa. "Terrence shot you."

I held my side. "He did."

"What kind of information do you need?"

I leaned forward, despite how it made the silver ache worse. "You were at the string quartet's concert at the museum last Wednesday evening."

"I was."

"You introduced yourself to a lot of people."

"I did. It's part of my job to foster good relationships with the community."

"Did you meet any vampires that night?"

Ms. Evans sat back in her seat.

A clock ticked in the kitchen.

"No one I knew to be a vampire," she said. "Not for certain."

"But you suspected someone." I moved to the edge of the cushion. "Was it in the baroque art room or the one next to it, by chance?"

"I met her in neither of those rooms."

My heart raced.

"In the Great Hall, I shook her hand," Ms. Evans said. "But I did not think her to be a vampire until later, until she uttered those awful words in the Renaissance art room."

"What did she say?"

"I do not care to repeat it."

"I could drink from you and know. I *must* know what she said—and her name."

Ms. Evans folded her hands so the crucifix at the end of her string of beads hung over her knees. "Please do not drink from me."

"But I *need* to know." My side throbbed. "And what she looked like."

"Why? Why do you need to know?"

"Because the woman I love is dying. Because she's mortal, and I'm this..." I glanced at my bloodied self. "Demon or whatever you think of me as. I thought if I became what I am that my blood would save her. But she wouldn't have it. She wouldn't let it save her. But I think I found another way to cure her, and what you heard might be that way." I winced. "And if I'm right, it could mean a lot of good for a lot more people than just her. But I need to find out if I'm right, so I really do need that name."

Ms. Evans closed her eyes and kissed her rosary crucifix. "Sublime." She opened her eyes. "Nadya Komarova was the fiend's name. She said, 'If it hadn't been a mortal's blood I drank, I might have guessed it the blood of a god.' The notion disgusted me."

"What did she look like?"

"Red hair, very light skin. Russian accent, though... I noticed the accent only when she introduced herself to me, not when she said those words."

Medium height, with blue eyes, she was in the background of Sadie's, Jenna's, and the cellist's memories.

I stood. "Thank you."

"I pray this leads to good," Ms. Evans said. "I pray you are wiser than your appearance says you are, and if you are not, and this brings evil, then let evil come to you. And in that case, I pray that God forgives me for not leaving my apartment when the Spectavi warned me."

I almost assured her she had nothing to worry about, but beyond my own intentions, I didn't really know where her information would lead, and I did not want to lie to Ms. Evans.

I nodded then left her apartment.

Replaying images of the redheaded vampire, I kept repeating "Nadya Komarova" in my head. "Nadya Komarova. Nadya Komarova." I had the name. I knew what she looked like. I had never hunted a particular vampire before, but I *had* to find her.

11

JOHN

My eyes opened. I sat up on the wide bed, atop a thick gray comforter, and shoved myself backward against the dark wooden headboard. The female vampire who had held Madison in the tunnel watched me from a leather armchair in the corner of a narrow room with steel-blue-colored walls. I must have passed out.

"Where am I?" I shouted. "Where's Madison?"

"She's here." The vampire's jacket was gone, and the sleeves of her white blouse had been rolled up her slender arms to her elbows. "She is safe, in another room."

"Let me see her." I glanced at the door near the vampire—the same blue as the walls—then to the door on the left, and a third on my right. A pair of recessed overhead bulbs gave off warm light. "What do you want with us?"

"You may see her. When, will depend." She stood, and her long legs brought her to the bedside.

I couldn't move any farther against the headboard. I could have screamed for help, but the vampire might not have liked that.

She sat right next to me on the bed. "My name is Mirabella. You two are my guests now. Mine and Bayard's."

Her subtle accent reinforced my assessment that she was French. Her long brown hair perfectly framed her gorgeous face. Her cheeks were high. Her nose was small, but not too small. She had the most inviting brown eyes.

"What do you want?"

She set her hands in her lap. "What do you think I want?"

I had spotted the tips of her sharp fangs. "Then take it, and let us go."

"I will take it. But you will not be going. Not tonight."

I shook my head. "Let me see Madison!"

"Shhh." Mirabella placed her hand on my thigh. "If you let me drink, you may see her."

"And if I say no?"

"Then I will drink all the same, and you will not see her." Mirabella leaned closer. "But I do not want that. I think Madison would like to see you."

Nausea built. Who would hear if I called for help? And would it matter? The Sanguan could have my blood anyway, and I had no doubt she possessed the strength to twist my neck, crush my throat, or do away with me however she deemed most enjoyable or efficient. And that would leave Madison all alone with those monsters.

"Fine," I said. "Drink."

Mirabella reached to my neck, where she carefully undid the highest shirt button I had fastened.

She slid closer and pushed my collar aside. She held my shoulder and leaned into me until her breasts pressed against my chest. I tilted my head, and she brought her mouth down to the side of my neck. Her warm breath hit my skin. I winced at two pricks. Mirabella sucked, and heat came with it.

She sucked, and heat built from her bite while I stared at the bedroom's side door. My eyes grew heavy. Mirabella drank and held me more tightly to her firm body.

Heat everywhere. I couldn't feel the bite. I couldn't feel the vampire. Only heat.

The heat layered. It surged... then quickly cooled. Mirabella leaned away from me. A tear slid down her cheek. "Sublime." She smiled and wiped the tear with her finger. "Thank you."

I had never made someone so pretty so happy.

"I'll see you tomorrow." She got up and gestured to the door to my right. "Madison is through there." Mirabella headed for the far end of the room past the foot of the bed.

I held my neck and waited until the Sanguan had gone and shut the door. I slid off the bed onto the concrete floor—where I had to steady my light-headed self. I checked my palm. Two dots of blood marked where her fangs had been. I checked again—blood didn't seem to be running.

I took two woozy steps to the door and braced myself for whatever I would find beyond it. I turned the silver knob and pulled open the door—to find a long closet with shelves of folded and stacked black, white, and gray clothes on both sides. At the far end was another door like the one I had just opened. I flicked a switch, and an overhead light came on. Halfway into the closet, vertical wooden boards divided the shelves.

Past the dividers in the same colors were similar clothes, but smaller—women's clothes. I checked behind me, and the door remained open. The lights in my room remained on. I shuddered at the thought—*my* room.

At the end of the closet, I held another doorknob and again braced myself. I pushed the door open.

Bayard sat on a bed like the one I had woken on, holding Madison, with his mouth at her neck, in a room just like mine. Her eyes were shut, and she still wore her dress. He leaned up from her and swallowed.

"Madison!" I cried.

"Shh…" Bayard looked to me with a finger at his lips. He laid Madison's head on the pillow. "She is well, John. Do not worry."

I rushed to the bedside. Her chest rose and fell with steady breaths.

"Rest, John." Bayard stood and walked to the door beyond the foot of the bed, near that room's armchair, where the jacket I had lent Madison lay folded. "You are safe, but you cannot escape. The walls are thick. You will not be heard. The window is mirrored. You will not be seen." He left and shut the door.

"Are you okay?" I asked Madison.

"Yes." She didn't open her eyes but got her shoes off with her feet, moved the comforter and sheets down the bed, and slid herself under them. She pulled down the sheets behind her and patted the bed there.

I took in the room again. It matched mine with everything positioned opposite.

Madison patted the bed once more. "Please."

I moved her shoes to the floor. I wanted to lie down with her and hold her. I wanted to *so badly*, but not there, not as prisoners of Sanguan vampires. What did they want with us? Our blood, sure. But why *ours*?

What was beyond the other doors? The vampires? Worse?

But before me, Madison asked for me. Bayard had said we were safe.

I went around to the other side of the bed. I untied my shoes, slid them off, and climbed under the covers.

Madison smiled. I moved to her and put my arm over her. She slid closer to me, and I held her tightly, thinking back to the basement of the club in Reims. Why had all those Sanguans liked my blood so much?

I woke holding Madison. She breathed calmly, and that aside, we might not have budged at all. I didn't want to budge. I wanted that moment to go on… except somewhere else.

I let go of Madison. My phone and wallet were in my pocket, as usual. I checked the phone. 8:37 a.m. Low battery. No cell service. That meant daytime, no vampires, and maybe the chance to find a way out of there, wherever we were.

I got out from under the sheets and off the bed. The door on my left went back to my room. In the long closet and beyond, the lights remained on. The bedrooms had no windows, I noted.

I went to the door on my right and opened it. Bathroom. Logical.

"Hey," Madison said.

"Hey, how are you?" I went around and sat on her side of the bed.

She sat up and touched fingers to the two fresh marks on her neck. "I'm fine."

"Did they hurt you? Did they—"

"No, just the bite."

"Me, too." I pointed to the closet. "My room's through there. It's the same as yours. There's a closet between the rooms with clothes." I pointed behind me. "Bathroom's there."

"And out there?" She nodded to the door at the end of the room.

"Don't know. That's as far as I got. I just woke up. That's where Bayard went, after he... drank. And Mirabella went out that door in my room."

"Mirabella?"

"The female vampire. The one who carried you from the Catacombs. Did you talk to Bayard? Did he say what they wanted with us?"

"Not really," Madison said. "He said we were their guests and that we couldn't escape. That's about it."

"Yeah, Mirabella said she'd be back tonight, but otherwise, that's all I got, too."

We both looked to the third door. I stood, Madison slid off her side of the bed, and we approached the door together. I glanced at her. She shrugged. I pulled it open.

Longer than it was wide, the room was painted the same blue as the others and shared the concrete floor. A plush leather couch, a big flat-screen television, tall stereo speakers, and a coffee table filled the space—an apartment living room. Beyond it was a kitchen with a stainless-steel fridge and an island with two barstools. A door was on the left side of the kitchen. A tall window ran the entire length of the wall opposite the television, with the Seine River and its distinctive Parisian banks beyond it.

We went to the kitchen, and I checked the door beside it. The handle twisted, but the deadbolt, which had no keyhole or latch, kept the door from opening. I pulled as hard as I could, but accomplished nothing. The oven, microwave, and dishwasher were spotlessly clean. I opened the cupboards and drawers to find ordinary plates, pots, pans, and utensils. I turned around. The apartment appeared very normal and very modern, with apparently soundproof walls.

I screamed, "Hey!" Then as loud as I could, I shrieked, "Hey!"

No echo. No response.

Madison opened the fridge. An unopened carton of milk sat on a shelf beside a block of cheese. On the shelf below were strip steaks and chicken breasts. Vegetables filled the bottom drawers.

"Looks like they expect us to be here a while," I said.

"Uh-huh."

We went to the wall-length window. The glass stretched nearly floor to ceiling.

Madison pointed at the Gothic buttresses across the river to the left. "That looks like the back of Notre Dame."

Nearer than the cathedral, we could see down to the city street, full of commuters surely headed to work.

I tapped my knuckle on the window. "Mirrored glass, Bayard said."

Behind us, a hallway ran off to the right of the television. Down it, we found a small room with workout mats, a treadmill, and an exercise bike. I felt ill. Madison shrugged.

Back in the main room, I pulled out my phone. "No service."

She went to the bedroom and returned with hers. "Me neither."

"I'm shutting mine off. Maybe it'll work later."

Madison powered hers off.

"What should we do?" I asked. "I mean, we have to get out of here. But I have no idea how."

"Yeah." Madison bit her lip. "I'm going to take a shower."

"Okay." I figured one of us should keep watch. "I'm going to look around some more." It was daytime, but vampires often employed humans, and I had no idea what Bayard or Mirabella could have planned for while they rested, wherever their coffins were.

Madison went to her room and shut the door. I powered my cell phone on and began checking every inch of the place for a signal.

My search yielded no cell service and nothing else that would help us escape the apartment. The locked door's thick deadbolt showed no weakness to the kitchen knives I stuck at it—butter *or* steak—or to my repeated efforts to pull at the door with all my meager mortal might.

When Madison emerged from her room in loose black pants and a matching T-shirt, with her long hair still damp, I again wished I could savor the moment of us having woken up together or just being with her in the morning after being with her at night. But our predicament spoiled the sensation.

I told Madison I would leave the bathroom door open while I showered and that she should yell if anyone came into the apartment. She never yelled, but I had never taken a quicker shower.

Wrapped in my towel afterward, I peered out into the main room, where she sat on the couch, watching what appeared to be a French soap opera. I put on black pants and a gray T-shirt from the closet then joined her there.

We made turkey sandwiches for lunch. While I cut them in half, Madison leaned in front of me and gave me a quick kiss. She smiled while filling glasses with water at the kitchen sink. I glanced at the door we could not open. The hell with it.

I brought my hand to Madison's side, turned her to me, and gave her a much longer kiss. Her smile after stretched wider.

I looked at the door—still shut. Who knew what Mirabella and Bayard would bring when they returned, but they hadn't really hurt us yet. If that door opened during the day, all bets were off.

We ate our sandwiches at the kitchen island, where I had a clear view of the door. I explained to Madison that my blood in particular seemed to interest Bayard and Mirabella. I shared with her the reaction I had gotten from Mirabella—but not my thought afterward about how beautiful I found the vampire.

I recounted my experience with Collette in Reims and how the other vampires had come down into the room to drink from me, though I did not know why.

Madison said Bayard seemed to enjoy drinking from her, but he hadn't used the word "sublime." I recalled Mirabella shaking her head after drinking from Madison in the Catacombs, but I kept that to myself. I hoped with all my heart that Mirabella had merely meant Madison's blood didn't stand out to the Sanguans like mine did.

Bayard had said we were safe, I reminded myself. But what were his words worth?

After lunch, back on the couch, we flipped through TV channels until stopping on one showing *Die Hard*, which we both immediately recognized, even though it had been dubbed over in French. We caught the end, and commercials indicated the channel consisted entirely of American movies shown in French. We watched all of *Die Hard 2*. We found a thin gray blanket in our shared closet, and Madison lay against me and covered us both with it. She dozed off, but I stayed awake, staring at the incredible view of the French capital city. I wondered if I could shatter the panoramic window with one of the kitchen barstools—and what Bayard and Mirabella would do to us if I tried and failed.

No one came through the locked front door, and when the clock on the microwave in the kitchen said 7:15, we cooked the steaks and roasted vegetables for dinner. We didn't share any kisses then. We didn't talk much. Sunset wouldn't be until almost ten, but I found myself checking the clock repeatedly. Could we run for the door when the vampires opened it? Of course not, they ran far faster than we could.

After dinner, Madison announced she was taking a nap, just like that, very matter-of-factly. She left the door to her bedroom cracked open, but I didn't follow. I sat on the couch, watching television—and the apartment door—as the sky darkened. I checked the time on the microwave over and over.

———————————

The door opened at 10:33. I stood. Wearing khakis and a navy shirt, Bayard entered first, then Mirabella followed, shut the door, and spun the deadbolt into place.

She had on tight jeans and a burgundy tank top. They each carried a black garment bag.

"Good evening." Bayard motioned to the couch. "Please have a seat." He laid the garment bag on the island in the kitchen.

Behind me, Madison's door remained open, but she hadn't come out. I sat down.

"I trust your day was uneventful?" Bayard sat beside me on the couch and crossed his legs.

Mirabella went into Madison's room with her bag and shut the door.

"Did you have all you needed?" Bayard asked.

"It was fine," I said. "We were fine."

"Good. Do let me know if there's anything we can provide to make you more comfortable."

Freedom, I thought, would have been nice, and I almost said it. "What do you want? How long are you going to keep us here?"

"The answer to the latter will depend on you."

"What do you mean?"

"In time, you will know," Bayard said. "It is not a game of deception."

"Then what kind of game is it?"

Bayard smiled.

"Why *my* blood?" I asked. "What's so special about it?"

"Soon, you will know. For now, know that you are correct. It is most special."

"*Why?* What is it?"

Bayard sat perfectly still.

"What about Madison's?"

"Lovely blood, from a lovely woman, but nothing like yours." Bayard checked his watch. "Time to get ready. We've a show to attend."

"A show?"

"Yes. But first, there is that oh-so-delectable blood of yours."

"I—"

"Hm?" Bayard raised an eyebrow. "Mirabella tells me she discussed this with you."

Madison's door remained closed.

"I—" I had to find a way out of that apartment, but had no way at that moment, and being separated from Madison would have been true torture. I tilted my neck to the side.

Bayard leaned close and brought his hard, heavy body against mine. I closed my eyes, and he must have bitten into the same spots, or the outsides of them, because I felt very little pain of broken skin before the warmth. My eyes shut. The heat permeated me.

Where Mirabella's had sung, Bayard's heat bellowed, building in layers. I couldn't feel my body against the couch, the floor, or Bayard. I felt only growing warmth, each wave came from deeper and lasted longer.

A way out of what? I didn't know. Where was I? I couldn't recall.

I knew only warmth. *Heat…*

And then cool, filtered apartment air covered me. Bayard's eyes remained closed while he swallowed. He let me go, and I sank into the soft leather cushions.

Madison's door opened, and Mirabella emerged.

Bayard stood. "You will fail if you try to break the window with a stool, this sofa, or anything in the apartment. Try something like that, and after you fail, you will not see Madison."

I gulped.

"Get changed. We'll return in an hour." He left, and Mirabella followed him out the door, which she locked.

My chest tightened. Even shallow breaths took great effort. I *couldn't* be separated from Madison. I couldn't leave her alone with them. I couldn't be alone with them myself.

Steadying myself on the couch back, I got up and called, "Madison?"

She didn't answer, so I went quickly to her room and found her on the bed, lying on her side, facing me.

"Madison?"

She opened her eyes. "I'm okay."

I breathed deeper. "I'm sorry." I sat beside her. "About all of this."

She took my hand. "It's all right." She smiled. "Really."

I didn't understand how she thought it was, but that she was not frantic, nor in terror, gave me some peace.

I shaved slowly. I felt slow and a little... foggy. I'd felt the same after Mirabella drank my blood the night before.

I changed into the tuxedo in the garment bag Bayard had brought and pondered what our evening had in store. "Show" could mean lots of different things. Where would it be? And would I get cell service there? Could I possibly risk making a phone call that Bayard would learn of? Of course not.

The shoes in my exact size shone, and that the pants and jacket fit perfectly added to the mounting evidence that Bayard had planned well. I highly doubted an opportunity to escape would present itself at the show, and he had made very clear what would happen if I tried anything and did not succeed. I would keep my eyes open, but I didn't have high hopes.

I heard the television come on in the main room. I turned off the lights and went out.

Standing behind the couch, Madison wore a long black satin gown with thin straps over her bony shoulders. She flipped through channels with the remote, holding a small purse in her other hand. She appeared taller—surely the bottom of her gown hid high heels. She might have noticed me staring, but she kept focused on the changing French stations.

When the front door opened, Bayard carried a small black bag by its handle. His tux could have been a copy of mine, except bigger to fit his frame. Mirabella wore an emerald-green gown similar to Madison's but with straps that sparkled with diamonds that matched her necklace. Her hair was pulled up into a tight bun, and her shoes clicked against the concrete floor.

"I'm glad to see you're both ready." Bayard set the bag on the kitchen island. "Come here, please."

Madison shut off the TV. Her heels clicked the same as Mirabella's on the way over, and her gown clung at every step.

Bayard pulled something black and round from the bag—a collar that was jet black, maybe an inch tall, not very thick. I stopped halfway to the kitchen.

"You'll be safe where we're going." Mirabella took a second collar from the bag. "But in case you get separated from us, you'll want to be wearing these."

"Or what?" I asked.

"In a theater full of thirsty Sanguans," Bayard said, "you'll be free game."

"I… I'll take my chances."

"No," Bayard said, "you will not. Come here."

Madison moved so her back was to Bayard and lifted her long hair to expose her neck. From a concealed hinge at the collar's front, Bayard opened it and brought the ring around Madison's neck. It appeared to fit snugly.

"Too tight?" he asked her as he closed it.

"No."

He took a silver ring off his left index finger and stuck its round face into the back of the collar. He turned the ring and, with a *click*, locked it. She let go of her hair.

"Couldn't a vampire break that off?" I asked.

"Yes." Bayard slid his ring back on his finger. "But they would not. Not the ones we'll be with tonight. They know who these collars belong to, and that will be respected."

So we weren't just property—we were explicitly the property of Bayard and Mirabella.

Mirabella held up the other collar. "Come here, John."

It was better than a brand burned into my flesh, I decided, while I walked across the room to the goddess in the green gown. She set the collar down and, with her pale fingers, undid the bowtie I had spent ten minutes getting right. She unfastened the top button of my shirt. She could have bitten me then. She could have leaned forward and had her pretty little fangs at my neck.

She might have kissed me first.

How could I think that?

Mirabella opened the collar and brought it around my neck. Rubber or a material softer than metal wrapped around what the noticeable weight suggested was steel or perhaps iron. Mirabella loosened and slid off the bracelet around her wrist, which included a round key like Bayard's ring. She reached around me and pulled my neck closer when she inserted the key into the collar.

Click.

"Relax." Mirabella redid my top shirt button over the collar. "I'll be with you there." With ease, she retied my bowtie.

I brought my hand to my neck. The bulge under my shirt must have looked strange, while Madison's collar might have been mistaken for a fashionable accessory of her own choosing.

The weight on my neck, though not overwhelming, was impossible to ignore. I hated knowing that same weight was locked onto Madison.

In a long limousine, with a driver we never saw, we rode through a Paris night muted by thick tinted windows. Bayard and Madison faced forward, and Mirabella and I sat on the opposite bench seat. From the apartment, we had been led down a hall with no other doors to an elevator that serviced only one other floor, a basement garage where the limo waited. From outside, its windows were opaque black. The vampires had taken our cell phones and said we would not be getting them back.

We were going to see an opera, Bayard explained while we drove. When asked if either of us had ever seen one, Madison and I both answered no.

I asked why they were taking us, and Bayard responded, "Because you don't want to sit around that apartment all night, do you?" But there had to be more to it. Bayard and Mirabella had not treated us cruelly, but surely, they had an agenda beyond our entertainment.

With my fingertips, I touched my collar under my shirt more than once. I never noticed Madison going for hers. She calmly watched out the window, where the *free* people of Paris were. I wanted to cry out to them. Maybe a Spectavi would hear and come to our aid. Or perhaps Bayard and Mirabella were so powerful that the Spectavi would need to gather a large force for an organized rescue. But because I could not hear a thing beyond the windows, I assumed no one would hear if I yelled, and I certainly could not risk anything that might fail.

Past the Palais de Tokyo Art Museum, the limo took us into a parking garage and circled as we descended. After a brief pause, we resumed, and out the rear window, a wall of stone slid closed, concealing our route. The garage grew narrower and darker until we stopped.

When the door beside Madison opened, someone in a suit reached in to help her out. Mirabella's door opened, and she got out. Bayard and I followed them onto a circular drive that wrapped around a smooth black wall with a lone red door. Two males in black suits and matching shirts held rifles at the entrance. Sanguans, not men, I figured.

The limo drove around and out of sight. Bayard extended his arm, which Madison took, and he led her through the red door, which one of the guards pulled open.

Mirabella lifted my arm into place so she could take it, and we followed.

In the darkness, walls of colorless stone lined the narrow tunnel. As we walked along the thin maroon carpet on the floor, light from beyond the tunnel made Bayard and Madison silhouettes. Voices in conversation gradually rose—a hubbub of people or vampires. Soon, I would be able to guess which.

Then I saw them, attired in gowns and tuxedos like ours, chatting and mingling. The tunnel opened to a long, tall space. High on the stone walls, lamps glowed. A huge chandelier hung from a long chain in the center of the room.

Every man and woman—I could tell they weren't vampires because they held champagne, wine, beer, or cocktail glasses—wore a collar like mine. Most collars were black, but some were silver or gold. Smiles abounded, both on the humans and on the vampires, whose especially pale skin, lack of collars, and, when I looked closely at their smiling mouths, fangs gave them away. I guessed maybe a hundred in total, mortals and immortals combined.

A young-looking vampire—which of course meant nothing of his true age—approached Bayard. After shaking his hand, Bayard introduced Madison. She smiled and shook the new vampire's hand. Then he brought her hand to his mouth and kissed it.

"Mirabella!" It came from our right.

She turned, so I did with her, to a radiant vampire wearing a golden gown that matched her long, blond hair. Alongside her was a brawny man in a tux, with a neatly trimmed beard.

"Vivienne," Mirabella said. The vampires greeted each other with a kiss to each cheek.

"*Voici* Ronell." Vivienne gestured to the man whose undone top shirt button exposed his black collar.

"This is John." Mirabella set her hand on my shoulder.

Vivienne clasped her hands and made a face like one might to a child. I feared she would pinch my cheek, but instead, she said to Mirabella, "*Très beau. Très, très beau.*"

"Vivienne!" Another couple approached. "Ronell! *Bonsoir.* Good evening."

He and Vivienne shifted their attention to the new couple, and Mirabella and I turned ours to approaching Bayard and Madison. She held a flute half full of champagne.

"Would you care for a drink?" Bayard asked.

Behind him, at the end of the lobby, a server with an empty tray neared a bar carved into the wall.

"No," I said.

Bayard nodded. "If you change your mind, feel free."

"I—" I felt ill, or that I should have felt ill. "Where's the restroom?"

"Past the bar."

I looked at Madison. She sipped her champagne. How could she be so calm? How could she be comfortable surrounded by bloodthirsty Sanguans, as property of Bayard's on display? I headed for the restroom.

"Find us," Mirabella called. "We'll be around."

I turned back, and while I kept going, let my gaze linger on Mirabella's magnificent figure. I had never spent so long with anyone so beautiful.

"Ugh." My cheek, then chest, hit a rock-hard, tuxedo-covered back. The huge man or vampire slowly turned.

I tilted my head up to his. "Sorry."

"*Pas de problem.*" He made a kind face. "No problem." He returned to his conversation with another in a tux and bowtie.

Some men and women around the room seemed about my age, while many must have been younger. Others were clearly older than me. And the vampires, while I had no idea their age, it struck me how old they might have been—what they could have seen and all they could have lived through, for better or for worse, over centuries. In any case, at least at that hour, on that night, everyone appeared happy, if not gleeful.

And in the middle of it all, Madison sipped champagne. She laughed... and was so pretty. Tall and thin, with a light in her eyes and a smile on her face that rivaled any in the room. Once more, I recalled Mirabella and Bayard's warnings. Better Madison smiling and me able to be with her and know she was smiling, than her in pain or being mistreated, or me separated from her, fearing she might have been. At the thought of her treated any way but well, I *did* feel nauseous. I continued to the restroom.

Beyond a plain door, black-speckled marble shone on the floor and the lower half of the walls, but aside from being a fancy restroom, nothing about it seemed out of the ordinary. No one occupied either of the stalls, and I found no air duct or passageway we might take to flee from the place.

I waited a minute but never actually got sick. I didn't feel any better, but after splashing water on my face and drying it off, I headed back out to the lobby, wondering if the Spectavi knew the theater existed. Surely, they couldn't. They could never know and let it continue to exist. They would send a small army if they had to, to destroy it and any Sanguans inside. But if that were true, that meant none of the mortals who had been there had reported on the place to the Spectavi. Had none of the mortals who came there *ever* been freed? Nausea filled me again as I hit the crowd, which had grown in both size and revelry.

A third of the way across the room, I found Bayard, Madison, and Mirabella chatting with two other couples. I joined the group at Mirabella's side and flashed her a fake smile.

Then I laughed genuinely at a joke about the President of the United States told by a vampire who had a Spanish accent and dark complexion. And I smiled while sharing a story I had read of how the president—an avid golfer—liked to award himself with mulligans and retake bad shots, blaming specific stressful matters across the globe, of which he had a limitless supply.

Eventually, those vampires left with their mortal guests, and others came. We moved around the room and met more couples, mostly consisting of a Sanguan and a mortal, but some were pairs of vampires, and some vampires had brought two or three mortal guests. Mirabella pointed out two Sanguans who had been companions for over four hundred years.

Then the crowd began to thin, and the lights dimmed.

Bayard checked his watch. "It's time."

Men, women, and vampires filed through a wide, open passageway opposite the bar. Bayard led us up a staircase beside it and into a balcony box with four seats. The wide, shallow theater below was filling in, as were the two boxes beside ours that faced the stage, where an orchestra sat before a red curtain.

Mirabella guided me to the leather-cushioned chair on the end. She sat next to me, with Bayard beside her, then Madison. I leaned forward and looked Madison's way, thinking she would do the same, looking for reassurance from me.

But she did not lean forward. She said something to Bayard I could not hear, and he laughed. I leaned back in my chair, touching my collar.

The dim overhead lights faded out. The long, heavy stroke of a cello reverberated in the darkness. The curtain lifted slowly, revealing the green plants and bright flowers of a garden setting. At the conductor's behest, more instruments joined the music. Mirabella took my hand and held it against the thin emerald satin covering her toned thigh. I should have yanked my hand away.

I looked to Madison, who was watching the performance. I turned to the stage.

A black cuff wrapped around a wrist of each violinist and flutist. A collar encircled the cellists' and percussionists' necks. One of the two devices on each of the other orchestra members meant they all must have been mortals. I assumed the cuffs and collars would have been a hindrance, but the musicians played with no sign of any. How long had they been playing with those on them, that they had learned to ignore their weight and bulk?

The opera quieted. A powerfully built man—or possibly vampire—walked to center stage. At once, his voice and the orchestra's string notes rose in short jabs. Then he sang for longer stretches, the instrumentals extended to match him, and I didn't understand any of it because he was singing in French.

When he finished, brief applause came, but not from our box. Mirabella still held my hand.

A woman in a crimson strapless gown of a heavy fabric, a thick cuff around her wrist, joined the man. Her song began with longer, undulating lines that the orchestra contrasted with short strokes and notes. I thought the slower pace might help me figure out the plot, but when the man joined in, that hope faded.

Mirabella lifted my hand and rotated my wrist upward. She unbuttoned my shirt sleeve cuff, rolled it and my jacket sleeve up my forearm, then got back to watching the stage. I watched her bring my wrist to her mouth.

I tried pulling my arm away, but she held firm without a glance. She set her teeth on my wrist. I closed my eyes. The deeper male voice onstage grew louder.

Warmth hit my wrist. Mirabella sucked gently, and heat crept down my arm, to my core. She sucked, and heat touched my legs and the top of my head.

Coolness came. Her fangs had left me. The woman's voice rose louder.

Mirabella held my hand loosely on her leg. I leaned

forward and saw Madison's eyes closed, her lips parted, and her wrist at Bayard's mouth. I settled back into my chair.

The orchestra played with no singing, and I preferred that to the rest of the performance to that point. But then the woman sang, and they did sound better together. I grew warmer—Mirabella held my wrist to her mouth. I shut my eyes and listened to notes rising and falling, and to voices over them, soaring and sinking, like the heat within me.

In the limousine, Madison took Bayard's hand, closed her eyes, and rested her head on his shoulder. I sat far from Mirabella but would not have resisted if the Sanguan slid over and leaned herself against me.

She had drunk from me on and off during the show, a little at a time. I enjoyed the performance immensely more as she did, though I could not describe the plot of the opera at all. In the end, the male singer had turned out to be a vampire. While onstage, for all to see, he drank from the female singer's neck.

We returned to the garage we had departed from, then went up the elevator, down the white-walled hall, and past the locking door to enter the apartment. In the kitchen, Bayard slid his silver ring off his finger, and when Madison held her hair aside, he used the ring to unlock the collar from her neck. "I hope you enjoyed yourself this evening."

"I did." She let her hair fall and smiled.

Mirabella undid my bowtie, unbuttoned my shirt, and unlocked my collar. "And you?"

I nodded. What could I do?

"I'm glad." She followed Bayard out with the collars in the small bag they had brought, and with a loud *thunk*, the door's deadbolt spun into place.

Madison looked at me with a blank face that gave me nothing to go on.

Should I tell her how upset seeing her with Bayard made me? Should I ask if she was all right? Or should I hold her and tell her everything will be all right?

In the cool air of the apartment, noting her bare arms and shoulders, and just how thin her gown appeared, I considered offering her my jacket.

"You look beautiful," I said. "You are beautiful."

Her face brightened.

I looked away. "Did Bayard tell you that?"

"He did." She stepped close. "But not like that."

I turned to her, and we kissed. My fingers touched the satin over her side, then I held her. She held me, and we kept kissing.

When we stopped, my heart was racing, and hers seemed to be, as well. She took my hand and led me to her bedroom. Standing at the foot of the bed, she helped me pull off my jacket. It dropped to the concrete floor, and I unbuttoned my shirt. Madison worked on my next shirt button, and I kissed her, which made things harder, but I couldn't help it. She pulled my shirt off while I got my arms out of its sleeves, then it fell to the floor.

I slid the straps of her gown off her shoulders, and it dropped around her. My bare body against hers, I held her and kissed her for a long time, before she led me to the side of the bed. We took off our shoes, she lay down, and I joined her there.

I awoke, naked like Madison, under the covers, with my arm around her. We had ended the night right there, except holding each other more tightly. Madison seemed to be at such peace.

Out the open bedroom door, sunlight filled the main room, but beyond that, I didn't know the time and wasn't about to get up to check.

Making love, Madison and I had shared something the vampires could not. The thought stung unexpectedly. It should have been solely about what Madison and I had shared, without vampires having anything to do with it. Though I wouldn't have chosen to be with anyone else in the world, I would have rather been with her anywhere else.

What had the night before been, for either of us? A tired blur, in part. Mirabella had taken a lot of blood by the time we got back to the apartment. But when the vampires left and I'd held Madison, I had woken up. Together in bed, I had wanted so badly to make it special for her. No blur there.

Mirabella at my wrist came to mind. I could almost feel the warmth. I moved my arm off Madison and rolled onto my back. I hadn't hated when Mirabella had done that, and the voices onstage and the orchestra's notes rose and fell as she sipped. And Madison had not appeared to have disliked Bayard's bites or his company one bit.

Madison clutched her pillow and opened her silver eyes. "Hey."

"Hey." I rolled over and put my arm around her.

She moved closer to me.

Just as we had the bright hours of daytime, Madison and I had been together in a way that the vampires could never be with either of us. The Sanguans were not human, and what Madison and I had shared was the most human thing I had ever done.

Madison and I didn't get out of bed until nearly noon that day, which we didn't know until the microwave clock told us. We had fallen asleep very late, and a different kind of lethargy slowed us both. Madison said it was because we'd lost so much blood the previous night. She had experienced it in Reims going to the club frequently. It didn't really matter that we'd slept late, though. We didn't have anywhere to go or anything to do before Bayard and Mirabella showed up after nightfall. At least I assumed they would show up.

While Madison and I cuddled on the couch and watched TV, wearing plain clothes from our closet, the realization that the vampires hadn't promised to come that night nagged at me. I would again ask Bayard what he wanted with me and would demand answers. That I hoped Mirabella would drink my blood came to mind more than once.

As the cloudless sky beyond the long window darkened, Madison gave me a kiss and said she was going to lie down. I watched her walk to her bedroom, wanting to reach out for her more each step she took. She left the door cracked open, and I stared at moving images on the television.

An hour after sunset, they arrived. They were dressed casually and carried no garment bags or anything with them.

I sat up straight on the couch, all my questions for Bayard ready, but not willing. After locking the apartment door, Bayard went to Madison's room and shut that door behind him.

Mirabella sat beside me. "I enjoyed last evening."

Thank goodness! I couldn't help the thought. It was wrong—everything was wrong, but I had been relieved to hear her say it. "I did, too."

The stunning creature smiled and leaned across me so her mouth could reach the far side of my neck. I put my arm around her waist, pulling her to me, and she did what I had been waiting all day for her to do.

Warmth and fire surged from her bite. I clutched Mirabella to me. She sucked harder. Heat, flame, nothing else in my mind, nothing else in my body. No couch, no fangs at my neck, no apartment, just rising fire.

It burned higher. And hotter! Then cooler. Mirabella leaned up from me. My heart raced as she swallowed my blood.

Madison's door opened. Mirabella stood and headed for the kitchen with Bayard.

"We'll see you tomorrow," he said. "Same time."

I steadied myself on the couch to stand. "What do you want from me?"

"Your blood," Bayard said. "And in time, your choice."

"My choice?"

"Do you believe in God?" he asked.

"Not really."

"Hm." He looked to Mirabella.

She smiled matter-of-factly.

Bayard opened the door. They left and locked the deadbolt.

"John," Madison called.

I marched that way and pushed open her door.

She lay face up, dressed as before atop the covers. She lifted her head from her pillow. "Lie down with me?"

I did, and she moved so I held her back to me.

I kissed the back of her neck. I kissed around toward its front.

Madison turned to me. I pulled off her shirt, and she pulled off mine. We each took our pants off and shared that human experience we had the night before, even better than the night before.

––––––––––––––

The next day and night went about the same. In fact, for better and worse, they had gone almost exactly the same. I got to spend nearly all day and night with Madison, with her in my arms for much of the time.

Yet when the vampires came, we were parted by more than the short distance between us, and when they took our blood, they left something that lingered, with me I knew for certain, and with Madison I had no doubt. And since the theater, it had all happened in the apartment.

At sunset, when Madison went to lie down, I stood at the window, watching Parisians and tourists strolling along the

Seine. To walk along that river with Madison would have filled me with such joy.

And then the vampires arrived, and I melted at Mirabella's touch before burning at her bite.

The following day, Madison and I watched TV nervously.

"Did Mirabella mention coming back tonight?" Madison asked.

"No, did Bayard?"

"No."

I wondered what that meant as the minutes crawled by, especially after their normal arrival time. What if they never showed up?

Half an hour later than usual, Bayard opened the apartment door. He wore a dark suit, and Mirabella a black dress. They carried garment bags and the small bag with them.

Bayard took Madison's garment bag to her in her room.

Mirabella handed me my bag. "Please get changed. We don't want to be late."

I went to my room as instructed. I shaved, and it didn't take long to change into the gray slacks, fitted black T-shirt, and nice brown shoes. I found the vampires waiting out in the main room. Had Mirabella been alone, I figured she would have drunk from me immediately.

"Where are we going?" I asked.

"A friend's," Bayard said.

I didn't know if it was that Mirabella had *not* yet drunk from me, or if the prospect of being out and some chance arising that might lead to our freedom stirred me, but I found myself energized. "What kind of friend?"

"An *old* friend," Mirabella said.

"How old?"

"More than a thousand years," Bayard said.

What does your friend do? That would have been a reasonable question about a mortal, but not a vampire. The immortals drank blood. Few, I supposed, did work jobs of sorts for a paycheck, and some were artists or actors, but I didn't think that was most. "Why there?"

"He's having a small gathering," Bayard said. "And *you* are the guest of honor. Ah…" He gestured past me. "There she is."

Madison stood outside her doorway in a mid-length, charcoal-gray dress with very short sleeves and a round neck. Her black pumps made her at least as tall as me. She had pulled her black hair back tightly, and her red lipstick contrasted starkly with her light skin.

She walked past me to Bayard and smiled at him. He took her hand and kissed it.

Madison faced him while he locked the collar on her neck. I went to Mirabella, and she locked mine on, as well.

Mirabella led the way down the hall. Madison hadn't asked where we were going. She might have heard from her room, but she might not have. Did she even care?

———————————

In the limo, Madison held Bayard's hand, watched the busy city streets, and turned his way when he commented about different buildings' origins or architecture or events he had witnessed long ago on streets we drove or passed.

Sitting on the bench seat opposite them, I watched out the window and tried not to look at the two of them together. When I failed, I repeatedly found myself longing for Madison to glance my way. She never did. I hated that my T-shirt left the collar on my neck completely exposed, but that notion faded as we drove.

At a stoplight, Mirabella brought my wrist to her lips and bit very briefly. Madison did watch that, then she watched Mirabella pull me forward and Bayard scoot to the edge of his seat to take a sip of his own.

He let go of my wrist and closed his eyes. "My God..." He opened his eyes. "You say you don't believe in God?"

"No," I said. "Not really."

"You talk to God," Mirabella said. "I know you, John. Bayard knows you. We've drunk more than enough of your blood to know that."

"It was one of the first things I searched for," Bayard said. "You speak to him sometimes, and spoke to him often when you were at your darkest."

"I..." I crossed my arms. "I don't know."

"You may know, after tonight," Bayard said. "What you witness may cement your opinion. Or it may not. We shall see."

We pulled into a parking garage and headed down.

"What's going to happen?" I asked.

"You will see." Bayard leaned forward. "And after tonight, you will be allowed to leave us."

My eyes widened.

"As a vampire," Bayard said. "Tomorrow night, or any

after, you may ask, and I will turn you—or Mirabella can, as you wish. And Madison may join you as an immortal, if she wishes. But it rests on you. Once *you* are mortal no longer, you will both be free to go."

The limo stopped. The doors beside Madison and Mirabella opened.

"But know this," Bayard said. "The gift in your blood will be lost as a vampire. That is the choice I reveal to you." He gestured to Madison, who slid out of the limo, and he followed.

Mirabella exited then I did. Another stretch limousine was parked beside ours. A red Ferrari, a blue Lamborghini, and a black Maserati were parked on the other side. Beyond an iron door, the four of us entered a narrow, shiny silver elevator.

Madison stood beside me in front of the vampires, the doors closed, and her hand found mine. She didn't turn— she didn't look—but her fingers interlocked with mine. She squeezed before letting go.

The elevator doors opened to a long apartment with dark-gray walls with a cloudy matte finish. At the opposite end, where logs burned in a marble fireplace, two males in suits stopped their chatting to look our way. Nearer, a female in a short blue dress with a very high neck closed her flip phone and stood from a leather sofa. Mirabella pushed at my back, and I led us forward on the hardwood floor.

"Friends," Bayard said. "Meet Madison and John."

The three nodded respectfully, then a female and a bald male came from around the corner and nodded, as well. A faded, cracking painting of the Virgin Mary hung in a golden frame to our left.

A short male in a pin-striped suit emerged from the dining room on the right. "Welcome, Bayard, Mira*bella*." He drew out the end of her name. "Madison." He took her hand and brought it to his lips for a kiss. "And most of all, welcome to you, John." He bowed slightly. "My name is Wilhelm."

I said nothing and, instead, tried to guess at what in the world Bayard had meant in the limo. I had no intention of becoming a vampire, though I supposed I would talk to Madison about it. What if she wanted to, and for me to, so we would be free? I couldn't imagine she wanted to be a vampire, but then, we had never discussed it. I had hardly known her before we became prisoners in the apartment, and in that short time, how could we have talked about *that*?

"Thank you, Wilhelm, for inviting us," Bayard said. "And thank you all for joining us this very special evening." He gestured to the dining room. "Shall we?"

Everyone headed that way. No one carried wineglasses or champagne flutes. All the others had light skin, and I didn't notice any collars besides mine and Madison's. I had seen two sets of fangs already—everyone except us had to be Sanguans.

Atop a long, polished table with rounded corners, a pair of golden candelabras had four arms each. The wicks of white candles burned with yellow flame. Covering most of the wall, a vibrant, panoramic painting depicted Greek gods at court—I recognized regal Zeus and Poseidon, with his trident, on a mountaintop that had to be Olympus.

At the head of the table, Wilhelm sat, with me and Mirabella around the corner to his left, and Bayard and Madison to his right. The other five took seats down the table.

Bayard waited for all to be settled. "I once heard a story that captured my imagination and would not let go. You all know it, and our host this evening played a crucial part in it. But for John's and Madison's sake, and for my own enjoyment, I will tell the tale. It is not a long one.

"In 1282, on the outskirts of a small village in southeast Hungary, a young man of fifteen named Odo lived with his dying mother, who was fever stricken and bedridden. Odo's father had passed the year before from the same affliction. Each day, Odo hunted for small game and had enough success to feed himself and his mother with his kill and what he traded it for. All in the village understood his situation and did not strike hard bargains.

"One day, Odo returned from his hunt and rushed to her bedside, for she lay motionless, her breaths nearly imperceptible. She cracked open her eyes and asked to see how Odo had done. He showed her the rabbit, and she told him to cook it well, for it might be her last meal on earth.

"Odo boiled the rabbit and cut vegetables, fearing he would lose his mother at any moment and be left all alone. His hands trembled, and he sliced his index finger with the knife. Odo yelled, but knowing his mother was dealing with far worse, he quieted down and hastily bandaged the wound. His mother asked to see it. She did not have the strength and dexterity in her fingers to help him, but she could tell him if he had done well enough. He placed his hand in her palm.

"It was okay, she said, despite the fresh red seeping into the bandage. She brought her son's injured finger to her mouth and kissed it. Then she took her deepest breath in a month. When her son finished cooking, she did not need him to cut her portions and feed them to her, as he had to of late. She found she had the strength to enjoy the meal with him. It was not her last meal, and afterward, she became animated in bed."

Madison looked to me. I didn't know how to respond.

"Weeks later," Bayard continued, "Odo's mother found her condition very grave once more. Fearful that when she shut her eyes to sleep, they would never reopen, she thought back to when she had improved the last time. They had the same meal as that evening, hoping an unknown medicine in it had revived her temporarily.

"The food didn't help. Odo hunted in the exact same spot the following day and caught a rabbit the same as the other, but that did not help, either. When they had run out of ideas, and her strength had nearly left her completely, Odo brought news to his mother he had heard while trading. A vampire had been hunting in the nearest village. Those in Odo's village feared the Sanguan would head their way next.

"At that, Odo's mother remembered the blood-soaked bandage she had kissed. Her son was no vampire, nor had he ever been bitten by one, but she wondered, had *his* blood from his cut finger healed her, as blood heals those demons from their wounds? It didn't take long to convince her son to try. With his hunting knife, Odo sliced his palm and let blood drip from it to his mother's mouth.

"At the first drop, she breathed easier. After the second, she could reach out and pull her son's hand to her lips. She drank for a few seconds, strength flowed through her body, and she got herself out of bed. She was healed."

Madison looked to me again. Back in our apartment prison, I had wished to be anywhere but that apartment. I would gladly have taken there, behind its locked door with her, over sitting at that candlelit table with vampires, listening to Bayard's story.

"The next day, to the astonishment of everyone, Odo and his mother showed up in the town center to trade for supplies. They attributed her good health to faith and prayer. On the way home, at the edge of town, an old man with a crudely braced leg struggled to limp toward Odo and his mother. His tattered clothes gave the impression he had been struggling for a while. 'I can help you,' Odo said to him. The man practically collapsed to the ground and wiped sweat from his brow. 'I'll take any help ya can give.'

"Odo cut his palm with his knife, and after some insistence from Odo, the old man licked and then drank the running blood. The man's broken, twisted leg straightened, mended, and was healed. Dumbfounded, the man got himself to his feet with ease. 'That has been my bane for twenty years. How can I repay you?'

"'No need,' Odo said. 'It was nothing. Only blood.' The man nodded. 'Then I will tell everyone the good you have done.'

"'No,' Odo's mother said. 'Tell no one.' The old man gave a confused look.

"'You are in my son's debt. Repay him by keeping his secret.'

"'As you wish.' He thanked Odo and walked into town.

"'They'll take you from me,' Odo's mother explained to her son.

"'Who?' he asked.

"'I don't know. But someone will learn of your gift and will want it for themselves.'"

Someone like the vampire telling the story, I thought. *Or the other vampires at the table. Someone* exactly *like them.*

I didn't believe the story, though. Surely, the tale was meant to scare Madison and me, to coax some reaction from us. Although, it would have explained the Sanguans flocking to drink my blood in Reims…

"Odo and his mother moved east," Bayard said. "To a village where no one knew them, and they could live far from the old man. It turned out to be a prudent decision, because the old man could not keep a secret. When Wilhelm"— Bayard motioned to the head of the table—"passed through Odo's original village in Hungary, word of Odo's feat had spread. Along with clear images of Odo and his mother, Wilhelm glimpsed the same tale with varying embellishments in many he drank from.

"Intrigued, Wilhelm moved fast, searching village after village for a year, until eventually finding Odo and his mother in their new village." Bayard gestured to Wilhelm. "I'll let you take it from here."

Wilhelm nodded. "I came across their home in the middle of the night and waited at a distance but didn't have to wait long. With his mother asleep inside, Odo went out to gaze at the stars as the young man often did. I raced over, grabbed him, sank my teeth into his neck, and knew all the stories were true."

"And his blood," Bayard said, "how did it taste to you?"

"Rich, yet pure," Wilhelm answered. "I had never tasted anything like it. It was like the blood of a god."

Eyes around the table shifted to me. The Sanguan in the blue dress licked her top lip from one fang to the other.

Wilhelm continued, "I brought Odo inside, and his mother woke up. I told them who I was, and what—that I had been a vampire then for nearly three hundred years. I assured them that I understood their fears, and that if Odo drank my blood and became a vampire, no one would *take* Odo anywhere. No one would dictate his life to him. He would be, well… a god.

"Odo had something none of us had. We can heal sick and injured mortals by turning them into vampires, but we have to turn them to do it. At the mere sip of our blood, mortals are *not* healed. We wait decades and centuries, searching for those most fit to bestow our immortal gifts on, but when I found Odo, no more searching needed to be done." Wilhelm shrugged. "I wanted to be sire to such a unique vampire."

I had no interest in being a vampire. I had no interest in being surrounded by them or listening to their stories.

"So I asked Odo," Wilhelm said. "He replied yes, he wished to become a vampire. His mother protested, but he convinced her, and then I turned him as we turn anyone. I drank his glorious blood, nearly all of it, until he teetered on the edge of life and death. I bit my wrist and let him drink from me until he grew strong, and he had fangs, craved mortal blood, and was a vampire."

Wilhelm sighed. "That night, we woke a man in a nearby home. Odo objected, but I had to see it for myself. I dragged the man from his bed, from his wife, and while she screamed and screamed, I snapped the man's arm. Odo cut his hand as he had before. We forced the man to drink, but nothing happened. The anguish on the man's face did not abate; his arm did not heal. Becoming a vampire had snuffed out the gift in Odo's blood. Odo tried to heal a sick woman the next night and tried with others for a long time, but his healing gift did not return."

Wilhelm looked to me. "I did not know any better."

"But now we know," Bayard said. "We know full well."

I shook my head. "I don't know why you think—"

"I have no doubt, John." Bayard paused. "But it is time for us all to become certain. Give Wilhelm your arm."

"I—"

"John," Bayard said. "Look around."

At the table, I didn't see bloodthirsty, crazed monsters. I saw thoughtful, calculating… monsters. Why had Bayard made his offer to me? Why did he *want* me to become a vampire? He had said my blood—if it really did what Odo's allegedly had—would lose its power. I had no idea, but he most certainly could have forced me to extend my arm, so I reached it out to Wilhelm.

The Sanguan took it in both hands. His face brightened. "It's been over seven hundred years. I stopped imagining I'd taste such blood again." Wilhelm raised my arm and lowered his fangs, and they sliced into me.

A scalding heat shut my eyes. An inferno spiraled, lashing against my insides. Where it hit, I wished it would hit again. The fire settled.

"Sublime," Wilhelm said. "Rich, yet so pure."

Bayard grinned.

Wilhelm released my arm, and I brought it back to me, knowing what the bite of a thousand-year-old vampire felt like. Wilhelm rose, moved behind Madison, and pulled a short, sheathed knife with an ornate golden handle from his pocket.

"Quinton," he said.

The lean, bald vampire beside Madison got up and rested his hand on her shoulder.

I stood. "Leave her alone."

Her eyes pleaded up at me.

Wilhelm slid the sheath off the blade and placed the cover on the table. "I only ever got to see it in memories." He brought Madison's left arm onto the table and held it there.

"Stop!" I shouted.

Wilhelm sliced the knife across Madison's wrist.

"No!" I screamed.

Blood poured from her artery onto the table in a puddle growing toward the candelabras.

Quinton held her down in her seat.

"Madison!" I ran around to her.

Blood dripped off the table to the floor. Wilhelm set the

knife on the table. Madison slumped forward.

"Help her!" I cried. "Bayard! Mirabella!"

"You help her," Bayard said. "Take the knife. Your blood will save her."

I grabbed the knife. "What if it doesn't?"

"Then we will have another decision to make, in very short order." Bayard cocked his head. "I'd hate to see Madison die tonight."

"John…" Madison's voice sounded weak. Her hand lay limp. Blood covered the table and her lap. She slouched in her chair, and Quinton switched from holding her down to holding her up.

I sliced my left palm with the knife. "Emgh." I reached near Madison's mouth. "Here!"

She brought her lips to my cut hand… and nothing happened.

"Drink! Madison!"

Her tongue licked the cut. Her wrist kept bleeding.

"Drink, *please*." I pushed my hand at her mouth. "Madison, *please*."

She sucked. At her wrist, the flowing blood slowed. Madison didn't slouch as far. She drank, stopped bleeding, and breathed deeper and faster. Skin formed, and the slice at her wrist closed, as though it had never been there.

Madison stopped drinking, her chest heaved, and she held her wrist. Tears ran down her cheeks.

I leaned close to her. "Are you okay?"

She nodded.

I gripped the knife handle tight and motioned the blade

around the table at the vampires. But that wouldn't work. I dropped the weapon into the puddle of blood.

Bayard opened his arms wide to the group. "Who would like a sip from the mortal with blood like that of a god?"

12

ETHAN

The nearest Sanguan club to Ms. Evans's apartment was called Cemetery, so with a name, a mental image of Nadya Komarova, and eight hours before sunrise remaining, I headed there. Silver from the Spectavi bullet coursed painfully through my veins and kept me from running fast, but I held my side, gritted my teeth, and did my best.

Nadya Komarova… She was average height with a narrow waist and wide hips. Her very pale skin suggested she had been a vampire for a long time, and her blue eyes and long fire-red hair would be hard to miss.

Pulsing music from Cemetery reached down the block at the edge of the French Quarter. The aching in my shot side throbbed with the beat.

As I approached, the Sanguan bouncer at the dingy club stared at me. He sniffed—yes, I also smelled the synthetic blood on my clothes, but I was one of us, not one of *them*.

"He's dead." I stopped at the door. "The Spectavi bastard bled all over me."

The bouncer nodded.

Inside, the stuffy, square room reeked of mortal sweat that, along with the excessively loud music and the mess of humanity dancing in near pitch black, reminded me why I rarely visited such places.

Bursts of strobe lights provided a better view of the crowd I wandered through. The pitiful, liquored-up, and drugged humans chatted or danced with immortals who preyed on just that type. Scanning the room for Nadya, I spotted a black-haired male vampire dancing and a blond-haired female sucking on a guy's throat. A brown-haired male danced with a blue-haired female and they didn't stop when drinking from each other's wrists. A Sanguan with bright-red hair was way too tall and had hair too short to be Nadya. A shirtless male in jeans held a blond woman tightly and kissed her neck. He kissed her cheek and bit her ear. Her face said she loved it, that she cherished each touch of his lips and each nibble.

Fine, I relented. My assessment had been too negative and general. *Some* in the club shared a real passion, a meaningful connection—the kind of thing, in fact, I had found as a teenager and desperately wanted back for myself with Ellie.

No Nadya, though. Above me along the rear wall, a grated metal pathway with a rickety railing made a balcony to feeding rooms. The doors were all shut, and barging into them indiscriminately might get me banned from all the clubs nearby. I winced, still holding my side.

"Hey!" Fingers tapped my shoulder.

I spun to a thin girl in a light-blue dress with a bob of blond hair.

"Whoa." She backed up. "What happened to you?"

"It's been a long night." I had to shout over the music and the din, but her heart beat clearly and forcefully to my ears. Twenty-three, I guessed her to be. The blue in her eyes had a familiar lightness to them.

"Looks like it," she said. "You all right?"

"I'm fine."

She put her hand on my shoulder. "Then dance with me."

I traced a long vein from the base of her wrist up her skinny arm.

The music pounded. The silver in me throbbed. I took the girl's other hand in mine, spun her, pulled her to me, and with my arm over her arm over her chest, held her back to me. My cheek pressed against hers. "Perhaps a drink, instead?"

"Okay." It came out sheepishly. She breathed faster. Her heart beat quicker. "Yes."

I brought her arm to my mouth and bit through her wrist's soft skin. Luscious liquid raced down my throat and combusted. I sucked, and blazing fire beat back the aching silver.

Twenty-two she was, starting law school in the fall. My side became more whole as I drank. The pure, awful, liquid metal retreated. I breathed an almost painless, full breath.

Law school at New York University—where Ellie had wanted to go after college. I pulled my fangs from the girl and clutched her young body to me. A tear slid down my cheek.

The girl breathed deeply. "What is it?"

"You remind me of someone."

"Someone bad?"

"No," I said. "My favorite person in the whole world."

"What happened to her?"

"She never really got to be your age." I let the girl go.

She turned to me with a confused look then glanced behind her. "I'll be right back. Will you be here?"

"No."

She frowned, and her shoulders sank. She kissed my cheek. "Then thank you, that was very nice."

As she walked away, I considered how Ellie and I would never have found ourselves in a club like that. Nothing was wrong with the girl, nothing wrong with the place, really. It was just not our scene. Ellie and I had been young, we'd both had plenty to learn, but we already knew so much about ourselves and what we wanted.

I closed my eyes. Ellie and I could be together again, and if I found Nadya Komarova, Ellie and I could be together again *soon*.

The girl's blood had healed my side significantly, dulling the wretched silver's sting. The vampire behind the bar seemed the correct height, but she had short black hair. Dark eye shadow blended to purple, the same color as her lips, and she wore different buckled cuffs on each wrist to complete the goth look. I nodded to her on the way over, and she waited for me there.

"Do you know a vampire named Nadya?"

The bartender shook her head.

"Nadya Komarova."

"Nope," she said.

"Anyone upstairs with long red hair?" I asked. "Russian, but she doesn't always have the accent, I don't think."

"Don't think so," the bartender said.

I started to leave.

"Why are you looking for her?"

I turned back. "I have questions for her."

"Regarding?"

"It's… a private matter."

She nodded and went down the bar to a customer brandishing a twenty-dollar bill.

I left and headed for the next nearest club in the French Quarter. It played hip-hop but was otherwise not dramatically different from Cemetery. I didn't drink from anyone there. I didn't see Nadya, and the bartender didn't know anything about her.

I spent the rest of the night checking other nearby lounges and clubs, getting the same result.

———————————

When I woke the following night, I went downstairs to my living room and called my maker—a vampire in New York City. He didn't answer his phone, and to my complete lack of surprise, he hadn't set up his voicemail. I texted:

Have you heard of a vampire named Nadya Komarova? Do you know her or know anything about her?

I'd explain when he got back to me. And he would, eventually. My maker had been a vampire a little over a hundred years and was still getting used to texting and cell phones in general. I missed him, and even though becoming a vampire hadn't worked out as I had planned, I remained grateful for what he had done for me.

When Ellie had gotten sick, I swore to try everything I could for her—every last thing. Vampires couldn't make fledglings all the time, but my maker had listened to my story, understood my need, and turned me, which enabled me to try the last thing I could think of for Ellie.

During our years dating, the subject of vampires had come up, of course. I had known Ellie considered them demons—all of them, Sanguans *and* Spectavi—which, I suppose back then, I agreed with. I told her I agreed with her, anyway, and since she had been adamant in her position, we didn't discuss it at length. Even so, I assumed that when she had no other choice, she would have preferred a vampire's life to none at all. I had been wrong.

I headed out, back to a reggae club in the French Quarter. Sanguan feeding grounds wouldn't be my whole strategy, but since a vampire new to a city might seek out dens of willing prey, they seemed the best places to start.

I recalled the soon-to-be law student from the prior night, and holding her body to mine. Eleven years before, Ellie had been thin like that girl. Ellie had become terribly frail. Like that girl, Ellie had full, radiant blond hair when I met her, but those strands had thinned and paled. The girl and Ellie had the same soft blue eyes.

I *would* find the source of the sublime blood. And when I brought it to Ellie, her eyes would melt me as they ever had. They first had in the seconds before halftime of a basketball game in our high school gym my sophomore year, when I should have been paying attention to the game I was playing in. Ellie was a freshman, and I had seen her in the hall a few times at her locker, but she had moved into town that year, so I hadn't met her.

The referee handed me the ball to throw in. My teammates ran and cut to get open from defenders, and in the bleachers full of classmates, parents, and townsfolk, in the third row, the prettiest girl smiled at me.

"Ethan!" my teammate yelled, and I inbounded the ball just in time.

"What the hell was that?" he asked me on the way into the locker room for halftime.

"A girl," I said.

He rolled his eyes, but I did not care.

The next day at school, she waited in the lunch line, a dozen people in front of me, and I was wondering how I would go about cutting in front of everyone to catch up with her, when she dropped back in line to me. I had never seen a girl do anything like that. It was so cool of her.

She introduced herself. I introduced myself. She congratulated me for inbounding the basketball in time. I told her if I hadn't, my coach might have killed me. She played tennis, and I asked if she'd ever gotten distracted like that in any of her matches. She said of course not. But she said it nicely, with a smile.

Our whole time talking, that she had moved back in the line to me stuck in my mind. It had been direct. She was direct. I had known direct people, but all struck me as cold and abrasive. Ellie was something I had never encountered before—direct *and* kind. A warmness surrounded her, and she just happened to get right to things. I loved the combination.

The smell of marijuana brought me back to New Orleans, where that remarkable girl who had never graduated high school lay in a coma. I headed into the club—the source of the roasted, earthy aroma. The instrumental reggae beat slower and quieter. The humans smoking pot in complete disregard for the law moved to match the music's pace, and there was significantly more lounging about, making it altogether more my speed than other clubs, but still, the place wasn't my scene.

I leaned against the bar and looked around. Plenty of Sanguans sipped on stoned men and women, but none of the vampires had bright-red hair.

Again, I approached a bartender who came close to matching Nadya's description, but Nadya did not have long blond dreadlocks.

"You need something?" she asked.

"Do you know a vampire named Nadya Komarova?"

"Nope. Why?"

"Personal matter," I said. "If you see her, tell her I'll be in the alley on the northeast side of Saint Louis Cathedral, two hours after sundown."

"Who should I say is looking?"

"Just tell her someone is, and that I'll be there, every night."

The bartender shrugged. "If I remember."

I leaned closer. "Remember."

I left. I had refused to leave my name so that it couldn't somehow lead to Ellie. There was no reason a vampire should want to harm her, but vampires with endless nights to fill could be curious creatures, and a curious vampire might sip her blood to learn her story and mine. I couldn't bear the thought of Ellie lying in a coma while a vampire drank from her.

The following evening, after leaving Ellie's bedside, I went to the alley as I had left word all over the Quarter and surrounding city districts that I would. Leaning back against the brightly lit, off-white, smooth stone wall, with my hands in my pockets, I debated whether Nadya would have stuck around New Orleans after the concert at the museum. I had never seen her in the city, which meant she was a visitor. But since the concert, I had not seen her, and none of the bartenders at a single Sanguan club had recognized her description or name. That wasn't conclusive at all, of course. Nadya might have had no interest in the clubs, just as I didn't.

But I thought one of the bartenders would have known or seen *something*, even if secondhand. Nadya had gone to the concert, and I found it unlikely she had come to New Orleans for that single event. Unless that was exactly what she had done, for a reason I would never know.

I forced away that bleak possibility and focused on what

would happen when I *did* find Nadya. I assumed her to be an ancient, full of answers. But what if she was a brand-new vampire who happened to have very light skin because she did as a mortal? What if she had stumbled upon a sentence in an old book like I had, and had simply liked the line? Or what if she liked it and had her own agenda? What if she were hot on the trail of the person with that blood, while I waited in that alley?

I shut my eyes and thought of Ellie. The weekend after the basketball game, a senior on my team was having a house party, and I invited Ellie. She told her parents she was staying at a friend's house then had that friend's older sister drop them off at the party. It was quite the production to attend a party where the main event was playing drinking games with cheap beer from a keg.

When Ellie walked in, I got up from the card game at the living room coffee table and asked if she wanted to join. Her friend did, but Ellie said no. I figured Ellie would join the next round, but when the next round started, I didn't see Ellie in the living room. I grabbed my beer and went looking. She was out back on the deck, leaning against the railing. She had her wool coat on and was sipping beer from a red plastic cup, looking up at the sky.

"We're about to start a new round, if you wanna play." I could see my breath in the cold air.

"That's okay," she said. "Those games aren't really my thing."

"It's kind of what we do here."

She smiled. "Go ahead then."

Without her, I didn't want to. "Nah." I stood beside her at the deck railing. "Maybe later, or something."

She pointed at three stars in a line. "That's Orion."

"I know."

"Do you know that one?" She pointed higher and right.

"Taurus." I pointed to a group of stars in a ring. "I'm sure you know that one?"

She gave a puzzled look.

"It's a basketball," I said. "There's, like, six stars in a circle. Sort of. They're circle*ish*."

She smiled. "I don't think that's a constellation."

"It should be."

Eventually, I got my jacket, and we talked out there for hours. While we made our way through a couple beers each, I found another reason to not want to be inside playing drinking games—I didn't want to be a drunken buffoon around Ellie. The feeling struck me as both brand-new and perfectly clear. I wanted her to see the real me.

I asked about the small silver cross hanging off her necklace.

She said, "God and his goodness are very important to me. Do you believe in God?"

"I don't know."

My phone buzzed in my pocket, in the alley beside Saint Louis Cathedral in New Orleans. A text from my maker read: *I know the name but have not had the pleasure of meeting Nadya. She's far older than I. Why do you ask about her?*

I responded: *I think she might know something about that blood I've long been looking for. I think she mentioned it in New Orleans last week.*

My maker responded: *She's powerful and known to be mischievous. She could be dangerous. Be careful. Good luck.*

I wrote, *I will be, thanks,* then closed my phone and put it away.

I headed north with a particular rooftop in mind, which offered a good vantage point of Bourbon Street. I'd get back to asking at clubs later but thought the chaos of Bourbon's nightly party might be to the liking of mischievous Nadya.

I hadn't spotted Nadya on Bourbon Street, but a lot of vampires I had never seen in the city had been hunting there, so the next night, after waiting in vain in the alley, I went back to watch Bourbon from above.

And it was a mess down there. The street was closed off to cars, so across its entire width, hordes of people wandered from one bar to another, with colorful, sugary, high-alcohol drink or drinks in hand. And they wandered very slowly. On countless nights past, I had drunk from enough to know that anyone out on Bourbon Street probably didn't have anywhere else to be. New Orleans *was* "The Big Easy," so the scene fit, but that didn't make the sea of people on the street any less of a mess.

Random music came from everywhere. As a vampire, I could hear farther than a mortal, and when I tried, could isolate particular sounds. But if I listened naturally, I heard the same combination of styles and sources that everyone did. Jazz horns sounded nice, but extremely amateur karaoke from a nearby bar mostly drowned them out. Dueling pianos played inside a bar, while outside its open doors, a small group did the Electric Slide to music blasting from a boom box, while the passing crowd separated to give them room to do their sliding, in all its electric glory.

Drunken men on balconies pelted drunken women of all ages on the street with bead necklaces so they would show their breasts. That it went on every night of the week, every week of the year, still amazed me, even after living in New Orleans for a decade.

Fancy hotels and restaurants operated on the same street! The juxtaposition in such proximity astounded me, and it was into those nicer establishments I watched many vampires walk, often arm in arm with—judging by their heartbeats—mostly nervous mortals. I spotted a few long-term couples I had met before, consisting of a vampire and a mortal. No shaky nerves with them. And occasional pairs of vampires walked the street, choosing their prey together, which was another thing I never had any interest in. I just wanted to be alone and to find a way to cure Ellie.

Had I really gotten any closer to doing that?

With a sigh, I sat down facing away from Bourbon and glanced at the stars. Then I lay down with my arm behind my head for more than a glance.

When Ellie and I had been together for a couple months, our parents didn't like us dating so seriously, so young. But eventually, they saw the same thing Ellie and I felt—just how much we enjoyed being with each other.

Ellie planned to go to law school but would study economics in undergrad. I was thinking finance, and that gave us plenty of common ground. We played tennis together, and I could hit harder, but since she practiced with the team and had been playing for longer, she placed the ball better around the court. We watched tennis on TV. We watched basketball and frequently shot hoops together in the park.

And as high schoolers, of course, we went to the mall with friends, to movies, and to parties, but always, it was about each other first. We were truly thankful to have such a great group of friends, but we cherished our time together more. We couldn't help it, and we didn't want to. We were in love.

We went to New York City for our one-year dating anniversary. We took the train in from New Jersey and spent the sunny afternoon walking around Central Park. We ate dinner in Little Italy before seeing a show on Broadway. It was a perfect day, I had thought, the first of many with Ellie to come. We both planned to go to college in New York City, where we would have years of perfect days, and we talked about visiting London, Paris, Rome, and so many other places. We were going to see the world together. But we never got to see any of it.

I sighed and rolled onto my side on the rooftop above Bourbon Street.

Below, against a brick building across the street, a big vampire in jeans and a motorcycle jacket had his mouth at the neck of a short woman with long bleach-blond hair. The Sanguan ripped out his fangs and let the woman drop to the ground.

The vampire wiped his bloody mouth on his jacket sleeve and casually disappeared into the crowd, while others passed the woman without a glance. I could discern no pulse or hint of movement in her.

Two women, still wearing what looked like that day's work attire, with ID badges hanging off their belts, holding tall green drinks with straws, stopped and knelt beside her. They moved her hair aside, revealing the bite and fresh blood on her neck. The women stood, and one pulled a cell phone out of her purse.

I got up and headed away on the rooftop. When the paramedics, along with the police or Spectavi, arrived to deal with the corpse, I didn't want to be anywhere nearby.

Nights of checking on Ellie, asking questions at clubs, then watching from rooftops stretched into weeks. Two hours after each sundown, I waited by the side of the cathedral for about an hour, under clear skies, clouds, or steady downpours, without fail and without a meaningful visitor.

I began to think Nadya Komarova must have moved on. I had missed my chance to save Ellie. I didn't even know what Nadya could offer. My weeks spent searching could have been a search for crushingly little, perhaps nothing more than another vampire fascinated by the same story I was.

Regardless, I called my maker one night to ask him to try to find additional information about Nadya. When he called back nights later, he hadn't discovered much new. "Mischievous," he repeated. "Maybe dangerous." He did learn that she had been a vampire for more than six hundred years.

Watching the occasional mortal murders around the Quarter, usually at the hands and fangs of Sanguans, but sometimes the result of bullets shot by fellow mortals, didn't help my mood. Each death reminded me of the fragile nature of Ellie's life.

I had to try something new. Yet Nadya was my only real lead in ten years of searching. My something new would be a new approach to learning about her, I decided. I would pay another visit to the woman whose word I had taken instead of drinking from her.

———————————

On my way to Ms. Evans's apartment, in the last hour of the night, I passed a Sanguan lounge. I checked my watch and figured the later, the better, in case Ms. Evans called the police after I drank from her. Ideally, I wouldn't leave them time to get the Spectavi involved at all before sunrise.

Inside the lounge, shockingly, mercifully, classical music played while the thin crowd chatted and relaxed. I sat at the end of the bar near the brick wall. In the far corner of the room, at a round booth table, a male and a female vampire drank from a man in fine suit. Two booths over, two males drank from a shirtless man.

The bartender came over—short black hair, gothic makeup, wrist cuffs—the same vampire from Cemetery the night I had gotten Nadya's name from Ms. Evans. The bartender stretched her hands out wide on the bar. "Find her yet?"

I slouched against the wall. "No."

"Why are you looking for her?"

"It's a private—"

The bartender raised an eyebrow.

"My… The woman I love is dying."

The bartender crossed her arms. "A mortal woman?"

"Yes, like I was." I let my head fall back against the brick. "She contracted meningitis suddenly. No idea how or why she got it. Antibiotics didn't help, and her brain and spinal cord swelled. She had small strokes before the swelling went down. She's been in a coma ever since."

"I'm sorry."

"Me, too."

"How long?"

"Eleven years," I said.

"And what can Nadya Komarova do for this woman? Your blood could make her a vampire. It would heal her."

"She won't have it. Not vampire blood. Her heart is starting to fail now."

The bartender brought a finger to her lips. "You think a different kind of blood could help her?"

A weary-eyed man staggered to the bar. "Hey, could I—"

"Shh!" The bartender pointed at him then past him. "Go away."

He did.

"I do think so," I said. "Nadya mentioned the blood, I'm fairly sure, at the museum of art."

"What did she say?"

"I wasn't there. I met someone who overheard her. Nadya described blood that tasted sublime. Rich, yet pure. It was like—" I leaned off the wall. "Do you know Nadya?"

"This woman, she is worth eleven years of waiting? Eleven years of devotion to what sounds like a chance hope?"

"She is," I said.

"You must have been quite young when you became a vampire. You think you understand 'love' well enough to make such a claim?"

I leaned farther forward. "I understood it then, and I understand it more now. This isn't the kind of love you walk away from."

"Hm."

"She's breathing, and so am I," I said. "As long as there's hope, chance or not, I will cling to it."

The bartender extended her right hand.

I raised an eyebrow.

She put her other hand on her hip.

I shook her hand.

With a thick Russian accent, she said, "Nadya Komarova. It is a pleasure to meet one so devoted to another."

"I…"

She pulled off her wig and let down her long bright-red hair.

"Why?" I asked.

"Why what?"

"Bartending."

"It's fun!" Nadya said. "I get to really see the people and the vampires in a new city. An old Sanguan can be intimidating, but no one thinks twice about acting themselves in front of a young bartender."

"Uh-huh." I shook my head fast. "So, the blood, did you drink it? What do you know? Where was it?"

"A friend drank it," Nadya said.

"When?"

"The night before the concert at the museum."

"My God," I said. "Where? Near here?"

"Not nearby."

"Whose blood was it?"

"Tomorrow."

"No." I got off the barstool. "*Please.* I've been waiting so long. I can't wait any longer."

"It's late. The sun will rise soon. We'll chat tomorrow. I'll meet you in your alley." She turned.

I grabbed her shoulder to spin her back to me. Nadya did not budge. I pulled, but nothing happened, so I let her go.

The six-hundred-year-old turned around. "I'll see you tomorrow, I promise."

With my heart pounding, I raced home to my coffin.

––––––––––––

First thing after waking, I told Ellie I had found Nadya. I told her the Russian vampire was real, the blood her friend had drunk was real, and so maybe all the rest of the story was real, too. I held Ellie's hand and told her to hold on just a little longer. Soon, I would return with someone who could help her, then we would be together again. Then I ran to the alley beside the cathedral.

No Nadya.

I paced back and forth in the short space between buildings.

I recalled, at eighteen, after an incredible summer with Ellie, leaving for Columbia University that fall. She had her senior year of high school to attend. I would see her on the weekends, and probably more depending on my class schedule, but I knew it would never be the same.

I thought an even better chapter was to come for us. I truly did, because we had our whole lives together. Still, when Ellie went back to high school, and I didn't, a chapter in our story ended.

Then, in the spring, an acceptance letter came in the mail for her from Columbia. We would be in school together again before long. After she read every word of it to me over the phone, she scanned the letter into her computer and emailed it. I remember reading it myself and grinning, picturing her grinning while I did.

I stopped pacing and stared at the wall.

Three days later, Ellie went to the high school nurse, complaining of aches and chills. The nurse said Ellie had a fever and sent her home for the day. Ellie called me, and we figured it was probably a cold or the flu, but that going to the doctor the next day made sense, to be sure.

The doctor gave Ellie antibiotics to be safe, so whenever I recalled her health's rapid spiral downward, I didn't find much to have done differently. Would medicine the day before have changed the outcome? Maybe. But we'd both been sicker many times and put up with it for far longer before seeing a doctor. In that case, Ellie actually went a lot sooner than she might have.

But the doctor didn't help. The medicine didn't stop the illness that had taken hold of her. Ellie went to the emergency room the next day, was admitted, and put on intravenous antibiotics. Those didn't work, either, and she slipped into her coma.

After a year, Ellie's parents moved her with them down to New Orleans, where they would be closer to Ellie's older sister and their granddaughter. In the years since then, they visited Ellie less and less.

"Hello, vampire whose name I do not know." Nadya approached, wearing black leggings, knee-high boots, and a loose short-sleeved black top. Her long fire-red hair framed her little face. Beaded bracelets wrapped around her left wrist. I remembered her comment about my age from the prior night and doubted she had been older when becoming a vampire.

"Where did your friend drink the blood?" I asked. "How'd she find out about it?"

"No." Nadya wagged her finger side to side. "Not how this works." The *W* in *works* sounded like a *V* in her Russian accent. "What do you think you know about this blood?"

"I know it could save the woman I love."

"*Know* how?"

"I found a drawing. In a book in an antique shop. In 1282, in Hungary, a young man's blood healed an old woman. The sun was shining outside. 'The taste is most sublime. Rich, yet pure. Blood of a mortal, like the blood of

God,' it said." I shook my head. "It sounds crazy, but I *know* that blood could cure her."

"I have seen crazier things," Nadya said.

"Have you heard that story? Have you seen those drawings?"

"No. But my friend raved about the blood. She used similar words and said it tasted like nothing she had ever experienced." Nadya shrugged. "You could be correct about what it can do."

"I am."

"Where is the girl?"

"Resting," I said. "Safe."

"May I see her?"

"No."

"Then how do I know *your* story is true?"

"It is."

Nadya crossed her arms. "But how do I *know*? How do I know you do not seek this unique blood for another reason?"

"What other reason? Do I look like I'm making this up?"

"You could sell blood like that for a fortune, to vampires as a snack, to humans as a life-saving meal. That blood is power."

"I don't want any of that. I just want to save Ellie." I had let her name slip.

"Ellie?" Nadya tapped her chin.

"Leave her be."

Nadya's bold blue eyes met mine.

"Please," I added.

"What is your name?"

"Ethan."

"Well, Ethan, race me to the football stadium."

"What?"

"You've told me plenty. Now show me what she means to you." Nadya looked up the side of the cathedral. She crouched, leapt, and landed hard on the roof. "See you at the Superdome!" She ran out of sight.

I spun to the south. When was the last time I *raced* anyone on foot? I darted to Chartres Street. I checked the rooftops but didn't see Nadya.

I bolted southwest, dodging people on the sidewalk. Why race me? Whoever won, what would it prove?

A group following a tour guide made me slow, which I regretted. I should have seen them sooner.

Past Canal, I hit wide three-lane Poydras Street. Rounding the corner, I bumped a man listening to headphones, but caught him as he flew away from the impact. "Sorry." I set him down and raced northwest.

The massive, white-domed football stadium loomed. Was an event going on there that evening? Where would I find Nadya? The stadium would dwarf the vampire.

At a taxi stand for the Superdome, Nadya stood, shaking her head. "This is sad, Ethan. How long have you lived here?"

"Ten years."

"I've been here one month!" She raised an index finger.

"You're faster," I said.

"You want me to tell you where my friend drank blood that was *so* delicious and *so* unique, she had to call me and gush about its every detail?"

"Yes. *Please!*"

"Then show me. Beat me to the French Market. Find a way to arrive there first." Nadya darted across Poydras Street in the direction we had come from, leapt to a rooftop, and stared down at me.

I couldn't jump like that. Actually, I hadn't tried in years. But forget it—I wouldn't beat her up on the roofs. And forget the French Quarter at all. Too many people there. I would stay north as long as I could. Rampart Street would be the fastest route.

I dashed over to Rampart, where few car taillights interrupted the wide pavement before me. With all the speed I could manage, I rushed east. I had never run so fast.

I turned south down narrower Ursulines Avenue. The French Market was six blocks ahead. I ran and leapt over a passing car at an intersection. I knocked a cyclist aside, gritted my teeth, and pushed on.

Nadya landed at the empty market, which had closed for the night, from the rooftop across the street, when I was a block and a half away. The sight of her slowed my last steps.

"Better!" She smiled. "Much better. *Séduisante*, do you know this boutique?"

"Yeah."

"Think you can get there first?"

"I—" I ran, imagining her eyes lighting up behind me. I wished I had shoved her to the ground first, to get a bigger head start.

Back in the Quarter, I weaved through foot traffic. I jumped onto the roof of a parked car, then one ahead, and another. I left dents behind, but they were just cars, and I was running for Ellie.

I leapt over the horde at Bourbon Street and kept running. Left onto Dauphine, there was *Séduisante*.

From above, Nadya landed between me and the front door, as I skidded to a halt.

"Very close." She extended her arm and put up her thumb. "Good job!"

"But I didn't win."

"Eh." She waved her hand. "I've been doing this a long time. You were not going to win."

"Bu—"

"Reims, France," Nadya said. "My friend drank from a man there with that delectable blood and called me to tell me how incredible it had been."

"Is he there, now?"

"Unlikely. I called my friend this evening." Nadya pulled open the door. "Come. Time for a new game."

Inside, a saleswoman with glasses looked up from arranging women's skirts and clasped her hands. "Nadya!" She came over to us and asked me, "Your name turned out to be?"

"Ethan."

"Fine. That's just fine." The saleswoman grabbed my wrist. "Everything is ready. All as we discussed earlier." She took Nadya's wrist with her other hand. "This way."

We followed her to the back of the shop, where the saleswoman selected the middle of three garment bags and handed it to me. She pointed to my feet then to a green shoebox and gave me that, too.

"What's this?" I asked.

"Tuxedo," Nadya said.

"You can change there." The saleswoman pointed left. "And, Nadya, you are this way." She pointed right.

I almost asked why, or what, or any of a dozen questions, but racing had yielded vital information, so getting whatever Nadya had planned over with seemed like the quickest way to learn more. I went to the small dressing room. The pants fit well, the jacket was a little tight, but I wouldn't say anything. The shoes were the correct size. I tied the bowtie and exited the dressing room.

Across the shop, Nadya came out in a long pale-blue strapless gown with a wide, sparkling diamond sash around her waist. "I look okay?"

For what? I had no idea what was to come. "Sure."

"Hmm…" She peered over her shoulder at a standing mirror. "I normally do better than 'sure.'"

She looked gorgeous. She was gorgeous. The gown's color went perfectly with her hair.

"Where are we headed?" I asked.

"Inn on Bourbon," Nadya said. "There's a party tonight."

She thanked the saleswoman, who thanked Nadya profusely for her business since she had been in New Orleans. The Inn on Bourbon, on the site of the Old French Opera House, was one of the nice places operating on the chaotic street.

On the walk, I asked Nadya, "What's the game?"

"You will see." A mortal wearing that gown would surely

have been in a limousine or a luxury car, but Nadya just held the thin fabric to keep it from the filthy street while we walked.

"Why the accent now, but not when you were bartending?"

"It's fun to blend in and keep myself unknown," she said. "It's not hard to speak another language and sound just like the locals." And she had, when she said that. Then the Russian accent returned. "But even easier not to bother."

The four-story Inn boasted two balcony levels and took up nearly the entire block, which helped it stand out from the street's typical, smaller establishments, though its cleanliness and classic design did even more so. Narrow, tall windows with white panes and arched tops lined each floor on street level. Beyond the windows, tuxedos and gowns set the party guests miles apart from everyone on Bourbon. Outside, a fire truck had parked, and four firemen in heavy, suspendered pants and navy-blue T-shirts chatted with three Spectavi in light-gray suits.

Perhaps the truck blocked some of the noise from the inn, or maybe the sight of civil authority was intended to keep the riffraff away. A horse-drawn carriage stopped behind the truck, and its passengers disembarked. We followed them inside.

A waiting host took a white card from the couple. He unfolded and read it before motioning them to pass. He gave Nadya a respectful nod and motioned us the same way.

"What's the party for?" I asked.

"Dancing." Nadya gestured past high tables where guests chatted and snacked on hors d'oeuvres, to the end of the room, where six couples glided around the wooden floor to the ballroom music.

"I mean who's throwing the party? What's it celebrating?"

Nadya shrugged. "Don't remember."

I counted twenty-eight mortals, three Sanguans—two male and one female—and us, apparently the lone vampire couple. Blue drapes partially covered the windows out to crowded Bourbon Street.

Nadya took my hand. "Let's dance!"

I pulled my hand from her. "I don't dance."

She frowned.

"Why dancing?" I shook my head. "What does this have to do with anything? We're wasting time!"

A few nearby looked over at us. Nadya flashed a smile, and they returned to their conversations.

"I need to know you can dance." She headed toward the far end of the room and struck up a conversation with two couples at the high table nearest the dancers. The song ended, and a couple headed off the dance floor. Nadya and a gentleman she had been talking with took their place.

He was taller than she was and, as his salt-and-pepper beard made clear, older than she must have been before becoming a vampire. But as the string and woodwind notes of a classical song rose, with one arm held high and his other at her waist, he led Nadya with a playful ease.

And that was why she had dragged me to the party, I decided. Nadya needed to *play*. First racing, then dancing, but I had no interest in games. I leaned against the wall with my arms crossed.

Nadya's partner kept a serious countenance, and she did likewise. If either missed a step, I didn't notice. When the song ended, he said something to Nadya. She nodded, and the younger man from his table joined her for the next song.

Horns and a light drum beat faster from overhead speakers. Nadya's new partner smiled warmly, and so did Nadya. She danced well and seemed to enjoy it thoroughly. Maybe the variety of it appealed to her, that each song and each dance came as something new, especially when they came with someone new.

When that song ended, Nadya kissed her partner's cheek, and during a break in the music, she came over to me.

She raised her eyebrows. "What if we are somewhere, you and me, and to blend in, to look like we belong, we *need* to dance?"

"We? Where would *we* be that we needed to?"

"Pardon me." A square-jawed man with brown hair stood behind Nadya.

She turned to him.

"Might I have this dance? Or one later, if this one is spoken for."

She put out her hand. "It is not."

He led her near the only other couple getting ready.

Nadya's new partner held her tightly, matching the other couple's poised position.

The song started fast, and with quick steps and quicker turns, they moved together to the dramatic music.

Where would we need to "blend in"? Did she mean to come with me, wherever that happened to be?

Focus filled Nadya's and her partner's faces.

Could we not simply go talk to the person with sublime blood? Was there more to it?

The quick turns continued on the dance floor, followed by long stretches of purposeful steps.

Recalling how I had been unable to budge Nadya when trying to spin her around at the bar, I didn't hate the idea of Nadya with me, tracking down the source of the sublime blood, as much as I'd expected to.

Nadya's partner bent her low, and after a moment there, she rose with him, into a long kiss, and the song ended. She was whatever the song or her partner called for, I realized. If it really was all a game to her, she did happen to be excellent at it.

Nadya came back over to me. "Are you ready to dance?"

"I—"

"I have ideas of who might be holding John," she said. "John, the one with the blood you seek. I can think of a dozen Sanguans who might want him for themselves, for many different reasons, depending on who it is."

I unfolded my arms. "Someone has him?"

"Almost certainly. He has disappeared since Reims, my friend tells me."

"Where to? Who has him?"

"Paris most probably. And who? Doubtless someone powerful. I've done many rescues, often successfully, and all are at least a little different. If we are going to get him…" Nadya tapped her chin and started for the high tables, then called back, shrugging, "Who knows what it might take?"

She found her second partner eager for another dance. They joined four couples on the dance floor.

I needed her help. The song began, and I watched her move with her partner, a smile, and perfect balance.

"Often successfully" was less assuring than other words she might have used, but she had been at the game for six hundred years. If she thought John was being held somewhere against his will, he likely was. How could I take him from there? How could I even find him to try?

I watched Nadya's moving feet, then her partner's, very closely.

My planning had never extended beyond verifying that the story about the blood was true and that a living mortal possessed that miraculous blood. I had never considered how I would bring the person to Ellie. And since apparently, I couldn't give John a call and meet him to chat, that *how* had become everything.

I pushed myself off the wall and headed toward Nadya. She noticed me and said something to her partner, who nodded and walked away, glancing at me as he passed. I shot him a look to say I would crush him if he got in my way. *I* would have the next dance.

I took Nadya's hand and her waist and moved when she did. My eyes fixed on the shoes of the man in the couple behind her, I matched his steps as best I could, while Nadya gently pulled me in the correct direction and pushed when the dance called for it. A soft nudge, a slight pull, watching shoes, and making my feet do the same, it went on for an eternity, or maybe five long minutes.

The music ended, and Nadya stopped.

I let her go. "I need your help."

"You will have it. Here..." She set her hand on my shoulder and, with her other hand, brought mine out wide. "And in France." The song started, and Nadya got me moving in the correct direction. "We leave tomorrow."

13

VERA

On Eure's campus in Virginia, I sat in the well-manicured grass on the hill overlooking the lake behind Edmond's home. A wall of drab clouds grew dimmer as the sun set beyond them. A warm, strengthening breeze blew my hair into my face. In the month since Edmond had pronounced his ultimatum, I had made no tangible progress on the Protice project. Every variation of every approach I had tried on past projects hadn't worked with Protice, and I had run out of ideas.

I had less than four weeks left, and *something* had to change, because I refused to fail. I would *not* miss my deadline. Something *would* change.

I pulled a clump of grass and let it drop. A ringing I had been unable to shake since the afternoon sharpened and roughened to a grating stinging in my mind. I doubted I would be free of it until Edmond woke and drank from me.

I had made no progress with my patients, either. In fact, I had been totally focused on Protice and hadn't tried anything new with them at all. Yet the stinging in my mind told me something needed to change with them, as well. Getting farther from them would have eased the pain, but I couldn't work as efficiently remotely.

On top of that—the stinging grew, and I brought my fingers to my temple—Edmond never left the patients for long stretches of time. I didn't like being parted from Edmond, and that meant I would always end up back near my patients, in order to be near him.

He frequently suggested I travel with Victoria, which I did sometimes and enjoyed, but it wasn't the same. Edmond had my heart, as I had his.

But would I have it if I failed with Protice?

The stinging spiked. I held my head, and it faded, like the fading light in the sky. A raindrop hit my arm. Low thunder rumbled in the distance.

Of course he would still love me, I told myself. But would Edmond think less of me? How could he not? The two patients aside, I had never failed him before, and Protice was the most important project I had ever known him to undertake.

In our war, all Spectavi vampires, except for a small group of their oldest and highest-ranking officials, drank synthetic blood. The Sanguans all drank mortals' blood, making the Sanguan threat to humanity very clear.

Since the Dark Ages, the Spectavi had protected humans and ensured humanity could chart its own destiny, free from the oppression of powerful vampires that men and women couldn't fight on their own. Spectavi vampires dealt with, usually in very swift, very permanent ways, Sanguans who attacked mortals. Sanguans who organized into gangs, cults, and armies that became a threat to humanity, Spectavi forces destroyed.

If no Sanguans existed, the world would have been a very different place. Mortals wouldn't have to live in fear of vampires. Even if the Sanguans needed mortal blood to survive, that didn't excuse drinking from people who didn't welcome their bites, terrorizing people, or murdering them.

The Spectavi couldn't catch every Sanguan in the act—or even come close. Edmond wanted all Sanguans, whether he could prove their crimes against humans or not, to drink synthetic blood instead. If any Sanguans refused, Edmond would use that as justification to hunt them down and destroy them.

But Sanguans didn't want to drink synthetic blood. Most loathed the idea of giving up the drinks from mortals they had become accustomed to. The synthetic blood didn't satisfy them the same way, and they argued no matter what we did to the synthetic, that would always be the case. Add in the fact that Sanguans generally didn't like being told what to do, and the question became, would the Spectavi force all Sanguans to comply and drink synthetic?

A majority of Spectavi wanted to do just that. They supported Edmond's plan. But too many felt such a directive against vampires who might be innocent of any crime was too extreme, even to deal with Sanguans. The argument had been raging for decades from leadership down through the rank and file. While Edmond served as the Spectavi's ultimate leader, he could not enact such a major policy change without near unanimous support. We intended to finally get that support with Protice.

The purpose behind Project Protice—and my task—was to chemically alter our synthetic blood so that those who drank it would be influenced in favor of Edmond's plan. Since nearly every Spectavi drank synthetic blood, Edmond would be assured the support he needed to turn his idea into official Spectavi policy. Sanguans would either drink synthetic blood, or be marked for death.

"Ah." I winced and grabbed my head again. I lay back in the grass, and the pain lessened. Another raindrop hit my arm, then two landed on my cheek.

Protice, which would alter the thoughts of Spectavi across the globe, was drastic, but Sanguans were drastic. They had killed and tormented so many humans. They had conquered nations and enslaved their people. And they had done it all over so many centuries. Those vampires *deserved* a drastic response.

I recalled my mom in her wedding dress, from a framed picture that had been on a shelf in our home. My dad held her. Then I saw my mom's neck ripped open. Blood poured and her skin melted, until my father's arms held nothing but a skeleton. The bones crumbled to dust and blew away in the wind.

A Sanguan had killed my mom, and I didn't know if my patients in Edmond's basement had sent me that image or if the horror was all my own.

My dad bled on a barroom floor in my mind. He, too,

turned to a skeleton, then ash, which a stiff breeze scattered into the air. Sanguans hadn't killed my father, and I didn't know if my patients had sent me that image, either.

I held my head and opened my eyes. Steady rain fell onto me. I couldn't fail with Protice. I *had* to complete the project.

There *were* Sanguans who abided by the law. But let that minority drink synthetic blood. Let them join our ranks. They had that option. Better to be rid of all the Sanguans who would not join the Spectavi, since that would include the truly vile Sanguans, than to let them all live, including the vile among them we didn't know about or couldn't prove guilty of their terrible crimes.

I would not fail. Edmond would have his mandate, we would hunt down all the Sanguans, and we would end the war.

Grass crunched up the hill. I rolled over, wiped water from my face, and watched Edmond approach, undeterred by the rain.

I resolved to get back to my patients immediately after completing Protice. I would not fail with them, either. I would bear their mental attacks, no matter how excruciating or how frequent, until I succeeded in my work. My patients would *not* win.

I tried to stand but grimaced at a stinging pain and only made it to a knee. Edmond crouched and wrapped his arms around me. He brought my head to his chest and moved my wet hair off my neck. In his bite, in the fire, the ringing, the stinging, and the images of my dead parents burned away.

He pulled my blood from me. The blue fire enveloped me.

Something *had* to change. *Let something change, but please, God, don't change how Edmond holds me and vanquishes my pain.*

14

JOHN

"Blood like that of a god." The night Bayard had said it, after all the vampires had drunk from me, we left Wilhelm's apartment. Riddled with fang marks, I lay in Mirabella's lap in the limousine, my hand bandaged. I was exhausted, and they had drained so much blood that I didn't even want *her* to take any more. We drove to our apartment, and across from me, Madison, still covered in dried blood, rested against Bayard's shoulder.

Bayard and Mirabella let us into the apartment, took off our collars, and left without a word. Madison helped me to her room and onto the bed, and in our clothes, we held each other and slept. I couldn't even muster the energy to kiss her before I passed out.

But I did kiss her when we woke around noon. She was fine. Her wrist was fine. No ill effects remained from her arm being sliced open and her blood pouring out of her.

We got cleaned up and put on our usual comfortable pants and plain shirts. I wrapped a fresh white bandage around my hand to cover my cut palm. Madison and I finally ate sandwiches around two.

"Why do you think Bayard gave me that choice?" I asked her. "Be free if I become a vampire, but lose… whatever my blood can do."

"I don't know."

I looked at the front door. We could walk through it that night for good, but we would be vampires if we did. Madison bit into the second half of her sandwich. I put mine down on my plate. I didn't want my life with her to be only part of a life—only the nights. I didn't want ours to be a monstrous existence spent hunting for others' blood. I had found Madison, and I wanted a real, whole life with her.

And what of my blood? An awful image of terminally ill, hospital-bound children came to mind. But I could heal them. I could heal just about anyone in a hospital, Bayard had told me, and he'd said we would go help someone one night soon, if I wished to. I had said yes, of course. But each time Bayard allowed me to heal someone, he would bring me back to our apartment. To our prison.

We watched TV, and Madison didn't go to her room to wait for Bayard. I prepared for the spectacle of her screaming at him about how he could have let her wrist be slashed open to bleed on Wilhelm's table. But when Bayard arrived, she got up from the couch and walked into his open arms for a long hug. She led him to her room.

Mirabella sat beside me. Beneath her knee-length skirt, she crossed her legs, then set her hands in her lap.

"Why give me the choice?" I asked.

"When Odo became a vampire, he didn't know his blood would lose its power to heal in the process, but you know that would happen."

"So?"

"Bayard wants to know what a man with your gift will choose, knowing fully what that choice will mean."

"Imprisonment shouldn't be part of my choice," I said. "If he let us go, right now, I would be truly free to choose."

"You would not be free, my dear John, if everyone knew what you could do. Bayard is doing you a favor. Besides…" She leaned across me to kiss the far side of my neck. "Is it so bad here?" She might have let me push her away, she might have let me ask more questions, but as she pressed her body into mine, then her fangs into my neck, I grew warm. I focused on the fire that I would have no choice but to think about as her drink went on.

I imagined being in bed with Madison, naked, with a fire raging around us and beneath us both, but leaving us unburned. Heat built, and I wasn't John with an enormous choice hanging before him. I was nothing but rising flame.

The following night, Bayard and Mirabella brought us clothes to go out, but the unexpectedly casual outfits included blue jeans and nice shirts. They did lock our collars on, however.

We were driven to an office building and led through a basement entrance to a dimly lit room with a wide window. Beyond the glass, in a bright room, a person lay in a hospital bed, bandaged all over, connected to IVs and monitors. A gap in the wrappings revealed closed, blackened eyelids.

"It's a mirrored window," Bayard said. "A fire in an apartment building in the Fourteenth District last evening burned him badly."

"He's a firefighter," Mirabella said. "He ran in to save a family and got half of them out before the ceiling caved in on him."

From the same door we had used, a man in a white lab coat entered the room.

"Doctor," Bayard said.

He nodded. "*Est-ce lui?*"

"It is he."

From the counter, the doctor brought over a tray with equipment, including short tubes and needles, and set it on a table beside a wooden chair. "Have a seat, John."

I did, and the doctor set my left arm face up on my leg. He rolled my sleeve as high as he could. He took an open cylinder with a long needle at the end, stuck the needle into a vein, and drew my blood into a thin tube.

The doctor withdrew the needle and centered a small Band-Aid where it had been. Using a door beside the mirrored window, he went into the patient's room. After securing the tube of my blood inside a larger tube near the IV bag, the doctor unwrapped bandages from the patient's arm, revealing black and red scalded flesh. Madison covered her mouth. The firefighter opened his eyes, and the doctor unwrapped bandages from his face, which appeared no better.

Where my blood hung, the doctor twisted a valve, and the red blood flowed through a clear thin plastic hose into the patient. The burned, bubbly skin of on his face lightened and smoothed. The skin on his arm did the same. The firefighter blinked and opened his eyes wider, his face full of astonishment. His chest rose with a fuller breath. His arm and his face healed until they appeared completely normal. The doctor smiled and explained to the firefighter—which we heard over a speaker and Bayard translated—that the experimental medicine had worked perfectly.

On the drive back, I asked Bayard if we could go help more people. He said we would, but not that night. I considered the setup that kept the patient from seeing me, and what Mirabella had said about my freedom. What if the firefighter *had* seen me and told his family and friends what my blood had done for him? When they all told their friends, and more and more people knew and came to me for help, what would I do? What if people just kept coming?

In the apartment, lying on my bed after Mirabella slid her fangs out of my neck, I pulled her head back to me.

She bit into me again, and heat returned quickly. She sucked, and flames rose. I didn't want to think about anything except that fire. When Mirabella finally left me and I crawled into bed with Madison, I managed to get my arm over her before I passed out.

The next afternoon, Madison rolled on her bed so her back was to me, and I held her.

"What do you want me to do?" I asked.

"Stay with me," she said.

I kissed her head and held her tighter. "Of course."

Mirabella and Bayard arrived that night as usual, and after they drank from us and departed, Madison and I stayed in. We did the same the night after. I asked Bayard if he worried other Sanguans who had drunk from us at Wilhelm's would know the location of our apartment from my blood and come for us. He said they respected him and the unwritten rules regarding humans from those events far too much to do that. The apartment was also booby-trapped, and any he'd misjudged would be met by an inferno of fire in the hallway and more than enough silver at the window or the walls to be lethal.

The next night, Mirabella and Bayard brought another tux for me and a stunning red gown for Madison. They locked on our collars, and we went to a play at the theater, which despite also being in French, was easier to follow than the opera. Mirabella wore black, and when she sipped from my wrist, I felt proud to be at the side of such a beauty, but my thoughts occasionally drifted to Madison. She appeared relaxed as ever with Bayard and when chatting with other people and Sanguans before the show. She seemed happy.

Two nights later, we went back to the doctor's office with the mirrored window. Two children, a boy and a girl, maybe ten years old, lay before us with bald heads. When the doctor went in to talk to them, they barely had the strength to respond, though the girl tried to smile. Cancer had spread throughout their bodies, the doctor told us while drawing two tubes of my blood. Chemotherapy had not helped.

The doctor administered my blood. The boy sat up and

smiled. When the girl smiled widely, I cried. Madison cried. Mirabella cried. Bayard smiled.

———————

Whenever we went out, we returned to the apartment to find fresh sheets on Madison's bed and our worn clothes replaced by clean clothes in our closet. Our refrigerator and counters were always restocked with food, though it required less and less fresh vegetables, meat, and bread to accomplish that, as Madison and I found our appetites only calling for small meals or snacks, and sometimes no meals at all.

At my request, Bayard brought magazines and newspapers written in English, along with a notepad and pencils for Madison. Her drawings from memory of European cities and landscapes weren't as grim as those in her old notebook, but the new ones all portrayed nighttime settings.

Bayard went to our hotel in Montmartre when Oluwaseun wasn't working. He paid for our stay and collected our things, which he discarded. I wondered what my web development customers thought of my absence, and if my parents were worried after having not heard from me, but neither seemed my most pressing concern. I could do nothing about either.

Each night, after Mirabella drank from me, I didn't worry about anything at all. Instead, once the vampires left, I found Madison waiting for me in her bed.

But then day would come, and hours waiting around the apartment for Mirabella's bite left a lot of time to think. I often dwelled on how I had ended up in the apartment, going all the way back to what brought me to Europe in the first place. My ended marriage seemed a lifetime ago, while my years of meeting women afterward and all the relationship starts and stops felt frighteningly fresh.

I asked God how I should respond to Bayard's choice, but he did not answer.

Bayard and Mirabella took us to another opera and a movie premiere. We visited the doctor's office every few nights, and the weeks flew by.

I buttoned my black dress shirt and put on a gray sport coat. We were headed to a club, Mirabella had said when she handed me my garment bag. I went out to the main room, eager to see Madison in whatever they had brought her.

She emerged from her room in a short red leather dress that clung to her lean body. Her black patent pumps included thin straps buckled around her ankles. She headed across the apartment for Bayard to lock on her collar. I imagined myself putting the collar on her instead of Bayard. If anyone *had* to, it should have been me.

Mirabella secured my collar, Bayard opened the apartment door, and we departed. While we drove, I couldn't take my eyes off Madison, especially her long legs. She noticed, I thought, in between glances at Bayard and out the window.

The club was small, dark, and high-end. A pair of collared women wearing leather corsets as tops worked the shiny silver-colored bar. The high-backed leather stools were all occupied, and other collared guests squeezed between them to order. Past the bar, six booths of varying sizes ran down and around the wall. The glass wall separating us from the crowded dance floor muffled electronic music but did nothing to block the colorful flashing lights.

Two Sanguans, a male and a female I recognized from our trips to the opera, arrived right after us, along with the same humans from those events, both female. They struck up a conversation with Bayard, Mirabella, and Madison, while I excused myself to order drinks. I picked out champagne for Madison, and the bartender recommended a concoction of whisky, vermouth, and Campari for me.

We stood for a while and talked, all eight of us, then squeezed into a big booth and ordered another round of drinks. Every person in our group was interesting, pretty, and in high spirits, but I wished the whole time to have been sitting beside Madison instead of across from her. The table's conversation over two or three more drinks distracted me in spurts, but my eyes always found their way back to Madison.

One of the other women turned to the vampire who had brought her. "Should we dance?"

"Certainly," she responded.

Madison glanced at me before taking Bayard's hand and following him past the bar, around the glass wall to the loud, crowded dance floor. I followed with Mirabella.

Blue, yellow, and purple shone from spotlights and flashed from strobes. The bass line punched quickly; higher electronic notes hit fast—and faster. Bayard held Madison, her eyes locked on his while they moved to the beat. A distorted female voice sang amid it all.

Mirabella took my hand and moved her back into me. She held my arm over her firm breasts, bit into my wrist, and sucked. I clutched her and leaned on her to keep from falling. When she pulled her fangs from me, we stayed like that and danced.

Madison's red dress made her easy to spot among so many others wearing dark colors. Her very light skin made her look like one of the many vampires in the crowd.

But by the end of the second song, Mirabella and her body moving in unison with mine had most of my attention. She sipped on my wrist briefly, frequently, and as ever, pleasing such a beautiful creature pleased me immensely. Why my blood tasted as it did, I could not say, but because of it, Mirabella chose to be with *me*.

At the end of a sip, with no music except bass rumbling low like thunder, she raised her arm over the crowd. From the sea of bodies, Bayard's hand reached out and found hers. He pulled Mirabella to him, and Madison came to me, as higher-pitched electronic notes resumed.

Madison kissed me. I wrapped my arm around her leather-covered body and wound my other around the back of her head. Pulling her close, I kissed her more deeply.

She said directly into my ear to be heard over the music, "I've never felt like this." She turned so I held her front, and her back pressed against me.

I said into her ear, "Me, neither."

We danced, and I didn't know what "this" was or what exactly Madison had meant. Did she mean about me, about me and our Sanguan captors, or about me, the vampires, and my miraculous blood?

I didn't even know what I had meant, or much at all, except that I wanted to keep holding Madison, letting the music move us and kissing her whenever I got the chance.

We got home near sunrise and slept until a few hours before sunset. Madison's dress and my clothes were strewn across the concrete floor. I held her in her bed.

"I've never felt as free as I did with you last night." She nuzzled her bare back closer to me.

I kissed her shoulder. Despite the collar having been locked on my neck, despite not having a choice about being brought to that club then returned to the apartment, I had a notion of what she meant.

The drinks helped dull our inhibitions. The music moved us. We knew many in the crowd, and Bayard and Mirabella wouldn't have let anything happen to us. Within those confines, once our vampires had gone to dance together, Madison and I had been free to focus totally on each other.

A few nights later, in the lobby of an underground theater before a symphony, I waited at the bar for our wine. Bayard came over, obviously not for wine of his own.

"Have you considered my offer?" he asked. "Not to imply any rush for a decision. You are welcome to stay with us as long as you like."

The bartender set our glasses down.

"Why is that my choice?" I asked Bayard. "What do you get out of it?"

He leaned back on the bar, looking out at the mingling vampires and mortals. "Where do you think our powers and vampiric thirst for blood come from? There have not always been immortals of our kind, but for more than a thousand years, there have been. What do you think bestowed our gifts on the first vampires, and, one might argue, cursed them with our need for blood and to rest during the daylight hours?"

"I don't know." I joined him looking out at the lobby.

"But you think it was probably the devil or another presence from hell." He knew because he had drunk my blood. "Or if not, then a pagan god or spirit from ages past."

"Which is it?"

"I do not know." Bayard shrugged. "I know all the legends and all the stories, but I do not know for certain which is true."

"Do you have a guess?"

He smiled. "I do. And evil is at its heart, which puts evil at each and every one of ours."

"Not the Spectavi," I said.

"Even theirs." He glanced at me. "As for yourself, you wonder if your blood's power is a gift from God. I wonder that, as well."

"But why set this all up? Why make me choose?"

"Because I've read all the histories there are to read, from every corner of the globe, religious and secular." Mirabella and Madison approached, and Bayard leaned off the bar. "Now I want to *see* history made, up close. I want to understand it intimately when I drink your blood. I want to know what you, in *this* age, at *this* moment will choose. Will you live with the good thing running through your veins to your heart, or will you root it out with evil?"

Madison scrunched her face as she neared. "Are you all right?"

I stared at and past her all at once.

She put her hand on my shoulder. "John, are you okay?"

I blinked. "Yeah, sorry." I grabbed the wine and handed her glass to her.

When Bayard put out his arm, she took it and headed into the theater.

I left my wine on the bar and walked with Mirabella.

While the orchestra played and Mirabella sipped from me in our box seats, I contemplated my situation: captive, yet curing men, women, and children who might never have been cured otherwise. What could I be were I free? How many people could I help?

But what kind of life would that be? When the world knew the power in my blood, the requests—no, the *pleas*—for my help would come constantly. And why shouldn't they? If I or someone I loved were ill, wouldn't I seek any cure, no matter what inconvenience that caused its source?

But thousands and millions of inconveniences would add up. Bayard's words replayed in my mind. Good or evil, the choice lay before me.

I woke late the next day, with a hope I had not put significant stock in for a while. Perhaps another vampire, maybe even a Spectavi, was looking for me. Bayard had found me after learning of my blood from a vampire who had drunk from me in Reims. Lots of vampires had drunk from me in that club's basement. Perhaps Bayard had been the first to find me, but others were searching. Although, other Sanguans could have been far worse than Bayard and Mirabella.

Later, Madison rested on me while we watched TV. I asked her, "If I decided to let one of them turn me into a vampire, so we could leave this place, would you have the other turn you?"

She sat up. "How could you choose that?"

"You'd rather stay here forever?"

She lay back down. "Is it that terrible here with me?"

"Of course not." I kissed her head. "But we aren't free."

She took my hand and interlocked our fingers. "We're safe, and we're together."

I let that settle then asked, "Do you ever see yourself having a family? Children of your own?"

"I used to… before my parents and my brother and sister were killed. The thought of that happening to my chil—" She sniffled. "What about you? Do you want to start a family someday?"

"Yes."

The next night at the doctor's office, my blood woke a woman from a coma, whose brain had hardly shown function for years. Another tube of it saved a bloodied car accident victim who had been hurried in on a stretcher. No tears that time, but a joy filled our side of the window, mirroring the joy beyond it.

With the sun sinking toward the horizon the following day, I watched Parisians walk along the Seine, while Madison read a magazine on the couch. Out our window, with the back of Notre Dame Cathedral rising through treetops in the distance, I spotted plenty walking alone, but mostly, I focused on couples, hand in hand or merely chatting or smiling. To be out there among them with Madison would have felt so right.

Yet soon, the sun would be gone from the sky, and all those I watched would have to worry about Sanguan vampires. Paris was a relatively safe city, but if a crazed Sanguan killed someone out there, Spectavi retaliation wouldn't bring the victim back. Inside our apartment, Madison and I shared no such fear.

When I sat beside her, she put her magazine on the coffee table, and as I lay against the couch's thickly padded arm, she leaned back on my chest.

I held her and brought my hand over hers on her stomach. "I love you."

Madison spread her fingers so ours interlocked. "I love you so much."

Our stomachs and hands rose and fell with a breath, another breath just like it, and one after.

I asked, "Do you love Bayard?"

A quiet breath came and went. Then another.

"I don't know," she said. "I love what he's given us. I love being here… I might. Do you love Mirabella?"

"I don't think so. I love that my blood makes her happy. I can't seem to help that." For a quiet breath, I watched our hands rise and fall. "But I'd leave her in tears if it meant the difference between seeing you smile or not."

Madison turned to me and kissed me. "I love you."

I kissed her and held her tightly.

15

VERA

In the waning minutes of nighttime, in the lab in Edmond's basement, I laid my head down on my arms on the counter. My latest mixture of synthetic blood had not had the desired effect on the Spectavi vampire test subjects. Three days before, in a stroke of inspiration, I had devised the fresh approach and rushed to try it. With the testing done and a failure, no further progress had been made on Protice.

"Hm." William stopped typing at his laptop at the counter behind me. His mouse clicked. "Hmm."

"What?" I said, my voice muffled by my arms.

"Take a look."

Slowly, I spun my chair around and rolled it over. An open email on his screen had the subject: *Top Secret.*

The other recipient was Edmond.

An informant in Reims, France, reports hearing of blood from a human male with a unique taste. Another Sanguan described the blood to him as being rich, pure, and sublime, like the blood of a god. The informant is seeking a source with firsthand knowledge or any additional information.

"It's blood related," I said. "I should have been copied on that email."

William nodded. "I'll remind him. What do you think? Interesting, isn't it?"

It was *different* and new, so it absolutely thrilled me. "Yeah."

William shut his laptop. "To investigate tomorrow." He got up. "Have a good day." He left the lab, no doubt headed for his home on the corporate campus and his mahogany coffin in the basement.

Blood like a god? *Interesting* only began to describe it. I looked through the lab window at the steel coffins. I rolled back over and opened my laptop. I double-clicked on the icon for the Spectavi historical archive application.

I typed my password, "Tomori."

Tons of new articles had been added since my last login—history never stopped being made.

In the search box, I entered "blood like a god." Results of titles and excerpts loaded, including lots of Sanguans who viewed themselves as gods and acted the part, all over the world, recently and back across the centuries. Scrolling down revealed that more than one Spectavi had considered themselves similarly divine. None of the results were about mortals with blood described that way.

I searched for "rich blood." Entries about wealthy vampires filled my screen—no value to me. "Rich, pure, sublime blood" led to results that shared little in common with each other, and seemed no more useful.

The sun would rise any minute, but I could ask Edmond as soon as it set. He was himself a Spectavi historical archive.

Which led me to an idea drastically preferable to waiting the day. I logged out of the application, which returned me to the login screen. I then logged in as Edmond, using the password he hadn't changed in three years, figuring his account might have access to more than mine did.

I searched again, and the first result was something I hadn't seen before: *1282: In Hungary, a human boy has blood that heals other humans.*

I clicked the title, sat back, and read Odo's story.

Right after sundown, I found Edmond in his drawing room, reading the early evening edition of the *New York Times*.

"Good evening," he said.

"Did you see that email?" I asked. "About the blood in Reims."

"I did." He turned a page in his paper.

"Think it could be like Odo's blood, from 1282 in Hungary?"

"Could be." He folded the paper down to look at me. "William showed you Odo's story?"

"Sure." Edmond would drink from me and know the truth before long, so I didn't feel like explaining it. "What's the plan? Are you going to Reims?"

The front door opened. Victoria entered.

"Not me." Edmond set the paper in his lap. He motioned to the chair to his left and the sofa across from him.

"I'm good standing." Victoria walked over to us.

"Me, too." I put my hands on my hips.

"Fine." Edmond gave a fake smile. "Victoria, did you read the email regarding Reims, and the article I attached?"

"I did," she said.

"What do you think?" he asked.

"That whoever possesses blood like that is in the hands of Sanguans, probably powerful ones. Whether or not they know what they have is another question, but Sanguans would not let a mortal with blood tasting like that remain free."

"Agreed," Edmond said. "I pray they do not know what they have. Think of all that blood could do. Think of all the good."

"It could do many things," Victoria said.

"Will you please bring its owner here?" Edmond asked.

"Sure," Victoria said.

"I want to go," I said.

"Why?" Edmond asked.

"Blood like a god? I wonder how my patients would respond to it. And if the blood really is different, it could offer fresh perspective that might help with Protice, too."

Edmond rubbed his chin. "Why not stay here and let Victoria bring the source of the blood to us? You'll certainly have all the access you want, for whatever tests you deem necessary."

I put my finger to my lips, imagining multiple consecutive days without massive psychological attacks from the inhabitants of the coffins in Edmond's basement. "Putting an ocean between me and my patients doesn't sound like the worst thing." I shrugged. "Maybe I can help find the source of the blood during the day or something."

"Hm."

While Edmond liked me getting away from the patients, he did not like when I left Spectavi-controlled campuses and military installations, especially at night. Sanguans were a threat to me, just like everyone else, but with me came a Spectavi security concern. I knew a lot about their inner workings, and any Sanguan who drank my blood would learn it all. That would not be an easy mess for Edmond to clean up, if he even could completely.

"She'll come no matter what," Victoria said. "If we say no, she'll pop out of a coffin on the tarmac after we land in France. Or maybe hide in a piece of luggage. I wonder if she'd prefer the surprise, actually."

"It does sound fun," I said. "Or I could fly over during daytime, you know, sitting in a regular seat."

"I guess that's that then," Edmond said. "Thank you, Victoria." The corners of his mouth turned upward. "Vera, find me before you leave?"

"Of course."

He got back to his paper. Victoria left, and I went upstairs to pack.

16

ETHAN

Nadya chartered us a private flight to France. She said she always flew that way, and when I asked, she confirmed that, like every ancient vampire I'd ever met, she had amassed substantial wealth over the centuries. In her case, over more than *six* centuries, the small fortune she'd inherited from the Sanguan who had made her a vampire had become a very big fortune.

We began our journey during daytime, resting in coffins, loaded onto the plane by employees of a company Nadya had worked with often and trusted with her life. Mid-flight, at nightfall, we awoke to a sky out the big windows as black as those in New Orleans, above an ocean colored to match it. We landed at private-aviation-focused Le Bourget Airport. While our things were brought to an apartment Nadya maintained in nearby Paris, a car drove us the hour and a half to Reims. Despite my reminders of the haste Ellie's recent heart attacks demanded, Nadya insisted on meeting her friend in person, rather than getting the information we needed over the phone.

In Reims, on a field of patchy grass before a third-century Roman triumphal arch with three passageways, our half a day of travel ended. A stiff breeze blew; clouds blocked every twinkle of starlight. I had dressed as I usually did in America, in slacks and a nice shirt. Nadya wore black pants, a short-sleeved top, and boots that partially closed the gap in our heights.

"You're sure she's coming?" I asked Nadya.

"Yes."

"Why here, exactly?"

The Russian vampire gestured to the arches.

"What do they have to do with anything?"

"We could meet anywhere in Reims. Why *not* pick a place with history?"

A pretty little vampire dressed for a night out smiled as she approached under the center arch.

"Collette!" Nadya ran to her.

"Nadya!" Collette put out her arms, and the two collided in a hug.

Collette finished kissing the second of Nadya's cheeks. "How are you, beautiful Nadya?" Her accent sounded French.

"My trip to America was cut short." Nadya motioned to me. "But now I have an adventure! So I am good. How are you?"

Thankfully, they had chosen English, though I figured Nadya could have opted for French if the mood had struck her.

"I am good," Collette said. "Fun times here in Reims. You will stay for a while?"

"No," I said.

They both turned to me.

"You said John went to Paris?" I asked.

"I believe so," Collette said.

"Collette, Ethan." Nadya gestured between us while she and Collette walked over. "Ethan, Collette."

"How do you know?" I asked.

Nadya frowned. "Ethan does not like fun."

Collette frowned. "And *he* is part of your adventure?"

"It's not an adventure," I said. "It's not a game. I need to find John."

Nadya put her hand on my shoulder. "It *is* an adventure. You will see."

"I—"

"But…" Nadya looked to Collette. "One which does call for haste. It's… part of the adventure."

"I see," Collette said. "Well, Ethan, yes, I do believe John went to Paris. Whether he is still there, I do not know."

"How do you know he went there?" I asked.

"The night after I met him in the club, he didn't get in touch with me like I assumed he would."

"How could he not?" Nadya asked.

"Right?" Collette put out her hands. "It's me! But he did not. So I took a walk around Reims and discovered why—Madison May."

"Who's Madison May?"

"A woman who went to the clubs in Reims every night for a month, with a vampire named Jacob. But he left the city. I drank from Madison not long after. She was quite upset to be alone with Jacob gone, and still being in Reims made it worse. She had plans to leave for Paris."

"What does that have to do with John?" I asked.

"Wait!" Nadya said. "I will guess. Did you see them together, John and Madison?"

Collette nodded. "Mm-hmm."

"Ah ha!" Nadya pointed at me. "See? I am good at this game."

"She is," Collette said to me. "I saw them walking back to Madison's hotel, and I followed them."

"Did you drink more?" Nadya asked.

"No." Collette shook her head. "They looked very happy together. But I did get near enough to hear Madison invite John to come with her to Paris, and John said that he would."

"What was it like?" I asked. "John's blood."

"Sublime." Collette bit her lip. "Glorious. Rich. So, so rich. Unlike anything I've tasted in my two hundred and fifty-four years on this earth."

———————————

We got physical descriptions of John and Madison from Collette, then she and Nadya chatted about Reims, New Orleans, music, clothes, people they had drunk from, people they wanted to drink from, and too many other inconsequential things before I finally convinced Nadya to leave.

We drove to Paris and spent the day in Nadya's third-story apartment there. Compared to my coffin back home, the one in her guest room had more ornate carvings on the outside and softer cushioning on the inside, yet still left me missing my own when I pulled the lid closed before sunrise. I woke with a thirst no different than each night in America.

An old-looking sofa occupied the middle of the apartment living room. Finely carved wood ran from its feet up to its arms. Matching upholstered chairs sat perpendicular to it, around a square wooden coffee table. No television served as the focal point of the room, and the whole place seemed out of a bygone era. The eighteenth century, I guessed. Nadya confirmed she had owned the apartment since before then.

Because Nadya was older than I was and therefore required less mortal blood to sustain her, I doubted her thirst screamed at her like mine did while we strolled to a lounge Nadya suspected would be a good source of information. I kept calm and walked at her pace, thankful she hadn't suggested anything more indirect than going to ask for information—I couldn't handle even the *idea* of another one of her games while John was potentially so close by.

The Sanguan lounge struck me with its cleanliness and had more modern furniture and fixtures than any in New Orleans. Its customers had all dressed in keeping with Paris's reputation as a fashion mecca. A woman in a white dress with a zipper the length of its front piqued my interest, though at that point, I would have drunk from pretty much anyone. But that would have to wait.

Nadya asked the bartender if he knew anything about a man with blood that tasted different than other people's. He said he did not. Though disappointed, I thought I had at least been conducting my investigation correctly when searching for Nadya.

Nadya wasn't done, though. We went upstairs, and at the end of a long row of identical doors, a huge vampire in a suit and black sunglasses, his hands behind his back, stood beside the last.

Nadya craned her neck up to him. "Hi."

"Hello." He stared straight ahead.

She looked at the silver door handle then back at him.

He glanced down at her.

She looked at the door handle again and put her hands on her hips.

"Can I help you?" the bouncer asked.

"Nadya Komarova!" She threw up her hands. "Here to see Jumaane."

The bouncer casually brought out his hand, turned the handle, and pushed the door in. "Go right ahead."

She did, I followed, and the door swung closed behind us.

An ebony-skinned vampire in an expensive-looking suit sat on a couch, his arm around a tall woman in a slinky golden dress, watching a flat-screen TV on a stand not far from them. In the rear of the room, a half-open panel door revealed a wide bed with a neatly made-up comforter.

"Komarova," the vampire said in a booming voice.

I expected Nadya to run over and plop herself on the couch with them. Instead, she bowed her head slightly. "Jumaane, thank you for seeing us."

"It is my pleasure." He sounded French. "Who is the young one?"

"Ethan," Nadya said. "A race car driver from America!"

I looked at Nadya.

"What kind of cars?" Jumaane asked.

"Uh, trucks, actually," I said, because for some reason, that's what popped into my head. "Pickup trucks. I don't know if you've seen them race, but they're fast. Not as fast as cars, but… also fast."

"I've seen 'em. That's cool." He asked Nadya, "What can I do for you?"

"We're looking for a man and a woman, and we think they're in Paris. Any new couples piquing interest of late?"

Jumaane smiled. "Men, women, couples… all of them pique my interest, all the time."

"He's a little over six feet. She's a little under," Nadya said. "He has brown hair. She has long black hair. And the man… he has… distinctive blood. Have you heard of anyone like that?"

He shrugged. "I hear things. I see things."

"Tell us," I said. "Please, tell us what you—"

Jumaane stood and glared.

Nadya shot her hand out to my chest. From her pocket, she pulled a green stone the size of a quarter. She tossed it to Jumaane. "What can you tell us?"

He held the emerald out before him and nodded. "They're on the Circuit."

"The Circuit?" I asked.

Jumaane sat down. "First time away from your pickup truck?"

"Ha!" Nadya enjoyed it.

"No, but—"

"They're with Sanguans," Jumaane said. "Hitting a lot of the underground events around the city. Shows, concerts, clubs. They're part of that crowd."

"You've seen them?" I asked.

"I have. Him, I recall vaguely, but only because of her. A mortal with skin as light as Nadya's, with hair as black as our nights—I don't forget a girl like that."

"When did you see them?" I asked.

"A week ago," Jumaane said. "At a symphony."

"Do you know who they were with?" I asked. "Which Sanguans?"

"There's a line." Jumaane put his arm around the woman beside him. "I don't think I'll cross it today."

"That's okay." Nadya grasped my shoulder. "We know what we need to know."

"I think you do," Jumaane said.

Nadya bowed. "Thank you, Jumaane."

He nodded. Nadya turned and headed out.

I followed and looked back. "Thank you."

"That line," Jumaane said. "I suggest you get acquainted with it."

Apparently the right question was the key to getting an informative answer from the bartender, because downstairs, it didn't cost Nadya another precious jewel to learn that the next big event on "the Circuit" was a play in three nights, Samuel Beckett's *En attendant Godot*, famous in English as *Waiting for Godot*.

Nadya said she needed to make a few calls, so while she

sat at the bar on her cell phone, I found the woman in the white dress standing at a high table with her tight-shirt-wearing boyfriend. They spoke enough English to make clear that a quick drink would be fine, as long as I drank from them both. I sipped from her wrist first, then his, and felt a whole lot better.

Back at the bar, Nadya told whoever was on the other end of the call that she would be attending the play with a guest, and that was that. Nadya hung up and reminded me how lucky I was to have her with me on the adventure. Still, I hated the prospect of waiting three nights.

Nadya explained the Paris Circuit in more detail, including how the mortals on it were collared guests of Sanguans. Since continuing to ask around could raise suspicion about us and our intentions with John and Madison, Nadya assured me that attending the play was the best approach. For all we knew, Jumaane had already told whoever was bringing John to the events that we were out looking for their mortals.

But Jumaane had mentioned a line, and if he wouldn't cross it by revealing who was keeping John, I hoped he wouldn't cross it by mentioning our interest to those Sanguans. Plus, Nadya had paid for the information with the emerald, which should have counted for something.

The following night, I called Ellie's nursing home and asked a nurse to check on her. They obliged and reported that Ellie was resting comfortably.

To pass the time until the play, we walked all over Paris. Nadya described the City of Light to me as it had been in centuries past. Jumaane hadn't been far off the mark, as I had never been outside New York, New Jersey, or Louisiana as a vampire.

From Nadya's apartment, we walked along the Seine River, past Notre Dame and the Musée d'Orsay. We strolled through a garden of Rodin's sculptures and passed the Musée de l'Armée on our way to the Eiffel Tower, which we didn't wait to climb. Later, we descended into the Catacombs, where the walls of skulls and dried-out mortal bones brought a sense of calm. I hadn't killed a mortal when drinking in years, and had only killed a few back then, yet the Catacombs felt welcoming and familiar, even though I had never been there before.

The next night, we visited the Louvre. Human security and Spectavi guards with assault rifles in hand and swords at their hips watched every step we took within the expansive halls and across the courtyard, not that we were the only Sanguans there. I enjoyed the Greek and Roman sculptures the most, while Nadya was partial to the impressionist paintings. I promised myself I'd take Ellie to that renowned museum once she drank John's blood and recovered.

After the museum, we walked west toward the Arc de Triomphe, which Nadya pointed out dwarfed the older Roman arch in Reims. I asked her how she came to be a vampire.

"Simple," she said. "My maker believed me to be the 'prettiest woman he'd ever seen.'"

I smiled.

"It's true. I don't make it up. He was very serious in all

things. He hated my games and hated when I acted parts and played music, but he was rich, and my family was not. So I stayed with him in his castle near Veliky Novgorod, in western Russia. And he said it over and over, 'Nadya Komarova, you are the prettiest woman I have ever seen.' And…" She shrugged. "He didn't want me getting any less pretty, I suppose, so one evening, on his soft bed, he drank my blood, and I don't remember while he did because I was lost in it, but I remember after thinking that he had drunk far more than normal. While I lay there, he bit open his wrist and brought it to my mouth. And I knew my choice. Except I had no choice. He would not have let me refuse."

She shook her head. "I did not like that—that he had not *asked* before draining my body until it lay at death's door. But I wanted his blood anyway. Immortal life? *Yes, please!* So I drank, and here I am, just as pretty as that night."

"You are certainly pretty," I said.

She nodded. "Thank you."

"What happened to your maker?" I figured worst case, Nadya would decline to answer the intrusive question.

"I killed him."

I stopped walking.

She stopped. "He wouldn't play! He wouldn't have fun. He demanded our nights be full of philosophical conversation at court or spent in his castle, reading together by the fire. Court, fine, but there's *dancing* and *gossip* and *fun* to be had at court. Reading by the fire was not for me."

"And you killed him over it?"

"I left him. But he found me, a week later, with a

handsome young vampire—he had been a prince as a man—and a few mortals, all together in bed." She looked away, as if remembering. "My maker drank them all dry, then he dragged me back to his castle with him.

"He was a powerful vampire. Three hundred years old by then. Born in the eleventh century. That night, he drank my blood and kept drinking, draining me until I was pitifully weak. He locked me away in the filthy castle dungeon. For a year, I never saw him or anyone, except the nearly drained mortals he threw down to me. I finished them off to survive, but the little blood in them did not give me the strength to escape.

"When he finally came to me in that dismal place, I apologized and begged his forgiveness. For a while, I played the part of the reserved, pretty face he enjoyed showing off at his side. And then at a ball, while he argued with other vampires about philosophy or logic… or whatever—I honestly don't remember—I ran and escaped.

"But I didn't go far, only south to the nearest town, where I waited for him with an axe. At an inn, I brought another vampire and a couple humans to my room, to set the scene as before. I closed the door, and while they had fun on the bed, I stood at the side of the door, opposite its hinges, with my weapon ready.

"Not twenty minutes later, my maker burst through the door. With a clean slice at his neck, his head fell off, and I was free of him."

"Wow." I scratched my head beneath my hair.

"It seems silly now," Nadya said. "The axe."

"Oh? You think you could have talked him into letting you go?"

"No, no. No chance. I should have used a sword." She smiled. "You should see me with my swords."

―――――――――――

The night of the play, the same driver who had met us at the airport picked us up at Nadya's apartment building in a limousine. While we drove, I pondered what we had discussed earlier, what we would do if John was at the event. Nadya spoke of more caution than I had expected or had any interest in.

"We observe them," she said. "If we are very lucky, we drink from them to know their minds."

"What do you mean?" I asked.

"They may be happy where they are. Most on the Circuit are. The shows, the clubs, the vampires they're in the company of… Most on the Circuit are living lives they love."

"So what if they are? I *need* John's blood."

"That may not be simple," Nadya said.

"It is exactly that simple."

She hadn't responded, and we hadn't spoken since.

Did John know what his blood was capable of? Or did his captors hold him purely for its unique taste? Drinking from him would reveal the answer. And I couldn't help wondering—despite always telling myself I *knew* my interpretation of the drawings to be correct—could John's blood really do what I needed it to?

We pulled into a parking garage and drove down through underground levels. We stopped, and an entire wall slid open for us to drive through. After two more corners, we stopped again.

"We are here," Nadya said. "When you see the crowd in the theater, you will appreciate my call for caution."

The driver opened the limo door, and I followed Nadya out. A pair of guards with swords and pistols at their sides opened the doors to a long, dark stone tunnel. Then our path opened to a theater lobby full of vampires and mortals with collars around their necks.

Age hit me. Nadya's black gown fit the scene, as did her sparkling diamond earrings and necklace with three rows of stones. And my tuxedo fit in perfectly. But a chasm of decades and centuries separated me from most of the Sanguans. Anyone with money could dress in fine attire, and anyone with focus and talent could compose themselves with the subtleties of a time gone by, but the lightness of an old vampire's skin to another vampire's eye was nearly impossible to fake. Even the most pale-skinned mortals found a way to go one shade lighter after enough years as a vampire.

I leaned close to Nadya. "All right, caution it is."

She nodded. "Let's see if we can find them."

I put out my arm, which she took, and we proceeded into the crowd. A brown-haired man didn't jump out to me as John, which didn't surprise me, considering all the tuxedos giving the men a similar appearance. I scanned for fair-skinned, dark-haired Madison.

"Nadya," a male voice said. "Nadya Komarova."

We turned to a Sanguan with a fair-skinned woman on

his arm, with a thick collar prominent on her neck above her blue dress. She had red hair and doe eyes.

"Fernand," Nadya said.

"I didn't know you were in Paris," he said. "This is Charee."

"Charee." Nadya gestured to me. "This is Ethan."

"He's young for your taste, no?"

Nadya smiled. "And Charee is perfect for you."

Fernand chuckled. "She *is* perfect." He brought the back of her hand to his mouth and kissed it. "Just you and Ethan tonight? Did you bring anyone?"

"Just us," Nadya said. "For tonight."

"Well, make some friends tomorrow, and then we should get together, us and our friends."

"We should." Nadya nodded to Fernand, and he and Charee went right, while we went left.

"How long have you known him?" I asked Nadya.

"Since eighteen… something. I don't remember. Met him in Spain."

I called myself an immortal sometimes, but she and Fernand were the real thing. I was just getting started.

"What did you think of Charee?" Nadya asked.

"Looked pretty pleased being at his side," I said.

"Uh-huh."

And that worried me. What if John and Madison were happy? Or beyond happy? What if they flat-out loved being with the vampires who brought them to the Circuit events?

"Nadya."

I spun to a thin Sanguan who had been older than most

when she became a vampire. On her arm was a man with short silver hair and a goatee.

"Yvette," Nadya said. "And who is this fine gentleman at your side tonight?"

"All nights of late, and perhaps all nights to come," Yvette said. "This is Douglas. He is a professor at the University of Oxford."

"Pleasure to meet you," Nadya said. "This is Ethan. He was a blimp pilot in America."

I laughed and turned it into a cough, to cover it up.

"Blimp pilot?" Douglas asked.

"Yup," I said. "The family business. Blimps, balloons… whatever's paying."

Yvette raised an eyebrow. "I didn't know blimps still flew in America."

"Oh yeah," I said. "Middle America, more than the rest. Like… Kansas, Nebraska. That's blimp country right there."

She nodded, and they went on their way.

"Blimp pilot?" I asked Nadya.

She shrugged, and I recalled what had happened to her maker, who hadn't enjoyed her games. I shook the idea away. That had been quite different.

At the entrance, a tall woman with raven-black hair, wearing a dark-purple gown, appeared on the arm of a tuxedo-wearing Sanguan. Through shifting gaps in the crowd, I spotted a man with brown hair following, alongside a striking brunette in green.

"There." I pointed.

Nadya lowered my hand. "Uh-huh."

"You know the vampires?" I asked.

"Uh-huh."

"Should we be worried?"

Nadya shrugged. "We'll see."

"What do we do?"

"Watch them." She led us to the far wall. "But don't stare. See if they look like they're enjoying themselves."

They did. I reminded myself that looks could be deceiving, but the two of them appeared happy and certainly not under duress. Madison—assuming it was Madison—hung on her vampire's arm. She laughed and smiled in conversations with other couples while they made their way around the room. John—assuming it was John—seemed to glow beside the vampire in green. And who could blame him? She could have been taken from the pages of a French fashion magazine or from one of its show's runways. Perhaps she had been. When he left for the bar, he held on to her hand and fingertips until moving absolutely beyond their reach.

Nadya pulled a passing vampire over by the tuxedo sleeve. "Who is that woman with Bayard?"

"Madison," the vampire said. "She's lovely."

"Is she?" Nadya responded. "I'll have to have a taste and find out. The man with Mirabella?"

"John."

Nadya nodded, and the vampire went on his way. "It's them," she said to me.

"They look happy."

"Thus far," Nadya said.

"What now?"

"Continue watching to see if anything changes with them, then we enjoy the play and leave."

———————————

Nothing changed. *Waiting for Godot* might have been good. Nadya did enjoy the play, but frustratingly little of consequence actually transpired onstage that I could tell. Regardless, seeing John and Madison in such apparently high spirits ruined my appetite for theater. Nadya and I had gotten close enough to hear Madison and John joking with Mirabella and Bayard about the first-timers they noticed among the humans in attendance. Aside from John's occasional trips to the bar for drinks, both stayed at their vampires' sides.

Nadya must have noticed my grim countenance on the ride home. "It was one night. We will see them again."

"And if they're just as happy?"

"Then perhaps we can appeal to them directly. Perhaps if we ask, John would let us take some of his blood. It could be as simple as that."

"And if he says no?" I asked.

"He would be cruel to say no."

"What if he is cruel? Or what if Bayard and Mirabella are, and they refuse to let him?" I shook my head. "What if his blood only works if it's fresh? Or what if a little of his blood isn't enough? I can't go back to Ellie with half a cure."

"Then perhaps a more drastic course of action is in order," Nadya said.

"Would you kill Bayard and Mirabella to get to him? I would."

"You could not," she said. "They are too strong for you. I hope I will not have to. I did not come here to kill anyone. But if circumstances demand it, I would take John from them so you could take him to Ellie. We would let John go after that, but I would help you do that much."

I nodded. "Thank you."

———————

At sundown, I woke to an alert on my phone that Ellie's heart had stopped. A subsequent alert reported that it had been restarted.

Sitting in my coffin, I called the nursing home and asked to be put on speakerphone with Ellie.

"Ellie, my love," I said. "Hold on. I'm close to finding your cure. It's in this city, and I've seen it! *Please* hold on, just a little longer."

I thanked the nurses for reviving her and promised them, as well, that I would be back soon with a cure for Ellie, though I did not describe it.

My insides ached. I leapt from the coffin and rushed downstairs. I couldn't handle that craving on top of the bleak news. Outside, I grabbed an old woman across the street. I sank my fangs into her neck and sucked her blood into me quickly.

Hold on Ellie, I thought. *Hold on a little longer.*

I withdrew my fangs. "No police, no Spectavi, or I'll find you." I let the terrified woman go. She stumbled then ran, while I sat down on the curb.

Nadya came outside. "Come on."

As we walked, I told her what had happened with Ellie. When we came to a gym with a padlocked door, Nadya broke the lock, and on the mat floor inside, she handed me a knife handle longer and wider than my own. I pressed an indentation on the side, and the blade shot out and locked into place.

"Try to stab me," she said.

I didn't come close. Nor did I come close to slicing her head off, which was, of course, the surest way to kill a vampire. Holding no weapon of her own, she dodged, ducked, and sidestepped my strikes with ease. Nadya worked with me on footwork, how to attack, and how to parry and avoid.

Nadya noted that, ideally, I would not end up needing to know any of those things. But I would be ready with whatever it took to bring John's blood to Ellie. Imagining Ellie unbreathing and the long, flat beep of her heart rate monitor, I gritted my teeth and got back to practicing.

———————

Three nights later, with bass-heavy electronic music pounding and white lights flashing through the club's persistent blue hue, I held Nadya and danced on a floor packed tightly with mortals and Sanguans. In a circular metal-barred cage hanging from the ceiling, a woman wearing only her collar and her underwear danced. An equally undressed man danced in the other cage.

"I *told you* we would have to dance." Nadya had to almost scream into my ear.

Over her shoulder, I watched Madison dancing with Bayard, and John with Mirabella.

Madison looked as though she loved both the music and being in Bayard's arms. I would have bet anything she did the latter, but I refused to leave that club without knowing for sure. John, on the other hand, glanced at Madison frequently while he danced with Mirabella. More than once, I noticed his eyes frantically searching for Madison. Madison bit at Bayard's neck, and John looked away as though he did not enjoy seeing it.

John moved Mirabella so that he didn't have to face Madison any longer, and he held the vampire more tightly while a song faded out. Mirabella turned John around and brought his wrist to her mouth. She pulled John to her, and sank her fangs in. She drank the sublime blood that could save my Ellie. Did Mirabella know the power of what she drank?

"There." I guided Nadya around to see. As a song faded in, Bayard took Mirabella's hand. He pulled her to him and put his arm around her. They danced, and the crowd enveloped them. Madison kissed John, and he hugged her and held her, until she moved just far enough away to kiss him again and dance with him.

I started that way.

Nadya grabbed my shoulder. "Wait."

I tried to pry her fingers off.

She moved close behind me. "Just a moment. Better we don't stand out to Bayard and Mirabella for our haste."

After what felt like forever, a male Sanguan made his way

to Madison and tried to cut into the dance. She held out her wrist but kept her eyes locked on John. The vampire bit in for a sip and moved on. A female came by and took a sip from John.

"All right." Nadya let me go, and I headed for John and Madison.

A couple danced themselves into my path, so I sidestepped them. I pushed aside a woman.

John held Madison close, and they moved as one. He kissed her sweaty neck below her collar. She laid her head against his cheek. Whether or not they were *in* love, they surely loved that moment. I'd find out for certain.

I reached for John's hand, assuming I would ruin their moment, but he kept focused on Madison while letting me lift his arm from her back.

Picturing Ellie smiling at me, I bit into John's wrist.
Sublime.

His blood was rich, pure… everything and nothing but glorious mortality, all at once. A perfect flame I had never known burned brilliantly.

It *was* love for Madison, in John's heart.

He *did* know the power of his blood.

He longed to be free of his captors, but he feared Madison would not leave Bayard.

I pulled my fangs from John, and he returned his arm to Madison's back. Nadya finished drinking from Madison and nodded to the front of the club.

I stared at John. His blood really could save Ellie. But what a terrible choice Bayard had given him. John wrestled

S.M. PERLOW

with it, he agonized over it, and he found peace in Mirabella's bites.

"Let's go," Nadya said.

I followed her out of the club and into the quiet of our waiting limousine.

"John wants to be free of them," I said.

"I know," Nadya said. "John has two wrists."

"What does Madison want?"

"It's complicated," she said.

"What do we do?"

"I do not believe Bayard will let John go without him making the choice he set before the poor man."

"And if John does choose freedom, he could no longer cure Ellie."

"A rescue then," Nadya said. "It is the only way."

I searched John's memories and saw the apartment where he lived, on the Seine River with a view of Notre Dame. "We know where Bayard's keeping them."

"We won't get to them there."

I found John's memory of Bayard explaining the booby traps.

"Fire, silver, and more, most certainly," Nadya said. "A cage for someone as unique as John would be a well-designed one."

"Where then? When? It has to be soon."

"There's always a next event on the Paris Circuit. We'll see what's coming up." She leaned closer. "And when we pick, and we take our chance, we must take it well. This is not the kind of thing you get a second try at."

"I've been waiting eleven years," I said. "Now Ellie's dying. When we take our chance—I promise you—I won't leave without John."

17

VERA

At Charles de Gaulle Airport outside Paris, a sleek Mercedes sedan was waiting for us when our Spectavi plane—a commercial passenger jet half converted to transport vampire coffins and half filled with first-class accommodations—rolled to a stop. I wore black pants and a matching turtleneck, one of the many high-necked tops I had to cover the bite mark on my neck when leaving Eure's campus or when I might meet those on campus who shouldn't see it.

A Spectavi guard opened the plane's door. I followed Victoria down the rolled-out steps with my laptop bag, a bag full of medical supplies I wasn't sure the lab in Paris would have, and my katana slung over my shoulder. My mess of windblown hair in my face aside, I was ready for anything.

Our driver took us to Eure's European headquarters south of the Seine in Paris. The skyscraper stuck out conspicuously downtown. It consisted of forty office floors used by Eure for business, four floors for residences at the top, and a number of basement levels for the purely military

Spectavi operations. I was staying on the top floor, in a room next to Victoria's.

She and I rode the elevator down together to a meeting room on the second basement level, where the two large, flat-screen televisions on the wall were powered off, and a Japanese vampire named Kioshi waited in a high-backed leather seat at the long conference table. He wore slacks, and his black T-shirt showed off his pale, muscular arms. Victoria often worked with Kioshi in France and wherever around the globe missions opposing Sanguans necessitated.

"Welcome, Victoria," Kioshi said.

She took a seat at the table. "Kioshi."

"Vera, welcome," he said. "How are you?"

I sat. "Fine. What do we know? Where's John?"

"I am well, Vera," Kioshi said. "Thank you for asking. Why, yes, it *has* been an interesting year since you were last here."

"You're right. My apologies." I leaned back in my chair. "We flew all the way here to talk to you about *that*, not to find this guy with blood that could change everything. Go on."

Kioshi smiled.

"What's the latest?" Victoria asked.

Kioshi turned to her. "John was last seen with a woman named Madison, here in Paris. They were guests of a Sanguan, or more than one Sanguan, we aren't sure. Our Sanguan informant couldn't confirm."

"Couldn't confirm?" Victoria asked. "Or wouldn't?"

"The latter, most likely," Kioshi said.

Victoria nodded.

"So what now?" I asked.

"We wait," she said.

"For what?"

"For our informant to be more forthcoming. And I'll reach out to other contacts. We gather all the information we can."

I had hoped for news that might let us act quickly, but I had also known that our most immediate course might involve waiting. "Kioshi, it's wonderful to see you. You'll have to catch me up on every single detail of what I'm sure was an *immensely* interesting year."

He smiled.

"But another time." I stood. "Will you call me when there's new information about John?"

"Of course."

I looked to Victoria.

"Yes?"

"Let me know if I can help you at all."

She nodded, and I left.

Like on Eure's campus back home, my access card would get me anywhere. I took the elevator to the roof. A Spectavi guard in fatigues pushed open the door for me, using the clunky metal bar. Stepping outside into the windy night, I crossed my arms. The vacant helipad lay before me, the lights of Paris all around.

I went as near to the edge as I could without stepping off the concrete path onto loose stones. The Eiffel Tower stood lonely, nearer than a skyline of office towers to the west.

Blocks of low buildings stretched in every direction.

What a life I had. Jetted over to Paris with the most powerful vampire warrior I knew existed in the world, leaving behind the oldest vampire I knew of, all to further my work on projects vital to the Spectavi.

My mother had never gotten farther from Virginia than neighboring Maryland; my father had taken exactly one road trip across the country with high school friends. They had worked hard to give me a good life and had always put me first. I remembered it, and my grandfather often reminded me of it. I needed to call him. It had been a while.

My parents' lives had been small in scale. Bless them for it, and for everything they had done for me. My eyes watered. I missed them so much. They got me started, their love made me, and I wished I could send them a picture and say, "Look where I am!" Of course, I would really mean, "Look where your start let me get to. Thank you." And they would know what I meant without me having to explain it.

I sniffled. My parents were gone. Long gone and not coming back. *Damn the Sanguans.*

I headed inside. *Damn the world.*

The next day, I lay in bed, with the thick black curtains pulled nearly closed. The sun shone through the gap, which I resolved to close later. I rolled over and checked the clock.

My patients had not attacked my mind in fifty-three hours. Years before, when the attacks first began, I had known even longer stretches of peace. Back then, one of

Edmond's or Victoria's bites had seemed to inoculate me. Unfortunately, the length of that protective effect had shortened considerably, and continued to shorten.

I closed my eyes, and instead of my patients' piercing images or hellfire, I saw myself with Edmond at the formal parties he brought me to when lab work didn't dominate my time. I recalled the last ball we had attended. He took my hand and led me away from the crowd and around a corner. He untied a ribbon concealing the fang marks on my neck and bit in for a quick drink. Imagined blue-hot fire blazed inside me, but its source was an ocean away.

I got out of bed, grabbed my green robe from the hook on the bathroom door, and threw it on. Barefoot, I stepped into the quiet carpeted hall. I held my card near the reader beside Victoria's door, the lock clicked open, and I went in.

She had remembered to shut *her* curtains, so I flicked on a light switch to see. In a room off the suite's main one, her black coffin rested beside a large bed with a black comforter. A long steel cross ran the length of the lid. Beneath it, she held her longsword atop her body. I'd seen her emerge with her most trusted weapon in that room, in her home's basement back in Virginia, and all over the world. She held it every night.

I pulled down the covers and got into bed. I laid my head on the pillow.

Edmond had a sword just like Victoria's. I pictured them in battle together, in tales Edmond had told me of ages past. But I had to imagine them.

Victoria, I had witnessed fighting. In her arena, she

slowed down sometimes so my mortal eyes could discern her technique. Out in the real world, she never slowed, she never stopped, and she never lost. No Sanguan could match her. I pulled the covers closer around me and watched her coffin.

How long until nightfall? How long until the warrior rose and held me in her strong arms?

How long until Victoria tasted my blood? Then I would taste the fire that said, "Vera, no Sanguan can touch you while you are with me."

———————————

By half an hour after nightfall, we had heard nothing new from the informant who had spotted John before and nothing from any other spies, either. Not thrilling, but also not shocking. Victoria said she would head out and see what information she could dig up on her own. Kioshi was doing the same.

I rode the elevator to the fifth basement level. After navigating a maze of locked doors and hallways, I reached the armory. Its official name was the "Weapons Laboratory and Research Wing," but Milo preferred "armory," so I'd taken up his cause of using the term. Milo's co-workers did not join us, leaving us alone in our crusade.

Beyond another guarded door, three shooting targets made a row at the end of a long room. Handguns and military-grade rifles hung on the wall to the left; swords, knives, and an exciting variety of sharp handheld weapons were displayed on the right. Miscellaneous grenades, explosives, and other fun devices filled shelves along the floor.

In the far corner, a thin young man threw a dart at a corkboard and hit the bull's-eye. Milo, who was twenty-four if memory served, was still as gangly as he'd been the year before.

I applauded. "You're keeping busy down here, I see."

He turned. "Vera!"

"Milo."

Grinning, he came my way. I thought he might hug me, but he didn't. He looked as if he would extend his hand, but he didn't do that either, and just said, "Hi."

"Hi."

"Um, no, I'm not very busy today. Mr. Leclerc is away."

"I see."

"How are you?" Milo asked. "What brings you to Paris?"

"I'm fine. I'm here with Victoria."

"Ah. Sanguan trouble?"

"Not directly, not this time. We're looking for a human of particular interest."

"How long are you here?"

"As long as it takes."

He nodded.

"How have you been?" I asked. "What are you working on?"

"I'm good. Busy, except today." He gestured to a counter beside the dartboard and led me over. "What do you think?"

Among two screwdrivers, a utility knife, and a bunch of tiny screws was a flat, textured gray disc with a clear circle at the center.

"What is it?" I asked.

He smiled. "Grenade."

"Grenade?"

"Light grenade. Push the center, wait two seconds, and a flash of all the wavelengths of the sun will fill a banquet hall. Sanguans—Spectavi also, unfortunately—it'll fry their skin. At least, that's the idea."

"And us?"

"For humans, it would be like a sun tan, like from a long day at the beach."

"Hm." I tapped my finger on my chin. "I want it."

Milo raised an eyebrow.

"I wonder if I could do something with the synthetic blood to offer resistance to this."

"Hm."

I pointed at the grenade. "*You* tweak that so it's not *exactly* like the sun. *I* tweak the blood…"

"Maybe, but this is the prototype. Let me build a few more, and I'll send one to you at home."

I picked up the disc. "But I want this one."

He grasped the disc, and I let him take it from me and put it back on the counter.

"Let's make a game of it." I walked to the board and pulled out the three darts. "If I win, I get the grenade."

"And if I win?"

"You asked me out for a drink last year, and I said no. If you win, we can go tonight."

He shook his head. "Do you play a lot?"

"Do we have a deal?"

"Fine."

I handed him the darts. "No. I honestly can't remember the last time I threw one of these."

"Twenty down?" he asked. "You have to hit the twenty, then the nineteen, and so on, all the way down to one, then bull's-eye. First one there wins."

"That's fine."

Milo stepped to a line of silver tape on the floor a few paces back from the board.

"Do you play often?" I asked. "With other people, I mean."

He raised a dart, aimed, brought his arm back then forward, and let it go. It landed in the middle of the triangular section for the twenty. "Yes." He threw another and hit nineteen. "At pubs, all the time." A dart hit eighteen. "I get to go again."

"Why?"

He walked to the board and pulled out the darts. "I hit with my third dart, so I get another turn."

"Convenient rule."

"Quite." Back at the silver tape, he threw and hit seventeen and sixteen. He missed fifteen, so his series of turns ended. He retrieved the darts and handed them to me.

I stepped to the line, right foot forward, put a dart in my palm, and judged its weight. I gripped it to throw, aimed, reached back, and let the dart fly. It landed in the section for twenty. Milo appeared concerned, and for good reason.

"I throw knives, training with Victoria." I threw again and hit nineteen, then eighteen to earn myself another turn. I went to the board, pulled out the darts, and returned to the silver tape. "We train a lot."

Seventeen, sixteen, fifteen—I retrieved the darts. I hit down to twelve, then down to nine, and finally missed trying to hit six. "Dammit."

Milo, perhaps tired of seeing me retrieve the darts, got them for himself. With an unsteady arm, he missed his first shot. Then he hit fifteen, but missed fourteen.

I hit the rest down to one, fetched the darts, stepped to the line, and, after an extra second of aim, nailed the bull's-eye. I handed the other two darts to Milo and picked up the disc from the counter.

He covered his forehead with his hand. "Don't tell anyone, okay?"

"That I beat you, or that I'm taking this?"

"The grenade. Losing at darts won't cost me my job."

"No problem." I slid the disc into my pocket and headed for the door. When I got there, I considered how many hours it would likely be before Victoria returned, whether she had new information about John or not. I spun around. "Hey, Milo."

He stopped organizing tiny screws on the counter.

"You wanna get out of here?" I asked. "Go have that drink?"

"Yeah, sure."

"Meet me in the lobby in half an hour?"

"Okay."

———

We took a cab to a bar Milo visited often. It was a little worse for the wear but surprisingly bright inside, and not in a bad part of town. Along with the thin crowd, I noticed the pair of dartboards in the back my first step inside. He suggested playing some regulars he knew who wouldn't suspect me to be any good. It sounded amusing, and I told him maybe after a drink.

Milo went to the bar, and I found a high table and draped my leather jacket over the back of the wooden chair where I sat. I didn't notice any vampires, but while I had a good eye for spotting them, I couldn't be certain. I'd worn a turtleneck in part to hide my bite marks from Milo and also because I didn't want them to suggest I would welcome a Sanguan's advance.

Years ago, in Virginia, Edmond had a team of Spectavi guards follow me off campus one night. When I returned, I made extremely clear that I would not be babysat, and that had settled it. In truth, if those guards could have guaranteed my safety from Sanguans without having to hover at my immediate side, I might have welcomed them.

If there were no Sanguans at all in the world, I could have sat waiting for Milo in complete comfort. *That* was the promise of Protice and why I *had* to complete the project. I *had* to find a way to alter the synthetic blood so Edmond could see our dream become real. Sanguans would become Spectavi and drink synthetic blood, or they would die.

Milo returned with a mug of beer for himself and a glass of red wine for me. At the first earthy sip, trusty Bordeaux came through again. Milo confirmed my suspicion that the wine had come from a vineyard on the right bank of the region, and then our conversation shifted to work, because it was my life, and as I found out, a huge part of Milo's, as well.

"Mr. Leclerc has me with a small group working on advanced projects," Milo said. "He sticks to conventional things usually—ensuring the stocks of weapons and ammunition are high, staying on top of the latest developments in the gun industry, things like that to ensure Sanguans never have more firepower than us."

"Guns, pshh." I waved my hand. "Give me a sword any day."

"*You* would actually do well with a gun, I'm sure." He squinted. "Are you fast enough with your sword to fight a vampire?"

I sipped my wine. "No."

"But pump a Sanguan full of silver bullets, and that will stop them in their tracks. Or slow them so you *can* fight them with your... what kind of sword is it?"

"Katana."

"Ah, yes. You ever think of that? The silver first?"

"Yeah." I shook my head. "I don't know. It's a good idea, especially against a young Sanguan. But I'm with Victoria and Edmond a lot and other ancient vampires. I sometimes wonder what it would take to bring down a Sanguan so old. I don't know that silver bullets would do it."

"Hm. True. Against an ancient, a gun may not help you." He drank some beer and pointed at me with his mug. "If you were a vampire, you'd be fast enough with your katana."

"I won't ever be."

"No? I'm sure Edmond would do it, or Victoria."

"They would," I said. "But I won't be a vampire. One mortal lifetime is plenty for me."

"Not me. In a few years, Mr. Leclerc said he would make sure it gets done." Milo smiled wide. "I will be immortal."

I lifted my glass. "Congratulations."

He lifted his. "Why don't you want to be? Forget fighting. Think of all you could do in your lab with forever before you."

I again scanned the room for Sanguans.

Milo looked all around, then back at me.

I didn't find any vampires. "A Sanguan killed my mother. My father was killed in a bar fight. I miss them every day. If I lived forever, I'd miss them forever, and I would lose so many others along the way."

"I'm sorry," he said. "I didn't know."

"It's all right. How could you have?"

"I do hope…"

"What?"

"Well, if it's going to be a mortal life for you, I hope you don't make it a lonely one, never getting close to anyone for fear of losing them."

"No, I won't make that mistake. It's not that I want to be *alone*. I have Edmond and Victoria, and they aren't going anywhere." I shrugged. "Who knows what's to come for me? It's only one lifetime, but I have a lot of it left to live."

Milo nodded.

"Besides," I said. "I like deadlines for my work, and I can't think of one more pressing than ever nearing death."

"Cheery."

"That's me!"

He drank more beer. "So what are you working on these days? Anything that would affect us in the armory?"

"Actually, yes. I'm working on a project that could change the war dramatically."

"Oh, how so?"

"I can't go into details, but let's just say that once I figure it out—and I will figure it out—you guys'll be busy, and before long, we won't have to worry about Sanguans in a bar like this."

"Sounds exciting."

"Mm-hmm." Buzzing and a soft ring came from my jacket behind me. I pulled my phone out of the inside pocket. "It's Victoria." I flipped it open. "Hi."

"Where are you?" she asked.

"Out."

"I'm on my way back with new information and am going to brief Kioshi. Want to join us?"

"Yes. I'll be right there."

"Good." She hung up.

"I have to get back," I said to Milo.

"I figured."

"Thanks for the drink, though."

"You're welcome."

I got up and put on my jacket. "You gonna stay?"

He glanced at the couple at the dartboards. "I know those two. I'm going to say hello."

"Okay." I smiled to him. "Have fun. Have a good night."

"You, too."

Outside, I hailed a cab and headed to the Spectavi tower. A dull sting in my forehead surprised me. I hadn't had much wine. The stinging grew, and I realized my patients had found me.

"His name is Sacha," Victoria said to Kioshi and me in the basement conference room. "He's the informant who supplied the original information about John. I persuaded him to give up significantly more."

"Persuaded how?" Kioshi asked.

"I beat him to a pulp," Victoria said. "He'll either become a significantly more valuable asset to us here in Paris, or he'll flee the city and never work for us again." She shrugged. "We shall see."

"What did he say?" The aching in my skull had grown since the bar, as if my patients knew I was closing in on blood that could cure them and end my torment.

"John Breen and Madison May are being held captive by Sanguans named Bayard and Mirabella. They all know the power John's blood has to heal mortals. Sacha wouldn't reveal where they were being held, but he said they're expected to be guests of honor at a small gathering for the Grand Climax, a satanic night of sacrifice in a week, at Hotel Vautour."

"So that's it—we go there in force and take him." I'd then have fourteen days to work with John's blood before Edmond's ultimatum with Protice was up.

"Sacha spoke to Bayard," Victoria continued. "The four of them are also planning to be at the theater in two weeks, for a performance of *Hamlet*."

I leaned forward in my seat. "But that's in *two* weeks, and it's a larger crowd."

"But think of the crowd," Kioshi said.

Victoria nodded.

"What do you mean?" I asked Kioshi.

"The Grand Climax is, to some, the most important night on the satanic calendar. I've witnessed the Sanguan rituals, and that small event will probably not include many humans other than John and Madison. All effort could be spent protecting them if we tried anything. But at the theater, each Sanguan will have their own mortal guests to worry about."

"The hotel venue troubles me, as well," Victoria said. "A raid on an underground theater, even a large theater, can be kept quiet. Such a theater will be literally underground and designed to be hidden. But a civilian hotel, while we might accomplish our mission, could bring significant media attention, the type Edmond would prefer to avoid."

I shook my aching head. "But the theater is in *two weeks*." I would have only a week before my deadline. "What if something happens to John before then? What if their plans change?"

"Mirabella met Bayard at a performance of *Hamlet*," Victoria said. "According to Sacha, he and Mirabella are celebrating that anniversary. I do not think their plans will change."

I sank into my chair. "But it's not for *two weeks*."

18

JOHN

The packed club's bright lights flashed through a pervasive blue hue. Bass pounded. Beats pulsed. A nearly naked man and a woman danced alone in a pair of circular cages hanging from the ceiling. I held Mirabella's firm body. Over her shoulder, as best I could in the crowd, I watched Madison dancing with Bayard, holding him, lost in him.

Madison bit at his neck. He smiled, and I looked away. I guided Mirabella so her back faced others I had met over the last weeks and months. Intense faces, faces full of glee, men, women, Sanguans, bare arms and legs, short skirts, tight pants, fitted shirts, low-cut dresses—I cared nothing for them, but I could watch them because they weren't Madison biting at a vampire's neck.

Mirabella held me to her with my arm and hers across my body. She brought my wrist to her mouth. She drank, and flames melted away the faces all around us. Flames danced to the music, flaring when beats hit and spiking when notes soared. I burned, and everyone disappeared, even Mirabella, Madison, and me.

My legs gave out as Mirabella finished drinking. So many faces... such commotion everywhere. The vampire held me from falling.

Madison and Bayard emerged from between dancing couples. Bayard extended his hand, and Mirabella took it. He pulled her to him and into the crowd. Madison smiled, and her eyes asked for me. I stepped to her and held her, then my lips found hers. No flames roared, but all the faces disappeared into the ocean of our kiss.

She took half a step back, or I might have held her forever. She kissed me quickly, and we danced. A man approached—no, a Sanguan. Madison held out her wrist but kept her eyes locked on me while the vampire sipped from her. He moved on, and a female came near. With my arm resting on Madison's shoulder, the Sanguan lifted my wrist and bit.

Fire burst—darker than Mirabella's, more sinister, snuffing out all around me. *Come back, Madison!*

And she was back, the drink was done, and I felt my arm on her. *Oh, Madison.*

I kissed her sweaty neck below her collar. She pressed her head against my cheek. We moved to the music as one.

More Sanguans—surely Sanguans—approached. The male appeared to be very young, and the female had vibrant-red hair and a pretty face. She drank from Madison, and he took my wrist from Madison's back. Again, I was lost among warmth and fire, lost without Madison.

The blaze burned with enduring hope and a young

passion seeded with a newborn spark. A second flame, powerful but playful, followed. It danced and toyed with the young fire. Burning streaks twisted around each other into long, thicker strands.

Both withdrew their fangs. Madison rested against me while the male gaped. The female ushered him away.

How much more could I take? How much more could I give? How much more that night and in the coming nights like it?

Madison moved us both gently to the bass track. How many more nights with her would I be lucky enough to have?

Madison and I passed out in her bed when we returned to the apartment a couple hours before sunrise, but we made love when we woke that afternoon. I held her after, her back to me and our fingers interlocked, and I thought about how much I loved her.

How many more afternoons like that would we have together? How many more afternoons like that could I *bear* to have? We were not free.

Bayard, at my request, brought me more often to the doctor's office to heal people. The evening before had begun that way, in fact. But I could have been doing even more if I were free of him and that apartment.

Yet I could not be free and retain my gift. That was not one of the options he had given me. None who had drunk from me had come to rescue us. Knowing what my heart said, what it cried out for, they had not taken pity on me and Madison. The Sanguans acted so civilized but were really so cruel.

Yet Mirabella's words rang with a truth I could not ignore. In a way, Bayard was doing me a favor. Life outside the apartment with my healing blood revealed to all would have been unlike anything I had ever known. I would have been seen as a saint or, while I disliked thinking the word, a savior.

I was no savior. My blood was a gift, though I did not know why I had it or where it came from. I enjoyed using the gift. But I had known love in different forms, and I did not feel *love* when using my gift.

Against Madison's stomach, I slid my thumb. She squeezed my hand and moved her body closer into mine.

When my blood healed a sick person, especially a child, I felt a profound happiness, but it was that *someone* or *something* had the power to heal as I just had, not that *I* had done it.

I loved Madison. I might have loved Mirabella in some other way—I didn't know. But Madison was everything, and I wondered what life as a savior for others would leave for me with Madison.

Bayard pitted good against evil when he described my choice. And maybe he was right. Maybe over hundreds of years, he had come to understand things that my thirty-one years hadn't allowed me to. Perhaps my choice truly was between living in the name of God's heaven or on the devil's path.

But I couldn't pick between them. I got lost trying to weigh good and evil, and my soul intertwined with either. Clarity came only when thinking about how much I loved Madison.

Surrounded by the glossy black walls of the Emperor's Suite, on the top floor of five-star Hotel Vautour, I sat in a high-backed chair at a polished wooden table. Madison and Mirabella sat on either side of me. Bayard, as usual, also sat beside Madison. Behind us, burgundy curtains adorned paned windows. According to Bayard, a disagreement over who would host the annual satanic "Grand Climax" had led to the compromise of the old hotel, where the entire floor had been closed off for us.

Eight other vampires sat around the table, some of whom I had met on the Paris Circuit. Clement, at the head, wore a charcoal-gray suit. He had been born back in 1051. Maurice, in 1108. Elnora, in the thirteenth century, if I remembered correctly. Nadya, a Russian vampire, sat across from me, wearing a tight black turtleneck. Her red hair evoked a hazy memory from the club a couple nights before. Ethan, the vampire at her side, looked very young. Priscila, Longin, and Claude rounded out the group.

Past Clement's end of the table, logs burned in the fireplace. I had never seen such a thing in a hotel, and tough as vampire skin was to most everything else, fire seared and singed it. In fact, a vampire's skin would burn much faster than a human's. I wondered if the ancient Sanguans in attendance had developed a resistance to the flame, if the proximity to danger excited the stoic group, or if they simply enjoyed the warmth and crackling of burning logs.

It was a little black dress for Madison, and slacks and a black T-shirt for me. I had come to realize that the more of Madison and me that was left exposed, the more the vampires would drink that night. However, even though all the introductions and conversations since our arrival had been in English, instead of French, I still had not figured out how that particular event would be about me. The Grand Climax meant blood sacrifice, and I did not think Bayard wanted me dead. I found it hard to believe he intended to sacrifice Madison, either.

Maurice stood from the table and went into a bedroom. A few of the Sanguans cracked smiles. Maurice returned, hand grasping the shoulder of a naked brown-haired woman. Of medium height, she was perhaps thirty years old, curvy, and clearly terrified. Maurice guided her to the head of the table and stood with her next to Clement. A short knife lay on a mat on the table before them.

"Each year," Clement said, "we gather for this Climax to offer a sacrifice. We enjoy the flesh and mortal blood as ever, but on these nights especially, as we drink, we thank Satan for the grand gifts he has bestowed upon us. We drink until God's gift of life is extinguished, utterly and irrevocably."

The woman whimpered. Maurice wrapped his arm around her and pulled her up until she stood on her tiptoes. He bit into her neck and sucked her blood.

Clement gestured to the woman. "Meet Camille." He gestured to me. "We have all met John, tonight or before. Together, they will help us see if we can extinguish more than merely a life this night." He shrugged. "Or less. We will risk that."

Maurice stopped drinking. Camille's eyes half opened while she was walked to Elnora, who held Camille's wrist and bit into it. Camille's body relaxed in Maurice's arms.

Elnora finished, and Nadya's eyes lit up as Camille's weak steps brought her nearer. Nadya took a long drink from Camille's unblemished wrist.

Ethan didn't seem to share Nadya's enthusiasm, but he found a fresh spot on Camille's forearm for his short bite.

Camille couldn't stand, and her legs didn't move, so Maurice lifted her and held her limp body. While Priscila drank, Clement said, "Camille is a secretary here in Paris, born in the city, though she understands English perfectly well. She is wife to Hugo, mother to Eliott—age six—and Olivia, who is four. We snatched Camille from her apartment two nights ago."

Longin drank.

I glanced at the sharp knife in front of Clement.

"She misses her family," he continued. "And she fears a grim fate awaits them once we are done with her here."

Maurice brought Camille to Claude, who bit into her thigh for a long drink.

"Tonight, she will have a choice. She may return to them, or not."

Mirabella drank from the woman's ankle. While she did, Bayard bit into her wrist.

Camille's head fell backward, and her mouth opened wide. Maurice carried the woman back to Clement. Bayard sat down.

"Camille will die," Clement said. "She has lost too much blood. Her life on this earth will be extinguished." Clement slid the knife across the table. It came to rest in front of me. "Unless John's blood saves her."

I grabbed the knife and stood. Camille's eyes cracked open.

"But." Clement raised a finger. "She may choose a different path." Clement stood and took off his suit coat. "She may choose to become one of us." He unbuttoned his shirt sleeve and rolled it up. "She may choose to extinguish the *idea* of her current life. That will be an even finer sacrifice on this important night, in the name of Satan."

In Maurice's arms, Camille looked from us at the table to Clement.

He brushed his fingers across her cheek. "Your time is short, sweet Camille. John's blood can return you to health and give you a little more time, or my blood can give you forever."

Camille tilted her head to again look down the table.

"Join us in nights everlasting, young, beautiful as you are now," Clement said. "Or return to your day job, to your crowded home, and grow old in your routine."

Tears slid down her face.

"Live forever," Clement said. "Or go home tonight, wilt, and die in the blink of an eye."

Camille lifted her neck to better see herself, then let her head fall so Maurice held it. Raspy, quietly but clearly, she said, "Vampire."

Clement leaned close. "You wish to be a vampire?"

"*Oui.*" Camille closed her eyes.

I set the knife on the table.

Clement bit into his wrist then brought the puncture wounds over Camille's closed mouth.

Drops of blood hit her lips. Blood ran onto them, but her mouth stayed shut.

Clement leaned to her. "You must drink, my dear."

Camille whimpered and looked to me.

19

ETHAN

Clement leaned over the naked woman. "You must drink, my dear."

Camille whimpered and managed to turn her head. "John."

John grabbed the knife from the table and hurried to her.

"*Désolée...* Sorry." Camille's eyes closed. "*Je suis désolée.*"

John cut his palm and held his hand up.

"Which will it be?" Clement asked. "Decide *now* and drink."

She opened her eyes and leaned her drained self toward John's hand. He tilted it to her, and she opened her mouth and drank his mortal blood.

Out the fifth-floor window, across the table from me behind Madison, I spotted the blinking green light of our approaching helicopter. My hand rested on my knife in my pants pocket.

Camille stopped drinking and breathed deeply. Maurice lowered her, and she stood on her own.

Why hadn't Nadya given the signal yet? The helicopter

looked nearly close enough. Two taps on the table, and we would act.

John returned to his chair beside Madison. He set down the knife, pulled a white bandage from his pocket, and wound it around his palm.

Maurice led Camille to his chair. "I'll get you a blanket." He disappeared into the bedroom.

"Unexpected." Clement sat down.

Had Nadya lost her nerve? Would she make me watch John's blood save Camille, then not go through with our plan?

"But fine," Clement continued. "We will fetch—"

I darted across the tabletop and wrapped my arms around John while lifting him from his chair, which fell behind him. Nadya leapt the same way and grabbed Madison. All eyes shot to us.

"Bayard!" Madison struggled against Nadya.

He stepped forward, and Nadya got her concealed knife to Madison's throat. Bayard stopped.

I glanced behind me—still too far to jump into the helicopter.

"What is this, Nadya?" Clement asked.

I held my knife's extended blade near John's throat. "We need him, and he's tired of being your prisoner, Bayard."

A small blade dug into my side, another my shoulder. Longin pulled a third knife from the inner lining of his jacket and threw it just over John's shoulder, slicing across my neck. I took my knife off John to hold the bleeding wound.

Longin flung knives at Nadya, who deflected them with her blade while still holding Madison.

The helicopter was near enough.

Claude grabbed the knife from the table.

I lifted John and toward the window gathered my speed to leap.

A deep slice into my back drove me, on top of John, to the floor. I let him go, rolled over, and crossed my arms to block Claude's downward stab at my head.

He slashed across my chest. I pushed him off me, and he slammed me back down. I pushed up again, but he didn't budge. Claude stabbed into my side. I slashed wildly but cut air. He stabbed my chest, and I coughed blood.

Nadya tackled him off me, tumbling with him to the floor. She jumped to her feet and kicked across his face. She grabbed me and leapt for the window, carrying me through the shattering glass.

We landed hard on the pavement, six stories down.

"John!" I reached up, holding my bleeding chest with my other hand.

"Ellie needs *you*, too," Nadya said. "We'll find another way to get him."

Our escape helicopter rose overhead without us. Why couldn't I have been patient?

Nadya's eyes lit up. "The adventure continues."

Ten more seconds would have done it.

Behind Nadya, Claude descended from the hotel window, followed by the two guards who had been stationed at the room's door. They landed, and the guards aimed their rifles, fired, and hit Nadya in the back while she raced us down the street.

20

VERA

In Hotel Vautour, one floor below the highest, I sat on the edge of my room's bed, trying to visualize the commotion coming from the Emperor's Suite above me. The white folding cane and oversized sunglasses I had purchased that day were on the end table. It sounded like glass shattering upstairs to my right near the wall—probably a window.

I brought my hands to my aching head. Piercing red didn't stab into my mind, and thunderous blows didn't rock my whole skull like at home, but the dull, occasionally throbbing pain had been nearly constant for days. I hadn't let Victoria drink from me and silence my pain because I didn't want her to discover what I had been plotting.

Above me to the left, a door flung open, and loud footsteps raced across the floor. More glass shattered. I didn't know if John was even still in the room. I stood and grabbed the cane and sunglasses. If John remained up there, broken windows might have meant fewer Sanguans with him. Regardless, I couldn't wait any longer.

I put on the big sunglasses. I also wore a wig of short black hair with long bangs. Sanguans who kept close watch on Spectavi leadership, and especially those who tracked Edmond, knew of me, and I didn't want to be recognized.

The black-walled hallway was empty, and even darker because of my shades. I unfolded the white cane and swept it from side to side as if I were blind. At the elevator, I pressed the up arrow.

The golden doors opened, and I stepped in. The top floor had been closed off for the night, the stairwell doors were locked, but Spectavi Intelligence had no trouble getting me a key for access. I inserted the key into the elevator control panel, turned it a quarter of the way, and hit 5—the button lit, and the elevator ascended. When the elevator stopped, its doors opened. I turned the key another quarter of the way around so the elevator would remain on that floor. I took a deep breath and, sweeping my cane before me, stepped into the hallway.

At the end of the hall, the door to the Emperor's Suite was half open. Planning the operation had been nothing short of thrilling. How would I get in? How would I get out with John? Would I bother trying to take Madison?

But I didn't relish the idea of walking into a room full of Sanguans. I hoped my concocted story so appalled them that they wouldn't launch themselves at me one by one, or all at once, to feast on my blood.

If they did drink from me, they would learn all the Spectavi secrets I knew before my blood ran out. Edmond and Victoria would hunt down every one of them and destroy them. One of those two outcomes seemed most likely.

I reached the suite and tapped my cane against the door and the frame. I pushed the door farther open and entered. Curtains blew around two vampire-sized holes out to the night sky, and at one end of the table, a woman in a black dress clung to a man in a T-shirt and slacks. Both wore collars around their necks. They had to be John and Madison, because I didn't see a collar on anyone else. Everyone around the table, including Bayard and Mirabella, whom I recognized from our file photos, stopped their conversations to stare at me.

Swinging my cane, I continued into the room. "John Breen? Is John Breen here?"

"I'm John," the man in the T-shirt said.

"And who might you be?" Bayard asked.

I kept going. "John, heal me!"

Bayard put out his hand. "Stop there."

I didn't.

"What do you know of John?" Mirabella asked.

I tapped my cane on John's leg and stood beside him. "I know his blood can restore my sight."

"How do you know this?" Bayard asked.

"Drink from her," an ancient-looking vampire said. "And know for certain."

"No!" I shook my head vigorously and pulled down my shirt collar to reveal my bite scar. "He would kill me!"

"Who?" Mirabella asked.

"Sacha," I said. Nods and rolling eyes went around the table. "He told me of John's miracles. He told me where to find him. Sacha blinded me for letting another drink from me, and I am sorry." I got to a knee before John. "I am so sorry for what I did." I took John's hand. "Restore my sight, I beg you! When I return to Sacha, let me look into his eyes and see him when I swear once more that I won't share my blood with anyone else, ever again."

John looked to Bayard.

"It is up to you," he said.

"Of course I will." John turned to me. "Of course."

"Thank you!" I dropped my cane to hug him with one arm and reached my other hand into my pocket.

"You'll be all right," he said.

"Thank you!" I whispered into John's ear. "Close your eyes and hold on to Madison."

He leaned away from me.

I held the disc grenade in my pocket and pressed its center.

"Close them." I slid the disc halfway across the table, and John shut his eyes. I grabbed his arm, and beyond my sunglasses, a burst of white light filled the room.

I pulled John off his chair. He pulled Madison.

"Bayard!" she yelled.

We hustled toward the door, away from screams, inhuman roars, and shattering glass.

"Come on!" I yelled when John slowed.

"Madison," he said. "Let's go!"

"No!" she screamed. "I can't see. Bayard!"

John got Madison out into the hall. Behind us, white filled the doorway. We ran into the elevator. I turned the key and pressed the button for the ground floor. While the elevator doors closed, I peeked out—the light in the room faded to dark.

We descended.

Madison clung to John. "I can't see!" She wept on his shoulder. "All I see is white."

"Shh… it'll be all right." He asked me, "Who are you?"

"Vera Clarke." I dropped my sunglasses to the floor.

"Are you Spectavi? Why didn't that light hurt you?"

"I'm with the Spectavi. I'm human."

"The Sanguans will be waiting at the bottom," John said.

One floor above the lobby, I hit the emergency stop. "Yup." I pushed the button to open the doors, grabbed John, and led him out of the elevator. He dragged Madison along with us.

At the end of the hall, I shoved open a room's door I had left ajar. At the rear of the room, I unlatched and pushed open the large swinging window. The delivery truck remained parked beside the blue sedan I had driven to the hotel earlier.

"Jump," I said to John.

"She can't see." John unwrapped his bleeding hand and brought it to Madison's lips. "Here. Drink and you'll be okay." He tilted his hand, and the blood dripped down to her mouth.

Madison found his hand, sucked on the wound, then blinked quickly. She stopped drinking and shut her eyes for a long second. She opened them. "I can see."

"Let's go," I said.

"John!" Madison tugged on his arm and started for the room's door. "We can't go." Her eyes watered. "We need to go back upstairs!"

"Shh…" John said. "We need to leave."

"No." Tears crept down her cheeks.

He moved closer to her. "Madison…"

"Please, John." She grasped both his hands. "They kept us safe!"

I flicked my knife open and pointed it at John. "I need *you*. I want to help her, but I don't need to."

"You'll be safe." John ran his thumb along Madison's collar and smiled. "That life in the apartment… it was wonderful, but it wasn't real life." He pointed to the window. "Real life is out there."

"It's not *safe* out there."

"I'll keep you safe."

"Time to go," I said.

"Come on." John led Madison to the window. "We'll go together." He got himself seated on the ledge, and she shook her head while taking off her high heels to carry them. Madison's shoulders sank, and John helped her up beside him.

She looked at him then down at the truck, and with his hand pushing her, they slid out. With a thud, they hit the truck roof. John jumped to the parking lot and helped Madison lower herself to him.

I followed to the truck then the parking lot, pressed the key fob to unlock the doors to our getaway car, and got behind the wheel. They got in the back. I started the car and hit the gas, pinning us against our seats. After a left out of the lot, in the rearview mirror, in the distance in the middle of the street, a shadowed figure did not pursue.

"What do you want with us?" John asked.

I looked to him in the mirror. "Your blood, of course."

"No," John said. "No way. We've been through that. We're leaving that."

I pulled out my phone and flipped it open—screen off, power button unresponsive. "Shit." Milo's light grenade must have fried it. "It won't be like that. I'm no Sanguan. In addition to being a highly skilled… operative, I'm a scientist. Your blood could be the key to a couple projects I'm working on." I pulled off the wig, threw it into the passenger's seat on top of my sheathed sword and medical bag, and let my long brown hair down.

———————

Just south of Paris, I pulled into a row house's one-car garage and clicked the remote to lower the door behind us.

"Whose house is this?" John asked.

"I rented it." I grabbed my sword and bag then got out of the car. John and Madison, who had finally quit weeping, followed me into the small kitchen.

"Is anyone else here?" John asked. "Don't the Spectavi have a base in Paris or something?"

"We do," I said. "A tower, actually. But those Sanguans might expect us to go there and be waiting on the way."

John nodded. "So what do we do?"

I dropped my medical bag onto the square dining table

and hung my sword by its strap on a chair. "Mostly, wait until sunrise, *then* go to the Spectavi tower."

"Mostly?"

I unzipped the bag and pulled out a small case, which I brought to the counter near John and Madison, beside the sink. "I need some of your blood."

"What for? Can't it wait?"

I unlatched the case and folded it open. Gray foam protected a needle and two glass collection tubes, as well as a blue elastic band, a few cotton balls, and Band-Aids. "I work with the Spectavi synthetic blood. One project in particular—" I winced and held my head. My neck ached. Yes, it was *two* projects. "One project in particular is very important to us. In case anything happens, I want to be sure to get a sample."

"How is my blood supposed to help?"

I took out the needle and a collection tube. "Honestly, I don't know."

Woosh-woosh-woosh-woosh… Overhead, outside the noise grew louder.

I set the needle and tube down on the counter, went back to the table, and pulled my katana from its sheath. "Helicopter."

"We shouldn't have left!" Madison cried.

"Do you have friends you can call?" John asked me. "Spectavi vampires?"

Woosh-whoosh-whoosh…

"That light grenade fried my phone." I stood between the kitchen and the living room, focused on the locked front door. "I'll be having words with the guy who made it."

"There's a landline." John pointed to the corded phone on the wall.

"Hm." I glanced at it. "Too late now."

John moved with Madison as far away as possible to the corner of the kitchen. "If it's Sanguans, can you fight them?"

I turned back to the front door, spun my katana end over end in my hand, then stopped it, gripped its leather-wrapped handle with both hands, and took an aggressive stance. "We shall see."

The door burst open, snapping the frame's wood. A female dressed in black with very light skin, red hair, and a knife entered.

"Sanguan!" Madison shouted.

A young male followed, his clothes covered in blood.

"They were at the hotel," John said.

"Yes, we were," the female said with a thick Russian accent. "I am Nadya Komarova. And who might you be, with such a fancy sword?"

I gripped it tightly. "Vera Clarke."

"We don't want to hurt you," the male said. "Or them… or anyone." Whatever wounds had bloodied him might have healed, as his words came out strong.

"This is Ethan. He is…" Nadya's eyes lit, but then she relaxed. "Eh…" She waved her hand in front of her. "He is from New Orleans."

Ethan gave her a surprised look that became a satisfied one.

"What do you want?" I asked.

"The woman I love is dying," Ethan said. "In New Orleans. John's blood can save her."

I relaxed my stance. "The woman you love?"

"She's mortal," Ethan said. "In a coma eleven years. She won't have my blood to save her, but she *would* have John's."

"Take a tube of it," I said. "I'll draw the blood for you right now."

Ethan shook his head. "What if it isn't enough? What if it only works if it's freshly drawn? I need John to come with me."

I glanced behind me.

"And then what?" John asked. "If I help her, what would you do with me after?"

"Nothing," Ethan said. "I... I could help you get anywhere you'd like, or leave you be. I need only this one thing of you, but I *need* it. I really do."

"And you?" I pointed my sword at Nadya. "What's your part in all this?"

"Adventure." She shrugged. "Small one." She tapped her knife on her chin. "But it is not over yet! New Orleans is thousands of kilometers away."

"Which is why we have to be going," Ethan said.

"I need some of that blood," I said.

"There's no time." Ethan shook his head. "There could be other Sanguans or Spectav—"

"There's time." John let go of Madison and stepped forward. "*Vera* rescued us, after all. I'll go with you to New Orleans, and I'll help you, but first, she gets her blood."

Ethan put out his hands. "Fine. Just hurry."

I backed up to the counter and, wishing I had enough hands to avoid doing it, put down my sword.

"Wait." John looked at Madison then at the Sanguans. He pointed to his collar. "Can you get this off?"

In the blink of an eye, Nadya was beside him. She put her knife on the counter and snapped the collar in two. She threw the pieces onto the counter and reached for Madison's neck.

Madison stepped back and brought her hand to her collar.

"It's all right," John said.

She looked at each of us, then looked at John. She lowered her hand.

Nadya pulled the metal apart. Madison touched the fang marks on her exposed skin.

I took John's wrist, extended his arm to me, and rubbed alcohol over a vein on the inside of his elbow. He watched while I stuck the needle in, attached the collection tube, and it filled with blood.

"What do you need this for?" Nadya asked.

"She works for the Spectavi," Madison said. "Some project."

Nadya crossed her arms. "What project?"

I disconnected the full tube from the needle and grabbed the second. "Can't say."

"Ooh." Nadya leaned over John's outstretched arm toward my katana. "Blue habaki…" She glanced at Ethan. "The collar around the blade at the handle guard is usually golden." She looked to me. "That really is a *magnificent* sword. May I hold it?"

I glared at her. "No." I connected the second tube, and it began filling with blood.

"No fun," she said.

"What's the plan?" John asked her.

"Helicopter to the airport, then private airplane to New Orleans."

"Good," John said. "I want to be done with all this, and then… I don't know. We'll figure something out."

I disconnected the tube, pulled the needle out of John's arm, and covered the spot with cotton.

"That sounds great to me," Ethan said. "Really, it's just this one thing."

I ripped open a small Band-Aid and stretched it over the cotton on John's arm. I set the tubes of his blood in my padded case. "Thank you for this."

"Thank *you*." John flexed his arm inward. "So much. Thank you for coming for us."

"Sure." I put the case in the fridge.

"Let's go," Ethan said.

"What will you do?" John asked me.

I grabbed my sword. "Hang out here until sunrise then head to the lab to see what I've got."

He nodded then took Madison's hand. "Let's go."

With sunken shoulders, she followed John, who followed Ethan and Nadya out the front door.

21

IN ROGABON, AFRICA

In the tropical territory of Rogabon in Central Africa, east of the nation of Gabon and west of the Republic of Congo, thousands of men, women, and children kneeled in the dirt clearing. Surrounded by jungle, before a stepped pyramid temple, and among bonfires that reached high into the starry sky, they chanted their god's name: "Unathi."

Six Sanguan vampires wearing black silk shirts with gold embroidery down the center, disciples of their god, stood in their usual positions up the pyramid steps.

The chanting grew quieter.

At the rear of the temple's platform top, which rose higher than the tallest trees in the jungle, stood Unathi. The huge Sanguan ruled over everyone and everything within the hundred miles of rainforest he had carved out of Africa for himself.

In French, he told Dosu, his chief disciple, the story of a thirteenth-century Hungarian man named Odo. At the story's conclusion, Unathi said, "It seems another mortal like

Odo walks this earth, an American man with blood as powerful and as precious. Word has come to me from Paris, from one who has drunk the nectar, and in that drink witnessed miraculous healing."

Dosu's eyes widened.

"The man's name is John Breen, and you must bring him here," Unathi said. "We *need* him here. He will be welcomed as a god, and his woman, a goddess."

Dosu nodded. "It will come to pass. I will convince them of our great need."

Unathi nodded and headed out to the firelight and his worshippers.

22

JOHN

Nadya's private plane was waiting at the airport outside Paris. Madison asked to sit alone so she could sleep, so I sat across the aisle to keep an eye on her. Still wearing her black dress, under a blanket Nadya had found in the back, Madison curled up against the side of the plane and closed her eyes before we lifted off the ground.

Ethan thanked me again for agreeing to help Ellie. I had lost count of how many times he had. I told him it was no problem and thanked him for attempting to rescue us, even though he hadn't succeeded. Ethan was just glad it had worked out and that we would soon be at Ellie's bedside.

Nadya was pleased with the outcome of their rescue, although she said she wouldn't have hated having a little more fun in the process.

We took off a few minutes before five in the morning, and, maybe because Madison was trying to sleep or maybe because everyone was exhausted from the night's events, we all kept quiet as we started westward.

I watched the peaceful sky out the big round window and considered what to do next. First, Ellie, but then... I had no idea. Madison and I hadn't discussed it. We had talked about loving each other and being together, but never anything *after* the apartment in Paris. We hadn't known there would *be* an after the apartment, away from Paris.

I had to buy a new cell phone. I needed to call my parents and let them know I was all right. I had to reach out to my web development customers and see if, after my long absence, they remained my customers.

But what I really wanted was to see Madison again with the sun shining on her, as it had on the hill in Montmartre. And I wanted her to want to be with me on that same sunny day. I didn't know if she did.

Hours into the flight, I asked Ethan how he had found me. I assumed he had heard from a Sanguan who had drunk from me in Paris. Ethan's story of ten years of searching shocked me. It also warmed my heart and made me very glad to be on the way to help Ellie. He told me more about her, as well.

Eventually our plane couldn't outrun the sun any longer, and daybreak loomed. Nadya and Ethan retired to coffins in the rear cabin. While they rested and Madison slept, I stared at the door to the cockpit or out the window at the lightening sky. I closed my eyes and tried to imagine what would happen next.

When I healed Ellie, it would be in a nursing home, where others surely suffered from illnesses or injuries. Should I cure any of them? How could I *not*? But could I give enough blood to cure them all? And what would they think when my blood healed them and I stood before them, instead of hiding on the other side of a mirrored window?

———————————

As Nadya had promised, a driver she trusted met Madison and me on the tarmac. He was mostly bald with gray hair on each side, and his name was Roy. The vampires would spend the day in their coffins in a secured airport hangar. Madison got into the silver Lincoln Continental without a word.

When I asked how she was doing, she answered with only, "Fine." Then she stared out the window the entire drive to Ethan's house, which was narrow and simple like all the rest on the street, a couple blocks from Ellie's nursing home, according to Roy.

Nadya had given Roy instructions to wait with us there until nightfall. If Ellie's condition became critical, we would rush to her aid, but otherwise, Ethan wanted to be by her side when she woke up. I would have preferred not to wait, but I didn't argue. Ethan *had* tried to rescue us, so I could certainly give him another half day of my time. I noticed a handgun in a holster on Roy's hip when he took off his sport coat and sat down at the small kitchen table to read a worn paperback book, with its cover folded over the spine.

Madison turned on the television in the living room, and I joined her there on the opposite end of the couch.

"How are you?" I asked.

She pressed the channel-up button on the remote. "I'm fine." She pressed up again. "How are you?"

"I don't know what to do at the nursing home. I'll cure Ellie, of course, but then what? Do I help all the rest?"

Madison looked to me. "That'd be a lot of people."

"I know. And *then* what happens, when they all see what my blood can do?"

"Maybe you shouldn't," she said.

"How can I not? I know I *can* help more than Ellie. Don't I have to?"

She shrugged. "Find a way to do it discreetly, like Bayar—" She looked away. "Like they did."

"Yeah." I recalled Mirabella holding my hand in the doctor's office in Paris, smiling at me. "I'll figure it out."

Madison turned back to the TV and left it on a decades-old rerun of *Family Feud*. Memories of Mirabella stole my attention from the game show. As I had loved that fire melting away everything else, I loved how the French Sanguan relished each sip of my blood. But her locking that collar on me, I had not loved.

Madison stared so intently at the TV that her focus could not truly have been there, either, and I knew which Sanguan she imagined. When Bayard had locked her collar, she might have loved it.

Another episode of the same show began, and before I knew it, had come to its end. When the credits rolled, I asked Madison, "What about after the nursing home? What... what do you want to do?"

She looked at me. "What do you want to do?"

"Be with you," I said. "Wherever, whatever we do. I have that much figured out."

She moved toward me. I put my arm over her, and as she had so many times in Paris, she lay back against my chest. "Not Seattle. My things are in storage there, but I don't want to go back yet."

"Okay. My things are in a friend's basement in Maryland, but they can wait, too. Maybe a hotel here for a couple nights while we figure it out?"

"Sounds good to me."

"Great." I reached into my pocket for a phone that wasn't there. "Hm. Think Roy would take us to the mall? If there's a mall around here. I want to get a phone, and we could buy some clothes."

"Yeah, good idea."

Mentioning a phone smacked me with the notion of reality. For all the wrong about our time in Paris, parts of it had been more right than any time I had ever known, and a new phone meant the end to a lingering aspect of that escaped season. But my new reality included Madison, so unlike ever before, reality sounded pretty great.

———————————

Roy had no objection to taking us to the mall, though he did stay nearby while we got new phones and bought clothes. The three of us ate lunch together in the food court. Roy was nice to talk with and had a kind air about him. He told us he had served in the Navy and known Nadya since he was a much younger man. He did all kinds of jobs for her when she visited the U.S.

On the drive back, I told Madison Ethan's story about

Ellie and his years of searching. She seemed close to tears hearing the beginning, but brightened at the end, which was us waiting for nightfall to go and heal Ellie.

At Ethan's house, Madison and I both wore brand-new blue jeans and tops—a light-gray polo for me and a black shirt for her. We watched sitcom reruns in the afternoon, and the news after that. Roy had pizza delivered for dinner, and after we ate, he remained in the kitchen with his book. Madison and I returned to the couch and sat in silence in front of the blank TV while the sun set.

Five minutes after it did, Ethan shoved open the front door. "You all right?"

Nadya followed him inside.

"We're fine." I got up, as did Madison.

Roy came in from the kitchen.

"No trouble today?" Ethan asked.

"No," Roy said. "None at all."

"Okay." Ethan took a deep breath. "Ready to go?"

I glanced at Madison.

She nodded.

"Sure," I said.

"Thank you, Roy," Nadya said. "As always."

Roy walked to her and took her hand. "Anytime, my dear." He kissed it. "Anytime at all." Roy left out the front door.

We all followed, and while he drove off, we began the two-block walk to the nursing home.

Discreetly curing a few others after Ellie sounded like a good plan, whatever the logistics of "discreetly" ended up being. I couldn't imagine what would happen if I started healing *everyone* in the building, room by room, and that scared me—I really could *not* imagine what would happen.

But what if it all changed when I got there? What if every room I passed had an open door to a patient in such sorry shape that I couldn't help myself but go in and heal them?

To think of something else, I asked Ethan to remind me how old Ellie had been when she got sick. Seventeen, he said, before she would have joined him at Columbia University in New York.

When our destination—a three-story building with two wings off its center—was in sight, my new phone buzzed with a text from an unknown number.

My offer stands—Bayard

"Who's that?" Nadya asked.

"No one important." I put my phone back in my pocket.

Inside the nursing home, Ethan greeted the receptionist at her desk. "Good evening, Bonnie."

She nodded and watched as we passed.

Down the beige-walled, blue-carpeted hallway, we came to the elevator. Ethan pressed Up and smiled widely. Madison and I smiled.

Finally, Nadya cracked her own. "Eleven years of devotion and searching—*that* is an adventure, Ethan, and one that will end so beautifully."

With a ding, the elevator doors opened, and we all stepped in.

"My adventure was with Ellie." Ethan hit the button, the doors closed, and we started up. "It began when I noticed her smiling in the crowd at my high school basketball game, and when we talked in the lunch line the next day. It went to hell when she got sick, and there, it lingered, just outside those fiery gates. Tonight, we turn our back on that pit, we rise from it, and our adventure continues."

The elevator doors opened.

Ethan stepped out. "Her room's around the corner, at the end of the hall."

We followed him past mostly closed doors. Beyond the occasional open door, a lonely man or woman in bed rested with their eyes closed, alongside at least one monitoring machine. A man changing channels on a tiny, ceiling-mounted television brightened my spirits. Nurses in blue scrubs with a woman meant the woman had company, but also that she required the attention of nurses. How could I choose who among them to heal?

We turned the corner, and Ethan sped up. "Down here, last door on the left."

Boom! The floor shook behind us. *Boom!* The ceiling shook. So did Nadya, Ethan, and Madison.

I put my arm around Madison as she crouched, holding her ears, and terror overtook her face.

Boom!

Ethan looked back. "No…"

Smoke and dust rounded the corner. Fire alarms sounded. The overhead lights flickered out.

Boom! The hallway before us erupted in flame. Strong hands lifted me and Madison.

"Ellie!" Ethan screamed.

Through a blur of smoke, a swinging, open door, and shattering glass, we flew in Nadya's arms from the third floor to the asphalt parking lot in front of the nursing home.

She set us down. "I'll find Ethan." Nadya stepped toward the burning building then ran so quickly that she disappeared to my mortal eyes.

I hugged Madison. "Are you okay?"

She didn't hug me back. Tears filled her eyes.

I leaned away. "Madison, are you okay?"

"It's not safe." She sniffled. "We were safe with Bayard."

I hugged her again.

"We aren't safe here." She wrapped her arms around me.

"We're safe now. We're all right."

Fire consumed the top floor of the far side of the building and half the side we had been on. Rooms burned, and flames curled out of windows up to the roof. Soot covered a nurse, her scrubs, and the patient whose arm draped over her shoulder as they hurried out the front door. They both appeared shaken, but were moving pretty well.

A doctor wheeled out a woman on a stretcher. A nurse held an IV bag high above the patient's blood-smeared face and shoulder.

A male nurse carried an old woman's limp body. Her gown was covered in blood. The nurse set her down in the grass in an island in the parking lot.

I stepped away from Madison. "I'm going to try and help."

She wiped her face with her arm. "You're going in there?"

"No, out here. Come on." I took her hand, and we headed for the old woman in the grass.

The woman's eyes were shut. The nurse held her side with both hands, but blood seeped through his fingers.

I let go of Madison's hand and knelt next to the nurse. "What happened?"

"Glass from a light," he said. "It fell from the ceiling and sliced into her. I got it out, but it hit somewhere bad. I can't stop the bleeding. She needs an ambulance."

I didn't hear any approaching sirens. Bloodied, soot-covered staff and patients staggered out of the nursing home, some together, some on their own.

The old woman whimpered.

"I need a knife," I said.

"Are you a doctor?" the nurse asked.

"No, but I can help her."

He squinted at me.

"My blood can help her." I showed him the scabbed cut on my palm. "I... Where can I get a knife?"

The nurse looked around. "Rita!" he shouted. "Rita, come here!"

A nurse left a stretcher and rushed over. "What is it? Are you okay?" She knelt next to the woman. "How's Mrs. Nelson?"

"Not good," the male nurse said. "You got your knife?"

"Yeah." She pulled a red Swiss Army knife from her pocket.

The male nurse nodded to me. "Give it to him."

Rita held it out. "What's going on?"

I took the knife, extended the biggest blade, and with my hand upturned, slit it open.

Rita stepped back.

The other nurse pulled Mrs. Nelson away from me. "You're a vampire?"

"No." I brought my palm above Mrs. Nelson's mouth and angled my hand downward.

Drops of blood hit her chin. I brought my hand closer, and my blood covered her lips. The nurses watched, wide-eyed. Mrs. Nelson's lips and mouth cracked open, and my blood ran in. Her mouth opened wider.

"Check her side," I said.

The nurse lifted his hands. He moved aside the red-stained gown. "The wound's closed."

I turned my palm up.

Mrs. Nelson's mouth shut. Her eyes opened.

I folded the knife closed, put it in my pocket, and rested my not-cut hand on her shoulder. "Are you all right?"

She nodded.

"What happened?" Rita asked. "Who are you?"

I stood up. Flashing lights and sirens approached, but from police cars and horn-blasting fire trucks, not ambulances. A doctor and two nurses surrounded a nearby stretcher. I headed there, checked that Madison was following, and positioned myself beside a nurse.

Soot covered the old man. His breaths came shallow and strained.

"This might just be too much for him," the doctor announced. "Weak as he already is from the pneumonia."

I brought my palm over his mouth and tilted it. Drops of blood hit his lips.

"Hey!" The doctor grabbed my wrist and moved my arm. "What are you doing?"

"Let him," Madison said.

"Look!" A nurse pointed at the man's chest—his deeper breath.

The doctor let me go. "Are you a vampire? Spectavi?"

I shook my head. "No." I brought my hand back over the man's mouth and let blood run into it. His breathing deepened, becoming regular, and he opened his eyes.

"He'll be all right." I lifted my hand.

All eyes around the bed were on me.

"Who are you?" the doctor asked.

"It doesn't matter. But I'm not a vampire, I swear."

"He's John Breen," a voice called from behind me, and I recognized it.

Madison gasped. Among the frantic, dirty, bloody crowd, Bayard and Mirabella stood like ivory pillars untouched by the chaos.

"Did you do this?" I yelled to him.

Bayard nodded.

"Why?"

"Enjoy your newfound fame," Bayard called. "My offer stands. Any night you want, it would be done." He smiled, then he and Mirabella ran at vampire speed and were gone.

"John," the doctor said. "Over here." He started for the crowd and looked back at me.

I glanced at Madison then caught up to the doctor.

"Who were those two?" he asked.

"Sanguans," I said.

The doctor nodded. "A woman fell. A shelf came down on her. She's bleeding on the inside, and we can't stop it." He pointed to an arriving ambulance. "They won't be able to, either, but maybe you can."

We found the woman on a stretcher, and my blood did save her. She smiled before we left. Madison and I followed the doctor through the mob of screaming people, with sirens whining and horns blaring all around. My blood healed another old woman and a young nurse injured in the explosions. Thick streams of water from fire trucks shot up at both wings of the burning building.

"John Breen!"

People called out to me to get my attention.

"Thank you, John," someone said while leaving a stretcher.

"Praise you, John," another said, sitting on the ground, after I'd cured him.

Madison followed me. I checked constantly. She usually had her arms crossed. She shook her head at me once, and she also wiped tears from her cheeks and squeezed my not-cut hand. When, after helping more people than I could count, I stumbled, she caught me.

"Maybe that's enough," she said. "You've given a lot of blood."

People were walking around the parking lot, no longer running. Ambulances treated patients at their open rear doors. The fires in the building only smoldered.

"A few more," I said. "Let's take another look around."

"Okay." She kissed my cheek.

I gave her a real kiss. I *did* have the strength to help a few more, I told myself. But I would rather have been far from there, far from the noise and the pain and the danger, safe with Madison.

"John," said another voice I recognized—Nadya's.

We turned to her.

"How's Ethan?" I asked.

"How's Ellie?" Madison added.

Nadya shook her head. "Ethan is fine. Ellie is not."

"Where?" I asked. "I can help her."

"Ellie is dead." Nadya pointed to the side of the nursing home. "Ethan got her out before the fire reached her room, but her heart stopped. They got it started again very briefly, twice, but finally, they could not."

We walked toward where Nadya had pointed.

"Eleven years," Madison said. "And one day too late."

I glanced back at three nurses following. One's cell phone aimed at us, and its camera flash went off. A staff member in a darker uniform crossed himself—forehead to chest, left to right.

"We should have come this afternoon," I said.

"How could you know?" Nadya asked.

"Bayard did this," I said. "We saw him and Mirabella after the explosions."

Nadya shook her head.

Two EMTs treated a soot-covered nurse sitting on the back ledge of an ambulance. Another tended to a man on the curb, wrapped in a blanket. Ethan bowed his head over a stretcher where a woman with thin blond hair lay. Her pretty face was calm, her eyes were shut, and her chest did not rise and fall with even the shallowest breaths. Ethan held her hand.

"Ellie," Nadya said.

When we got there, Madison stood with me. Nadya went to the other side the stretcher with Ethan and the defibrillator cart. Those behind us stayed back, heads bowed, one muttering.

I looked to Ethan. "I'm sorry."

He rubbed Ellie's hand with his thumb.

"It's my fault," I said. "Bayard and Mirabella did this so everyone would know what my blood can do. You and Ellie just got caught in the middle of it."

"It's their fault." Ethan glanced skyward. "Or God's, that salvation for Ellie, for one so faithful to him despite the tremendous cost, would be made at hand, yet *minutes* too late." He dropped his head. "Or it's my fault for not asking you to come here this afternoon."

"No," I said.

"Yes. I was selfish."

A camera flashed behind me. I thought of Ellie jolted back to life by the defibrillator paddles across from me. Twice, Nadya had said.

Four others had joined the group of onlookers. More approached. Another camera flashed.

I pictured Ellie jolted again. The wound on my palm was barely bleeding. I looked at Ellie, the crowd behind me, then at Ethan. I pulled the Swiss Army knife from my pocket. With trembling hands, I unfolded the longest blade.

Madison covered her mouth. Nadya's eyes widened. Deeper than before I cut open my palm. I winced, and blood flowed.

Leaving a red trail across Ellie, I moved my hand to her mouth. Nothing happened.

Blood ran over her lips. I couldn't aim it any better. Nothing happened.

"Come on," I said. "Come on, dammit!" I glanced to the stars where Ethan had laid blame. "*Please.*"

Ellie's chest rose with a breath.

Madison gasped.

Ellie's lips parted, and blood flowed into her mouth. Her eyes opened.

"Ellie!" Ethan leaned closer. "Oh, Ellie!"

A tear slid down Nadya's cheek.

My world spun. Cameras flashed. I slumped.

Madison caught me. Nadya came over and helped her.

Ellie wiped her mouth with her arm. "Ethan?"

"Ellie!" He leaned down and hugged her. "Ellie." He kissed her cheek.

"Ethan, where am I?"

"Outside the nursing home," he said. "In New Orleans. There were explosions and a fire."

"You died." Nadya nodded to me while holding me up. "He brought you back."

More flashes came from the growing crowd behind me, along with prayers in English and languages I didn't know. A steadily held cell phone might have been shooting video.

"He's mortal," Ethan said. "Human blood saved you. He… he has a gift."

"John Breen," I heard behind me.

"It's a miracle," someone else said. "His name is John."

"Are you okay?" I asked Ellie.

"I think so." She sat up. "I think I am. Are you?"

"There!" a woman shouted, pointing, rushing our way. Her dress shirt wasn't covered by soot. She held a microphone, and a cameraman followed her.

"I need to get out of here," I said. "I need to rest."

Ethan grasped my shoulder. "Thank you!"

I nodded. "I'll see you again?"

I hadn't expected to ask it, but felt such relief when he said, "Yes, of course."

Nadya lifted me, then Madison, and ran with us from the scene.

23

VERA

I had been awake all day, working at a small desk in the corner of the basement lab in our Paris tower. Technicians in the main area focused on their own projects. No windows meant I only knew the sun wouldn't set for a couple hours because of the old clock on the wall. But I didn't need the sun or to take a break for restful sleep. I had the invigorating fascination of John's blood. A few drops from the tube I had drawn were smeared across the center of a slide under the microscope I peered into. Other drops, I had run through the computer analyzer earlier. The lab didn't have everything I did in Virginia, but it had enough for me to determine that John's blood was unlike anything I had ever seen or heard of.

Victoria, asleep in her coffin since before I returned after sunrise, had apparently been curious about my whereabouts the prior night, and she might have called or texted, but I hadn't tried charging my phone or gotten a new one to check. How mad could she be when she woke? I had John's blood.

The corded phone on the counter rang. Lab technicians glanced my way, but I wouldn't answer it. *Who could know to call me here?* It rang another five times before it stopped.

I peered into the microscope.

The phone rang again. The clock read 7:36 p.m. Still daytime. It rang, and everyone looked my way once more.

I lifted the receiver. "Hello?"

"Vera," Edmond said.

"Edmond?" I spun in my chair to face the wall. "Where are you?"

"Istanbul."

"Ah." Night had fallen there already. I wished for a window just then. Since I couldn't be out in the sun *with* Edmond, I enjoyed the rare occasion to talk to him when at least the sun shone on me, and I pretended he was by my side.

"Are you all right?" Edmond asked. "I heard you were missing yesterday."

"Heard from who?"

"Are you all right?"

"I'm fine," I said.

"Good." He exhaled. "I worry; that's all."

"You don't need to."

"But I do. I always will."

I hated it. I shook my head. And I liked it. And he hadn't asked for details of where I had been, which I appreciated. I switched the receiver to my other ear. "I have good news."

"Oh?"

"John Breen's blood is like nothing I've ever seen."

"You have it? You have him?"

"It," I said. "Not him."

"How? How much?"

"Last night. And, uh… enough. Plenty to run all kinds of tests. Already, it's incredible. There's more to his blood, yet in some ways, there's less. It'll be easier to show you."

"Okay," he said. "Do you think it'll help with Protice or your patients?"

"It might. I have ideas for how it could with both. I'm assuming we'll be heading back to Virginia tonight, so we'll see when I get there."

"Yes, head home tonight. I'll do the same."

"Good," I said. "I miss you."

"I miss you, my love. I miss you in my arms, and I miss you smiling in your lab. I don't believe I've seen you happy at your work for ages. I pray this blood will have you smiling when I return."

"It will," I said. "I really think it will."

24

JOHN

Soft knocking came from outside our hotel room the morning after the chaos at Ellie's nursing home. Fluffy pillow surrounded my head. My arms were straight at my sides. I opened my eyes. Madison's were on me. I would have gone back to sleep for days had she not been beside me.

"Hey," I said.

"Hey."

Knocking came again.

"Is that our door?" I asked.

"Yeah," Madison said.

"What time is it?"

"Seven. I'll get it."

"No." I reached out and stopped her. "I will."

"You're tired."

"It's fine." I found I was still wearing my shirt. With considerable effort, I got out of bed. I grabbed my jeans off the floor, put them on, and went to the door. Madison had the covers pulled up to her neck.

I cracked the door open to a short young woman with straight black hair and an older woman who looked similar.

"Hi," the younger woman said. A small silver cross hung at the end of her necklace.

"Hi," I responded.

"I'm Maria," she said. "I was working the front desk when you checked in last night. You came in with that vampire. I saw you on the news when I got home."

I vaguely remembered Nadya racing us across town, putting the room in her name, and paying for it for a few days.

"You're John Breen?" the younger woman asked.

"Yes."

"This is my mother."

"I have terrible arthritis," the older woman said. "I'm in such pain, whatever I do. Whenever I move at all."

"She has been for years," Maria added.

"The doctors give me pain pills," her mother said. "But they don't really work, and they make it so I can't think. I fall asleep. I'm not myself. I can't take them anymore. Can you help me?"

I glanced back at Madison, who had sat up in bed, but that didn't yield an answer to the woman's question. I checked my pocket—the Swiss Army knife was still there.

"Yeah." I opened the door wide. "Uh…" I motioned to the bathroom beside me. "Here, I guess."

Maria helped her mother take slow steps inside. "How does it work?"

I unwrapped the red-stained bandage from my palm. "Drink from here, and you'll be healed."

"But how? You're not a vampire, right? *Why* does it work?"

"I am not a vampire." I unfolded the knife. "Why it works, I do not know."

I cut open my palm, and Maria's mother slowly reached for my hand. I brought it to her mouth. Blood ran past her teeth. She wrapped her hand around my wrist. She pressed her mouth to the wound and sucked hard.

Maria watched wide-eyed. Her mother stopped.

I moved my hand away, and a tear ran down the older woman's cheek.

"Mama?" Maria asked. "Are you okay? Are you better?"

Maria's mother let slip two more tears and a smile. "I am." She rolled her wrists around. "Nothing… the pain is gone."

Her daughter hugged me. "Praise you, John. Praise you!"

I backed up from her.

Her face brightened. "Are you God?"

I exited the bathroom and opened the room's door. "No."

"You've given me my life back." Maria's mother walked to me. "Thank you."

I nodded, and she left with her daughter, who glanced back while I shut the door.

"That was nice of you," Madison said.

I rewrapped the bandage around my hand. "How could I say no?" I slid my pants off, crawled into bed, and put my arm around Madison as she lay down. My head crashed into my thick pillow, and I fell asleep.

Knocking at the door woke me. Madison hopped out of bed before I could say anything.

"Housekeeping," came from the hall.

Madison peered through the peephole. "Can you come back later?"

"Okay."

Madison hung the Do Not Disturb sign outside the door.

The clock read 11:04 a.m.

"Were you up already?" I asked.

"Yeah." She got back into bed.

"Sorry."

"It's all right," she said. "You must be exhausted."

"I am. But better now."

"Good."

"I'm hungry."

She smiled. "Me, too."

Knock-knock.

"Later," I called to the door.

Knock-knock-knock.

I went over, looked into the peephole, and hung my head. "Not housekeeping." I grabbed my jeans. "One second." When I had them on, I opened the door to a bald woman in a wheelchair in a medical gown and a man standing beside her.

"Are you John Breen?" the man asked.

"Yeah." I opened the door wide.

"I'm sorry to bother you." He pushed the wheelchair into

our room and looked at Madison. "Hi, I'm sorry."

"It's fine," she said.

"This is my wife, Lena," the man said. "Chemotherapy isn't working for her. I snuck her out of the hospital. I saw what you did last night on the news. Can you help her? I can pay you. Whatever you want. I brought money. We have more I can wire you."

"No," I said.

Their faces fell.

I shook my head. "No money, I mean. Yes, I can help. Shut the door?"

He brightened. "Sure." He wheeled her farther in and let the door close behind him.

"Thank you," she said.

"Of course." I cut my palm and let her drink. When she smiled and breathed easy, they both hugged me, him even more tightly than her, before they left.

I shut the door behind them. "We should get out of here." As the words slipped my lips, they felt horrible to say after what I had just done. "I guess."

Madison got out of bed. "We need food, if nothing else."

———————————

Neither of us knew New Orleans well, so we asked what was nearby at the front desk. The first answer of McDonald's sounded perfect to us both. We figured later we would take the time for locally authentic cuisine, but at that moment, proximity and speed trumped everything else.

No one paid us any mind on the walk, but in line to

order, a couple of teenagers pointed and whispered. I turned away, and they didn't bother us. We ordered then headed for a booth to eat. After we scarfed down the sandwiches and fries, I went back up for the chicken nuggets Madison had eagerly agreed to my suggestion for.

Standing in line, I thought of the couple in the hotel. I had not wanted their money. But my savings wouldn't last forever, and eventually, I would need to work. Yet, I had a gift people would pay for. They would pay *fortunes*, without hesitation, if I asked them to—which of course, I would not do.

But… how could I work normal hours for a normal wage, knowing I could earn all the money I would ever need merely sharing my blood? And if I worked a regular job, when would I have time to help others, whether for profit or not? I looked across the restaurant at Madison. When would I have time for her? Time when I wasn't exhausted from a lack of blood in my system?

I'll figure it out, I told myself, and ordered our twenty nuggets.

While I waited for them, Bayard came to mind. I couldn't believe he had caused such destruction and pain to expose me. Pushing me to choose was *that* important to him. And since he had texted, I had his phone number and could text him back, but I didn't want to. I didn't want to become a vampire and lose my gift.

I didn't want to lose the ability to enjoy lunch with Madison or to do a lot of other things with her. I longed to *be* with her, sharing every aspect of life. Real, human life.

While things might have been closer to normal than they were in Paris, we had not found real life yet.

———————————

Rejuvenated after our meals, we found a pharmacy, bought fresh bandages for my hand, then returned to the hotel. That proved to be a mistake—depending on how I thought about it.

A blind man, a woman with failing kidneys, an older man with lung cancer, and a father and his crippled daughter stood outside our room. I let them in and had them wait while I cut open my palm in the bathroom and healed them one at a time in there. They all thanked me profusely before they left, and I felt drained again.

When Madison and I were alone in the room, I sat down beside her on the bed. I kissed her and thought of continuing to kiss her while taking off all her clothes and holding her tightly, but I was exhausted, and something nagged at me.

I lay back on my pillow. "I'm worried what will happen when the sun sets."

"Yeah. I am, too." Madison laid her head on the bed's other pillow. "If all these people found out about you so quickly, I'm sure Sanguans will."

"Exactly." I pictured vile Sanguans, more vicious than our captors in France, feasting on my blood. They drained Madison until she died, because her blood didn't have the rich, sublime taste mine did, and they saw no need to keep her around. "What should we do?"

"I don't know," Madison said.

"We could go to the Spectavi. The police could get us in touch, I'm sure."

"Have you ever actually met any Spectavi?"

"Not really," I said.

"Me neither, and I'd feel safer at night with a vampire we know we can trust."

"So would I. Maybe we call Nadya later? See if she's still in town."

"That sounds good." Madison scooted closer.

"If she wanted to harm us, I guess she would have already."

"Yeah." Madison kissed me. "I like this idea." She kissed me again and pulled the bottom of my shirt up.

I leaned up to help—

Knock-knock.

She pulled my shirt back down.

The large man at the door had such a persistent cough that I couldn't figure out what he said. I healed him, and he didn't explain his ailment before departing.

Madison and I left the hotel and found a coffee shop with an eclectic mix of chairs and sofas inside. They poured our drinks into blue and green handmade ceramic mugs, and we sat at one of the many vacant tables.

"What do you think about Ellie?" I asked. "How it happened. That my blood brought her back."

"It's incredible. It's… a miracle. I'm so glad it worked."

"Absolutely. But it's kind of scary, too. I wonder if it was because she had recently died, or if there's a limit to how long it could have been, or what."

Madison sipped her black coffee. "That is scary."

We stayed there until the third person recognized me, and instead of asking for a picture like the first two had, she called a friend, and amid a conversation in Chinese, she said my name repeatedly while pointing.

We found a better restaurant than McDonald's—which did not take long—a diner offering lots of Cajun options. The waitress recognized me, but aside from mentioning that, she treated us not out of the ordinary. We made it a slow meal, with appetizers we took our time picking at, big main courses, and desserts we both said we didn't need, but eventually finished.

When the sky began darkening outside, we headed back to the hotel. Three people were waiting outside our room. I cured them while Madison called Nadya. It turned out she had re-rented the apartment she stayed in before traveling to Paris with Ethan, and she said of course we could join her there if we would feel safer. Madison agreed without asking me, but I would have had the same answer.

We took a taxi from our hotel, and when it pulled up to Nadya's luxury apartment building, the driver refused my money.

He put out both hands. "I cannot accept payment from a saint. God is with you, John Breen."

We got out, he drove off, and I had no doubt he would immediately start spreading word that we had been his passengers—and where he had taken us. Being with Nadya still seemed like our best bet, though, so we used the intercom to call her unit. She buzzed us in, and we rode the elevator to the top floor.

It was a big building, but there were only six apartments on her floor. Hers was huge, with lots of large windows and a long balcony out back.

"Do you like it?" she asked when we entered. "I like it."

"It's really nice," Madison said.

"Yeah," I added, wondering if the tall, leafy plants in the room's corners were real or fake.

"Not cheap." Nadya shrugged. "Come, sit." She gestured to the gray leather couch. We sat across from a big powered-off television, and she plopped onto the single-cushion love seat and sat Indian style. "How are you two?"

"Fine," Madison said. "I guess."

"People kept showing up at the hotel," I said. "They saw me on the news."

"Hm." Nadya scratched her chin. "That is a problem."

"Yeah," I said.

"What will you do?" Nadya asked.

"We don't know," Madison said.

"Maybe this will all blow over," I said. "We hide here for a couple days and nights, don't go out, and people assume we left New Orleans."

"You are welcome to stay here," Nadya said. "Day, night, as long as you like. But Bayard will not let this simply 'blow over.' You said he caused the explosions at the nursing home. He knew exactly where to find you. He must have followed us after the rescue in Paris. That helicopter was not inconspicuous."

"Do you think he's still here?" Madison asked.

"Maybe," Nadya said. "Maybe not."

Knock-knock.

I shook my head. "Son of a bitch."

"I'll get it." Nadya jumped up and went to the door.

A uniformed, middle-aged police officer stood with his hat in his hands. "Hi, are you"—he looked over Nadya's shoulder—"John Breen?"

I stood. "I am."

"I was going to see you at your hotel, but you got in that cab, so I followed you here. Wanted to give you a second to settle in."

I figured he had—barely. "Thanks."

"Is it true what they say your blood can do?"

"It is."

The officer stepped around Nadya. "It's my partner. He's in the hospital. He got shot two nights ago, in the chest near his heart, and a bullet to his gut that caught his spine. Surgeon didn't think he'd live the night, but he's a fighter. He pulled through. Now he's come around, and they're telling him he won't walk again. Not ever. He's two years on the force, got a wife, and two kids, and he's a fine young man, and—"

"I'll help him," I said.

At the nearby hospital, a nurse drew my blood, and it healed Officer O'Leary's partner. His two children were at home, but he sat up in his bed, planted his feet on the ground, and stepped to his wife, who sobbed as they embraced.

We had planned to head straight back to Nadya's after that, but I couldn't bring myself to leave the hospital without curing anyone else. We were an interesting group walking from room to room: me, the nurse, Madison keeping a close eye in case I stumbled from exhaustion, Nadya with a sheathed short sword on each hip—she had refused to leave them at home—and Officer O'Leary. He said that ensuring I could help others was the least he could do and, in fact, was his duty to me and the patients.

On the way to the sixth room, an older nurse found us and asked us to go with her down to the morgue. Her husband had died of a sudden heart attack two nights before and would be moved to a funeral home in the morning. She asked if my blood would help him.

It terrified me the whole way to the basement, picturing a man two days dead rising, as though he had never left. Where would I be bringing him back from? What if he didn't want to come back?

But the nurse's tears and solemn assurance that of course he wanted to keep living with her and seeing their grandchildren he so adored, along with my own need to know, convinced me to try.

The younger nurse drew my blood and injected it into the corpse. Nothing happened. I cut my palm like I had with Ellie. My blood ran over the dead man's mouth, and he did not take a breath. His lips did not part. The nurse held open his mouth to be sure blood ran into it, but the man did not stir.

After significantly more blood than Ellie had taken, I rebandaged my hand. It seemed I had been able to revive Ellie only because she had been very recently deceased.

The older nurse dried her tears and thanked me for

trying. She said she was grateful because it meant everything possible had been done for her husband.

It relieved me immensely that I could not be the answer to *everyone's* prayers. I couldn't imagine that burden on myself.

Back upstairs, we went into every room we passed and cured the patients inside. I lost count at a dozen, and leaving a room sometime later, I stumbled and couldn't walk on my own. All agreed I couldn't give any more blood, and Officer O'Leary drove us to Nadya's in his police car.

Nadya asked if she could play with the lights and sirens, but O'Leary said no. She asked again, and again he said no. She kept asking until finally he agreed to let her turn them on once. She played with them the rest of the ride back.

Nadya gave us the bedroom her coffin wasn't in, and Madison and I shut the door and lay down. Madison put her arm around me, and I don't know if she slept, because I passed out immediately.

———————————

When I woke up, Madison wasn't beside me, and the windows were dark. I found her in the living room watching television with Nadya—the local news.

"Hey," Madison said.

"Hey."

"How are you feeling?" she asked.

I noted my head didn't spin. "Better."

"Good."

"What time is it?" I asked.

"Five-thirty in the morning," Madison said.

A grainy picture of me popped up in the lower corner of the TV, with "John Breen" written below it. Video filling the rest of the screen showed the scene outside Ellie's nursing home after we had left.

Madison powered off the TV.

"What have you two been up to?" I asked.

"Watching stories about you," Nadya said. "And organizing things."

"Organizing?"

"*All* the people," Nadya said.

"They've been coming since we got back," Madison said. "One or two every hour. Faster now, I think. There's an empty apartment on the floor below, so we got the key from the building manager and sent them there to wait. Officer O'Leary is with them, and he called for a nurse to draw your blood, who should be there by now. Is that all right?"

I closed my eyes.

"We didn't know what to do," Madison said. "We didn't think you'd want us to send them away."

"No," I said. "It's okay, thank you."

Knock-knock.

"They should be downstairs, not here." Nadya got up and went to the door. She opened it. "Oh."

A tall, ghostly figure in a light suit stood with his arms straight at his sides. "Good evening."

"He's a Spectavi vampire," Nadya announced.

"I am," he said. "My name is Wesley. May I come in for a word with John?"

315

"Sure," I said, relieved at the delay a conversation of any length would bring before I had to cut my hand back open and exhaust myself.

The Spectavi looked to Nadya.

"Come in." She made an overly grand gesture of it. "But I will chaperone this conversation, if you do not mind." She put a finger to her lips. "Or if you do, actually, I will all the same. Madison, my swords are on the kitchen table. Would you bring one to me?"

Madison got up, while Wesley came in and Nadya shut the door.

Madison carried the sheathed blade over, and Nadya drew it. "Thank you." She pointed the sword's tip at the Spectavi then at me, and back to the vampire. "Well, talk."

Wesley flashed her a fake smile then clasped his hands, turning to me. "John, I wish you no harm. No Spectavi wishes to harm you. You need to know that fact, most of all." He raised his eyebrows. "I cannot say the same about *all* Sanguans."

"That's the fun about us Sanguans," Nadya said. "You never know what you're going to get."

I trusted Nadya, but her notion didn't sound *fun* to me.

"Well," Wesley said. "Be that as it may, John, we want to do more than *not harm you*. We want to help you."

"How can you help me?"

"I noticed all the people in the apartment downstairs, and the line growing out its door."

"Line?"

"Oh, yes," Wesley said. "Word of your ability is spreading.

People want to be healed by you. Others simply want to witness the miracle for themselves."

I looked at Madison. It was all wrong. *She* was not wrong. *She* was right, but the rest was a mess.

"I can't just ignore them," I said.

Wesley shrugged. "Who said you should?"

"What do you propose?"

"Come under our protection, and we'll figure it out."

"Your protection?" I asked.

"Come stay with us at Eure, on our main campus in Virginia."

"Do you want to *protect* him?" Nadya touched her sword's end to his shirt. "Or do you wish to *possess* him and his ability?"

Wesley gently pushed the blade away. "The former, I assure you. And Madison, as well, is more than welcome."

"I don't know…" I said. "We just got back. We're still figuring things out."

Wesley stepped toward me. Nadya slapped the flat side of her sword across his chest. He glared and showed her his fangs. She showed hers before settling to a confident smile.

He calmed, looked back at me, and adjusted his jacket. From its inside pocket, he pulled a gray business card. "Call anytime." He held it out. "After dark or leave a message."

I took it. Nadya guided the Spectavi back using her sword's flat side.

Wesley opened the front door. "I enjoyed meeting you, John. Based on all you've done already, you seem like a man who desires to do much good. Together, we could." He left.

I inspected the card, nothing but a name and a phone number. "How did you know he's Spectavi?"

"Synthetic blood, he stinks of it." Nadya took her sword sheath from Madison and leaned the weapon against her couch.

The smell offended her, but the Spectavi meant something very different to me. I put the business card in my pocket and wondered when I would really be able to consider his offer. When would things slow down?

"Well." I took a deep breath. "I guess I'd better get out there and see how many I can help."

25

IN PARIS, FRANCE

Dosu's private jet from Rogabon landed outside Paris. He got into a Mercedes waiting on the runway, so he didn't pass any televisions where he would have seen news of the miracles being performed in the southeastern United States. His driver headed into the city, where Dosu's contact would reveal where Bayard and Mirabella were keeping John and lay out a plan of how to get at the unique mortal.

Dosu thought of his people in the African jungle. Unathi was their god, whom they worshiped above all. But Dosu and the other Sanguans were venerated also, as lesser deities.

Dosu thought of John in the hands of the Spectavi. He could not allow that to happen. He owed it to his people not to.

In Paris, Dosu arrived at a wine bar filled with few sources of light and many conversing mortals. He sat at a small table to wait for his contact, and his vampire hearing picked up whispers in French all around him.

"… in New Orleans," a woman three tables away said.

"It's unbelievable," her date responded.

"I saw it on the news earlier," a woman at the table behind them said. "Brought a woman back from the dead, allegedly."

"John Breen," the bartender told another customer.

"And the woman with him?" the customer asked.

"Madison… something," the bartender responded. "I don't recall, but they were here in Paris recently, doing who knows what."

"Well, now his blood is healing people all over New Orleans."

Dosu got up and went out to his waiting car. Whatever information his contact had must have been incorrect or out of date. He got in the back seat, told the driver to return to the airport, and called his plane's pilot. Dosu informed him they would be heading to New Orleans the minute Dosu stepped back aboard the aircraft.

26

ETHAN

"I want to take you to Paris," I said, sitting across the kitchen table from Ellie, who wrapped her hands around a cup of steaming tea.

"So take me to Paris."

I leaned forward and took her hands from the cup to hold them. "And to Rome and Athens and to Madrid. I want to do it all."

"Then let's do it all. I've been in New Orleans long enough. I think I'm due a vacation."

I leaned back. "We should have done it before."

"When?" Ellie shrugged. "We were so young."

"We still are."

"*You* are. You haven't aged a bit, but I have, and I will."

"You're beautiful," I said. "More than ever."

She smiled.

"You don't have to age. Not anymore." I leaned forward again. "Doesn't this—me—prove something to you?"

"Prove what?"

"That I'm not evil. I'm a vampire, but we aren't all evil, and I'm among the good."

"Ethan." She took my hands. "My love. You are not evil, like the Spectavi are not evil. But an evil has changed you—"

"It has empowered me!"

"An evil *is* there." She shook her head. "And perhaps if it weren't, I wouldn't be here talking to you. I don't hate you. But I hate the thing the devil planted inside you."

"That thing isn't *me*. It's just a source of strength."

"It's your essence," Ellie said. "You drink human blood to live. You crave it, don't you?"

"Yes, but—"

"Do you hunt for it?"

"I—"

"Do you?"

"I hunted hoping to find a cure for you or any clue that could help," I said. "Like the one I found that led me to John."

"Now that you've saved me, will you hunt for more blood?" Ellie asked.

"I have to."

"Right. *That* is your very being."

I shook my head.

"You will not drink my blood."

"No," I said. "If you don't want me to, I never will."

"See." She held my hands tightly. "You thought I might. And you'll want me to change my mind. And I won't hate you for it. I love you. I love you, and I'll be with you as long as you want. But that ends in fifty years or sixty or whenever God sees fit for it to end."

"And then what? You'll be with him in heaven, while I'm down here on earth?"

"Yes," she said. "If I've earned it. And I'll weep that you cannot join me there."

"No weeping. There's been too much weeping already." I lifted her hands and kissed her fingers.

I looked away. I fought against pulling her hands closer and biting into her wrist. I'd salivated for a taste since we got home from the nursing home.

More than anything, I longed to drink nearly all her blood, and for her to drink from me and become a vampire. We could be together forever and share kisses and drinks from each other every night.

I turned back to her. "Is Paris okay to start?"

She smiled. "Give me a few days, then yes, Paris with you would be amazing."

I nodded. Maybe seeing the city illuminated and alive would change her mind. Or if not Paris, perhaps somewhere else would do it.

Maybe just being with me would make her love take a deeper hold. Maybe after months or years, she would refuse to let what we had continue marching toward its end, even if it meant changing her relationship with God. Maybe.

27

VERA

Edmond found me in the lab in Virginia. I was smiling, despite the hellish, patient-induced nightmare that had jolted me awake earlier and had only faded to a persistent pain at my temple.

He smiled. I hugged him and kissed him. I wanted him to do more, and when I slid my tongue across his fang so its sharp point nicked it and he tasted my blood, he could not have had any doubt about that.

But he leaned back, so I did the same.

"How's your work coming along?" he asked.

"Well," I said. "With Protice."

"How well?"

"Very. It took three tries, three different mixtures, but on the third, the effect was remarkable. The test is ongoing, but so far, the subject is responding exactly as intended."

"Good," Edmond said. "More than good. Was it John's blood?"

"Yes," I said. "And no. John's blood gave me the ideas. I

324

don't know that I ever would have had them on my own, or at least I wouldn't have anytime soon, but his blood isn't in the mixture."

"I see." Edmond gestured to the patients in their coffins. "Have you tried John's blood to treat them?"

My smile faded. "I have. For a few minutes, it seemed to help." I pointed to a brain activity printout on the counter. "The calming effect lasted a little longer on Patient One than Patient Two, but then they both reverted to their wild patterns. The effect of John's blood didn't last as long the second time and had no effect at all the third."

"I see." Edmond rubbed his chin. "I'm sorry to hear that."

"I was very sorry to discover it."

"Have you seen what's going on in New Orleans?" he asked.

"A little. I've been working. Is John still there?"

"He is. His secret's out. He's healing people night and day. It's all over the news and the internet."

"Good for him."

"Perhaps," Edmond said. "His gift is quite a responsibility. Correct to assume that if your test with Protice continues to go as it has and is repeatable, you won't need more of his blood?"

"Correct," I said. "And I have a whole unused vial at the moment."

"Nevertheless," Edmond said. "He would be safer here. He can't heal *everyone*, and once he starts choosing, the unchosen masses will no longer hold him in utter reverence."

"I can't imagine that responsibility." I remembered

Madison being terrified leaving the Sanguans in Paris. I wondered how she was dealing with John's sudden fame.

"I sent someone," Edmond said. "He invited John here."

"Here?"

"Where else? I should see to his protection personally."

"You really want all that attention on this campus?"

"God gave John a gift," Edmond said. "But he also gave it to the world. It is in my power to protect that gift. It is my duty, in fact, to protect it. John is working out of an apartment, I'm told, with a growing line wrapping down the hall and a crowd of onlookers gathering outside. I can bring order to what he's doing. He can't heal everyone, and once John is here and safe, I can guide him to those most in need, those most worthy of his gift."

28

JOHN

I'd cured roughly twenty people that night—more than ten for sure. Thirty sounded like too many, but I couldn't recall for certain how many it had been before Officer O'Leary and Madison helped me back to Nadya's apartment. The sun had risen by then, so she had already retired to her coffin.

When I woke that afternoon, Madison reheated pizza that she had ordered for lunch. She used the microwave at my request, because I didn't feel like waiting for the oven.

I sat sprawled out in a kitchen table chair.

The microwave beeped, and Madison brought over a napkin and two triangular slices of greasy pepperoni pizza on a white plate. "How long can you keep this up?"

"I don't know," I said. "How can I turn those people away?"

"I don't know." She sat next to me. "I really don't. You're doing something incredible, and... meaningful, so meaningful, for all those people. But you can't keep up this pace forever."

"I know." I bit off the pizza's tip and felt a little better as soon as I swallowed. "What did you think of that Spectavi last night?"

"Unsettling." Madison shrugged. "But I don't know why."

"Me, too, and me, neither." I took another bite of pizza. "Then there's…" I didn't like saying his name because of what it seemed to trigger in Madison. "What our captors offered."

"Become a vampire?"

I nodded.

"Then your blood couldn't heal anymore."

"Yeah. It feels like giving up." I had a bite and chewed it quickly. "Remember when we walked around Montmartre, all morning and after lunch, waiting for our hotel to be ready?"

"Of course."

"I remember the sun on my face. I remember you in the sun. I don't want that day to be my only memory of you like that."

"I don't, either." She leaned over and kissed my cheek. "How's your pizza?"

I swallowed a big mouthful. "Good."

Taking my hand, she pulled me up from my chair then led me across the living room. "I'll microwave it for you again." A step into the bedroom, she stopped, turned, and let me catch up to her. "If it gets col—"

I kissed her then ran my fingers from her neck to her hair and through it. We kissed until she pulled off my shirt, then I pulled off hers.

"Madison May," I said. "You are beautiful."

She kissed me hard and unbuttoned my jeans. I unbuttoned hers. I couldn't take Bayard's way out. I couldn't give in. I could not give up that most human thing that I had with my Madison.

When I finally made it out into the painting-and-plant-decorated hallway, I heard a clamor on the floor below. I pulled open the door to the concrete stairwell—the line of men, women, and children wrapped down the stairs, from the floor below to the bottom of the building. The conversations nearest me stopped, and the quiet progressed downward.

I nodded to them all then made my way down. The line of people extended from the stairwell into the hall, all the way to the end, wrapping around to the apartment where I was curing people.

When I stepped into the hallway, a man from the stairwell shouted, "John, save me! I'm dying. Please save me now!"

"John!" another called, but I proceeded to the apartment where Officer O'Leary stood guard.

I passed more people shouting my name before O'Leary opened the door and I went in. Two police officers in the kitchen turned to me. I didn't see the nurse anywhere. The apartment door closed.

"John." The officer with a bar on his shoulder indicating his rank extended his hand. "I'm Lieutenant Jones. This is Sergeant Palmer."

I shook their hands.

"It's incredible what you're doing," Jones said.

"It really is," Palmer added.

"But this crowd"—Jones gestured to the door—"has gotten out of control. People keep coming, and with the stories hitting the national news, people are coming from farther away. It's getting worse."

"It is," I said.

"God has a plan!" a woman screamed outside the apartment. "It's not for you to change!"

Booing and shouting rose from the hall.

"These people can't stay here," Sergeant Palmer said.

Jones put out both hands. "You haven't done anything wrong. It's a safety issue, and the fire marshal is concerned."

"Okay," I said.

"We'll take care of it as nicely as we can."

Sergeant Palmer spoke into his radio. "Go ahead."

"What should I do?" I asked.

"What do you mean?" Jones responded.

"Where should I go? How should I help people? *Should* I keep helping people?"

The lieutenant rubbed his chin. "We can put you in touch with the Spectavi, if you'd like. They might have the resources and a facility to handle this kind of thing, long term."

Long term… the words sank into my stomach.

"I can give you a name and a phone number," Jones said. "Or they have an office in town you can stop by. At night."

I shook my head. "I already have a phone number."

"John!" a scream came from the hall.

"Please head downstairs," a firm voice outside the apartment said. "Let's go."

"Sorry," Sergeant Palmer said.

"John! Help me, John!" someone screamed. "John! Save me!"

I went into the bedroom, and when I shut the door, the screams became harder to distinguish from one another.

———————————

Before they left, the two police officers asked me if I had any idea who might have been behind the nursing home explosions. I said I didn't but that I had seen two Sanguans flee from the scene. Answering with the full truth felt like betraying Bayard and Mirabella, which I wasn't prepared to do. At least not yet.

An hour into the night, Nadya, Madison, and I met Officer O'Leary in the lobby. He had talked his commander into letting him escort us to a hospital in Slidell, forty minutes north of New Orleans. He assumed anywhere local would mean chaos, and we all agreed the less of that, the better. I didn't think I could keep up the routine indefinitely, either physically or mentally, but since the screams of the crowd being forced away that afternoon, I had thought of little aside from curing people.

Although none of those people who had been waiting for me at the apartment were likely to be in Slidell, I was doing my best, I told myself. I was helping *someone*.

Nadya had us hold her swords in the back seat, and she mostly resisted the urge to play with the police car sirens during the drive. No crowd greeted us at the hospital when we pulled up, thank goodness. But when O'Leary led us through the doors past the receptionist, doctors and nurses looked up from clipboards and stopped their conversations and writing. Jaws dropped, camera phones flipped open, and thankfully, one nurse came forward to say hello and ask how she could help us.

"Are there kids?" I asked. "Like, a section of the hospital for them we could go to."

"Not all together." The nurse smiled. "But here and there, I know some children who would be very excited to see you. Come on."

We followed her, and in the first room, Andy had leukemia, and it was awful, until my drawn blood ran into his arm, and it wasn't awful anymore. We visited Holly, and it crushed me to see her breathing only with the help of a machine, because what if my blood didn't save her? But it did save her, and she breathed deeply, hugged me, and smiled widely. Thank God.

In that moment, I believed God existed. I did because no *natural* mutation could possibly have caused my blood to heal a person. But when we went to see Shawn, who had an inoperable brain tumor, I wasn't so sure. How could there be a God who would let that happen to an eight-year-old?

My blood healed him, too. And it healed child after child until I tripped over my own feet and Madison had to catch me from falling to the floor. With my arm over her shoulder, she steadied me while we walked so I could heal more. When I grew dizzy, I asked Nadya to help, too, and she did, until finally, I could barely keep my eyes open.

As we left, doctors and nurses again stopped working to applaud—and it didn't feel right. I didn't deserve it, but when they whistled and cheered, I couldn't help smiling.

When the doors closed, the sound of the applause died out. Officer O'Leary's police car was at the near edge of the big parking lot. An old brown sedan was parked behind it. The driver's door opened, and a pudgy-faced man with a long beard emerged. He was wearing a jean jacket, and a faded cross tattoo marked his forehead. "Who do you think you are?"

"Hold it." O'Leary put out his hand and had his other on the pistol at his hip.

"You think you're *God*?" The tattooed man held his arms at his sides so that the car obscured my view of his hands. "You think you're *Jesus Christ*?"

"No." I managed to stand on my own. "I don't."

"You ain't," the man said.

"I know."

"Calm down," O'Leary said. "Just calm down and let me see your hands."

"I'll *prove* you ain't." The man raised a handgun.

I heard O'Leary drawing his.

Nadya stood at the decapitated man's side, her sword horizontal past his stump of a neck. His body crumpled to the ground. She had moved too quickly for me to see.

A gunshot fired from the lot. Glass shattered behind me. I ducked, pulling Madison down with me, while the shot echoed.

Nadya stood thirty rows into the parking lot with her sword low, a second body at her feet. A rifle lay on the roof of the car beside her.

"Madison!" I had my hand on her back.

"I'm fine. Are you?"

I looked myself over. "Yeah."

"Inside!" O'Leary pushed us toward the door next to the bullet-shattered glass panel.

I pulled open the door. In the hospital, we turned the corner, got low near the wall, and O'Leary checked left and right, pointing his gun as he did.

The receptionist was crouching beside her desk, describing the situation over the phone. The police arrived minutes later.

No other shots had been fired. Nadya had already searched the parking lot, but the police conducted their own sweep of the whole area. O'Leary vouched for Nadya when she explained the events that had led her to decapitating my two assailants. Dread filled me the entire ride back to New Orleans.

———————

For a change, I didn't pass out immediately upon entering the apartment. My adrenaline rush was subsiding, but my mind raced.

"Pizza?" Madison asked.

"Yeah." I sat on the couch and left the TV off, so it didn't turn on to a news story about me. "Please."

"I'll order something else tomorrow." She pulled open the fridge and took out the box. "Maybe Indian?"

Tomorrow—I imagined it. What if people attacked us tomorrow? What if they did any *day*, when Nadya couldn't move at vampire speed to slice their heads off? In my mind, I heard the rifle shot and its long echo again. What if tomorrow's shooter had better aim?

Knock-knock.

It never ended.

Nadya opened the door to a thin African priest. Her sword went to his throat. "Sanguan." His black shirt and white collar gave him away as Catholic.

"Yes." He put out his hands. "My name is Dosu. I come in peace."

"And I thought we'd already had tonight's excitement," Nadya said.

"What happened?" Dosu asked.

I stood. "Someone shot at us."

"Who?"

"A religious fanatic," I said. "I guess. He's dead now."

"I am sorry to hear that," Dosu said. "But glad to see you are unharmed, and, I hope, up for a quick chat?"

"How can a Sanguan be a priest?" I asked.

"Why not?" Dosu responded.

"Doesn't... Isn't the devil's power what makes you a vampire?"

"Is it? Do you know that for certain because of the power God has given you?"

"No," I said.

"I do not know for certain." Dosu gestured to Nadya. "I do not think she knows the source of our dark power, and unless Miss May does, that means none in this room do." He motioned to the living room. "May I sit?"

"I can hold this sword at his throat anywhere," Nadya said.

"All right," I said.

Dosu came in and took the love seat perpendicular to the couch.

Madison stayed in the kitchen, leaning against the counter, with her arms folded.

Nadya stood as promised, with her blade pressing into the white of Dosu's collar. "Do you think you are fast enough to get away before I slice?"

"No," he said.

Nadya nodded. "Nor do I."

I sat down on the couch. "You really believe in God?"

"I do," Dosu said. "And I think he would be proud of the works you've done in his name."

I shook my head. "But if I can do them, why are there people who need me to? I mean, why are they in the hospital in the first place?"

"The Lord has a different plan for each of us."

"But how can *that* be his plan?"

"We cannot know his plan," Dosu said. "What happens to one person may happen for another, or for some other end bigger than one person. In any case, I believe his plans for us do not end on this earth."

"It's still cruel," I said.

Dosu crossed his leg over his other knee. "It is cruel."

I hadn't expected to win the point. "Why are you here?

What do you want from me?"

"What do you intend to do with your gift?" Dosu asked. "Long term."

"I don't know."

"Tonight's shooter will not be the last to make such an attempt. You may not be safe in this city."

"I know." I had thought of little else since leaving Slidell. "Are you here on behalf of the Church to offer me protection? The Spectavi have."

"No. In truth, any protection the Church could offer would be in concert with the Spectavi."

That combined protection didn't sound so bad.

"But no," Dosu said. "That is not why I am here." He reached for his shirt collar and took hold of the white tab in the middle of it. It scraped against the sharp edge of Nadya's sword as he removed it. He tossed it on the coffee table. "Also in truth, I was a priest as a mortal man, but have been neither human nor Catholic for some time."

Nadya's face focused.

"But I needed to talk to you," Dosu said. "And that was my way in the door. I come from Rogabon, a territory in Central Africa. Our leader, Unathi, sent me to bring you back there."

"Is he a Sanguan?" I asked.

"He is. There are a hundred Sanguans there, and to the Spectavi, Unathi is a warlord, and we are all their enemies. But to the twenty thousand humans living there, we vampires are like gods, Unathi chief among us. The people worship him and us, and we protect them from any enemy and live off their blood. These people choose to live there. They are free to leave anytime they wish, but few ever do. It is a very different way of life than here in America, but it is one we have lived for centuries. It is *our* life."

Madison stepped forward. "So why do you need John?"

"Because four years ago, we encountered a terrible enemy we failed to protect our people from. Men, women, and children started growing ill in a small settlement miles from our most central. At first one, then two people a week. They ached all over, which are symptoms that unfortunately come from other diseases prevalent in Africa. But then these people's eyes became cloudy, and they could not see." He pointed to his ears. "They heard a ringing that would not stop. When it finally did stop, they heard nothing. This disease was unlike any in Africa or anywhere else."

Nadya inched her blade away as he continued. "No treatment worked. We have doctors among us, including Sanguans with more extensive experience than any mortal, and they could do nothing. More became ill, and faster, and after their hearing went, they could not taste, and they could not distinguish one smell from another, and so they lived, but like zombies—alive, yet hardly able to sense life at all."

"When more than a hundred had contracted the terrible disease, Unathi asked for help—no small step for a god. He reached out to neighboring nations, to the World Health Organization, and even to your country's president, but no help came."

"Why not?" I asked.

"Because of Edmond Duchart, leader of the Spectavi.

Perhaps because of Victoria, as well, as revenge for all we've cost her, but Edmond for sure. Edmond craves power. He needs control, and we, as much as any Sanguans on earth, refuse to kneel before him. Our nation is independent. We do not acknowledge Spectavi authority. They do *some* good for humanity—I can admit that—but we want no part of it, and Edmond refuses to tolerate us."

"Three times in the last hundred years, Victoria has led an army of Spectavi against us. Three times, the great crusader warrior has been beaten back and, amid heavy casualties, ordered a retreat. We are a hundred plus Unathi, but others nearby answer our call when the Spectavi come, and together…" Dosu made a fist. "We are strong." He relaxed his hand. "Edmond blocked any effort to aid us, so this disease would wipe out our people entirely, eliminating our source of mortal blood. Their end would end our way of life and, with it, our nation."

"How'd you stop it?" Madison asked. "Did you stop it?"

"We stopped it. Eventually, we guessed the disease's source—the temple in that small settlement where people grew ill. We burned the temple and the surrounding area, and in the years since that fire, we haven't had a new case."

"Meaning it's not contagious?" I asked.

"It seems not," Dosu said. "But for the four hundred who contracted the disease before we burned the temple, that fact is of little comfort. We do all we can for them, but they are miserable."

"Could you turn them?" Nadya asked.

"Two, we did," Dosu said. "They became vampires, and

it healed them, thank God. But many are too young, and others are too old, and it would be ages before we could turn them all."

That made sense, based on my understanding that vampires could only make fledglings of reasonable strength once every ten years or so.

Dosu leaned forward until the skin of his neck touched Nadya's sword. "*You* could cure them, John. All of them."

"I can't," I said. "How do I even know this is true? Nadya, have you heard of Unathi?"

"I have," she said. "He is a Sanguan warlord in Africa. But of this disease, I have heard nothing."

"Come with me," Dosu said. "My jet is waiting at the airport. Let me show you. You will be convinced in an instant, I assure you."

"I want to believe you," I said. "I've met a couple Sanguans worth believing in recently. Sanguans of virtue and compassion. So I *could* believe you. But I can't fly halfway around the world to a warlord's jungle territory."

"Nadya is welcome," Dosu said. "And Madison, of course."

"It's too dangerous for Madison, which is part of the problem, and no matter how well Nadya fought, one against a hundred is pretty bad odds."

Dosu shook his head. "There would be no fight. You would be treated as gods. You would be *revered!*"

I slammed my hand on the couch. "I don't want to be revered!"

Dosu sat back.

I pulled the gray card with the Spectavi's phone number

from my pocket. "Madison, I don't think we're safe in New Orleans. I don't know if we'd be safe in Africa, either. If I call this number, and the protection they offer sounds reasonable, will you come with me to Virginia? Maybe we can be safe there."

She sat beside me and took my hand. "Yes."

Dosu leaned forward. "John—"

"I'll ask to speak to Edmond," I said. "I'll tell him I want to help your people."

"And if he says no?" Dosu asked.

"I'll tell him… I'll tell him I won't go stay with the Spectavi unless he agrees to let me help you."

"He'll talk you out of it," Dosu said.

"He won't."

"Edmond is cunning. He may delay your trip. He may discredit my story. You will never come to the aid of my people." Dosu stood. "I wish you would believe me and return there with me now. But since you will not, I wish it were because you did not find our cause worthy, not because you are running to Edmond Duchart. He will not allow you to come, but if you change your mind before you join him, if you search your heart and know, deep down, that you should help us, know that we are waiting eagerly for your arrival." He set a green business card on the table. "Know that four hundred of us, especially, are waiting."

Dosu headed for the door, while Nadya kept her sword a flick of her wrist away from slicing his neck.

"I'm sorry," I said.

He opened the door. "As am I."

29

VERA

We sat in the grass by the lake behind Edmond's home. He pulled his fangs from my neck. The fire subsided, he lay down, and I rested my head against his chest while I cooled. It was late, and the sun would rise soon. The blue-hot flame of his bite had quieted the thundering red attack on my mind hours earlier. He had taken that latest drink, and we still lay there then, because neither of us wanted to be anywhere else.

My continued work with John's blood had led to no lasting improvement with my patients. In the midst of one of their assaults on me, I drank half a vial of John's blood, and while the years-old bite scar at my neck turned to smooth, fresh skin, the hellish imagery, the stinging pain, and the awful noise in my brain did not abate. I supposed it spoke to the inhuman nature of the connection that had formed between my patients and me.

But my test for Protice had concluded successfully, with synthetic blood modified in a way that only John's blood could have inspired. Follow-up tests yielded the same results. Drinking the altered synthetic blood swayed the minds of Spectavi in favor of Edmond's call to eliminate any Sanguans who wouldn't switch to synthetic blood, and as long as the Spectavi continued drinking the altered synthetic, their minds would remain swayed.

My role in the project was complete. We didn't need any more of John's blood, and our factories could produce as much modified synthetic as necessary, for as long as necessary. Edmond had his new weapon to fight the Sanguans—he just had to decide when to use it.

His cell phone rang.

We both sat up.

Edmond answered it. "Yes… Did he? That is excellent to hear… Her, too, sure… Hm… Tell him we can discuss it here, in person… Insist. Tell him it's a sensitive subject, details are classified, and I'd rather not discuss it over the phone… Okay… Sure, she can be there… Sounds good. Thank you." He flipped his phone closed.

"Who was that?"

"Wesley, down in New Orleans. John Breen called him and wants our protection here in Virginia. The woman with him, as well."

"Wow."

"Wonderful, in fact," Edmond said.

"What was that about something being classified?"

"Oh. A Sanguan got to John and told him a story about a warlord in Africa and an illness afflicting his tribe. John wants to go and help them."

"Is it true?"

"The warlord is real, yes. His name is Unathi. He is a Sanguan who controls a territory in Central Africa. Him, I know well. The illness? In truth, I do not know. It's likely a trick to lure John there. Unathi might want him to be the next spectacular sacrifice atop his fiery temple or for him to be a prisoner, trotted out to perform miracles to further Unathi's glory and reputation."

"Couldn't you send someone to verify the claims? If people are sick and only John can cure them—"

"They are savage people led by especially savage Sanguans," Edmond said. "Unathi and I have been at war since long before you were born. I will send no aid to my enemy."

"So you won't let John go?"

"No. Our conflict aside, it's far too risky. John is too important. I have big plans for him."

"Like what?"

"Consider the attention he's garnered in Louisiana, based on grainy cell-phone-shot pictures and reports which people around the world are struggling to believe. But it's all true, and it's also becoming chaos. Think of the positive light that will shine on the Spectavi from all over the globe when *we* present that truth and control the narrative. John can perform miracles not in hospitals in New Orleans, but from Saint Patrick's Cathedral in New York, or Saint Peter's in Rome. *Then* people everywhere will believe, and we can be selective in who we choose to cure."

"What do you mean 'selective'?" I asked.

"John can't heal everyone. He's learning that. Since he cannot, he should heal those most worthy, and those in cases that would help us progress toward our more far-reaching goals."

"And you'll decide who those people are?"

"How could he, once he lives here? It's not safe for him out there, so when he's not at a prearranged event, he'll have to remain on our campus, meaning he won't ever meet a needy passerby on the street. He couldn't have a publicly known email address or phone number, because he'd receive millions of messages he'd never have time to read or listen to. If he stumbles across some cause on the internet, I suppose we could consider it." Edmond raised a finger to his chin. "Responding to natural disasters seems a prudent use of his gift, considering the certain media coverage."

I imagined Madison dragged around to John's carefully selected appearances. Would *she* be allowed to have an email address? Could *she* leave Eure's campus? Probably not. I wouldn't tolerate such a life. I would rage against it.

Edmond stood. A shade of almost blue stretched across the treetops beyond the water.

"John asked if you could be there in New Orleans," Edmond said. "He told Wesley he'd feel better seeing someone he trusts already. I said you would go."

"Okay."

"Fly at sundown. I want Spectavi with you. I'll see you when you return." He pulled out his phone and flipped it open. I heard him discussing the plans while heading to his house.

I stayed in the grass, by myself, as I would be for the rapidly approaching day. That was not my favorite side of Edmond to see. He usually dealt with world events, politicians, religious leaders, and war between vampires, rather than treating the lives of individual humans as tools to advance the Spectavi agenda.

Or maybe all of Edmond's means caused very personal repercussions, and I only worried for Madison and John because I had met them and they seemed so naïve to what awaited them with the Spectavi. They didn't know Edmond as I did. They couldn't know what their life at Eure would be like.

I recalled Madison clutching John during the hotel escape, pleading with him not to leave. She had not seemed strong. Perhaps nothing mattered to her except being safe. Or perhaps she had hated leaving the vampires who surely drank from her often, because of the hold those bites had on her. Perhaps it was both of those things.

I hated being parted from Edmond and Victoria. I loathed nights without their bites—without the fire burning inside me, while they held me and knew me completely. Yet I craved freedom, too, and I had it. I demanded of Edmond that I be allowed to leave the campus at any time, and he allowed it.

And, always, I had Edmond and Victoria to come back to. I had their protection against the world's evils. I could not imagine my life without them. I could not imagine being alone.

With the Spectavi, John and Madison would have

protection like mine. But they would not have my freedom. Did that matter to them? I wished I knew them better and that they knew Edmond better.

30

JOHN

Two officers stood sentry at the entrance to Nadya's building. Behind their police car were two black Mercedes sedans with tinted windows.

Madison and I didn't have any luggage, and Nadya was accompanying us only as far as the car. Wesley, the Spectavi who had visited the apartment, had said that whatever we needed would be provided and we could have things shipped to us later. I hoped I would see Nadya again, though I could not imagine when or the circumstances that would lead to it.

"They're on time," I said as we headed toward the awaiting Spectavi. "That's a good start."

Madison gave a small smile.

A male in a gray business suit stepped out of the lead car. From the rear door, wearing a black pantsuit with a white high-necked top, Vera emerged, then waited with a familiar determined expression, her hands clasped in front of her. Three Spectavi came out of the rear car.

Out the door, I scanned left and right. Would a sniper's gunshot ring out at any moment?

"Hello," Vera said. "It's good to see you all."

I looked to her. "Thanks for coming."

"Happy to. Thanks for trusting me to be here."

I nodded.

Nadya pointed at the vampire beside Vera. "If harm befalls either of them…" She shifted her finger to Vera. "I will find you, and significant harm will befall *you*, I promise."

The Spectavi smiled. "You have nothing to worry about."

Vera extended her hand to Nadya, palm faced mostly down, which seemed odd. "Thank you for seeing them here safely."

Nadya took Vera's hand.

Vera clasped her other hand over Nadya's. "Thank you."

The Sanguan nodded.

Vera gestured to her car. "We should be going."

I let Madison slide in first then sat next to her. Vera went around to the other side. The Spectavi got back in the passenger side up front, and as soon as his door shut, the driver pulled away from the building.

"How long's the flight to Virginia?" I asked.

"Two hours." Vera picked up her sheathed katana from near our feet and held it in her lap. "Edmond sent our newest business jet. It's really nice."

"Great," I said. "And we'll be able to talk to him, once we're there?"

"Yup. He's looking forward to it."

"We are, too." I took Madison's hand, and she smiled.

The jet waiting on the tarmac was slightly larger than I had pictured. I followed Madison up the short staircase built into the door. Wide gray leather seats on each side took up the front of the cabin, and two pairs in the rear faced each other. Polished wood trim ran along the windows.

Two Spectavi in the same style suits stood from their seats. Vera got on board and peered out the door behind her. From the cockpit, the pilot—human, I guessed—emerged. He had a neat beard but was older, tanned, and wore slacks and a light-blue, short-sleeved, button-down shirt.

"Are we ready to go?" he asked.

"Almost." Vera looked at us. "Please have a seat, wherever you'd like."

Madison and I made our way back, past the Spectavi, and sat in the seats next to each other.

Outside, police car sirens grew louder.

"Out there." One of the Spectavi pointed to the windows.

I recognized the number on the side of the car speeding across the tarmac. It stopped beside our jet, and out came Officer O'Leary, Ethan, and Nadya. The Sanguans were dressed in gray suits like the Spectavi, and Nadya wore thick-framed glasses and a short black wig. She had a sword on each hip.

"What's going on?" Madison whispered to me.

The three from the police car spoke to the Spectavi who had driven us, who responded by nodding and stepping aside.

"I don't know," I whispered back.

Ethan and Nadya ascended the stairs. Vera stepped back to let them on the plane.

"Edmond wanted a couple more," Nadya announced. "Just in case."

"In case what?" a Spectavi asked. "We're about to leave."

Ethan pulled a gray handle from his pocket, and a knife blade extended from it.

Nadya drew a sword. "In case of Sanguans."

Vera unsheathed her katana and stepped backward into the cockpit doorway.

Nadya darted to the Spectavi nearest us, so quickly that I only saw when she got there.

Ethan grappled with the other. Nadya hurled her Spectavi out the plane door then stabbed her sword through Ethan's foe's side. The Spectavi groaned, and with the bottom of her shoe, Nadya pushed him out the door.

"Take off," Vera called into the cockpit. "Now!"

Ethan put away his knife and closed and latched the plane door as we started moving.

"What's going on?" I asked. "What are you doing here?"

Nadya sheathed her sword. "Ask Vera."

She stuck her head out of the cockpit. "Ethan, would you watch him?" To the pilot in the seat beside hers, she said, "No radio."

Ethan took his knife back out, stepped past Vera, and sat in the copilot's chair.

The plane picked up speed, and Nadya sat in the window seat across from us. Vera gave her a long look then took the aisle seat.

"Edmond won't let you go to Africa." Vera sheathed her sword. "I don't know how much you care about that. I don't know how much you care about what your life would be like with the Spectavi."

The plane lifted off the ground.

"I wanted you to know," Vera continued. "So *then* you could decide what to do."

"Where are we headed?" I asked.

"Wherever you want," Vera said. "Virginia included."

"What would things be like with the Spectavi?" Madison asked.

"You would be safe," Vera said. "Edmond is completely capable of providing that. You would be on a campus protected by a small army during the day and Spectavi vampires at night, where... essentially no vampires drink human blood. You would be as safe as you could be." She shrugged. "But that safety would cost you."

"Cost us what?" I asked.

"Freedom. Free will. Edmond sees you as a chess piece, John. You would heal many, but *Edmond* would decide who, when, and where. If you don't care who you heal, maybe that's fine with you. But you won't be allowed to leave Eure's campuses, except as part of carefully planned excursions surrounded by Spectavi. Edmond would control you, be certain of that."

"What about Madison?" I asked.

"I'm sure she'll be completely comfortable there, and at your side at events where Edmond shows you off."

I glanced at Madison. She glanced back.

"How do you know all this?" I asked.

"Edmond told me," Vera said. "Most of it, in very similar words. The rest... I just know."

"What exactly is your relationship with him?"

Vera's eyes shifted sideways, then back. "I'm a chemist, and we discussed your situation since your blood is important to my work."

"Did it help your projects?" I asked.

"One of them."

"Would you take more, if I lived on that campus?"

"I'm sure he would make me," Vera said. "I'm sure we would conduct all kinds of tests on it and on you."

"That much I figured." I asked Madison, "What do *you* want? Most of all, I want you to be safe."

"I want that, too." Madison made a contemplative face. "And I want to stop running. I have been for so long, and I don't want to anymore, as long as I'm with you wherever I end up. And I want *you* to be happy. Does that kind of life with the Spectavi sound like a good one to you?"

"I can imagine worse." I saw and heard the parking lot gunshot in my mind. "And I can imagine better, but I can't guarantee it." I pulled Dosu's green business card from my pocket and handed it to Vera. "What do you know about Unathi? A Sanguan in Rogabon, Africa."

She flipped the card over to the pen-written latitude and longitude on the back. "I know he's a warlord with followers who consider him a god."

"Do you know anything about a horrible disease in his territory, four years ago?"

"I don't," Vera said. "Edmond didn't know if it was true, either."

I said to Madison, "If we go, and it's true, and I heal those people, maybe we could live there. Dosu seemed all right. He seemed passionate about helping his people."

"The Spectavi will track this plane, wherever it goes," Vera said. "Edmond will send Spectavi to try to rescue you— and me, since he thinks I'm also a prisoner of Nadya and Ethan."

"Dosu told us they fought off the Spectavi a few times," I said. "If they do again, maybe Vera escapes during the rescue attempt, so she can go home, but Madison and I stay in the jungle and disappear among Unathi's people for a while."

"That could work," Vera said. "If the Spectavi rescue fails, Edmond might not want to admit it to the world. He might prefer to let you two be forgotten."

"After a time," I said. "If we think it's safe, we could take trips from there to heal some in need. It wouldn't be as many, but I could still help people. And even if we couldn't do that, I wouldn't be used for my blood, and we wouldn't be shot at by crazed fanatics."

"It could be a home for us," Madison said. "It would be so different than here, but… that's exciting. It's new, and just saying it, 'new' sounds wonderful, as long as it's with you."

I smiled then shrugged. "If the Spectavi succeed in rescuing us, we wind up with Edmond anyway."

"He'll learn every detail of our plan," Vera said.

"How?" I asked.

"He'll drink from me," Vera said.

I raised my eyebrows. "The leader of the Spectavi drinks mortal blood?"

"Yes," Vera said.

I looked at Nadya.

"Not surprising," she said.

"Hm. Well…" I turned to Vera. "When he learns about the plan, how do you think he'll react? Do you think he'll be vindictive?"

"No, actually," she said. "He'll be content to have you with him, and he'll expect you to fall in line, as he would have expected anyway."

"What will he do to Nadya and Ethan?" Madison asked.

"He'd go through them to get to John or me," Vera said. "But whether he succeeds or not, that would probably be the end of it. Revenge is rarely his priority."

"Uh-huh. Well, that's the plan then," I said. "We fly to Africa and cure Unathi's people. When the Spectavi come, Vera goes to them so she can get out of there, but Madison and I will stay back. With luck, the Spectavi fail to rescue me and Madison, and we have some kind of life there. If the Spectavi succeed and we're all rescued, then we go to Virginia with them, and that's fine."

"And if Dosu was lying?" Nadya asked. "You are correct that I can, most probably, not fight off a hundred skilled Sanguan warriors."

"Then we'll face whatever that means together." Madison took my hand. "I like your plan. We're aiming high. It's far away, it's foreign, but life there could be the adventure of our lifetimes. If we end up in Virginia, we're still together, and we're safe. Or if Dosu was lying, and things go badly, I'd rather face that with you than know you're miserable as a Spectavi political tool, having never tried for something better."

I squeezed her hand. "Thank you."

Vera walked to the cockpit. "Can this thing make it to Africa?"

"What part?" the pilot asked.

"Central." Vera handed him Dosu's business card with the coordinates.

"Maybe," the pilot answered. "It's thirteen, fourteen hours."

Vera turned back to us. "Sound good to you?"

"Yeah," I said.

"More interesting than flying to Virginia," the pilot said. "To be honest."

As the plane angled eastward, Vera returned and sat down.

"How'd you get past the Spectavi back there?" I asked Nadya. "And how'd you know to come?"

Nadya finally took off her wig and glasses. "This one." She pointed to Vera. "She gave me a note at the apartment when she shook my hand, and a vial that I *did not* want to drink, but for you two, I did."

"It was an additive that made their blood smell synthetic," Vera said. "Like a Spectavi's. It'll wear off in a few hours."

"Wow," I said.

"Yup." Vera took off her suit coat. "I developed it myself, two years ago."

"Will things be okay for you after this?" Madison asked. "What will Edmond do to you?"

Vera put her index finger to her chin. "He'll forgive me. We don't need more of John's blood for the projects I'm working on." She shrugged. "He might be upset at first, but eventually, he'll forgive me. Whatever I've done, he always has."

31

VERA

So far so good with the Sanguans, I thought as we neared Africa. I reminded myself that John and Madison trusted them, Nadya especially. And both Nadya and Ethan had trusted me and come to the airport in New Orleans.

"We could land in Libreville," our pilot, Gary, called back. "It's on the west coast in Gabon. Otherwise, it's on to Rogabon, and we won't have fuel to do anything but land there, assuming we make it all the way there."

Ethan, who had returned from his coffin in the rear cabin after nightfall and taken my place beside Gary, stuck his head out of the cockpit and looked to us. I turned to John and Madison. Nadya did the same.

Madison lifted her head off John's shoulder.

"I say we go on," he said. "I trust Dosu."

"I've been thinking about Unathi," I said. "Edmond described him as savage, but it sounded to me like Edmond considered him a rival. Except those two things don't add up. Edmond, for all his faults, is certainly wise and clever. I don't know how a *savage* could be a rival to Edmond. I don't have any new facts, but I don't think we're going to find someone uncivilized there. I say we keep going."

"Fine with me." Nadya tapped her nail against one of her sheathed swords in her lap. "We're either doing a very brave thing or a very stupid one. It will be interesting either way."

Ethan told the pilot, "We go on."

"All righty," Gary said. "There's like a thirty percent chance we run out of gas and don't make it anyway."

John, Madison, and I all smiled.

———————————

"We should be over Rogabon," Gary said. "Oh! Wow."

"What?" I called to the front.

"A fire sprouted up," Ethan said. "Out of nowhere. Look."

I went to the cockpit door. Ahead, the bonfire reached above the treetops, illuminating the green rainforest canopy not far below us. We had flown over a blanket of nearly uninterrupted darkness since the coast.

A second fire shot up. I stepped aside so Madison and John could see.

"There's the runway." Gary pointed. "I was getting worried."

I peered over John's shoulder—in a clearing, red lights lined a long, straight strip, which gave me a little comfort. A primitive jungle *savage* might not have had electricity.

A nearer fire rose, then another in the distance.

"What's the plan when we land?" Ethan asked.

"Hope someone's there to greet us," I said.

"Dosu, ideally," John added.

"Take your seats," Gary said. "We're close, and also, we're out of fuel."

We all sat down, and I watched our descent out the side window. Two new fires lit the night, and I could make out the top of a black stone temple. I wondered how much a few runway lights really meant, and what Unathi would be like. I wished I'd been able to judge Dosu's character for myself.

We descended beneath the treetops. Edmond had surely tracked the plane and likely knew our destination once it became clear we were headed for Africa. But I did not see an army of Spectavi out the window. How far behind us would his rescue attempt be?

With a thud, the rear wheels hit the ground, then the nose touched down more softly. We slowed and came to a stop. In the silence, my leather seat creaked loudly when I turned to look out the window on the other side of the cabin.

"There." I pointed at two sets of approaching headlights.

Nadya stood. "No choice now." She opened the side door and lowered the staircase.

Our plane's lights shone on two open-air jeeps, each with a driver and passenger up front, all four dark-skinned males.

"That's Dosu," Madison said. "In the second jeep."

They stopped beside the plane and hopped out. They wore loose black pants. Two were shirtless, and two wore black shirts with golden embroidery down the center. I wondered which, if any other than Dosu, were vampires.

Nadya descended the stairs.

"Let's go." Ethan motioned out of the cockpit, Gary got up, and they headed outside.

John and Madison followed.

I left my suit coat on my seat, threw the strap of my sword scabbard over my shoulder, and stepped out into the warm, sticky air and down the staircase. Insects' creaking came from all directions. Dark trees surrounded us.

"John." Dosu grinned. "You changed your mind."

"I did," John said.

"I am so glad." Dosu gestured to the other in an embroidered shirt, which up close appeared made of silk or another fine material. "This is Kwasi." He gestured to the two shirtless males, whose chests shone in the mugginess. "Wasswa and Opeyemi."

They nodded.

"You know Nadya and Madison," John said. "This is Ethan and Vera, and Gary, our pilot."

Dosu's eyes met mine. "It is a pleasure to meet you." He looked to John. "Did you fly directly from the United States?"

"Yes."

"Then after such a long trip, shall we enjoy a dinner, for starters?"

"Thank you," John said. "But could we see the afflicted first? If there are four hundred, it'll take me some time, and I don't know how much time we have."

"Oh?" Dosu crossed his arms. "How long before you must leave us?"

"Hard to say," John said. "This is a Spectavi plane. We

361

borrowed it, but I'm sure they tracked it and will want it back."

"And you," Dosu said. "They will surely want you along with it."

"I'm sorry," John said. "It's the best we could do."

"Nonsense." Dosu shook his head. "Any help at all is a true blessing. But I do agree—considering the circumstances, we should begin at once. They are a few miles from here, in a hospital of sorts we built to meet their unique needs." He gestured to the jeeps. "Please. We will have your aircraft towed off the center of our runway."

John, Madison, and Nadya got in the back of the jeep with Dosu up front. I went with Ethan and Gary in the other, and taking the same dirt path the jeeps had come by, we headed into the jungle.

Our headlights hardly penetrated the dense vegetation. Our tires and suspension made the only sound aside from a constant chirring of insects.

I called to the front seats, "Why all the fires? We saw them from the plane."

The one in the fine shirt, Kwasi, looked back, and I spotted his fangs. "Special night."

"Special why?"

"Your arrival. Unathi foresaw it."

"He knew we were coming *tonight*?"

"Yes." Kwasi faced forward.

Ethan and Gary did not appear pleased by that answer.

"Très belle," Wasswa said.

"Oui," Kwasi responded.

"Very beautiful," Wasswa had said, probably about Madison or me.

It didn't feel right. At any moment, the other jeep would peel off onto a separate path, I feared. Eyes glowed in the jungle. On the plane, I had found myself glad we would arrive at night, when Nadya and Ethan would be awake with us, but gripping my sword tightly, I wished it had been daytime.

A bonfire burned high in the middle of a clearing ahead. We pulled into the grassy circular area. A small thatched-roof house stood at the far tree line. We stopped between the fire and the house, behind the other jeep.

"Where's the hospital?" Ethan asked.

"It's here." Kwasi opened the door and stepped out. Wasswa did the same. The house was not remotely large enough to fit four hundred people.

"Come," Kwasi said. "Please."

John, Madison, and Nadya got out of the jeep in front of us, along with Dosu and Opeyemi.

Ethan, Gary, and I exchanged glances and shrugs, then got out.

"Where's the hospital?" John asked.

Shvwt! A curved silver blade stuck in Nadya's chest—some kind of three-pointed weapon. Another flew from the trees and hit Ethan. Nadya dropped to a knee and drew her swords. Ethan, holding his knife handle with its blade still retracted, bled from a slash across his gut and crumpled to the ground. Above him, Kwasi's long knife dripped red.

Shvwt-shvwt! Two more knives flew into Nadya.

Clang-clang!—thwak—shvwt. She dropped to the ground, blood pouring from multiple wounds. Dosu stood over her, his knife at her neck, but my human eyes hadn't caught the vampire-speed action.

Shvwt. A tri-pointed knife lodged in Gary's forehead. Blood trickled, and he collapsed.

Madison clutched John's arm.

From the door of the house, another of Unathi's warriors in a fine shirt emerged. He sped to Dosu's side, took Dosu's knife, and knelt next to Nadya.

"No hospital." Dosu stepped away from Nadya. "No four hundred sick. No incurable disease."

I drew my katana.

Wasswa walked to the lead jeep. "Pretty girl, with a pretty sword." From the trunk, he grabbed a short sword with a blade narrower at its base than its end. He smiled and approached me.

I dropped my scabbard to hold my sword with both hands. Wasswa neared. I stepped to him and cut high.

He parried—at mortal speed, so he had to be human— and stepped back, his smile gone. I moved toward him and cut low. He blocked with his blade and retreated farther. I kept pressing.

I cut high, and he blocked. Low—block.

Faster, I cut—high—low—high.

And faster! Low-high-high across his bicep.

I slashed open his chest, and he fell backward to the grass, arms outstretched. Wasswa coughed blood. He tilted his head to the side then stopped moving.

From the jeep, Dosu threw Opeyemi a long, curved sword. Opeyemi caught it and ran at me. He reached the blade back.

I stood tall.

He swung hard.

I ducked, slashing his hamstrings as he passed.

"Aggh!" He tumbled to the ground and held his leg. Blood gushed between his fingers.

I stood up, and a wind whipped across me. Dosu's arm wrapped around my neck from behind.

"Pretty girl, with a pretty sword." He held his other hand outstretched over my right on my katana. "That was not untrue."

I struggled for a breath. I pulled my arms into me, but against Dosu's strength, I accomplished nothing. I dropped my left hand from my sword and elbowed backward at the Sanguan's stone-hard body.

Dosu tightened his arm around my neck, and I couldn't breathe at all. I grasped his constricting arm and pulled, but it didn't budge. A shirtless male came out from the house and went to John and Madison.

Kwasi still pointed his knife at motionless Ethan's throat. The other in an embroidered shirt held his blade steady, kneeling over Nadya.

I closed my eyes and inhaled with all my might, but nothing reached my lungs. I cracked my eyes open and got my second hand back on my sword handle. I pulled inward again, to no avail.

The newly arrived man pushed John and Madison toward the house.

My eyes closed, I gripped my sword tightly.

No air. Everything went black.

32

JOHN

"Let's go." A shirtless man shoved Madison toward the thatched-roof house he had come out of. He pushed me and held a short knife with a wooden handle inches from Madison's back.

I glanced behind me. Vera's body went limp. It took Dosu considerable effort to pry her sword out of her grasp, then he lifted her and carried her into the lead jeep.

Another man—also shirtless, which appeared to be what distinguished the humans from the Sanguans, who wore the embroidered shirts—pulled a heap of thick chains from the jeep's trunk and dropped half near Ethan and the rest near Nadya.

"Inside." Our captor pulled open the door, and we went into the lone room. On the dirt floor was a low bed in the corner, and a small table and chairs near us.

He left and shut the door, blocking the light from the fire in the clearing.

In the darkness, I held Madison. "Are you okay?"

"Yes." She sniffled.

"I'm so sorry."

"It's all right. We knew the risk."

I heard the jeeps start and drive away. "I never thought… I just… I trusted Dosu."

"I did, too."

Madison stepped back, and my eyes had adjusted enough that, from the slivers of light that found their way through the walls' wooden strips, I saw her wipe her face with her hands.

"You'll be fine," she said. "I'm sure they won't hurt you."

I took her hand. "I won't let them hurt you. I'll do whatever they want, but only if they don't hurt you."

"And Vera?" she asked. "And Nadya and Ethan?"

I looked at the ground.

"It's okay," Madison said.

"I'll try."

"I know you will. I came here with you because you were trying, trying to do good, but more because you were trying for better than the easy choice. When I lost my family, nothing mattered to me. Then I thought being safe was all that mattered. We had that in Paris. We had something good in that apartment."

"I'll never forget it," I said.

"I won't, either. But the apartment wasn't enough for you. And I saw that. I know I didn't show it all the time, but the more I saw it in you, the more I remembered the same thing in me, a dream about what I *really* wanted my life to be. Something beyond ordinary and routine—something exciting. My dream had been buried and was dying, until you brought it back. You gave it new life. And as it grew, the more I loved you and the less I loved Bayard. I got so excited when he went to Mirabella at the clubs and left me to be alone with you."

"I love you." I kissed her.

She wrapped her arms around me and dug her head into my neck, and her tears wet my skin.

"I hated leaving Paris," she said, "because I was scared. Not because I didn't want to be with you."

"It's all right."

"I love you," she said. "You need to know how much I love you in case..." She sniffled. "In case this is the end."

"It's not." I kissed her wet cheek and held her more tightly. "I won't let it be."

The door swung open.

With my arm, I blocked the sudden light.

A huge black male in a dark, sleeveless robe stepped into the room. Firelight illuminated half of his bald head and the silver ring pattern covering the side of his robe. He had a broad chest and the biggest biceps I had ever seen in person. He grabbed Madison.

"Hey!" I shouted.

He shoved me to the ground, drew a long knife, and slashed it across Madison's throat. He held her upright while her eyes widened. She gagged and clutched her neck. Blood poured through her fingers.

I scrambled to my feet. "Give me the knife!"

He spun it and held out the handle.

I took it and sliced deep into my palm, which I brought over Madison's mouth. "Drink!"

She moved toward it, but her head fell aside.

"Please!" I lifted her head and got my blood running onto her closed mouth. "Please, Madison. Please!"

Her lips opened, her mouth opened, and she had the strength to hold her neck up herself. The blood from her neck slowed, the wound closed, and the bleeding stopped. She took a calm breath.

I brought her to me and held her away from the monster.

"I am Unathi," he said. "Welcome, John and Madison, to Rogabon. I am sorry to have done that in such haste, but I needed proof."

"You could have drunk from me and known!" I shouted.

He grinned, revealing huge fangs. "Yes, and I look forward to doing so. I am told your blood is nothing short of sublime." He walked to the doorway, knelt, and reached outside to the left. He returned with a short stack of clothes. "Please change into these for the ceremony."

"Ceremony?"

"Tomorrow," Unathi said. "The bidding will begin to see who in Africa will pay the most for your services. And you will provide those services when you are told, if you wish for Miss May to remain at your side. She is beautiful, doubtless tasty, but otherwise of no use to me." Unathi handed me the clothes. "But that is tomorrow. Tonight, at our ceremony, Vera will die. You will revive her. If I wish it, she will die again, and again you will bring her back." He walked to the doorway and turned around. "My people must know of your power beyond any doubt, so their stories of it will spread far and wide, and the price for your services, whether paid in money, goods, or other favors, will be sufficiently high." He went outside. "Change your clothes." He shut the door.

I whispered to Madison, "Edmond will come."

The door flew open.

"You think *Edmond* will come for *you two*?" Unathi shook his head. "You have a gift, and Edmond wants it, no doubt. But let me explain something about Edmond Duchart, the CEO, the businessman. When he noticed your plane headed for my jungle, before he lay down to rest in his plush coffin in Virginia, Edmond may have dispatched a team of Spectavi. He might even have sent his white knight in black leather, Victoria, and she is a mighty warrior. But she will not be your savior, either. Whatever she does anywhere else on this earth, every time she comes *here*, she leaves bloodied and beaten." His face grew grave. "You may see a battle, but let me snuff out any hope it might bring and tell you what will happen. The Spectavi will lose here, as always. They will leave, and you will remain in this jungle, my prisoners." Unathi went back outside. "Change now. It's time to go." He slammed the door shut.

33

VERA

My eyes cracked open. My arms were stretched above me. *Where is my sword?*

Bonfires, maybe twenty spaced unevenly across a large dirt clearing surrounded by dense jungle, roared high into the cloudless sky between me and the stone temple I had spotted from the plane. Heat hit me hard. Everything appeared wavy, in a haze.

Dark-skinned people—presumably humans, because I saw a lot more than the hundred Sanguans who supposedly lived there—gathered in the clearing, paid no mind to me, and greeted one another. The women wore black, brown, or gray skirts, with tops that left their stomachs exposed. Bead necklaces, bracelets, and belts wrapped around them. Most men wore no tops and simpler jewelry. Many had painted their faces, chests, and arms with white and might have been as prepared for battle as they were a ceremony.

Sweat beaded on my face. In the abundant firelight, I could see my wrists had been tied to a stone column. I still wore my top and pants. Blood covered my right side.

And my side throbbed. I twisted my body to see fresh blood running under my cut top from a stab wound. My head ached. Red flashed. I shook my head, but red flashed again. My patients had found me, from seven thousand miles away.

To my left, across the clearing, Nadya and Ethan, their bodies slouched forward and their heads drooping, were chained to their own columns. Their skin had tinted a sickly blue, and hardly any blood could have remained in their bodies if they couldn't break the metal and be free.

Between the fires, the people of Rogabon concluded their greetings and kneeled, facing the temple. They began chanting.

I pulled my wrists down, but they didn't budge. I twisted my hands and arms, but the rope held them.

"Agh." My side. I must have had precious little blood left in me, as well.

The chanting became more uniform.

My eyes grew heavy.

The chanting grew quieter.

My eyes shut.

Where is my sword?

I opened my eyes. I couldn't drift away. If black overtook me, I might not return from it.

The red-orange fires raged before me.

Where is Edmond? Victoria?

My head flashed red. My mother, unmoving, bleeding from the neck, shot to mind. My father, beaten and dead, joined her.

The people of Rogabon raised their arms and chanted louder.

Where are my parents? In death, did they find themselves some place better than this godforsaken jungle?

The chanting stopped. I glanced at Nadya and Ethan. Neither moved. I strained to see the temple's top platform through the haze. Madison, John, and a huge African male stood there. Madison wore a long, narrow black dress, and John wore black pants and a white shirt.

"Unathi!" The crowd confirmed the identity of the vampire in the sleeveless robe.

He took Madison's hand, and all three started down the steps. Others wearing embroidered shirts like Dosu's and Kwasi's emerged from the temple and followed them. The chanting in the clearing resumed.

My eyes shut. My head fell to the side. Would I get to see my parents when I died?

"Vera."

I opened my eyes. Dosu stood before me, holding my sword in one hand.

He cut it through the air then did it again. "An impressively crafted weapon. Thank you for this gift."

I spat at him. The bloody saliva hit the ground short of his feet.

"Save your blood," he said. "Save your strength. It will be a long night for you."

"What will you do to me?"

"*We* have a gift for *you*," Dosu said. "Have you ever imagined what death tastes like? Not the specter of death, but actual death—having died? I have, but I could never know, lest it be the last thing I ever tasted. But you? You will taste it and return to us. Perhaps we will see how long you can drink it in, before even John's blood cannot bring you back."

"You're sick."

Dosu shrugged.

"You're worse than sick," I said. "You're a monster to lie about four hundred ill people, to lure John here. Forget *death*—how can you *live* with yourself?" I spat hard and hit his face.

Dosu wiped it off, smiled briefly, and came near. "I did play on John's compassion to get him here, but compassion is a wasted emotion. I was a priest a long time ago. When you are dead, ask God how he spat in the face of my mortal compassion, only to show me pain and suffering everywhere." Dosu leaned closer. "No, Vera, I am not a monster. I am a *demon*, walking the earth, serving a much more fulfilling master than God."

Woosh—woosh—woosh—woosh... Two long helicopters cleared the treetops ahead near the temple. Dosu bared his fangs at the descending choppers.

A dozen Spectavi soldiers in gray fatigues dropped from the first helicopter, wearing swords on their backs. Another dozen followed from the second. Last, a large figure in a black sleeveless top jumped down. I recognized him and his longsword, though I'd only seen him hold the old weapon three times before, and never outside our headquarters in Virginia.

I smiled.

The helicopters ascended. The people of Rogabon stopped chanting. Most wearing skirts rushed away from the temple, but some of the women stayed and took swords or knives from the men, who all remained. Together, walking or sprinting with menacing faces, the warriors headed for the Spectavi.

My eyes closed. If they didn't reopen, at least I would die knowing that Edmond had come for me.

34

ETHAN

Mortals hustled past me. Crackling fire heated the air and my face. The smell of African skin filled my nostrils. I sniffed. Sweat and blood... So much blood.

I opened my eyes. Blood!

My arms were stretched high, fixed to stone tightly by chains. I pulled my wrists forward, but they didn't budge. How could that be?

Blood!

It came back to me—where I was and the wounds that had left me so drained and weak. Bonfires roared before me, helicopters rose in the sky ahead near the temple. From beneath them, the sound of metal on metal surely meant a battle. The Spectavi must have come to rescue John.

Nadya was bound to my left. She looked drained and awful. Her eyes shot open. She kicked out at a passing woman. Her legs reached short of another. She might find a way to break free and survive, I thought, but not me. I would never see Ellie again.

Away from the temple, a woman ran past me, pulling a screaming child by the hand.

Eleven years I had held on and fought for Ellie. And I had won that fight... sort of. I got Ellie back, and it had been glorious... almost. It had also been torment, and I was fooling myself by ignoring that.

My whole body slumped. Better to die than to live with Ellie again, only to lose her permanently when her mortal life reached its end. I wanted her for all time. I craved her blood and for her to be a vampire by my side, every night, forever. Even if she lived to be eighty or ninety, it would kill me to lose her again, so better that death took me before it did her.

Nadya lashed her body out and wrapped her legs around a passing woman. The woman struggled while Nadya used her legs to pull her prey in and lift it up. Nadya sank her fangs into the woman's neck. Two women hurried by to my right.

Nadya had blood, and I needed it. She would survive. I would die.

I kicked my legs and smacked a running bearded old man in the head. He crumpled to the ground. With my heel, I dragged him to me, nearer and nearer.

Blood—I heard the unconscious man's heart beating it around his wrinkly body. I pulled him closer and got both my feet around him.

My dearest Ellie, I will see you again.

With my legs, I lifted the man. I could taste his blood already. I pulled my legs up hard, and the man's head and neck came near, but fell back.

Ellie, I will hold you again.

I pulled the man to me, and as I caught his leathery neck with my mouth, my fangs dug in. I sucked hot blood. The flame burned low, but it burned. I sucked harder, and it burned higher.

I will return to you, Ellie. I will suffer that torture.

I sucked blood full of a long life's wisdom and memories of children and grandchildren. *Vwoooosh!* The inferno at my core ignited. I sucked but only a trickle of blood came, then none. I hadn't caught any of the wisdom. I had raced past the faces of his family members. I let the dead man fall to the ground like a sack.

"Argrah!" I pulled my wrists down, the metal around them snapped, and I was free. I breathed deeply. Nadya had freed herself and drank from another woman, which seemed the perfect idea.

I darted to the nearest woman fleeing the battle at the temple, wrapped my arms around her sweaty body, and sank my fangs in. Because I needed *all* her blood, I sucked hard.

Let her die when I drink the last drops.

I pulled her blood out and gulped it into my inhuman body.

So that I can live, so that I can be strong enough to return to Ellie and help my friends survive this hell of a jungle, damn my conscience, damn my soul. I'd killed before that night, and I would again. *Let her die.*

And she died. I pulled my fangs from her, breathed a huge breath, and dropped her drained body.

"Ethan!" Nadya walked over with a short sword in each

hand and a devilish grin. "Not as nice as my swords…" She did a little jig. "But finally, a proper battle."

"Where's John?" I asked.

"I don't know."

People ran frantically across the clearing and into the jungle. Bloodied warriors limped back our way, grimacing in pain.

"But there's Vera." Nadya pointed past me with a sword.

Her eyes were shut, and her head drooped atop her limp body. Nadya and I ran that way.

We skidded to a halt.

Huge Edmond Duchart swung a longsword at Dosu, who parried with a katana but retreated toward Vera. With both hands gripping his mighty weapon, Edmond cut down hard. Dosu blocked and stepped backward.

Edmond swung faster, harder, faster, and—*shvt!*—clean through Dosu's neck. The Sanguan's head fell and rolled along the ground. Nadya and I went over.

Edmond pointed his blade at us.

I put both hands out. "We're friends."

"Vera asked us to come," Nadya said.

"To New Orleans," I added. "To help John."

"They are." Vera's eyes stayed shut. "Friends."

Edmond cut the rope between her hands and caught her falling body. "Vera." He kissed her neck.

"Edmond." She smiled. Then anguish overtook her face.

"You'll die." Edmond dropped his sword and knelt with her. "You've lost too much blood. As they attack your mind, you'll die in this jungle." He leaned closer. "Drink my blood.

End their assaults on you. Join me. Be a vampire and truly join me. Make what we have not a fleeting light, but a fire that burns for all time."

So slightly, she shook her head no.

"Vera." Tears filled Edmond's eyes. "You can't die on me."

"But I am," she whispered.

Edmond looked away then back at her, and his voice took on a serious tone. "You have a project to finish. You'll die before you do?"

Vera's face grew more pained.

"You'll give up on your patients?" Edmond asked sternly. "You promised me you'd bring them peace. You promised!"

Tears slid down Vera's cheeks.

Edmond held his wrist to his mouth, ready to bite it. "Drink my blood. Be a vampire!"

"John," Vera said. "Unathi has him."

Edmond dropped his head.

"John…" Vera's head fell backward.

A huge breath of air filled Edmond's chest. He let it out. "Then I must fight him again, after so many years." Edmond stood with Vera and bit her neck through her top's collar for no longer than a second. The anguish on her face abated. He passed her to me, grabbed his sword, then picked up the katana Dosu had been fighting with and handed it to me. "Protect her."

"I don't know how to fight with this," I said.

"That is not for you. It's her sword. If we get John, when she wakes up, it's the first thing she'll ask for." He shook his head. "Even before me. Follow me, but stay out of it. Protect her, and protect that sword, or you will die in this jungle tonight." He looked to Nadya. "Komarova, keep Unathi's forces busy."

She nodded. "Nice to see you again, Edmond."

"This is no game," he said.

She scraped the sharp edges of her swords against one another. "It's all a game. This is just one of those parts that is not a joke. It's a part you play with resolve because you cannot afford to lose."

They sprinted toward the temple, where the sound of metal weapons colliding with metal still filled the air. With Vera in my arms and her katana in my hand, I followed.

Across the clearing, we weaved around fires, stepping over the dying and dead whose retreat from the battle hadn't made it far. Living mortals grew scarce. Near the temple steps, Unathi and twenty of his vampires surrounded eight Spectavi, their backs close together, katanas parrying defensively far more than they attacked. Madison and John stood a few steps up the temple, in the clutches of one of Unathi's vampires.

Unathi cut a Spectavi in two with his longsword. He looked our way. "Edmond."

Edmond kept going, slicing his blade through two Sanguans before they fully turned to him. Nadya hacked apart another, and the Spectavi odds had improved.

I stopped, not full of the fear and anguish of before. I didn't whine for Ellie or for myself, but I would have died in that battle. No amount of passion or courage would have gotten me to its end. I didn't have the skill to match those Sanguans, so I knelt, held Vera, and listened to her slowing heartbeat.

Unathi marched toward Edmond, but before he got there, Edmond cut down a few more Sanguans. They weren't weak foes. *They* were not unskilled, but Edmond's sword struck with such precision and power, both surely developed over such a long life, that his enemies crumbled before him.

Nadya whirled with her two blades as though it might have been a dance. But no smile covered her face with each step and sword strike. Focus drove her through the melee. Nadya slashed across legs and spun to slice off arms. She engaged one foe only to leave and engage two others, before returning to the first at an opening to take off his head. Then her swords swung again before the decapitated body hit the ground.

Unathi's blade met Edmond's with a force that seemed to match the Spectavi lord's.

"I didn't think you'd ever come back here," Unathi said.

"Nor did I." Edmond swung his blade.

Unathi's met it. "Where is Victoria?"

"On her way."

"And you didn't wait?" Unathi swung. "John is *that* important to you?"

"No." Edmond chopped down hard. Unathi parried and gritted his teeth.

Edmond chopped. Unathi blocked and whipped his sword across Edmond's side. Edmond stepped back and glanced to the cut—not deep. Unathi showed his fangs. Edmond showed his, and the vampires swung their swords. *Clang!* They met, and they swung again.

With Nadya's help, the Spectavi's position had improved. The numbers on each side grew closer to even, and the Spectavi attacked occasionally, instead of fighting purely defensively. With each Sanguan the spinning, slashing, whirling Russian took out, the Spectavi position improved further.

Edmond swung at Unathi. Unathi swung at Edmond. The colossuses did not dance. They didn't break off to engage other foes. They traded massive swings and parries. They ducked and dodged just in time, only to lunge into another purposeful swing.

Edmond reached his longsword high and cut down hard. Unathi blocked and backed up. Edmond stepped forward and swung. Unathi dodged it and slashed deep across Edmond's thigh.

As Edmond thrust his sword into Unathi's gut.

Wide-eyed, Unathi punched Edmond's face, driving him backward and the Spectavi's blade out of his stomach. Unathi staggered and clutched his bleeding side. He glanced at John and Madison then at his dwindling force of fighters. He snarled at Edmond and raced away into the jungle.

Nadya threw a sword end over end into the forehead of the Sanguan holding John. The vampire fell backward on the temple steps. Unathi's remaining Sanguans exchanged glances then raced into the trees where their leader had gone.

Nadya, Edmond, and I all ran up the steps to John and

Madison. With her other sword, Nadya beheaded the Sanguan lying at John's feet. "Are you hurt?"

"Please help Vera." Edmond favored his bleeding leg.

"We're fine," Madison said.

John knelt to Vera. "Is she alive?"

"Barely." I moved her closer to him.

John put out his palm, and Nadya sliced her sword across it. He brought his hand above Vera's lips.

The first drops of blood hit them, and when the blood ran, she opened her mouth for it. She drank, swallowed, and breathed easier. She opened her eyes.

I held out her sword.

She took it and clutched it to her. "Edmond."

He lifted her from me and held her tightly. "Vera." He let her stand on her own. "Are you all right?"

"I'm fine." She smiled. "Thanks to you." She turned. "Thanks to John. Thanks to you all." She spun her katana end over end in her hand. "And I didn't even lose Tomori."

Edmond looked at me. "See?"

"What?" Vera asked.

"Nothing." Edmond gazed at the battlefield—the diminishing bonfires and the unmoving bodies of Sanguans, Spectavi, and mortals. Five of his soldiers remained. "We need to go. Unathi will return with reinforcements. He always does."

"Go where?" John asked.

Edmond pointed in the direction opposite where Unathi had gone. "Half a mile that way. Our helicopter will meet us and bring us to Kinshasa, where our plane is on the runway, waiting to take us home."

35

JOHN

Our helicopter landed in Kinshasa, in the Democratic Republic of the Congo, beside the Spectavi 747. Armed guards stood outside the jumbo jet and growled at Nadya and Ethan, but when Edmond told them to settle down, they let the Sanguans pass without incident. We boarded, and even with the rear reserved for vampire coffins and a middle cabin we were told included conference rooms, bedrooms, and something like a living room, the forward cabin was cavernous compared to the small jet we had flown over on. Pairs of big gray leather seats lined each side, and four round tables with swiveling chairs ran spaced out up the middle.

Edmond and Vera sat together near the front. The Spectavi soldiers who had fought in the jungle were local, so they stayed behind. In the middle of the cabin, I sat against the window, and Madison sat next to me. Ethan and Nadya chose seats on opposite sides of the plane, in the back of the cabin.

Edmond had explained in the helicopter, answering Vera's questions but for all to hear, that after the incident at the airport in New Orleans, he figured out our likely destination almost immediately. The superior speed of the four-engine 747 had allowed him to land in Africa before we did. Victoria had been on her way, but because she'd started in Los Angeles, she would have arrived hours later. Since the fighting had concluded, she was headed to Virginia to meet us.

The plane started rolling. Madison laid her head on my shoulder, and I put my arm around her.

From behind us, a woman in a gray skirt suit approached. She smiled warmly and handed me a stack of clothes—soft black pants, hooded sweatshirts, and white T-shirts. "Edmond thought you might like to change."

"Thank you." I took the clothes. "Actually." I handed them back to her. "Could you put them on the seat behind us? We'll change later."

"Certainly." She set them down. "Can I get you anything else? Drinks? Something to eat?"

"Later, I'm sure. Thank you."

"Of course." She walked to the front of the plane and had a word with Edmond.

Madison leaned up to give me a kiss then settled in again. At that moment, all I wanted to do was hold her.

The big jet lifted off the ground, and the cabin lights dimmed. I closed my eyes and held Madison more tightly. Tears welled up, tears I had been holding back and did not want her to see.

We should never have gone to Africa. We had been lied to, and our plan came from good intentions, but it had been way too risky. Madison had lost *so much blood* when Unathi sliced her neck open...

I thought of Paris, and of Madison in the black satin gown at the underground theater before the opera. I recalled dancing with her in the red leather dress at the high-end club. I remembered those clothes and all the rest coming off before being with her those nights and when we woke after the sun had risen, then lying with her for hours after. I missed it all.

I could still hear the *click* of the collar's lock when Mirabella put it on me. As much as I had loathed that collar, I hadn't loathed when she drank from me while I wore it. Sanguans far worse than her roamed the night. Far worse than Bayard, too. I'd hated seeing him with Madison, but he'd kept her safe and made her happy, which was all I wanted to do.

And he really had been doing me a favor, keeping word of my ability from spreading like wildfire. Sure, other Sanguans who drank from me knew, but it was nothing like what happened in New Orleans after the nursing home explosions.

Which was his doing, I reminded myself. If I'd taken him up on his offer, Africa would never have happened.

I rubbed my temple with my free hand. Nothing was settled. I rubbed the dried tears beneath my eyes. Or everything was settled, and I just hadn't gotten used to it yet.

A new beginning awaited us, the beginning we had fled

from. Edmond had proven valiant and did not seem *bad* at all. Yet Vera's warnings about him still concerned me. Seeing them together, I had no doubt she was close enough to him to know him well.

Edmond had saved us, which I would forever be grateful for, but he remained the businessman and calculating politician who lied about drinking mortal blood and would use me for his benefit, the benefit of his Spectavi, and their company, Eure.

Besides the safety he offered, maybe I owed him that much for the rescue, I reasoned. And if so, Madison did, as well. But what would her role be in our future? To be at my side while my blood did its work and… just *be* there? She had chosen Africa because she wanted more than that. She didn't want routine. She sought an *exciting* life. After all she had been through, she had begun to dream big again.

And I yearned to make her dreams come true. They were my dreams, too. We'd seen a tiny bit of France together, and I wanted to see the rest of it. I wanted to see the world with her, to experience all the sights, sounds, tastes, and adventures it had to offer.

The black-and-white T-shirts and pants on the seat behind us reminded me of the clothes we'd worn in the Paris apartment. The stewardess's suit reminded me of the suits Vera and the Spectavi had worn in New Orleans. That uniform awaited us in Virginia, in our "home," as Edmond had called it at the steps of Unathi's temple.

"Are you awake?" Madison asked.

"Yes," I said, loud enough for her to hear over the noisy jet engines.

She tilted her head up. "How are you?"

"Fine. How are you?"

She shrugged. "I'm worried about Virginia."

"Me, too."

She sat up. "I play it out in my head, and today, to be there, safe and with you, it sounds wonderful. So does tomorrow, and maybe it would be for a while. But then what?"

"I know what you mean."

"I'm sure we'll have a nice apartment, or maybe even a house. They'll treat us well, but it'll be a new cage. We won't be free."

"No," I said. "We won't be. But with my blood, and the fact that my name and my face have been all over the news and the internet, I don't know what to do about it."

Madison took my hand. "There's another way." She glanced to the back of the cabin at Ethan, who stared out his window, and Nadya, who held a magazine, clicked her overhead light on, then stretched her arm and fingers to click on the light for the seat next to hers.

"Live with them?" I asked.

"Live *like* them," Madison said. "They could make us vampires, right now, on this plane. I'm sure they would do it. I'm tired of running, and I'm tired of being afraid."

"My blood would lose its power."

"But Edmond wouldn't want you anymore. People everywhere wouldn't want your blood anymore. We could be together, unafraid, able to live *our* lives."

"Except they wouldn't be human lives."

Madison let go of my hand. "Is that most important to you?"

"No." She was most important to me.

I thought of the firefighter in the doctor's office in Paris whose terrible burns had faded before our eyes and the first woman I had healed outside the burning nursing home. I recalled the children with incurable diseases. I wouldn't be able to save them from God's plan or his indifference. Or if he did not rule on high, I wouldn't be able to save anyone from the cruel randomness of the world anymore.

"Even with Edmond," I said, "my blood would help a lot of people. It would save so many lives."

"It doesn't have to."

"Shouldn't it? Shouldn't I want it to?"

She shrugged. "You want what you want. You want what your heart tells you. You have one life to spend how you choose, and I know firsthand it can end in an instant."

I sat back in my seat.

Surely, she meant her family, but I thought of Madison with her wrist slashed open in Wilhelm's apartment in Paris, before the first time my blood healed her. I recalled my blood restoring her sight during our rescue. Unathi had sliced her neck hours earlier. How many more times would I let that happen?

We would be safe on the Spectavi campus, but only relatively. What would happen when a hundred Sanguans came for me? Or a thousand?

What if Madison were kidnapped, and I wasn't with her the next time her wrist was cut open? What if someone cut mine first, or while I was away from Eure, a single bullet caught me in the wrong spot? A skilled marksman could make a shot like that from a considerable distance. No mortal's blood could save me, and Madison would lose someone else close to her. She would be alone again.

Yet maybe I needed to risk all that because my gift could do so much good, for so many people.

Or I could be selfish.

I asked Madison, "You could drink people's blood to live?"

"I could," she said. "Exactly for that reason. To *live*. To truly live, free and strong. But only if it's with you. I would only be immortal with you."

"I would do anything for you."

"I know it's a lot to ask."

"It isn't," I said. "You're asking me to live an immortal life with the woman I love more than anything in the world. Of course I will."

"I love you."

We kissed and held each other. We had found a solution. We had a way forward, with each other, that wasn't resigning ourselves to a fate neither of our hearts were in. I would lose my gift, but I had never wanted it in the first place. I had wanted Madison! Always, even before I went to Reims and met the tall, fair-skinned beauty with long raven-black hair.

We rested our foreheads on each other's.

Bayard had framed my decision as one between good and evil. I didn't choose either. I chose life with the woman I loved.

"I'm excited," I said.

"Me, too." She smiled.

I glanced toward the rear of the cabin. "You go to Nadya. She's older, so her blood will make you stronger."

"No. You should go to her."

I shook my head. "If anything ever happened, if we got caught up in the war between the Sanguans and the Spectavi, I want her looking out for you first, because you're of her blood. She's crazy, but she fought incredibly well back there."

Madison smiled again. "She *is* crazy. But okay."

We kissed and held each other, and when I squeezed her to me, I reminded myself that we would be able to do those things as vampires. That embrace wasn't goodbye. We were suddenly on the brink of a whole new world, but we would be in it together.

Madison got up and headed for the back. I saw Edmond and Vera sitting up front as they had been the entire flight, then crossed the cabin toward the rear, and the notion that I wouldn't be able to father children as a vampire came to mind. When I thought of my children used as leverage to influence me for my healing mortal blood, my resolve deepened.

Madison took the aisle seat next to Nadya.

I sat beside Ethan. "Hi."

"Hello," he said.

"Would you make me a vampire?"

He raised his eyebrows. "Now?"

"Yes. It needs to be now, before we get to Virginia and

are surrounded by Spectavi. Madison is asking Nadya."

"She'll say yes. She'll think it's fun."

I glanced over, and though the overhead lights were off, I could see Nadya smiling gleefully as Madison spoke.

"Indeed." I turned back to Ethan. "We think life with Edmond, while a relatively safe one, would be life in a different kind of cage. I'd be his political tool."

"He'd let you help a lot of people," Ethan said.

"Yes, but people of his choosing."

"Nevertheless, your blood would heal many."

"You don't think I should do this?" I asked.

"I didn't say that. I just think you should be sure."

"I am. I never asked for my gift. *Everyone* isn't my responsibility."

Ethan nodded.

"And what kind of life would that be for Madison?" I asked. "Following me around while I healed people."

"A safe one."

"Maybe. But you saw Unathi's Sanguans with the upper hand against the Spectavi for a while. Maybe on Eure's campus, she'd be safe with me. But outside that campus, would either of us really be? And maybe Edmond would realize that, and he'd never let us leave. The safer they made us, the more they'd keep us from living anything remotely resembling real lives. And *that* is what Madison and I want. To *live* together."

"It sounds like you really do," Ethan said. "I've never made another vampire, but I've considered this possibility for you. In fact, the only reason I didn't ask if you wanted me to turn you was because I wanted to see if Ellie would change her mind and would be turned herself. But she has not changed her mind." He looked me in the eye. "You are certain?"

I turned to Madison, who looked back at me. "Yes," I said to Ethan.

"I will drink your blood until you are nearly dead. As I recall, you may feel death has taken hold of you. Then from my wrist, drink my blood and feel mortal death be banished, never able to touch you again."

Madison nodded to me. I nodded back.

Nadya held her, smirked, and chomped her fangs into Madison's neck.

Ethan bit into mine. Warmth ran down my neck to my arms and legs. Ethan sucked hard, and heat surged at my core then oozed outward.

I breathed faster. I watched Madison do the same, watching me. I closed my eyes and saw fire. Flame everywhere. I forced my eyes open. Madison opened hers.

Nadya drank. Madison smiled at me. Ethan drank. I smiled at Madison.

My eyes closed. Heat burst against my insides, built, and burst again. So hot.

Fire roared, touching each inch of me, warming every part of me, consuming everything. *Too* hot.

Black seeped into the flame. It spread among the yellow, orange, and red. It towered over the fire, then curled and a wave of it crashed.

Fire rose. A fresh wave of black hit. Flames flared

repeatedly, but black waves battered them mercilessly.

Upon smoldering embers, black slammed down hard, until all was black.

What happens after the black?

A flame crackled. My eyes shot open. I couldn't breathe. Madison's head lay back. Nadya bit into her own wrist and tore her fangs out of it.

Ethan held his bitten-open wrist inches above my mouth. A drop of blood seared my tongue. The next burned it. But, God, *let it burn*. I raised my mouth to the source. Heat flowed into me, and I could breathe again. I held Ethan's wrist and sucked his blood.

The fire within built anew. A low wave of flame curled and crashed.

Flames rose higher over the black and crashed upon it. The dark tide receded.

Vwoosh!—an inferno at my core ignited.

I watched Madison holding Nadya's pale wrist, sucking hard. I loved Madison.

I clutched Ethan's arm and drank. I loved the blood.

Ethan lifted his wrist. I pulled it back to me and kept sucking. Damn the young vampire! I needed more. I needed it all!

He jerked his arm back and pushed me away with his other hand. Ethan held his wound as I sat back. My chest heaved. I looked to Madison, and hers did too. My heart raced. I ran my tongue across my top row of teeth, finding two fangs a little longer than the teeth had been, and a lot sharper.

The wound on my palm I had repeatedly cut open had closed and healed completely, leaving fresh skin, perhaps a little paler than before.

My hands went to my growling stomach. I leaned forward, my eyes widened, and my stomach growled louder... deeper. I grimaced. I held a cavernous pit I needed to fill. I *needed* to.

Ethan put his hand on my shoulder. "It's hard at first. It gets easier, but you will need blood."

I took a slower breath. Then another. "Could be tough on an airplane in the middle of the Atlantic."

Ethan reached up and pushed the stewardess call button. "You'll find that there's always someone to hunt."

Across the cabin, the call light above Madison and Nadya was already lit.

36

VERA

By the time we landed at Dulles Airport in Virginia, Edmond knew what John and Madison had done. Night had turned to day for the last few hours of the flight, and when the two of them joined Ethan and Nadya heading for the coffins in the rear of the plane, Edmond figured it out pretty quickly. For their part in my rescue, Edmond allowed the four Sanguans to go in peace.

Left alone in the forward cabin, I had smiled to no one but myself. *Good for them,* I decided. Edmond didn't *need* John; he had only wanted him.

What a life John and Madison could have together as vampires. *As Sanguans...* My face darkened each time I thought it.

They wouldn't be like the Sanguans I dreaded, though. John and Madison *couldn't* be like them. I couldn't imagine it. They had Ethan and Nadya to learn from, and those two Sanguans certainly seemed honorable.

Edmond had drunk from me on the plane and learned

my role in everything that had led us to Africa. Beyond acknowledging it, we didn't discuss it. Back at his house, even though I had slept during the flight, I slept the whole day. Edmond had drunk quite a bit from me.

In my robe, I walked downstairs shortly after sundown. Edmond, wearing a dark business suit, sat down in his favorite chair in the drawing room and picked up the waiting newspaper.

I walked past him to the sofa.

"Good evening," he said.

"Good evening." I sat. "Are you mad?"

He scanned his paper. "About what?"

"What I did. That John's blood has become like any other vampire's."

"No."

"No? You don't wish he were here now, and still mortal?"

"I do wish that." Edmond turned the page. "But it cannot be, so I will let that wish go." He looked up. "There, I just did."

Unamused, I crossed my arms.

He lowered the newspaper. "I'm disappointed John isn't here. I think we could have accomplished great things. However, you did what you judged to be best, which I respect."

"So I was right about how you would have used John?"

"More or less. And you were well acquainted with the facts… most of them." He wagged his finger at me. "Please don't make decisions like this on a hunch."

"Okay," I said. "*Give me* all the facts, and I won't have to."

"Hm. You know more than most. You know plenty." He smiled. "But I will tell you one other thing. One other reason I am not overly upset today. John is not the first with blood like that."

"I know. There was Odo in the thirteenth century."

"And Sophia in the ninth, and Julio in the seventeenth. There were likely others, there may be others now, and in time, there surely will be others."

"What happened to Sophia and Julio?"

"They died. Once their power became known, everyone wanted it for themselves, to control it, or to destroy it, and they didn't last long."

"Why isn't that in the archives?"

"Not everything is in the archives."

Shaking my head, I smiled. "Tell me more that isn't in the archives. Please?"

Edmond nodded. "I will."

"Thank you."

He checked his watch. "We need to be going soon. You'd better get changed."

I got up, gave him a long kiss on the way past, and headed upstairs.

37

JOHN

Shortly after sundown, at a dimly lit hotel bar near Dulles Airport in Virginia, on opposite sides of a small booth in the back corner, Madison and I sat with two new friends, a young couple on vacation.

With my fangs in the woman's wrist, I sucked her blood, quieting the savage thirst I had woken to for the first time. Her sweet blood filled the void then fueled the fire raging in its place and came with a torrent of her memories, thoughts, and emotions.

She was twenty-six and had come to the bar for one last beer before taking the shuttle to the airport at the end of her vacation from Norman, Oklahoma. She loved her boyfriend, whose blood Madison sucked across the table from me, and wished he would get around to asking her to marry him. Later, I would ask Madison if he planned to.

Her uncle had died in his hospital bed two months before. She had been there at the end of his long battle with—

Ethan tapped me and Madison on our shoulders. I pulled my fangs from the woman, Madison pulled hers from the woman's boyfriend, and Ethan raced away faster than the mortals could have seen. I needed to learn how to stop short of killing people without Ethan's help.

"Mmm…" The woman opened her eyes. "Why can't our vacation be *starting*, not *ending*?"

I smiled.

The man opened his eyes. "Yeah."

I looked at the time on my phone. "You should get going, or you'll miss your flight."

He checked his watch. "Oh, yeah." He got up. "C'mon."

His girlfriend threw her head back. "*Fine.*" She stood. "Thank you, John."

"Thank you. Thank you both. Safe travels."

They wheeled their suitcases across the bar and into the hotel lobby.

Madison wiped blood from the corner of her mouth and came around the booth to my side. I scooted in, leaned against the wall, and put my arm around her when she rested against me.

The woman's uncle had been a doctor. He'd spent years researching different approaches to battling diseases like the one that took his life. I didn't know that I would be working in a lab anytime soon, but the *years* of his work stuck with me. *I* had years—all the years. I had forever.

The quick cure in my mortal blood was gone, and that hurt. But I could find other ways to help people. As a vampire, I could do that on a timeline infinitely longer than

I could have as a human. "What do you think?"

"About what?" Madison asked. "About him?"

"About all of it. What we chose."

"I love it." She stretched her head up and kissed me. "How 'bout you?"

"I love it, and I love you." I kissed her and thought of an infinitely longer timeline doing that, as well.

"I love you." Madison tapped her chin with her finger. "But I do think we can do better than a hotel bar near Dulles Airport."

"Ha. Blame Vera. We'd be on our way to New Orleans if we didn't have to wait for her."

"Okay." Madison kissed me. "We blame Vera."

I kissed her, and as she sat up, I kissed her neck. Then she kissed mine. I pulled her to me, and she sank her fangs into my neck. I bit into hers, and we sucked each other's blood.

38

VERA

On the way to Washington, DC, to a charity gala at the residence of Spain's ambassador to the United States, I rode with Edmond in a limousine with dark-tinted windows. He wore a tuxedo, and I had on an emerald-green satin dress with thin shoulder straps and a very low back. Edmond liked to see me in green, and based on what I'd seen in the mirror before we left, I could not blame him. My hair was up, and a thick diamond choker covered the fang marks on my neck.

We stopped at a hotel bar near the airport for a meeting I had arranged the night before.

"I won't be long," I said as the car pulled around the hotel's circular drive.

Edmond flipped open his cell phone. "I'll be here."

The hotel doorman opened the limo door and took my hand to help me out. Another doorman pulled open the glass door, and across the lobby, at a high table near the bar, my four Sanguan friends sat on high-backed stools, chatting and laughing.

Sanguan friends… I was still getting used to the idea, and in fact, it had been part of the reason I'd insisted on seeing them.

Ethan noticed me first, then the others looked my way.

"My, my," Nadya said. "That is quite a gown."

"And those diamonds…" Madison added.

"Thank you," I said. "We're on our way to a charity gala in DC."

"Lucky you," Ethan said. "We have to get on another plane."

Nadya grabbed John's wrist and Madison's. "New Orleans awaits the arrival of young, thirsty vampires!"

John rolled his eyes but smiled. Madison just smiled.

"You'll stay with them there?" I asked.

"I will," Nadya said. "They have to learn how to do it right. It is one thing to have the chance at immortal life, but quite another to take that gift, to survive the centuries, and make them count."

"And *you* are going to teach them?"

She threw up her arms. "Of course!"

Ethan lowered her nearer arm. "I'll be there for a week or two, as well. To be sure they have a second point of view about everything."

"Phew!" I smiled. "And then you're off to Paris with Ellie?"

"I am."

"Good for you. Good for you both. John, has anyone recognized you here?"

"Yes," he said. "But being with these three helps. The 'John Breen' with miraculous blood was very specifically not a vampire. Now I am, and they all are. It's easy to convince people they have the wrong guy."

"Ah, yes. I see how that could be quite convincing." I looked at each of them, unable to ask the question I needed to. "Well, I guess this is goodbye."

"For now," Nadya said. "We'll see each other again."

John got off his barstool and came over. "Thank you." He hugged me. "Thank you for giving us the chance to make an informed choice."

"I'm glad I could."

Madison came over and gave me a hug. "Thank you."

"You're welcome."

She returned to her stool.

"I'm so happy for you two," I said.

Ethan gave me a hug. "Thank you, Vera, and Ellie says thank you."

"You're both welcome. I hope I get to meet her before long."

"We'll make it happen."

Nadya came over, and we hugged.

"John told me about the two you chopped down in Africa with your katana," she said. "I would have liked to have seen that."

"Oh, they were nothing. But who knows? Maybe you'll see me in action someday."

"I hope I do."

I looked them over again. "I really do have to go." I wouldn't ruin it. We would always have that happy goodbye, and I would find another way to warn them. "Bye." With a wave, I turned and took a step. Then I stopped and dropped my head.

"What is it?" Ethan asked.

I turned back around. "Would you ever consider becoming Spectavi?"

"What?" Nadya gave a stern look. "No."

Ethan shook his head.

"We just chose *not* to be with the Spectavi," John said.

"Yeah." Madison folded her arms. "Why would you ask that?"

"I wasn't sure I'd tell you," I said. "I didn't want to ruin… everything. But maybe I already have, and now all I can do is warn you of what's coming your way."

"What's coming?" Nadya asked.

"Things are going to get hard for Sanguans soon," I said. "Not only for you, but for all Sanguans, all over the world."

"Why?" Ethan asked. "What are you talking about?"

"One of the projects I've been working on will change the war, for the worse for Sanguans."

Nadya scowled. "Worse how?"

"I trust you. You're not like the rest." My eyes watered. "You're the first Sanguans I ever trusted, but I can't stop what's coming. You won't be able to stay out of the war. Following the law won't keep you out of it anymore."

Ethan crossed his arms. "Why not?"

"I can't say more. Edmond might *actually* be mad this time, that I've said as much as I have."

John and Madison slouched with sunken faces.

"I'm sorry." I shook my head. "It won't be for months,

or longer, but… consider joining the Spectavi, and if you won't, be careful out there." I hated how each of them looked at me. "I'm sorry."

I turned and marched across the hotel lobby, expecting Nadya especially to slap her hand on my shoulder, spin me around, and demand more answers. They could drink my blood to know everything. If Edmond saw it, he would storm in and have no choice but to kill any who learned his plans.

But the man at the door opened it, and another opened the limousine door.

As I slid in, Edmond put his cell phone in his pocket. "What is it?"

I believe in my work, I told myself. I believed in a world without savage Sanguans who roamed the streets of Washington, DC, Paris, or anywhere, waiting to pounce and leave humans drained, dead, or both. I hated that Nadya, Ethan, John, and Madison—my friends—were going to get caught up in the change to come. I *didn't* hate Sanguans like them, and there had to be others like them. But they had a choice, and at the expense of those few who refused to become Spectavi, the world would be far better off. Humans would stand a chance in that world.

"Nothing." I knew Edmond would learn the truth with his next bite.

Our limo pulled away.

Red flashed. Thunder struck. I fell into Edmond.

Lightning crackled across my brain, into it, searing it, singeing it, and finally exploding into balls of fire that burned my mind.

I looked up at Edmond. "Help me."

His fingers were undoing my choker.

Pillars of electrified storm clouds were all I saw.

Crack-boom! Boom!

I felt for his arm and squeezed it. "Please!"

Blue fire roared, sucking lightning into it. The thunder quieted. The clouds rolled out. The storm passed.

Cool blue enveloped me. I opened my eyes.

"I've never seen it hit you so fast," Edmond said.

"It hasn't."

"I hate seeing you like this."

"I hate being like this." I brought his arm across my body and held it tightly to me. "I'll cure my patients, and these attacks will stop."

"And if you can't?" he asked. "This is torture for us both."

"Have I failed you yet?"

"No."

"And I won't with them. Whatever it takes, I will finish what I started."

THE END OF BOOK I

CONNECT ONLINE

Thanks for reading. If you enjoyed the story, please leave a review at your favorite online retailer.

Get the latest updates about S.M. Perlow's works by signing up for his newsletter:

smperlow.com/newsletter

Find him online at:

smperlow.com

twitter.com/smperlow

facebook.com/smperlow

WORKS BY S.M. PERLOW

Vampires and the Life of Erin Rose

Novels
Choosing a Master
Alone
Lion
Hope
War

Short Stories
Alice Stood Up

—

The Grand Crucible

Novels
Golden Dragons, Gilded Age

—

Other Works

Short Stories
The Girl Who Was Always Single

CPSIA information can be obtained
at www.ICGtesting.com
Printed in the USA
LVHW03s1713100618
580220LV00003B/524/P